ELIZABETH KINGSTON

Desire Lines

Other books by Elizabeth Kingston:

Welsh Blades
THE KING'S MAN
FAIR, BRIGHT, AND TERRIBLE
DESIRE LINES

Ladies of Scandal
A FALLEN LADY
HOUSE OF CADS

In collaboration with Susanna Malcolm:
THE MISADVENTURES OF A TITIAN-HAIRED GODDESS AND AN OUTRAGEOUS HELLION

DESIRE LINES

First edition. March 21, 2019.

ISBN: 9781795514798

For Taffy

If they don't give you a way, love, then make one.

Character List & Other Notes

WELSH BLADES CHARACTERS
Lady Eluned - Lady of Darian, Gwenllian's mother
Lord Robert (de Lascaux) - Lord of Darian
William (Will) - Lord of Ruardean, Eluned's son
Robin Manton - son of Lord Robert's best friend
Gwenllian - Lady of Morency
Ranulf - Lord of Morency
Sir Gerald - a knight of Morency

HISTORICAL FIGURES
Edward I, King of England
Llewellyn, last Prince of Wales
Dafydd, Llewellyn's brother

FICTIONAL PLACES
Darian: Lord Robert's lands in Wales
Dinwen: Eluned's childhood home now part of Darian
Morency: Ranulf's lands in Suffolk
Ruardean: Will's lands in the Welsh Marches

PRONUNCIATIONS (simplified)
Eluned: Ell-*in*-id
Gruffydd: Griffith
Gwenllian: Gwen-*lee*-an
Iorwerth: *Yor*-worth
Rhodri: *Rod*-ree
Rhys: Reese

Desire lines (or desire paths): a planning term referring to the paths created by pedestrians or cyclists when a constructed route is unsatisfactory or nonexistent

Aderinyth

✠

Philip Walch was his favorite, because he only cared about the birds. Not who was in command, or how high or low anyone's birth, or if you were English or Welsh or Norman. All that mattered were the birds and how you treated them.

"Do we have to sew his eyes shut?"

"They are not like men," answered Phillip. "A falcon is calmed by the dark. Her fears do not live in the night."

Her. Gryff looked down at the covered basket he'd insisted on carrying once they'd caught the falcon not far from its nest. He would have looked under the cloth to see it again, if Philip hadn't warned him they must wait until they were back in the mews. Females were the fiercer hunters, everyone knew that.

"Where do her fears live, then, if not in the dark?"

This made Philip Walch smile, but he didn't laugh at Gryff. He was never cruel. "She knows naught of fear, and never will. You have heard us speak of their fear when they are handled, if you move too fast or cause them harm. But it's not fear such as we have. A bird will trust you, or it will not. Now she does not know or trust any man, and so we say she fears us. It is our arrogance, that we see our own fearful hearts in them so that we may say we conquer that fear."

Gryff knew already that there was no conquering. Not with any of the falcons, or the hawks. It was a partnership, always: the man took care of the bird and in return, the bird would hunt for the man.

"Then why must her eyes be stitched closed?" he insisted. This was his chance to learn as much as he could and he intended not to waste it. His father gave each of his sons one spring and summer of their boyhood to catch and train a bird with the master falconer so that they could learn the art of it. But after that, Gryff must return to only hunting with a trained bird, instead of devoting every hour to their care and keeping.

"I see no greater merit in the old way of seeling closed the eyes. It's the hood she'll wear, and a dark room she'll stay in, so that we need do no stitching." They had reached the mews, and Philip pushed the door open for Gryff to enter. "It is done because she sees more in one glance than you will ever see in your life. All of this is strange to her, and is best she become accustomed slowly. You will see."

They were careful in lifting her out, Philip's hands gently closing over her wings and his voice soothing as he instructed Gryff to attach the jesses to her legs. It was hard to see in the gloom and Gryff sweated all the while, afraid of doing it wrong, worried she would bite him. She was only a little more than a baby, just beginning to venture from the nest when they caught her, but she looked at him with eyes that seemed ancient. It made him feel much younger than his seven years.

"There she is," said Philip approvingly, when Gryff had attached the leash and handed it over. At a glance, the falcon seemed perfectly calm. But anyone could feel she was ready to bate and scream, to bolt away from them for as far as the leash would let her. Only Philip's practiced hands kept her still.

Gryff found the hood and held it up.

"I will train her, truly?" he asked, and Philip nodded. He could hardly believe he'd be allowed that much time at the task, for it took weeks. Every hour of the day must be spent in the mews with her. He had heard Philip tell his father already that Gryff was possessed of a falconer's steady temperament, unusually patient and observant for such a young boy. It made him glow with pride when he heard it.

"How long until she is tame?"

"You will both be trained, but is only you who will be tamed, little fool." It was affectionate, but serious. There were few who were permitted to call Gryff a fool, though he was only a boy. But Philip could. "You could raise her from the egg and still she would not think you her master. Never will she truly need you. She will stay with you so long as it suits her. But she will never be tame."

They began the long process of coaxing the falcon to accept the hood. All the while, Philip explained that the fiercer the creature, the more gentle must be the man, or they would never be in accord. This was why his father wanted him to learn this art, so that he would know what it was to be a servant to one who served you, to have dominance but never complete control.

Gryff looked at the bright eyes of the young falcon, and was glad it could never be tame.

Chapter One
1288

It began in beauty and in blood.

He saw her face in an improbable moment, amid chaos and carnage – startling blue eyes and a soft mouth set in perfect, graceful lines – and then he saw the blood. Not a drop of it touched her. It was all around her, and all of her own doing. Ferocity and beauty, that's how it began.

At first he only saw men dropping on the road, an incomprehensible sight. Eight men, vicious criminals, who had lain in wait behind the trees and sprung themselves on the small party with whom she traveled. They had done everything as they always did, Baudry and his men. Their habit was to fall on the armed knights first, while the women and children screamed in terrified confusion. It was always over quickly.

But this time Baudry and his men only crumpled to the ground one after the other, though it was clearly not the armed knights who caused it. Gryff looked up to the trees for archers, but there were none. This was not a rain of arrows. The horses reared and the women screamed and the attackers merely fell down dead, as though from a plague.

She was the plague.

In the moment he realized it, she looked at him. Briefly, her eyes came to rest on Gryff where he stood beside the road and somehow she did not kill him too. He had raised his hands without thinking, arms extended and palms open, as though he could halt her with a gesture – or at least show he was unarmed. She saw it, just a blink down to his hands and back up to his face again before she was turning away. It was fast. She was so fast, in a way that made him think of a snake striking at its prey. Even before she had finished turning away from him, she drew a fresh blade from somewhere and threw it at Cuddy. Impossibly, it found the half inch gap in his hard leather collar and sank into his throat.

Fitting, for Cuddy to die on his knees with naught but a look of surprise. Even more fitting, that it was the hand of a woman that did it. All that violent lust was ended at last with the almost leisurely flick of a woman's wrist, and her barely looking at him as she did it.

Gryff watched him die, trying and failing to relish it. It was all too sudden. One minute he had been bracing himself to watch as Baudry and his men slaughtered yet another group of innocent people, and the next minute – this.

Cuddy was the last to fall. Now she stood with her back to Gryff as she looked over the scene, and he did the same. Baudry and all his men were in the road, lifeless. Among the travelers, one of the knights was injured and the other appeared dead. A woman clutched two children to her while one of the unarmed men of the traveling party stumbled over bodies to reach her. The last was a monk with a bloodied eye and a stunned look.

The beautiful woman took it all in at a glance and turned back to Gryff. Now he saw she was a young maid. She wore no veil, and she was slim and straight, few womanly curves on her slight frame. There was no distress in her. No fear, no sign of what she'd just done. Months he'd spent with these murderous men, and he had learned something about this kind of unceremonious violence, and the kind of person capable of it. Her brows drew together, a look of concern or curiosity or both as she met his eyes again. It made her seem entirely human for the first time.

He tried to tell her that he wasn't one of the thieves, but it came out as a weak and wordless croak. She was coming toward him with a purpose. He was strangely calm about it, though he didn't want to die. Not yet. Let him go home first, just once. He only wanted to see his home again in this life.

If he died like this he couldn't even be buried there. No one would know it was where he belonged. Even in death, he could not go home.

The panic only came on him in the moment she stumbled. It was Baudry himself – not dead after all – reaching up from his place on the ground as she stepped over him. He grasped her leg and pulled her down and Gryff saw suddenly how small she was. Baudry was more than twice her size, and she disappeared completely beneath his bulk.

"No!" Gryff shouted it over and over, as though that might do any good. He could not reach them, though he tried. The rope that attached his ankle to a tree barely allowed him up onto the road, but he strained against it anyway. He could be no help to her or to anyone, the state he was in, but he had seen her face as Baudry pulled her down. She had not expected it. She had had no weapon in her hand. She was so small. She would die and be left broken and lifeless in the road, and so he shouted, "No! No!"

But somehow it was Baudry who died. Gryff only saw the broad back, muscles contracting, undoubtedly moving to snap her neck, and then he was motionless. Baudry became a lump of heavy flesh that she struggled to push off.

In the end, she had to slide out from beneath his dead weight. Now there was blood on her. The shoulder of her very fine woolen gown was soaked in it. None of it was hers.

"By what mischance are you tied to a tree?"

The uninjured man of the traveling party had appeared beside him, completely unnoticed. He looked to be a merchant of some kind. The monk was tending to the wounded knight, the woman and children huddled near. This merchant disregarded all of it and greeted Gryff like it was a perfectly normal afternoon.

He must think of some way to explain it.

"They have held me as prisoner." He felt on the verge of babbling. Too much relief, too much fear and uncertainty. The girl had turned back to the scattered bodies in the road, leaning down to each one in turn as a little dog scurried among them. "Since the Epiphany. Just before. Two days before."

"They sought your ransom?" The man looked doubtful, and with good reason: Gryff knew he looked even worse than the thieves. Dirty and ragged, more bones than flesh, clothes that were never more than rags, and wearing no cloak in this cold – only a fool would think anyone would pay money for his release.

"Nay," he said finally. "Not ransom. They kept me. As a servant, of sorts."

He found he could not say more. There was too much to explain and a kind of creeping fear was coming over him in the calm. He watched the girl as she went among the bodies. He kept expecting another one to rise up when her back was turned, and come for him this time. It seemed impossible that Baudry and his men and all their torment were finished, in only a few short minutes.

But they *were* dead. She was pulling free the weapons that had killed them. They were strange short knives with no hilt, the blade a few inches long with only a flat circle of metal where the handle should be. Instead of a handle there was a small hole where she inserted something like a nail to pull the blade free. It was the only way to get enough grip, he saw, especially when the blade was slick red and buried deep.

"I am Alfred Brant," said the man at his side, and looked at him expectantly.

Names. This was conversation. This was how people spoke to one another when they met. He remembered it. It shouldn't be so hard to do.

"Gruffydd," he said without thinking, swallowing the *ab Iorwerth* in time. But it was too late. His name was enough.

"You are Welsh?"

It was no crime only to be Welsh. Not here, anyway. So he said, "Aye, born of a Welshman. I'm called Gryff. Just Gryff."

"Well met, Gryff, and God give you good morrow. There is a priory ahead, not two miles. They'll bury our dead and care for Sir Gerald," he said with a nod toward the injured knight. "And for you, do you come with us."

Alfred had a kindly face, as though that meant anything. Gryff looked at it for too long without speaking. He knew it was too long, but he could not help it. Words seemed almost as foreign as the idea that he might be able to move among decent people again, and have food to eat and not fear he would be killed in his sleep.

"Better you share the road with us than journey alone," Alfred advised with a patient look, and Gryff finally nodded. It *was* better. Safer. And he did not know where else to go. He did not even know where exactly he was.

"First I must… There's something," he said, gesturing to the trees behind him. "It wants only a moment. Not far. If you will cut me free of this rope."

"There are more of your company?" asked Alfred, his kindly face turned hard. "They wait for you?"

"Nay." He said it with a shake of his head so vehement that it likely damned him. "On my soul, I swear it. There is only what few things were theirs, and the hawks. I must bring the hawks. I cannot leave them. Go ahead if you will, only free me and I will meet you on the road before you have gone even half a mile."

There was only suspicion in the man's face. Gryff did not know what to do. He could not even contemplate leaving the birds behind, alone. He stared at this stranger who seemed to want him to choose between his own freedom and the hawks. But there was no choice. He could not leave them.

So they looked at each other, Alfred with suspicion and Gryff silently pleading, until suddenly the girl was there. She pulled a long and elegant knife from her boot, knelt down without a word, and cut the rope that Baudry had tied around his ankle not an hour ago. Her eyes swept over him when she stood, taking in the threadbare tunic he wore, the lack of cloak, the shoes that were hardly worthy of the name. She looked a long time at his face – silent, always silent. Was she a mute?

In her, there was no suspicion. It was something else. Compassion, he thought. It had been so long since he had seen it that he almost did not recognize it.

In the same moment he saw it, she turned her eyes to Alfred and some understanding passed between them. She had no words, it seemed, but she held sway among this party. Alfred nodded at her and walked to where the others were gathered around the injured knight. The girl went to the mule that had stood calm and imperturbable throughout the attack. She reached into a pack on its saddle and pulled out a round loaf of bread, stepped forward, and handed it to Gryff. With a snap of her fingers, the dog came to her side and she made some other quick gestures that ended in her pointing at Gryff. Then she walked away.

The dog seemed to understand whatever she meant, and sat looking up at Gryff. Little thing, velvety brown fur and ears standing up on its head, friendly face watching him curiously. The man named Alfred was lifting the dead knight onto the mule while the girl and the monk helped the injured knight onto a horse.

They were going ahead without him, leaving him with a loaf, a dog, and his life. He was free.

Gryff stared down at the bread in his hands. The smell of it was breaking his heart.

He was free.

1277

It was his brother Aiden who was supposed to go as hostage, not Gryff. Even their mother had said so. She'd left off her prayers for a whole afternoon to argue with Father about it. Their oldest brother Rhodri had already been sent to live with a great Norman lord years ago.

But Rhodri was a bastard born of another woman, so Mother had been happy to see him sent away. For the Welsh, a bastard son had the same value as a child born in wedlock, with all the same rights and claims as any other child. His father loved Rhodri, but he said, "We must follow Norman ways in this matter – all the Welsh must, if we are to survive." The Norman way was to give everything to the eldest trueborn son. Bastards did not matter at all under their law.

So Rhodri was sent to foster in England, a gesture to show that there was no ill will, that good and sensible Welshmen trusted the Normans and should be trusted in turn. Years later when there was a battle against the English king – the latest in a series of battles that stretched back generations – his father sided with the Welsh prince Llewellyn. They lost, because the Welsh always lost, and all the Welshmen of consequence who had risen up against English rule were made to give over hostages. It was normal. It happened all the time. It was how peace was kept.

If Father had been more important, the English would not have let him send Gryff as hostage. They would have demanded Aiden, his first trueborn son.

"You're not important at all," Gryff said to him at some point in the journey that took him from his home. He'd made a point of saying very little since the scene days before when he'd shouted and wept and begged to stay. The humiliation of it was still with him. He was too old to act so childishly, but it had seemed impossible to control himself.

It was just as hard when he'd kissed his mother goodbye, but at least he'd only cried quietly. Later, on the journey, he wept for the loss of his trueborn brothers, too. He stopped being envious that the two of them could stay at home, and began to realize what it would mean not to see them every day. Maybe never again. He missed them already. How alone he would be, among the Normans.

For his father, he had naught but hatred. Never once did Father say he regretted any of it, and still he stood by Prince Llewellyn no matter what price his family must pay for it. He never even said he was sorry that they hadn't fought well enough to win their stupid battle.

"You have no power against the Normans *or* Llewellyn, and you can't even win a fight." Gryff stopped himself from saying *I hate you I hate you*, only because he knew it would make him sound like a baby. He was twelve, and the only thing his father said that was true was that Gryff must be a man and not a sniveling child.

Father only ignored these outbursts. When they arrived at the massive Norman castle where many great lords and soldiers waited, Gryff wanted to run. It wasn't fair. He barely even spoke their language, and none of them would know Welsh.

"There can be no profit in fear, Gruffydd." Father looked grim, but not sad to say goodbye. "Nor in pride. Is humility that will serve you well among the Normans. There is much to learn of their ways, and I command you to learn it well. But never forget you are Welsh." He gripped Gryff's shoulder hard, and looked earnestly at him. "You are Welsh. They cannot take that from you without you permit it."

"I am your son," he said, and pushed his father's hand away with disgust. "They cannot take me from you without you permit it."

He walked toward the Normans without looking back.

He never saw his father again.

Chapter Two
1288

As he walked back to the thieves' camp and chewed very slowly on the bread, Gryff gradually came to realize that the dog was meant to keep watch on him. By the time they reached the place that Baudry and his men had days ago claimed as their own – the latest in a series of spots deemed "likely" – Gryff had seen enough signs to know it was a dog with a purpose. A dog with a mission. Its task was to pay very close attention to whatever Gryff was doing.

It seemed a little wary of the birds, though, and kept glancing back at them suspiciously while it trotted around the clearing, investigating, always alert.

Gryff found his old, worn falconer's bag and slung it over his shoulder so that it crossed his chest. Everything he needed was inside. He'd learned to be efficient, always ready to move at a moment's notice. It was the matter of a moment to put on the glove and coax the goshawk from the branch to his hand, then transfer him into the cage. Gryff worried the cage was too small and fretted about it every time he was forced to use it. But it was only two miles to the priory, the merchant had said. Not long.

The dog came to investigate, darting in to sniff gingerly at the cage and then jumping back from the hawk. It caused Gryff to smile, which first felt natural, and then strange. He had not really smiled for months, and was amazed his face remembered how. But he did not want to think of that.

"Well for you that he is hooded," he said to the dog, who spared him a dubious glance. "You are close enough and so small that he may strike at you. Keep well away from them both. If aught should happen to you, I fear your mistress would skewer me."

Reminded of the girl and her gift, he took another careful bite of the bread before stowing it in his bag and turning to the falcon. She came to him readily, as she always did. Her perch was a padded mound atop a stake driven into the ground, made for travel. Gryff pulled it up and tucked it into the crook of the arm that held her, then picked up the cage and headed back to the road. Away from this place. He would never have to think of Baudry or his men again.

He made sure to aim a little north so he could rejoin the road far from the place where the bodies were. Don't see them, don't think of them, just go on with life and one day he would find he had forgotten most of it, and struggle to remember the details. There was an art to letting go of memories. He had learned it well.

Now the dog walked jauntily alongside Gryff, casting worried glances up at the goshawk in the cage.

"This is Ned." Gryff decided to make a practice of civil conversation, so that he might be more coherent when he met with people again. Besides, it distracted him from the intense longing for another bite of the bread he could not reach while his hands were otherwise occupied. "Ned the goshawk. Nor would I have you repeat it, but I will tell you I named him for Edward the king."

The dog looked up as though to acknowledge it before veering off to nose quickly through the brush. Gryff tensed, the strange fear coming over him again – as though Baudry might rise from the dead and hide among the overgrowth, waiting to spring at him. But the vigilant little dog found nothing of interest and returned to Gryff's side again.

He kept speaking, to ease himself away from the senseless fear.

"The custom is to give the bird a meek name. It makes for a fierce hunter. A grand name tempts fate, so to give a bird a warrior's name is to risk having the laziest hawk you ever knew," he explained. Now he lowered his voice as though the King of England might hear him. "It amused me to think I might have a timid Edward, a Ned that no one need fear. Alas 'twas an ill plan. He is as much a killer as his namesake."

This seemed not to disturb the dog at all. It only looked up expectantly, waiting for further introductions. Gryff turned a little as he walked to show the falcon to the dog.

"She is just as fierce, and fitting of her name. Tiffany. Named for the Epiphany. Because I trained her to give as a gift on that feast day, for the abbot."

He felt a familiar weight on his chest, a burn in his lungs. Brother Clement had called her Theophania, the proper Greek form, until he gave in and simply called her Tiffin. When Gryff called to her in the hunt, it was just Tiff, which Clement had said was not elegant enough.

Eager to think of anything other than Brother Clement, Gryff looked to the dog again. He didn't know its name.

"What will I call you? A mighty name, I think. You are no hawk." It looked cheerfully up at him, tongue lolling as it walked. "Bran. I'll call you Bran. A giant and a king."

A Welsh name for a long-ago king. The little dog was nothing like a giant, but the name fit him anyway. Innocent and earnest, like he and his brothers had once been when they had asked the bard to sing the legend again and again. "Does it agree with you, little Bran, or is it too Welsh?"

But Bran was running ahead through the trees, in the direction where the road should be, and disappeared quickly. Either there was some danger, or the party of travelers was there beyond the trees. Gryff stood, his breath suspended. There was only the sound of the dog barking in the distance and his imagination to keep him company while he tried to convince himself there was no danger. He cursed Baudry to hell for turning him into this timid ghost of himself, and tried to make his feet move. It was the weight of the birds on his arms, though, that finally spurred him to move in the direction of the road.

The sound of the barking grew louder until Gryff came to the road, where the travelers were tensed and watchful. The deadly girl was nowhere to be seen. Bran made more noise than he could have dreamt possible for something so small.

"The dog does not care for my birds, I think," he called as he approached.

"He envies their beauty," answered Alfred, looking in admiration at the falcon, and the whole party seemed to relax.

While Alfred helped him affix the cage to a saddle, the girl appeared. Gryff thought she came from the trees, but he had not heard or seen her. She looked warily at the birds, and he tried not to stare at her. It felt impossible that the others could so easily keep their eyes from her. But then, they were likely used to her. He had not been in the presence of any woman, whether plain or comely, for longer than a few minutes – not in years. Little wonder he was transfixed.

Bran only stopped barking when she stamped her foot on the ground before him and made a kind of short hissing sound. "*Fss*," she said, the only sound that had passed her lips in Gryff's hearing, and then she leaned down to scratch the dog's head. Little Bran quieted immediately, but continued to look between her and the hawks as though nothing was more imperative than that she should know they were there and they troubled him. He looked ready to break out into noise again at any second.

But she made another signal with her hand and pointed to the west side of the road, where the dog kept its attentive patrol as the party resumed its progress toward the priory. The girl herself moved to the opposite side of the road, just as watchful, her eyes scanning the trees as they made their way.

"Tell us, if you will – how came you to fall in with the knaves?" Alfred asked.

Gryff had put another bit of bread in his mouth and he chewed slowly, not just to savor it but to have time before he answered. "Months ago," he began, and then stopped. Months ago, only three months. It felt like years. Maybe he should start it from that point years ago, when he'd fled. He almost did that, then remembered in time that it would invite questions of what he had fled, and why. Bad enough he had already given a part of his true name.

"I was at an abbey. A small place. Less than a dozen brothers. Franciscans. And me." He heard himself, how he could not seem to say more than a few words together before pausing. It made him sound like a liar, like he was inventing it as he spoke, but he could not make it come out any other way. Men were harder to talk to than dogs or hawks.

"You are a monk?"

"Nay." Once he would have laughed at that. Now nothing about it seemed humorous. "I kept hawks for the monks. They let me stay. For charity. It was deep in the wilds, away from all. It burned. All the buildings, just before the Epiphany, in the night. None but myself and two brothers survived."

Alfred sucked in a deep breath of shock. "God assoil them," he said, and waited to hear more.

Gryff tried to tell him the rest in as few words as possible. The chapel and dormitory were already engulfed in flames by the time he and Brother Clement even knew it was happening. In their tiny rooms in the hawk-house, they were woken by the shouts of the brothers who had stumbled out of the smoke. Only three of them emerged, burned badly. Two died in the snow before morning. The fire moved so quickly that as it spread to the hawk-house, Gryff had no time to do more than cut free two hawks. Now there was no falconer to call them back, and so they would return to the wild. They could easily survive there. Trained but never tamed, and God be praised for it.

"These two I kept only by chance," he said, and it was not really a lie. It *was* chance. It was all chance. These two birds had been most in his mind, so he had reached for them first and saw them safely away from the fire before returning to free the others. It was chance that he got out of the burning hawk-house in time, despite the blinding smoke. Chance that the snow was deep enough to quench the flames that had caught his clothes.

"And what of those brothers who lived?"

Gryff looked over his shoulder and saw only empty road. On the far side of the road there only the tip of Bran's tail as the dog walked along. The girl was on the near side, walking a little ahead of them – not quite close enough to hear their conversation, he thought, if she even had hearing.

"Baudry," he finally answered. "The thieves. We meant to go to the village. It was far." He looked at her hair as he spoke, a single golden braid tied with a scrap of cloth. The sunlight bounced off it, an impossibly beautiful color. "They killed one brother when they attacked." He pushed away the memory of Brother Julian's staring eyes, the surprise still on his face in death. Baudry's men would not have done it if they'd seen he was a monk – some for care of their immortal souls, others because there was no profit in killing a monk with no possessions. None of them saw any profit in preventing Brother Clement's death. "The other died of the cold. He was very old."

He stopped talking. There was nowhere to look that didn't fill him with sorrow and anger. The wounded knight slumped in his saddle, the body of the knight who had died was tied to another mule, the weeping woman and her silent children – all caused by the same men who had watched Clement freeze to death.

Though his appetite was gone, he shoved more bread into his mouth and let his eyes wander to the girl again. Not a girl – a woman. Young, but not at all a child. He wished he could see where she had hidden away the blades she had recovered. She looked so harmless now.

"Yet did they let you live," Alfred observed after a long moment.

Gryff wanted more than anything to ignore that and ask instead what trade Alfred was in. But he must answer lest they think him one of Baudry's men, so he swallowed and replied.

"I know the hawks, how to hunt with them. The thieves did not, and it was a hard winter. Better to keep the birds and have meat, than to sell them and watch the coin run out."

Baudry had enjoyed having a falcon, too, imagining it made him the equal of a nobleman. To hunt with a peregrine meant he had come up in the world, even though he must rely on Gryff to keep the bird in good health. He liked having a servant, too. Even one who must be kept tied to prevent escape. Even one who he likely had planned to kill in full summer, when food was not so scarce.

"How then is it that you are so starved?"

"They wasted nothing on me except what they must." Some weeks ago – a month, he thought – Tiffin had brought down two herons in one day, and he had had a full portion of meat.

There would be more, he suddenly realized. At the end of this road, there would be a priory and they would offer a meal. He could fly the birds now and they might bring down a duck, a goose, and he could eat it all himself. Every day now, he could eat his fill and choose where he would go and what he would do. He had only to decide his direction.

Home. That was the first thought, of course. There was no way to know if it was safe to return to Wales, and his rusty tongue could think of no easy way to ask it. Not without saying too much. What he needed was a friend. One who was not dead or hundreds of miles away, or overly loyal to the English king. One who would care about keeping him safe.

That thought of safety brought the strange girl to mind again. He raised his eyes from the bread she had given him to watch her as she walked ahead of them. Her hair was like a candle's flame, a glowing sliver of gold against her dark cloak. Fine traveling clothes, good shoes, shining hair, and that fair face.

She looked like a Norman lady, one of those he had known who flirted as easily as they breathed, who sometimes had dared meet him in secret to open their mouths or their legs to him, to welcome him in for a hot moment of sin. Then they, with their smooth skin and bright eyes, would pull the finest silks and furs over their nakedness and melt away into the night.

There was a familiar pang at the thought of that lost life. Let the world fade away, Brother Clement had so often said. All worldly desires and the things of the flesh, let the memory of them fade. But Gryff was not a monk, for all that he had lived like one for years. He turned his eyes away from the girl and his mind away from how starved he was. Instead he tried to calculate how many years he'd lived, hidden and deprived, in the wilderness.

Four, he thought. Definitely more than three. He'd stopped counting on purpose.

When they reached the priory, he gave the birds over to the austringer and made his way to the guest house. It took more time than should have been necessary, to scrub every inch of his skin and trim his unruly beard down to almost nothing. Hunger, relief, fear – all of these conspired to fatigue him so easily that he almost could not keep his eyes open.

As he sat shivering, clean and wrapped only in a length of borrowed linen, one of the brothers came to say that the sheriff had recovered the outlaws' bodies to be hanged at the crossroad and serve as the usual warning. They had been stripped first, and the monk held out the familiar garments, shoes, and the handful of possessions that had been found on Baudry's men. Everything salvaged would go to the poor.

When he was offered a pair of boots, Gryff only shook his head. He did not say that he had watched the original owner kick a man to death while wearing them. He refused it all and instead chose clothes that had been left with the monks by some other nameless donor. His body almost did not feel real, covered in cloth that was not stiff with dirt and sweat, the sweet sensation of the air moving across his freshly unearthed skin. It was like moving in a dream, to walk to the little hawk-house and check on the birds with his legs unfettered.

Back in the guest house, he shared a room with the wounded knight, Sir Gerald, who was silent as Gryff curled onto his own pallet. There was a covered plate waiting for him, set on his blanket. It held a thick slice of cheese and a little bread, though the brothers had already given him his meal when he'd bathed. A kindness, this extra little portion for the starving guest. He ate it slowly and was trying to convince himself that he was safe now, when the wounded knight spoke.

"Is not her usual way, to kill." His voice was stronger than Gryff would have expected for one who looked so near to death. "They were too many, and so intent on murder that she must kill them in all haste, that no innocents would die. More often she maims. A hand or a foot, or any wound well-placed to make a man stop fighting but not kill him – that is her way."

Gryff wanted to ask more: how this knight knew her, if she was truly deaf and dumb, and why she had habits of maiming and killing. Above all, he wanted to know how this man or any man could be immune to her beauty. Haps he had forgotten how comely women could be, so long had he been away from them. She might be only ordinarily pretty and his eyes unaccustomed.

Ordinary or not, her beauty was all the more unnerving because it came with such a casually lethal skill. Even if it was not her usual way, she had not hesitated. Sir Gerald's words were meant as reassurance that there was nothing to fear.

Or so he thought, until the knight spoke again.

"When next you think to look on her with lust, remember it. She'll cool your blood by spilling it, and let you live with the shame and the scar." He smiled a little, as though it were a pleasant thought, and looked toward Gryff. "But if truly you are no villain, there is naught to fear of her. I vow it, and you may sleep easy in that promise."

He did sleep, but it was not easy. It never was.

1277

At first among the Normans, only Will paid him any attention at all – and that was because he wanted to learn Welsh. Will never said that, of course, he just always greeted Gryff in the language and then fumbled for words beyond the simple greeting, obviously hoping for help.

Gryff pointedly answered in Norman French, or in English when he wanted to practice that language. He never spoke in Welsh anymore. He wanted everyone to forget he was from Wales. Not that they ever would – all they did was remind him how backward he was. Savage and poor and stupid, worthless even to his own father. Well, they never said that last part, but they didn't have to.

"My mother is Welsh," said Will, who at ten years old could not be expected to understand how little his mother mattered to this conversation. "There are Welsh and Norman *and* English at my home in Ruardean and all are treated as equal. They are all alike except in their speech. It's not like that here."

Will reminded Gryff of his little brother Owain, never wanting to leave his side in work or in play, imitating Gryff in every gesture. Will didn't have a brother, and he'd been brought here to foster under Lancaster when he was only a baby. He didn't have a father, either – not one he'd ever known – and he barely even knew this home he spoke of with such authority.

"It's not like that here because Lancaster's wife is more Norman than he is himself, and all the household too." Gryff stabbed at the dirt with his wooden sword and wished he had a real one. The master at arms said he wasn't ready for it yet, but Gryff knew it was because he was Welsh. He'd overheard the men saying that he shouldn't be taught to fight at all. "Lancaster would never marry a Welshwoman, nor let her rule."

Will shrugged. "They say my father is mad. Better my Welsh mother rules than a madman."

"It's your Norman uncle who rules," Gryff corrected him, angry suddenly. "They don't give marcher castles over to Welsh people. There's naught in Wales like these manors, we could never – *they* could never build anything this grand."

Will just used the tip of his own wooden sword to dig up a clump of earth, and didn't look at him. It was obvious he disagreed but didn't want to argue. "Do you want to go see the destrier?" he asked instead.

It had become a favorite thing to do, visiting the new war horse that had been brought to Lancaster's stables. Not that Gryff would ever get to ride a destrier in his life. Will would. He'd also probably get a real sword before Gryff did, even though he was younger.

"Nay, I want the kitchen. There will be pears in confit left, and Agnes will have saved some for me." Agnes was the cook's daughter and had taken a liking to him.

Will began to follow him as he headed through the tilting yard toward the kitchen. Gryff frowned at him. "You know well you cannot come with me. Kitchens are for servants."

"*You're* not a servant." He got that mulish look, just like Owain used to before a tantrum. Will wouldn't start shouting and insisting to come along, though. He was too smart for that.

"I am no servant," Gryff agreed. "But nor am I the son of a great Norman lord. Go you to the hall and call for pears confit, and the kitchen will bring it to you fresh."

He walked away and tried not to care that he'd seen the hurt in the younger boy's face. He liked Will but he wasn't sure if Will really liked *him*, or just wanted to pretend to be Welsh. He was too young anyway. Ten years old was practically a baby. In two years, Gryff would be fourteen and that was the age of manhood.

He wondered if that meant they'd send him back to his father in Wales in two years. He'd asked how long he would remain hostage and no one could give him an answer. It had stopped mattering to him because he didn't want to go back to Wales. It *was* a backward place, and poor, and there was nothing there for him. They were still fighting now, the Welsh Prince Llewellyn against the English king. The Welsh would lose because they *always* lost, and then they would have even less and the king would treat the people even worse.

It was stupid. Gryff was glad now that he'd been sent to the Normans. Everything was better here. The food, the buildings, the horses, the weapons. Five months he'd been here, and he'd seen enough to convince him that he should obey his father's command to learn everything he could of Norman ways. Not to please his father, but to please himself.

In the kitchen, he had to wait to get Agnes' attention. There was a boy there, about Gryff's age, pleading with her and almost shouting about some bit of meat that was cooked wrong. He wasn't rude about it. He was just desperate. Agnes was saying that she'd happily give him a bit of pigeon pie instead.

"That's no help!" the boy despaired. "It must be from the duck she killed, and it shouldn't be cooked at all. I was to keep it apart from the meat for the kitchens and bring it to the hawk-house myself. Father will skin me like a rabbit, she's his favorite falcon. Haven't you got any fresh offal, at least?"

"I've the pigeon pie or a nice roasted capon."

"You can't give her cooked meat!"

Gryff said this at the same time and in exactly the same scornful tone as the boy, who looked at him, startled. It made Gryff embarrassed somehow. He could feel the heat creeping into his cheeks as they both looked at him.

"A falcon cannot eat cooked meat," he explained to Agnes. "And you must not wait too long to feed her. It doesn't have to be the same duck she killed, though. Any duck, as long as it's not cooked."

Agnes pointed to the larder and said they were welcome to find one. The boy passed by Gryff on his way out of the kitchen, paused, and announced, "You're coming."

They found a fresh duck laid out on the cold stone and though the other boy declared it insufficiently fat, he scooped it up and said they would go to the hawk-house now. Gryff had been avoiding the place, because everyone seemed to expect him to go there. But he followed now, for lack of a good argument against it.

The boy was named Hal. He talked without stopping and walked almost too quickly and he had skin dark as night. When he demanded to know Gryff's name and where he was from, the answer actually made him stop in his tracks.

"But the best falconers are from Aderinyth, and the gyrfalcons!" Hal said, and Gryff could not help but be pleased at the look of awe. "The peregrines too, of course, and once we had some goshawks. How many nests are there really? My father says it must be at least a hundred."

"No one knows," mumbled Gryff.

It wasn't a lie, really. There might be more than the three gyrfalcon nests they knew of, and the eighty-two nesting places of other kinds of falcons and hawks that his family knew. But the number of them and their locations were a secret known only to a select few. It was the only wealth they had, and the Normans would steal it if they could.

Gryff didn't care about keeping any promises to his father, or keeping Welsh secrets safe. But he stayed silent about the nests.

When they came to the hawk-house, Hal went immediately to his father and confessed everything about the missing duck and its replacement, then moved on quickly to introduce Gryff and say where he was from.

Gryff barely heard any of it. He hardly even noticed Hal's father at first, though the man was taller than anyone he'd ever seen and had a voice so deep it would shake mountains loose from the moorings of the earth. He just looked at the row of birds on their perches and breathed in the familiar smell and could not move.

"That's Amabel," came the deep voice of Hal's father who, he was to discover, was the master falconer.

Amabel was a gyrfalcon, snow white and in perfect health, sitting peacefully on her perch with one leg tucked up under her feathers. The price of her, when sold, might have kept a family for a year. More, even. Gryff could not help but think of Philip Walch, pointing at the place in the cliff where the nest of the whitest gyrfalcons hid, explaining how blessed they were to have such rare birds.

She was beautiful and perfect. She looked like an old friend, patiently waiting for him here in a quiet corner of this strange new home. To look at her made his heart ache.

"God give you good, Amabel." He whispered the greeting in Welsh, because in that moment it was the only way he knew how to be.

Chapter Three

1288

In the black hours before dawn, she lingered in the shadows outside the church as the brothers prayed their nocturns. The rise and fall of their voices was soothing, though the sound barely reached her. She waited until an answer came to her, finally, in the little silence between prayers.

Be selfish.

She had promised it years ago. Somewhere along the way it had become the only course she trusted in moments of uncertainty. To swear fealty to no one, to serve no one and nothing unless it be the leading of her own heart.

But her heart was divided. It told her to go ahead without delay and finally find word of her sister. It told her also to stay with Sir Gerald, care for his wound, take him safely back to Morency to heal. Two duties, two urgent needs. How to choose between them?

Be selfish. She did not want to return to Morency, or tend Sir Gerald's wounds. He would fare as well without her, and she did not want to lose another day that might be spent in finding her sister.

It was her haste that had led them to travel in so small a party on the main road, vulnerable to attack. Nine men dead, eight by her hand and one because she had been too slow. As soon as she thought it – *too slow* – she could hear Gwenllian contradict her. Not too slow. No one could be that fast, her teacher would say, *not even you*. Still she felt her heart pulled in two directions again: remorse on one side, cold indifference on the other.

It was necessary. They were villains. None would mourn them.

They were men. They were alive. Now they were not.

Be selfish. Guilt changed nothing, served no one. It was a luxury she could ill afford, and so she would let it go. She would confess, say her penance, and move forward with a spirit unencumbered.

There was the ragged man, little more than bones and beard and filth. Dark eyes and desperation. It had been years since she had seen hunger so deep. In her memories, it wore her sister's face. But even more than the hunger was the way he shied from shadows that were not there, how he shrank from any contact with others, how even now when he was safe he could not sleep soundly.

She saw herself there, the girl she once was. The girl she would be still if not for the selfless care of a kind stranger.

And he was Welsh. That was not easily dismissed. Of all things, a Welshman in need. It felt like God's own hand had put him in her path.

What was owed? *Everything*, her heart answered. *Nothing*, said her mind.

Be selfish. The brothers would care for him. Her task was more important. Her dog did not like his hawk. It should be an easy thing to turn her back upon.

But even to think it caused her pain. It would disturb her dreams. Already it disturbed her dreams – why else was she here, surrounded by prayers in the dead of night? For years she had prayed too, every day, giving thanks for her own rescue from a fear that had nearly swallowed her. In spite of her promise to swear fealty to no one, she had loyalties that were bound by love if not by her word: her sister, her lady, her teacher, her friends. She did not need another.

Yet she could not banish the memory of his eyes fixed on the bread in her hands. He looked at it like it was his own heart she offered to him, cupped in her outstretched palms.

✠ ✠ ✠

He woke to find her leaning over him, her cool hand laid along his cheek. Slowly the dream dissipated, screams fading and fire dwindling to darkness. Her brows were drawn into a frown of concern, and he knew he must have cried out in his sleep. She meant to soothe him, but it was like waking into a different kind of nightmare. Instead of sharp terror, it was the slow press of reality – this new life, this changed body.

He could feel every knob of his spine where it pressed against the pallet, the product of long hunger.

Her hand moved to the scarred mess at the side of his head, her fingertips outlining his ruined ear. At least enough of his hair had grown back to hide the worst damage, leaving only the edge of the scar visible. It would always be there, though, a permanent reminder. He could ignore the memories until they faded into nothing, but there would always be evidence of it. It had happened. He lived now in the aftermath, where beautiful women looked on him with pity instead of desire, and visited his bed only to quiet his ravings.

"The pain is gone from it," he said even though he did not know if she could hear it, because it seemed to him that was the question in her eyes. "I buried my face in the snow to stop the flames." He was lucky it had not taken half his face and scalp. "In my dreams the snows are not there, and I burn." He licked his lips. "I burn and burn."

Her beauty was even more unearthly in the candlelight. It was overwhelming, to be so near to a woman after so many years. Near enough that, beneath the mingled fragrance of wood-smoke and fresh bread on her sleeve, he caught the scent of her. The salt sweat and musk of her skin.

It made his mouth ache, a ravenous hunger that had been dulled by the more urgent demands of survival. With a vicious suddenness, he wanted to devour her, to slide his hands beneath her skirt to find bare flesh and push her thighs open, to put his mouth on her skin and thrust into her. His breath came short, so vividly did he imagine the feel of her tight heat around him.

There was only silence from her as she withdrew her hand and stood. He watched her feet as she walked to the door where her little dog was stationed. The feet paused, stopped, turned back to him, and waited. He raised his eyes to her. The flame of the lamp she held flickered in the draft from the door, but he saw her perfect face, perfectly clearly. Her look told him she had seen the lust in him. As clearly as though she had spoken it directly in his ear, that look told him: *No.*

He dropped his eyes to the knife that hung at her belt. A simple eating knife, like any common woman would carry. But what she could do with it spoke more loudly than any words or any look. It made the lust in him curdle into nothing.

He turned his face up to contemplate the ceiling, and listened to the even breaths of the wounded knight who slept only a few feet away. Such easy, deep, unbroken sleep.

There was a faint sound at the door, a little rustling. Then the dog was at Gryff's side. It looked at him, then back at her where she still stood in the doorway. She made a gesture, gently patting the air with her hand and holding her palm up, and the dog came closer to Gryff. It curled up next to him, the warm little body pressing against his ribs as the girl left.

"Bran," he said, and put a hand to the dog's head. It gave a very big sigh for something so small, and settled in to sleep.

✠ ✠ ✠

It was day when next he woke, which seemed miracle enough. He had not slept so many hours together since…before.

Almost as miraculous was the still intact meat pie that was wrapped and set near to his head, while patient little Bran sat inches away and stared longingly at it. It smelled heavenly.

"It is pork," he informed the dog. "And you are well trained."

Bran only looked at him hopefully, restraining himself from leaping on the pie as Gryff picked it up and broke off a bit of the crust. The smell made his mouth water painfully. He put the bit in his mouth and blinked back the rush of tears. So pitiful had he become that he was unmanned by a pork pie.

He broke off another piece and held it out to Bran. The dog came forward slowly, never taking its hopeful eyes off Gryff as it took the most careful, gentle bite he'd ever seen from man or beast. Laughter escaped him, jagged and rusty, stabbing the quiet. He kept laughing as the dog nibbled almost daintily from his hand until the portion was gone. Then Bran retreated to a spot several feet away and sat, watching solemnly while Gryff ate the rest.

Just as he finished it, two brothers came. One examined Sir Gerald's wounds while the other merely handed a bowl of bread soaked in broth to Gryff, and left. More food. It did not look to be a very wealthy priory, but they were generous.

"By God's grace there is no fever, and you will mend in good time," the brother was saying to Sir Gerald. "But to journey ahead to Lincoln or back to Morency would be foolhardy."

Morency. Lincoln. Gryff gripped the bowl, assailed by memories that he could not seem to sort fast enough. They were somewhere on the road between Morency and Lincoln. He should avoid Morency; he might have a friend in Lincoln.

"I am told you are Welsh." Sir Gerald had managed to sit upright and now held his own bowl of sop. The monk was exiting, leaving them alone.

"I was," Gryff answered, taking as much of the Welsh out of his voice as he could. He had not realized how much of it had crept back in. "I have not dwelt there since I was a boy. I called Monmouth my home these many years."

It wasn't true, but it was close enough. Monmouth was near to Lancaster's keep, and he had visited enough times to know it well. It was something he must remember, now, another little lie to commit to memory: he came from Monmouth.

In the next minute, he wished he had chosen anywhere else.

"Monmouth is near to Ruardean, whence comes the lady of Morency. Do you know that place? Her brother rules Ruardean now. Lord William, I think his name is."

William, whom he had taught to fly a hawk. Will, who had been so amazed when his beloved sister had married Morency. Little Will was a Marcher lord now. His father must have finally died.

"In those days, it was not a William who ruled," was his only reply.

"Five years then, at the least, that you have lived away from there."

It was a simple statement of fact that answered the nagging question: five years since Wales had fallen. Five years since he had run in fear of his life.

"What task sends you and your party to Lincoln?" Gryff asked, to turn the conversation away from himself.

"Alfred journeys only as far as Godmanchester, for the market. My business in Lincoln is at my Lord Morency's command." He looked ruefully at his injured leg. "Now it falls to Nan alone."

Gryff fought against the urge to repeat her name aloud, to feel the simplicity of it on his tongue. It was such a humble name. Nan. Achingly beautiful Nan. Deadly Nan, who could guarantee safety from any dangers on the road.

"If she journeys on to Lincoln, I would join the party," he said between bites of the sop. "The goshawk I will sell, but the falcon I keep for my own. I would take her to a man I know in Lincoln."

A friend who might tell him everything he wanted to know: if anyone still searched for him, if it was safe to go home to Wales, if there was anything left to go home to. Sir Gerald would likely know these things too, but unless the world had changed very much in five years, it would be the gravest mistake to trust a Norman knight who served the king's bosom friend.

"Nan goes first to a village near to Lincoln, and then on to the town as it please her." The knight leaned his head against the wall, overcome with weariness. "She has her own business and will not wait for a party to gather, so impatient is she. And she needs her no companions to keep her safe from harm."

"I will be glad to leave this place even today. This minute, if I must." A stop on the way to Lincoln was no hardship. "I will pay her if she requires it, to act as guard on the journey. The hawk will fetch a good price."

The thick mustache twitched a little, a quick smile. "She goes where she will and as she likes. Nor will she travel with you if she does not wish it. Your coin will not change that."

Gryff did not reply to this, privately musing that a woman who went where she would and as she liked could decide for herself whose coin she would or would not take. There seemed to be nothing ordinary about her. "Strange though it be, I can believe she is as much protection against rogues as any king's guard. How comes it that a lady has such a skill?"

This produced a short grunt of a laugh. "She is no lady, but servant to Morency. It is a rare villain who will come through his lands, for they have learned it is well guarded. Few know it is a woman who is most like to be their reckoning."

All these words spoken, and still he had not answered the question. But to learn she was servant and not lady was a relief. Little chance, then, that she would know anyone from his old life.

Gryff looked over to find that the dog had gone – slipped away to find his mistress, no doubt, or another bit of pork pie. The guarded tone in the knight's voice told him it was pointless to ask why Morency sent a woman more lethal than a band of thieves to Lincoln with a dog in tow.

"She was trained by Lord Morency's own hand?" he asked. She must be. There was no one else in all of England with both the skill and the disregard for what anyone might think of the strangeness of it.

But Sir Gerald had put his head back against the wall and drifted to sleep that quickly, exhausted by the effort of eating. Gryff poked at the sodden bread with his spoon. His belly would not stand more, but he could not make himself loosen his grip on the bowl. He would want it later; he must just keep it near until he could swallow more. Another reason to curse Baudry and his men, that they had made him worse than a dog with a juicy bone – or a bit of pork pie – jealously hoarding every morsel.

Within the hour, he managed it, then made himself rise and go to the hawk-house. He found Tiffin sunning herself outside, her feathers spread out in the sunlight while Ned looked on from a perch. Gryff had flown them both two days ago, and they were in as good health as he could hope for. The monk who kept birds for the priory informed him that the market at Godmanchester would be a likely place to sell the goshawk.

He should sell the falcon too. He knew it. It was a miracle he had kept both birds alive and well, that they had not flown away and abandoned him the many times he had struggled to keep them fed. He knew it was foolish to think he could keep it up with Tiffin, especially while he journeyed to Lincoln and even more when he could not guess what the future would bring. But she was like a piece of home. She had calmed and comforted him through these months of despair. He could not bear to part with her unless he might give her into the hands of a friend.

"We leave at first light," said Alfred, who was waiting for him back in the guest house some hours later.

The girl Nan was there, too, kneeling over Sir Gerald to carefully put some kind of salve on his wound. She did not look up when he entered, but her dog immediately began to bark. It did not stop until she made that noise again, the quick huffing hiss of a sound that reduced the barking to little more than a canine grumble.

"Godmanchester is but a day's journey on the old north road," Alfred said when he could be heard again. He held out a length of rough wool. "You will find finer cloth there, but this I give you gladly to keep off the chill of morning, until you may purchase better."

Gryff took it and thanked him. He supposed this meant that Nan had agreed to let him accompany her to Lincoln. She did not look up at him, though. She only went about her business, sharing out a portion of the unguent into a smaller jar. Gryff looked away from the sight of her smoothing the knight's hair from his brow, the fond look she gave him, and turned to his own pallet.

Alfred talked on – about the road, the market, the need to bathe here as the inn at Godmanchester never seemed able to provide any but the filthiest water. Gryff sat, exhausted at the thought of walking for a full day tomorrow. He had taken his evening meal of porridge outside, after an afternoon of exercising the goshawk had left him too tired to make his way back here.

The dog appeared at his feet just as Alfred was bidding them goodnight.

"Will you sleep with me again, Bran?" He whispered it, ashamed of how much he wanted it. Embarrassing enough to crave the comfort and warmth of it, but he knew what he wanted most was the security in knowing the dog would act as guard and wake him if anyone entered while he slept. Just for now, he promised himself. Soon he would be himself again.

Bran stayed where he was and it was a long time until Gryff realized the girl had left without his noticing, as silent as ever. He looked to find a small sack of almonds waiting for him in the place where he would lay his head.

"None for you, little Bran," he said, and turned his attention to eating all that he could while there was still food to be had. Then he slept.

In the hour before dawn he woke with a jerk of alarm and struck out at the figure that hovered over him. It was instinct, and a bad one – if he were still tied to a tree among the thieves, they would have beaten him bloody for lashing out. But he was not among the thieves, nor tied by rope. It was the girl again. Nan.

He had not touched her. She was too quick, and had leapt away before his fist could land. Now she stood over him, a lamp in her hand, her startling blue eyes locked on his until his breathing began to calm. Then she blinked and gave a small, apologetic nod of her head before looking down at his pallet, just a few inches from his head. He followed her eyes to the spot and found a strip of dried meat there, and a bit of bread.

It took a moment for him to realize that she had put it there – that she, and not the monks, had left all the other little gifts of food. It took longer for him to realize that she had already slipped away before he could find words to thank her.

1280

Before Rhodri tried to kill him, Gryff had thought they would be great friends.

"A bastard brother is still a brother," Gryff had said to him, and to his own surprise he truly meant it. There was some Welsh still left in him, he supposed.

He had only faint memories of his half-brother, who was six years older and had been sent to foster so long ago, but they were mostly fond memories. Then Rhodri came to Lancaster's court to celebrate Michaelmas and immediately sought out Gryff. They found they had a mutual admiration for many Norman ways, and a shared resentment of their father.

"Owain and Aiden still think him perfect," Rhodri reported of their other brothers. "They do not care that he has sent us away. Two brothers instead of four – that's half the trouble for father. And for Aiden, less than half."

Inheritance. It all came down to that, for Rhodri. Perhaps it was the same with his other brothers, but Gryff had never felt it so strongly from them. It hurt to hear that they did not miss him. It hurt even more to know that Rhodri was allowed to visit family. Even if Gryff wanted to, he could not. His fourteenth birthday had passed last year without fanfare, making him a man in the eyes of the Welsh, but he could not go anywhere without royal permission.

Still, it had been nice to have Rhodri there. He never spoke a word of Welsh, and he too thought Wales was a wretched country. They were in agreement on the superiority of Norman laws and English ale, and they did not even argue over which of the serving girls in Lancaster's hall each would flirt with.

It was only when he showed the white gyrfalcon to Rhodri that there was some little unease between them. There was anger behind the admiration in his half-brother's eye as he said that unlike Gryff, he had never been allowed the year of falconry study that their father gave to his legitimate sons.

Perhaps Rhodri thought this confession would make Gryff sympathetic, but it only made him suspicious. The year of study was a tradition in their family that went back generations. It was no small thing to deny this to a son, and if their father had not allowed Rhodri to live among the falconers, there must be a very good reason for it.

That was why, when Rhodri asked him about the nesting places, he lied.

Gryff said, "Father wants only Aiden to inherit the land, and that means everything of value in it." Then he gave Rhodri the same lie he gave to any outsider who asked: "No one person in Aderinyth knows them all. Is a secret shared among the falconers of old, and kept from all others. Even the princes were never told."

A fleeting stab of annoyance crossed Rhodri's face, like he knew it was not true but could not say so. It passed, and Gryff thought no more of it until some days later when they drank together in a corner of the hall during the holiday feast. He had turned away briefly when he saw Agnes across the hall, her hair decorated with Michaelmas daisies, giving him a knowing wink. He wondered if she would wait for him behind the bakehouse again or if there was anywhere more private she preferred to lift her skirts for him. Then he reached for his cup as he turned back to his friends.

Hal knocked it from his hands. He pretended it was an accident, that he was clumsy with too much wine, but Gryff knew his friend. Hal never drank so much that he was clumsy, and the look he gave Gryff was too sharp and clear-eyed to mistake for anything other than a warning. Rhodri laughed and said he'd find more ale for them, and when he had gone Hal leaned forward to whisper in Gryff's ear.

"Have a care with your brother. He dropped aught in your ale."

When Gryff protested it could not be true, Hal reached down to retrieve the cup where it had fallen. There was still a swallow left in it and Will (who of course had observed the exchange and missed nothing – he never did) said that they should feed it to a rat and see if it died or only became drunk.

The rat died. Gryff stared at it and fought down a kind of panic. He let Will explain it to a confused Hal, all about the old Welsh laws and how this particular tradition had been the downfall of so many Welsh families of property. "When every son inherits an equal portion," said Will, "greed is like to strangle brotherly love. It has torn Wales apart from within, how they fight each other. It has done more damage than any English king could hope to do."

He wondered if Rhodri had tried to kill Owain and Aiden, too. He'd have to kill all of them, to have a hope of inheriting. Gryff supposed he himself was the easiest to get at, and the least likely to be missed.

He found Rhodri the next day and dropped the dead rat before him. "It drank too much ale," he explained, and his bastard brother only gave him a long and belligerent look, then shrugged and turned away. There was no more pretending that they were friends or loving family. They did not speak again.

It was only because Gryff could not bear to think anything might happen to his real brothers that he sent a warning in secret to them. Will carried the message to a member of his own household, a Welsh kinsman whom he swore could be trusted with anything. When the Welshman returned and said the warning was delivered to his brothers, he said also that Gryff's father had given him some words to deliver in return.

It was a message for Hal, thanking him for saving Gryff's life.

Chapter Four
1288

When he closed his eyes, night or day, the gold of her hair lingered in his vision. It was like a beam of searing sunlight that had left an indelible mark across his eyes, and he was not sure he wanted it ever to fade. It was better than every other thing that waited for him in the dark.

For three silent days he had walked behind her on narrow paths and byways, avoiding the main road after they had left Godmanchester and the merchant Alfred behind. Three days of waking to find another little offering of food had been left next to him as he slept. Three days of staring too much at the braid that fell down her back and between her shoulder blades, shining like a thin river of gold flowing through a forbidden landscape. After two days of silence and staring he had finally looked beyond the tip of that braid and noticed that the thickening at one side of her leather belt was not poor craftsmanship, but rather the hilt of a knife. The belt was also a kind of sheath, the weapon parallel to her waist and the grip made of the same leather as the belt, very cleverly hidden in plain view.

She wore leather braces buckled to her forearms, thin and supple, fashioned to fit closely beneath the split sleeves of her dress. In the braces were eight of the strange, short blades with no grip – four on each arm. These were in addition to the simple eating knife that hung from her belt and another concealed in her boot.

Five years without a woman, and the first one God put in his path was beautiful enough to tempt angels to sin – and covered in weapons.

Now she came dripping from the river where she had stopped to wash the mud from her dress – his fault, because the falcon's dive to the lure this morning had caused the dog to run between her ankles and her to slip in the mud. Wading into the water, she had pulled the filthy gown off and left only her linen undertunic to cover her as she scrubbed. For shame, he had turned away from the sight of her bathing. She might only be a servant, but he was mannered enough for the king's court, not an uncouth lout.

When she came out of the water, holding the wet gown modestly before her linen-clad form, he looked and saw another knife between her breasts. He turned away again to allow her to put on a fresh gown and wondered where else there might be blades hidden beneath her clothes, tucked against skin that was as golden and glowing as her hair.

She was silent – she never made a sound except for that odd hissing noise she employed to call or quiet the dog – but he knew she was dressed again when she led the mule ahead on the path. Unlike the gown she had dirtied, the one she wore now was made of rough material, the kind of garment only the meanest peasant would wear. She had tucked the skirt of it up into her belt, to let the linen beneath dry as they walked. He had seen servant women tuck their skirts up like that, to scrub floors.

The splatters of mud had been washed from her hair, too, and now it hung loose to dry. It spread across her shoulders, a veil of sunlight on this gray day.

"Come ahead little Bran," he called, though there was no need. The dog was well trained to keep up with its mistress. It was only that Gryff grew weary of the silence, and had taken to speaking to the animals only to hear words again.

He had become aware at some point that though Nan might be mute, she was not deaf. Once he had realized that she could hear, he spoke his nonsense only in Welsh – and no matter how hard he tried it was memories of his childhood that came out. He found himself talking idly of walks with his brothers in the hills, claiming the hawks and eagles that wheeled against the sky as their own, arguing over it, searching for the lake where a fairy was supposed to live. Pointless reminiscing. A world that was gone. It meant nothing to anyone, these memories of a lost life. Fitting, then, to talk to a dog, a mule, a falcon about it.

He had mumbled in Welsh for no more than a mile or so, about how according to legend the fairy in the lake would name one of the brothers king, when

Nan stopped abruptly and turned to look at the falcon, and then at him.

"Aye, she must hunt," he answered, for that was the polite question in her face. She did not need words, so uncommonly skilled was she at communicating without them. Now she swept her eyes back toward the river and nodded slightly. He looked to see a mallard floating peacefully by.

He said a quick prayer for better luck than this morning, when Tiffin had missed two coneys and a fat partridge, and he had the falcon in the air. "Quickly, quickly," he whispered, because there was no way to know if this seemingly empty stretch of land belonged to someone who would call them poachers. Nan was looking up at the falcon, rapt. After a time she inhaled sharply, he looked up too to see that Tiffin had gone into a dive.

It did not take long. When the hunt was done they had two mallards, both kills blessedly fallen to the ground and not in the cold water. Gryff came back with the second one and found Nan already dressing the first. She pulled out the feathers over its belly before cutting it open and removing the viscera. She looked like she had done it every day of her life, and yet she seemed ignorant of every other aspect of the hunt.

He watched her hesitate, shy of the falcon.

"The heart belongs to the hunter," he said, and pointed to it in the red mound. She picked it up and looked at Tiffin. He could feel it in her, the breathlessness and the awe, the fascination with the falcon, the fear of making a wrong move.

He pointed a finger to his falconer's glove, just below where Tiffin sat waiting for her reward. Nan looked at the place and then at him, as skittish and hopeful as a shy child. She held her breath as she placed the scrap next to the falcon, and her face transformed as she watched the bird take it. There was the start of a smile on her parted lips, a quiet rush of air escaping her, watchful eyes softened with delight. The sight of it took his own breath away.

Then she turned back to the ducks and tended to the kill better even than he could have. Beauty and blood.

It was not just her skill with the knife that was remarkable. She plucked the mallards as quickly as a kitchen maid. She packed the carcasses with grass and hung them from the saddle, then took a cake of soap from her bag and washed her hands in the river. Not even a feather clung to her when she was finished, and they were on their way once more with her leading the mule before him on the path.

He walked behind her, blinded by something as simple as her hair, and thought of her face looking up at the falcon's flight. How the soft pink of her lips parted in that small smile, the way the wet linen clung to her legs. More images to keep him company when he closed his eyes.

Hair like spun gold floated in waves down her back. It mesmerized him. He reached out a hand to touch it, an impulse he seemed unable to control.

The contact was so slight that it seemed impossible she could feel it, yet she immediately halted. Her hair was like cool silk against his fingers, a miracle of softness in the midst of this harsh world.

Because she did not move, did not pull away or protest, his hand gathered a sheaf of it and let it fall over his palm, his thumb brushing lightly over the strands.

She was perfectly still while he held the shining wave, tilting it this way and that to catch the light. Warmth rose from her body to touch the back of his hand, setting off a cascade of lustful thoughts. Her face turned toward her shoulder until she was in profile to him, and now the pulse in her neck was visible. He was sure he did not imagine it, though the sight of it beating so fast made him almost lightheaded.

Here was something he knew well, that he could recognize even without the heat of her skin or the evidence of her heartbeat. Curiosity. Hidden desire. The sudden and unmistakable tension in her body.

She was not indifferent to him. All these silent hours together, she had hidden this. It made his own pulse race. God save, that she might actually want him.

He let his fist fall gently to the place where her neck met her shoulder and watched her pulse leap, her shallow breaths quicken. The feel of her tender skin against his knuckles raised the lust in him so sharply that if she turned now he would fall on her, devour her, slide himself into her and take her here in the mud like an animal.

She must sense it, but still she did not move. She might almost be carved of marble.

A fingertip traced up the side of her neck and felt her tremble sweetly, faintly. His hand turned over and opened over the smooth skin at last, palm sliding around the curve of her throat, and now relief and excitement flooded him as she turned – a quick, bewildering flurry of movement that happened in the blink of his eye – and then she was perfectly still again, facing him and holding the point of her knife to his belly.

The swiftness of it stunned him utterly. There was no trace of desire in her look; there was only a cool, hard warning. He stood with his heart hammering, his skin turning cold, his vision blurring.

He blinked, mortified less by the thought that he had imagined her response than by the way he was now frozen in fear. Utterly frozen.

Not fear of her. Not really. It was only a warning, clearly communicated without words, as she communicated everything. It was not fury and the promise of retribution, as it had been the only time he'd escaped the thieves. A day of running, sure of his freedom, relaxed and finally believing it was over when Baudry appeared from behind a tree and held a dagger to his throat.

This was not that. But it felt like it.

He looked down at the knife, blinking. A shape was carved into the grip, and he seemed only able to consider the question of what it was – a circle, a snake, the letter G? – instead of what might happen if she pressed the blade forward. He knew he must say something. Once, long ago, courtly words had come so easily to him, smooth and polished, the accepted ways a man would beg pardon of a lady. But now his mind was a desert. If only she would take the blade away.

When she finally did, concern ceased her features. She looked at him with her brows drawn together, obviously wondering what ailed him. All the warning in her had dissolved into uncertainty, and she seemed to become smaller. It was a trick of his mind – she had always been this small, coming only barely to his shoulder and so slight of frame that it would take no great strength to overpower her.

She stepped back from him and returned the knife to its place at the back of her belt, never fumbling for the hidden sheath. He waited to feel relief, but it did not come. Her eyes flicked over to the hooded falcon in the cage, then roamed over the baggage strapped to the mule, an aimless wandering of her attention. He gradually became aware that she was waiting for him to move from this place where he had turned to stone, so that they might resume their journey.

It was mortifying. She saw it in him, this outsized fear, and knew what it was.

The shame brought him to his senses, and he concentrated on forcing the memory of Baudry away. It was quickly done; he knew how to forget better than he knew anything. He let himself think only of the road ahead, the little dog, the freedom he finally had for the first time in his life. He would not squander it in fear.

"I'll have you walk ahead or beside me, if you please, and not behind."

For a long moment, he thought it was the mule that had spoken and that he was going mad. When he finally comprehended that it was Nan, he could do nothing but blink in astonishment. She only picked up the rope that served as the mule's rein from where it had fallen, and began wiping the mud from it.

"You can speak." It was a witless thing to say, but he seemed incapable of anything else.

She paused only slightly in her work, glancing up at him and giving a brief nod to acknowledge it – but no more words. He struggled to find any himself.

"But…wherefore have you played at being mute these many days?"

She looked disconcerted at the question. "It is not play." When he only blinked at her, she said simply, "When words are needed, I speak them."

With that, she gave a little jerk of her chin that asked him to take a place beside the mule so that they could begin walking again.

He would have refused to move until she explained more fully, but the sound of her voice still echoed in his head. The fact of her speaking was easier to accustom himself to than the manner in which she spoke. Even in so few words he could hear that her voice was unrefined, with none of the polished tones of Norman nobility. It matched the way she had tucked up her skirt and gutted the birds with no squeamishness, and how she was busily braiding her own hair with quick, efficient moves.

A servant. Her speech matched exactly what she was, but her face had made him forget it.

"Do you think to pretend a higher station, and so hide your speech?"

The look of affront that crept over her was more eloquent than any words she might have spoken.

"Your pardon," he said hastily. "I mean you no insult. I thought…"

He had thought of his own pretending, how he had spent so many years trying to hide the Welsh in his voice. But he didn't say so. He just walked with her in silence until he could stand it no more.

"Where do we travel? What village?"

She made no answer, nor acknowledged the question. It was as though he had not spoken at all.

"What business have you there?" he tried.

But it seemed she thought words were not needed on the subject, and she only walked ahead without speaking again.

They continued all afternoon in a silence that felt both more companionable and more strained until the sun was low in the sky. They moved off the path to find a likely place to camp for the night. She went, as she did every evening, to bring water from the river while he built a fire and roasted the meat. As she always did, she gave him two oat cakes to her one, and a thick slice of the hard cheese that she never seemed to eat.

He almost refused it. He did not know if she did it out of practicality – for even in his recently starved state he was considerably larger than she was – or out of pity for him. But she did it so naturally and easily that he worried he would offend her further if he refused it now.

After he had smothered the fire and made his bed on the ground, she made one of her gestures to the dog that began their nightly ritual: she would choose a spot within sight of the little camp and wait there in the dark, and the dog would do the same at a spot in the opposite direction. They were silent sentries, keeping vigil while the night fell and then creeping back quietly after a time to sleep. Gryff had spent the last three nights trying not to remember things that the thieves had done to travelers who wandered off the road at night. He would wait, only able to sleep when both girl and dog returned to the camp.

As the dog trotted by him on its way to keep watch, Gryff called out softly. "God grant you a peaceful night, mighty Bran."

The dog went on to its duty, but Nan stopped where she was. She turned to Gryff, a peevishness in her face he had never seen before.

"He's named Fuss," she scowled. "Nor would I never give him such a name as Bran."

He blinked in surprise that something so insignificant would cause her to speak again. He remembered the strange huffing hiss she used to call the dog. It wasn't a hiss. It was a word. Fuss.

"Fuss?" he asked, skeptical, and she nodded. "Is not a fitting name for such a steadfast creature. He answers well to Bran."

Her own look was far more skeptical than his own, with more than a hint of scorn in it.

"You would have us called Nan and Bran?"

She gave a delicate snort of disgust as she walked away in the failing light.

If she had been more good-humored about it, he would have given in to his amusement and laughed. Nan and Bran was no more absurd than Gryff and Tiff, he should have said. But he had somehow managed to annoy her several times in just this one day, from causing her to fall in the mud to misnaming her dog, and he saw no need to antagonize her further.

He lay in the dark and remembered the feel of her hair, her throat. In the moment, he'd been so sure that she wanted his touch. He even thought he had felt her lean toward him. The prolonged hunger must have addled his brain. Or it was just her and all her contradictions that addled him. Golden beauty and lowly manners, a dozen blades and a friendly dog, days without speaking and then breaking her silence for a trivial request. It spun his head.

When she came back from her vigil among the trees and settled on the ground a little away from him, she spun his head even more.

"I speak Welsh," she said, in that language. It struck his ear with a sweetness, the sound of his lost home floating toward him in the dark. "Nor was it my intent to deceive you. If you have said aught you would not wish me to hear, I am full sorry. Be assured I will repeat none of it. Idle talk is not in my nature."

It stunned him into silence. All of it: that she had spoken at all, that she understood Welsh, that she had heard all his meandering memories, that she was contrite. But the most stunning fact of all was that her Welsh was perfect. She had only the slightest accent, and every word as polished and correct as a Welsh princess.

She was at every turn a mystery and a contradiction.

"How come you to know Welsh?" he asked finally.

There was a long pause. He could hear her draw a slow, deep breath before she spoke. "I am sorry," she said softly, reverting back to English. "Truly, I am. Good night to you."

That was all. Explanations, it would seem, were considered idle talk.

He stared up at the branches against the clear night sky, sure he would not sleep. But he did, and when he woke in the morning he found she had left a small gift of food beside him as usual, as though nothing had passed between them at all.

1281

In his years of living in Lancaster's household, Gryff had convinced himself of many foolish things, but none was as all-encompassing in its stupidity as his belief that Isabel was in love with him too. He was barely seventeen, which was a perfect time to be a fool in love – that's what Hal's father said – and she was so beguiling that it was impossible to resist her.

"Tell me again, this word for when a Welshman misses his home."

They were huddled together in a shadowed corner of the crumbling west tower of the keep. He and Hal had discovered long ago that it was the perfect place to hide and now that they were grown, they employed it frequently for less childish endeavors. Isabel's soft curves were pressed against him, seeking warmth after the chilled air had cooled the sweat of their lovemaking.

"Hiraeth," he answered her. After many years of swearing he would never do so again, he found himself almost eager to speak his native tongue whenever she asked. Isabel had a seemingly insatiable appetite for stories about Wales, and since she was equally insatiable in ways profoundly more pleasing to Gryff, he did not hesitate to indulge her.

"Hiraeth," she repeated in perfect imitation. "It means to miss your family? But I feel this too, so it cannot be true when you say there is no word in my language."

He didn't know her language. She came from Aragon and would return there soon, so her father could marry her to a new husband – one who might live longer than the Norman one had. She seemed determined to make the most of her freedom as a widow before that happened.

"Hiraeth is more than just missing family," he explained. "It is the land and the people, the smell and the sounds, and more. Like a flavor on your tongue from a fruit that no longer grows. You ache to taste it again, but you cannot, and so you are never satisfied. Hiraeth means to long for a place that is lost to you, or impossible to reach. To know a great part of your soul dwells in a place you cannot be – that is hiraeth."

Her lips had begun to kiss his throat before he was finished, her hands moving under his tunic. "Mm, do not stop," she sighed. "I love the sound of it."

Belatedly he realized he had said all of it in Welsh. It had felt entirely natural, because all the words he knew to describe hiraeth had been learned from Welsh bards. He wanted to confess to her what he had discovered through all her questioning about his homeland, what he could barely admit to himself: he missed it. All of it. His brothers, his mother, and even his father. The hills and the sea, the rain and the mists, the bards and the falconers. He did not want to miss it, but he did. He did.

He could not tell her in this mood. She was urging him down on her, and he was more than happy to oblige her. Later he would tell her all his heart, he thought. Finally there would be someone who would understand him.

The only thing that happened later was that he learned what she really thought of him.

He and Hal were strolling in the ornamental garden, in the last stages of manning a new hawk. Gryff had spent four days patiently waiting in the dark mews with the bird, until finally it took food from his hand. Now it must be carefully introduced to the wider world so that it was not shy among people, and the almost empty garden was a perfect place.

Near the bower of gilliflowers, they paused when they heard the voices of ladies. The sound was accompanied by soft laughter, so they grinned at each other and crept closer to hear through the thick screen of pink petals.

"He is even more satisfying than I hoped for. The only disappointment is that he is not unwashed, or even a little pagan. I was promised a true savage!"

It was Isabel's voice, gossiping with a friend. She went on to wonder if there was time to find an Irishman to seduce, and wondered how long to enjoy her sport with Gryff before taking a new lover. The new lover would be Scottish, because she hoped to sample every kind of man the island offered before leaving.

Gryff thought he hid it well from Hal, the swift stab of pain she caused. He should have walked away then, but the need to pretend it didn't matter kept him standing there, listening while she laughed and described how satisfyingly unsophisticated he was. She took his descriptions of his home in Wales –

spoken to her at her eager insistence – and made them laughable. Nothing but sheep shit and rain, she said, and the manor houses sounded like no more than tiny heaps of slate and stone not even worthy of the name.

"I thought the Normans were provincial! The Welsh truly are worse. But I take what amusements I can in this dung heap at the edge of the world. They will never believe me when I return to Aragon, how this little island thinks itself so important, so grand."

The worst wasn't even the look of pity on Hal's face – it was the slight embarrassment, the uncomfortable manner. Savage, backward, uncouth. Years here, living as one of them, educated as one of them, and nearly all the Normans still thought it about him. They liked him, but they saw him that way, and she had learned this scorn from them.

Hal was different, and so was his father. When they made their silent way back to the mews, Hal's father awaited them. He asked what ailed Gryff and when he received only a shrug in reply, he peered closely at Gryff's frown.

"Ah, a fair maid," he divined. The rumble of his voice was as soothing as always, despite his words. "Who has turned your head this week? Agnes again, or is it still Lady Julia?" There was no hope of hiding these things from Hal's father, who seemed to know everything.

"I miss my home." Gryff had not meant to say it at all, much less for it to come out half-choked, like he might weep at any moment. He burned with the shame of being Welsh, and the anger at knowing he should not be ashamed. "I do not belong here."

Hal's father was better than his own. He put a hand to Gryff's shoulder and said, quietly insistent, "You belong *here*."

And he was right. This mews was like the best part of home had been transported here. It was like the magical places in tales and legends, where two realms overlapped and he could briefly pass from one world into the other.

He picked up the leather strips held out to him and made new jesses for the gyrfalcon. Working with hawks required a steady hand and a quiet mind; they could sense turmoil in a man, and would not trust him if he was not calm.

Hal's father kept him busy for days, for weeks – for as long as was needed to soothe the heartbreak, he said, for there was no better cure for it.

Hal himself suggested that a better cure would be for Gryff to seduce the friend with whom Isabel had been gossiping. "Or whichever lady at court is most likely to stir her envy."

They narrowed it down to three friends who may have gossiped with her, and three more who would make her writhe with jealousy. Gryff had all but one in his bed within a fortnight, and found Hal was right – it worked nearly as well to help him forget as the falconry did. When Isabel cursed him for his faithlessness and called him a swyving whoreson, no better than a rutting beast in heat, he apologized most cordially and explained she could not expect better behavior from an ignorant savage.

Chapter Five
1288

Walking at Nan's side with the mule between them was far less distracting, but he did miss the view of her golden braid trailing down her back. He had thought she would speak more now that the silence between them had been broken, but three more wordless days proved him a fool to expect it.

Well, the days were not entirely wordless. "Which bit should I give her?" she had asked yesterday, beaming at the falcon from afar, one hunter admiring the skill of another as she cleaned the small heron that Tiffin had brought down. Nan bade him good night every evening, and good morning too, almost like those few words were a duty she had neglected. And of course when the dog made too much noise she hissed his name in admonishment. Fuss.

No more words than that did she ever speak, nor did she need to. When he offered her coin for serving as guide to Lincoln, she only looked at his outstretched hand, shook her head, and stayed silent.

Her expression said that though she was not offended at the offer, she had no interest in his payment. It said that she let him travel with her because she wanted to, and no other reason. This morning when she turned the mule eastward, he asked why – and her answering look said as plainly as any words that they went this way because it would lead to their destination.

The paths they had traveled ran parallel to the wide north road and now that they turned east, they must cross over it. As she did so often, she sent the dog ahead before them. When it came trotting back from the road with an expectant look, her obvious relief told him without words that she was no more eager than he to encounter other travelers.

They emerged at a crossroads. Lincoln was to the north, and Gryff had opened his mouth to ask her which villages lay to the east and west when he saw the gibbet. It was empty, and looked as if no criminal had rotted there in recent memory.

Sometimes he dreamt he was hung on one just like this, burning in a desert sun, bored. He would ask passing travelers who had put him here and why, and the answers were always different: the sheriff because he was a thief; the king because he was a traitor; his father for no reason at all. When he woke, it always took too long to remember that it was only a dream.

Gryff did not realize he had stopped to stare at the gibbet until something at his feet drew his attention away from the grim sight. It was little Bran. "Fuss," he said, trying out the name.

He followed the dog to where Nan waited on the far side of the road, and they walked into the trees together. It was true forest here, and on the narrow way he must walk behind her. But this place made him uneasy, and he could take no pleasure in the sight of her now.

As if to confirm his fears well-founded, the dog began to bark at something ahead of them. It was a frantic noise, and caused Gryff to grip the only thing he had that could serve as weapon: an eating knife he had bought in the same market where he had sold the hawk.

It was nothing. He knew it was nothing even before he saw her quick movement, a flash of something in the underbrush and then stillness. He could see it was nothing by how unconcerned she was, how she only tried to quiet the excited dog, how no one and nothing came at them through the trees.

It was nothing, but he could not convince his body of it.

He stood tensed, not thinking about how Brother Clement had begged for his life among trees just like these. He was not thinking of it. He would not think of it ever again.

Nan was suddenly before him. She had stepped closer, only inches from him now. She put a hand to his wrist, a soft touch against the tight muscle above where he gripped his knife.

"Gruffydd," she said, and waited until he met her eyes. "There is naught to fear." She held up a lifeless hare, and he understood this was what had startled the dog. "I will make it a stew, and your falcon may rest from the hunt for a day."

For the space of a heartbeat, he did not see her beauty. She was only an ordinary person, calm and sensible, who soothed him even as she startled him by saying his full name. It was the first time in years he had heard it, and pronounced perfectly. It brought him back to himself. He blinked, and she was unbearably lovely again, the forest was just a forest, the dog was still making too much noise.

The look she gave Gryff was piercing, bright blue eyes assessing him keenly until she turned away and silenced the dog with a scornful, "Fuss!"

It was only a moment – a strange moment, but easily forgotten. Or so he thought.

They walked on in silence and at midday they came upon a stream where they rested and let the mule drink. Gryff shut everything out of his mind except for the sound of the birdsong in the trees, a joyful riot. Then her voice came, as it always did, unexpected and startling.

"Is a mistake, to hide from the memory, whatever it is." She did not look at him as she tied the newly filled flask of water to the mule's pack. "You only give it strength."

It made his breath speed up, the quiet confidence in her. She spoke as if she answered a question he had not asked. After a long pause to think how he should respond, he said, "You confound me."

He only meant he was baffled that she spoke now to say this, when she had withheld her speech so carefully.

"I see you. You try to make yourself forget." She looked at him, held him in her frank gaze. "You won't. You make it worse."

It was how she spoke, so bold and yet in the accents of a servant, that gave an edge to the anger that sparked in him. He bit his tongue against asking how she dared speak to him so. After all these years, it seemed he was still capable of haughty disapproval.

It must have shown in his face, for she lowered her eyes even as he unclenched his jaw enough to scoff, "What do you know of it?"

Her answer was to fall back into silence, and this time he was grateful for it. They resumed the journey, with only birdsong echoing in their ears.

✠ ✠ ✠

When they stopped for the day, he watched her as she prepared the hare with practiced, efficient movements. He had tried to help by cleaning the game, but she had taken it from his hands. Whether this was from habit or because she was particular about the cooking, he did not know.

In truth, he knew nothing about her, or about her life. This was what he had been thinking as they walked all afternoon, after she had spoken so bold. She was servant to Morency, clearly lowborn, but like no servant he'd ever known. She inexplicably spoke perfect Welsh, and gutted rabbits and men with equal skill.

She never spoke idle words, and he was a fool to have dismissed anything she said only because some remnant of pride still lived in his breast.

"What *do* you know of it?" he asked, and this time without scorn. She looked up from cutting the meat. "What see you, when you look at me? How am I so mistaken?"

It was a long time her steady eyes held his, her hands stilled. It meant something, that look, but he did not know what. Eventually she turned to her work again, carefully placing the bits of meat into the pot on the fire.

"I'll tell you a story," she said over the sizzle of the meat. "I had a husband once. Oliver was his name, and he worked in the stables. We were very young. Nor did I want a husband, but I thought it would be my protection from a great lord who lusted after me." She reached for the wooden spoon beside her and peered into the pot. "This was long before I came to Morency. I worked in kitchens, and for a time served ale in the hall of the king himself."

His heart reacted to this news, a thump of alarm in his chest as he wondered if she had ever served him on his visits to court. But he knew that was impossible. He would have remembered her. He could never forget such a face, even on a serving girl.

"There were many there who chased me, as men will always do when there is too much drink and not enough maidens. But this lord made sport of me, and I feared him. So I married Oliver as my protection, but still the great lord chased me. He commanded me to his bed, and before the night I was to go to him, Oliver tried to kill him." She gave a little shake of her head, rueful. "It were not in Oliver's nature, murder, and he was caught when he tried it."

She stirred the sizzling meat, only looking up to glance to where the dog sat. He was meant to be keeping guard, but kept looking back at the smell of the meat. She paused to wash her hands before pouring water into the pot. Then she pulled out the sacks of spices she kept, carefully measuring handfuls and pinches, methodically sifting them into the pot as she spoke.

"Well then, the lord thought it were a plot by a rival to have him murdered. He sent his men to drag me from the kitchen because he knew I had served a lord he suspected. He bade me tell him all I knew of this rival and this plot. I knew naught but said whatever would please him – anything at all, for he held a knife to Oliver's throat." Her spoon stirred, scraping along the bottom, a hollow sound. "But naught pleased him, and he killed Oliver. Right there before my eyes."

The words were very calm. She pulled an onion and two turnips from the sack. The knife sliced into the onion first, peeling off the outer layer. Her hands were perfectly steady.

It was more than she had ever spoken, and he did not know if this was the end of her story. Questions rose up in him, impatient and hot, but she had said *I'll tell you a story*. He knew he was not meant to interrupt, that she must say her piece and his only task was to listen well. So he held his breath, attuned to her smallest movement, and waited. It was a discipline born of years spent in training fierce creatures to trust him.

"He was a very great and powerful lord. He kept me there as his amusement. It was a hunting lodge, for he had been on the hunt. Oliver served him and his men, kept the horses for them. Nor can I remember what game they hunted." She furrowed her brow a little, like it troubled her to forget this detail. "It were more than a week, I think, haps two. I did not count the nights."

She sliced the onion to pieces and added it to the pot before looking him in the eye. "You would know more?"

There was no belligerence in it. She asked it a little indifferently. He wanted to say no, that there was no need to tell him. But he did want to know more. He wanted to know so many things.

"Did you kill this great lord?"

She laughed with real humor, a short yelp of a sound that broke the spell she had woven. Lines of mirth appeared at the corner of her eyes.

"Nay, I did not know how then, and would not have dared. I would never have dared. I was no more than a timid mouse." The laughter faded from her face as she looked down at the turnip she now held. "A mouse that he wanted, that's what I was, and there was naught to stop him having me. But he did not, in the end. Not in that way."

Gryff opened his mouth to ask how she had been spared rape, but he found he could not say the words. She saw his curiosity, though, and returned her attention to the turnip. Her knife began to cut away the peel in one slow, long strip.

"I was all over terror, every minute, until he reached for me. But each time he pulled me close, the fear died in me. It were like a miracle, though I prayed no saints to intercede. I only…" She paused, looking hard at her turnip. "When his breath fell on me, I would think – let him do what he will, for it won't be worse than what he done to poor Oliver, left to die and rot on the floor. And the thought would stop my trembling, and that ruined his sport." Now she pulled the long curl of peel free and held it in her hand. A look of wry amusement came over her face. "It were a good lesson I learned: a woman without fear is like a winter wind on a stiff cock. For a man like him, anyway. If I looked him in the eye and did not cringe, it withered him without fail. And lucky for me it did."

She cut the peeled turnip to pieces, dropped it in the pot, and picked up the other. All the while, his mind raced. A great lord, cruel and lecherous. Name after name passed through his mind, all men he would have thought too chivalrous for acts so vile. But then, chivalry was reserved for ladies, not their servants. Indeed her lack of outrage, as though her story were the most common of tales, seemed to mock his assumptions. If he asked her to name her tormentor, would he find it was someone he had called friend?

"How came you to be free of him?" he asked, because that was an easier question.

Her hand paused. She looked into the fire and seemed to glow. "A great lady saved me." There was reverence in her voice. "I tell you true, it was only her goodness that saved me, for I was not worthy of her regard."

"Who–"

"It was her who taught me this, after. How to go on, I mean." She raised her eyes to look squarely at him now. "That's my purpose in telling you the tale. You ask what I see when I look at you, and I see you cringe and shrink as I did in the days after. Not just from shadows and hares, but from your memories of it. You look to hide from it, and that is what I call a mistake."

He could feel heat flare in his face. Cringing and shrinking. That was what she saw, and he would only look more foolish if he tried to deny it.

He dropped his gaze to the half-peeled turnip in her hands, too distracted by her face to think clearly. He turned her words over and over in his mind.

"A great lady taught you – what? To throw knives at villains and play the mute for days?"

Nan shook her head. "She said, 'even do you never care to speak again in your life, Nan, you must not lose your voice.'" Her hands resumed the slow paring. "She taught me when you run and hide from a thing, you make it into a monster that can only live in your darkest dreams. Without your running, it's naught but a thing that happened once. Now it is only a story for me, and not a great beast that seeks to tear me apart."

He raised his eyes to her face in the firelight and saw she was completely serious. Baudry and his men – what they had done, what he had seen…and she thought it was a simple matter of words. He fought against scoffing outright, but there was still a trace of scorn when he said, "This is your great wisdom, that it is but a story that needs telling?"

There was a stubborn set to her jaw. "I claim no wisdom, but I know what I know. When you make it a thing you can hold in your two hands, it belongs to you. Until then, you belong to it."

It was better to say nothing than to tell her she was wrong. Or even if she was not, he preferred forgetting, and was far more skilled at it. He let the silence stretch out between them, and thought how he had spent days wishing she would speak. He watched her hands remember their task, gripping the knife, carefully sliding the blade under the peel as she spoke softly into the hush.

"I was made to strip my clothes every night, and his men threw water on me to clean me before they took me to him. They tethered me with a rope, same as you." Her hand faltered, a minute slip of the blade that cut the perfect curl of peel that had almost come away in one piece. She looked at where it fell in the dirt, the only moment in all her recitation that was not dispassionate. She pointed at him with the knife still in her hand, a faint but emphatic gesture. "So don't think I don't know how it is."

She finished peeling the turnip in quick, efficient strokes, sliced and dropped it into the pot. She gave it a stir as the quiet settled over them again.

He watched her over many long minutes as the light waned, as the forest sounds around them changed from day to night. She had small hands, not rough or calloused like the servants he had known in Lancaster's household. She salvaged the turnip peels and washed them, storing them away in a jar of brine so that even the meanest scraps would not be wasted. A serving girl. Widowed of a stable boy.

Blessed are the meek, Brother Clement would have said. He was always urging Gryff to look on others with compassion, to see the divine in the ordinary. Five years spent hidden in the wilds with monks, and still he struggled with humility. Or maybe it was just her – it was that he wanted to look at her only with desire and not compassion, and thus compounded his sins.

"Never could I speak of it as you do." He was sure of that. He stared hard at the last bit of sunlight that sifted through the trees and imagined his father, alive, hearing what had happened to his least favored son. "Never."

The sound of her spooning the stew into a bowl did not rouse the same overwrought hunger as in the past. A week of eating every day had calmed his desperate appetite. She had seen to that, so determined to care for him. Now she rose from her place beside the fire and took the few steps to reach him.

"I do not say you must tell it as I do, not even to your confessor. Only that you must not look away from it." She handed the portion of stew to him, the rich smell rising up from the bowl. "It's plain to see you were born to finer folk, and lived in fine estate once. But you are in the muck now, if you'll pardon me saying it, and none down here will shame you for being powerless. It's only what we all are."

She went back to her place by the fire and set about eating her supper.

He heard her words echoing in his ears and thought of his father and brothers, and of the way their lives had likely ended. He thought of his people, of what might have happened in Aderinyth since the defeat of Wales five years ago. The fear and the sorrow of it rose in a lump to his throat.

This time, for the first time, he did not push the thought away. He let it sit in his mind until the visions were too terrible to bear, and then he turned his attention to his supper as best he could.

Chapter Six

Nan paused before the little house, and leaned forward until her forehead touched the doorpost. She needed a moment to gather herself. Just a moment. She could feel him behind her, heat all along her back, like he was fire and not flesh. He stood well away, but she could feel him.

The Welshman distracted her. So much so that she could not think of him by his name. Him. He. The Welshman. She had tied his life to hers by feeding him, traveling with him. She bound them further by giving him her story. It felt right, all of it. But it did not feel right to call him by his name. Not when her skin would not forget the brush of his hand.

It did not matter. What was behind her mattered less than what was before her, waiting beyond this door. She put a hand to the rough wood, trying to forget the Welshman, trying to prepare herself for this long awaited moment. The village priest had directed her here, sniffing in disapproval despite the paper that bore the seal of Morency. Nan had handed it to him, hearing Lady Gwenllian's voice in her memory, reading it out to her before it was sealed so she would know what it said.

Take her to her Aunt Mary, it said. And that was the power of a great name like Morency, that though the priest looked at her like she was naught but a whore who traveled alone with a man she did not call husband, still he did as the paper told him.

The Welshman did not like the contempt in the priest, but he had not shown anything more than displeasure. She was waiting every minute for his anger to burst forth. It would. It was the only thing missing. For days she had expected it, tensed at each spark of temper that appeared and then vanished, amazed at his lack of rage. Her own fury still pressed under her breast, dulled with time but always beating. *It is a rare anger in you, Nan*, her lady had said, and it was true. But that was years ago and she had since learned how to pour the hot anger into steel, to hone the edge of it and confine its damage to the path her blade traveled.

She could see no such fury in him yet. When the village priest had sneered at them, the Welshman only stood taller and spoke haughtily. Like one who had imitated it his whole life, he summoned the arrogance of the highborn and wielded it easily, until the priest was scraping and scurrying to placate him.

The Welshman had served a lord, or was born to one, she was sure of it. A bastard son, perhaps, but more likely a master falconer to a great lord – they were among the highest members of any household, that would account for his airs. But she did not care to know, and pushed the thought away. She was always pushing away the thought of him. Even now when what she searched for waited just inside this door, her thoughts were on him. How well he looked now that the edge of starvation was gone from his face, the soft and longing way he spoke of his home in Wales, the smiles he gave to Fuss, the searching looks he gave to her – it all crowded her mind, and she pushed it away.

Mary. Mary was inside, with answers that would break her heart. She was ready to hear them. She would never be ready.

At her back there was the heat of his lust. Within it, she felt the pull of his fascination with her. But over it all, the buffer to these potent forces, was his infinite patience.

That was the one thought of him she did not push away now: his face as he waited for the falcon while it moved through the sky, diving and missing over and over again. How he stood serene and untroubled, like time had no meaning, calmly waiting for the moment to arrive.

She gathered that calm to herself, willed it to seep beneath her skin and to her bones, and raised her hand to the door.

✠ ✠ ✠

Gryff did not know if he was meant to follow. He had felt the tension gathering in her all morning, and had bitten his tongue against asking why today was different. She had taken extra time to clean herself, put on fresh linen and her finer gown, and emerged with her hair carefully coiled into neat braids at the sides of her head, crowned with a crisp white linen fillet. Her forearms held no weapons now, the split in the sleeves tied closed. When she led them into the town and headed for the church, he thought she meant to attend mass.

Instead they stood before a house so humble it was little more than a hut. The place was called Wragby and, despite the priest's fulsome description of its weekly market, it was no more impressive than this tiny home at its far edge. Nan stood before the door, so still for so long that he was sure she had frozen to the spot. If he had been able to see the letter from Morency, he might know her business here. But he knew only that she had journeyed to meet whoever was inside, and it did not endear her to the ill-mannered priest.

He watched her move at last, heard her call softly to ask for entry and open the door. Her mood had infected him – his breath was held, his heart hammering as she stepped inside – and suddenly he found himself there on the threshold. Though he thought she did not want him and knew she did not need him, he could not resist following.

She stood in the gloom of the hut, her hair reflecting what little light there was, before an old woman seated on a crude bench. The house was only a single room with a hearth at the center, the wooden beams above black with soot. The woman sat with her hands gripping a shallow bowl in her lap, work of some sort, and squinted up at Nan. *Her eyes have seen better days,* the priest had said.

"Come closer," said the old woman, setting the bowl aside and gesturing her forward. "I won't know you if I can't see you."

Nan took a deep breath and swallowed. She knelt before the woman and whispered, "Aunt Mary. I've found you, Aunt Mary. I've come to you."

There was a hitch in her voice on these last words, and the old woman's face softened, crumpled. Her hands came up to hold Nan's face.

"Oh bless me," she exclaimed softly. She drank in the sight of her niece. "If it ain't our own sweet Nan. You live." Tears dripped down her face. "I did not dare to hope you still lived."

It was the sight of tears forming in Nan's eyes that made Gryff turn away. He was not meant to see this. Now the old woman was saying that when the priest claimed he had received word from Morency that her niece searched for her, she had thought it must be a cruel trick. She wept and laughed as she said it, patting Nan's cheek. He should wait outside, or walk all the long way down the lane until he reached the center of the town. Something, anything to avoid the pain of seeing this love overflowing, this homecoming, this joy he would never know for himself.

But as the old woman was saying, "You've your mother's beauty, you always did," the dog began to howl. In a corner of the room it had discovered some chickens, evidently a very alarming sight that called for a great deal of noise.

Gryff stepped past Nan and said, "Bran!" in the same moment she cried, "Fuss!" This had the advantage of confusing the dog, who immediately paused in his outcry to look at them both in turn. Before he started up again, Gryff crossed the floor and knelt down to distract him amid a cloud of feathers. At the edge of his vision he could see Nan pressing the tears from her eyes.

"Is this your lad?" asked the old woman. "Oh aye, you're of an age to be married now! Come let me see him."

She held Nan's hand tight and beckoned Gryff to come nearer. He looked to Nan, unsure.

"Nay, Aunt Mary, I have me no husband. We only journey together for safety on the road to Lincoln."

She said no more than this, whether from circumspection or her natural disinclination to speech, and dismay came into the old woman's face. She looked as if she might begin to weep again, but for different reasons.

"You were ever a good girl, Nan. I did my best by you, and if you have been brought so low that you must prostitute yourself then all I would hope–"

"Nay, goodwife, never would she dishonor herself or your good name. I beg you will not slander your niece for the charity she has shown me." He came to her so she could see him well, his words striking a jarring note even in his own ears. They spoke so plain and humble, and he did not. "So urgent was her need to find you that she would not be delayed in waiting for the safety of a larger party, yet did she take pity on me in my distress and allows me to accompany her to Lincoln. By my hope of heaven do I swear there is no dishonor in it."

He bent lower to be sure she could see him. She squinted up at him, the disapproval fading from her face as he spoke. Her eyes went round, and she gave a little gasp, turning to Nan.

"Oh he speaks fine words, and I've been forgetting you are a favorite of the lady of Morency!" She sat up straight but lowered her eyes, suddenly meek. She patted the grimy kerchief that covered her hair, as though a worried touch could turn it into a silk veil. "You won't be in the habit no more of humble ways, though I'll welcome ye as best I can. The winter stores are all but gone now, but Edmer will bring a bit of cheese. And there's always the chickens–"

"You won't kill a chicken for us," Nan said firmly, looking abashed at this change in demeanor. "And may God strike me down in my arrogance if ever I think myself too good to sit at your table." She put a hand atop Mary's and spoke gently. "I am only Nan, Aunt Mary. And as for any good fortune I have had, it all started with you looking out for me."

After that she turned briskly to business, asking Mary to tell her of her life in their years apart and instructing Gryff to bring in the packs from the mule that was tied outside. She was a whirlwind. She took over the grinding of the millet in the bowl that Mary had set aside, and had the task done even before he finished bringing in the baggage. She swept feathers from the floor and cobwebs from dark corners without pausing.

All the while Mary explained that after Nan had gone into service, she had married a widowed man and come to live here, then was widowed in turn. Now she lived with her husband's grown son, Edmer, whom they would meet when he returned from his day of work in town. He was simple-minded, she told them, but a good boy whom she would have loved as well as her own, if ever she had had any of her own.

When Gryff brought the hooded falcon out of the cage and set up the perch just outside the only window, he almost regretted it. He must keep Tiffin near, as her value was too great to leave unwatched, but the sight of her caused Mary to become even more deferential.

"There's a very fine bird," she said, craning her neck through the window. "Not like them ordinary hawks I seen in town. This one is fit for a king, it is."

Fit for a king. It's what Baudry had said, his eyes full of greed and wonder, his hands still stained with the blood of the man he had killed. He had been reaching for Gryff and stopped when he saw the falcon.

It was not so bad, to think of that moment – to think of how he had been spared only because of the value of a bird. He could not look squarely at the moments surrounding it. Not yet. But he would do as she advised. He would try, and if she was right then perhaps for the first time in his life he would not be ruled by shame.

He found the bag that held the woodcocks – Tiffin had brought down two this morning but there had been no time to spare for plucking them. Nan began to rise from the mending she now bent over, but he waved at her to sit back down on the bench next to her aunt, who was asking to know everything of Nan's life. He sat just outside the door and methodically pulled feathers as he listened.

Nan said she had worked first for a weaver's wife, and then went to serve in a kitchen in Chester. "From there I served in other places, and now I am at Morency these four years past." She made no mention of any of the things she had told Gryff last night, nor even that she too had been married and widowed. When asked what her duties were at Morency if not in the kitchen, she did not say she could kill a man twice her size with a flick of her wrist. She only said her duties were to attend to whatever tasks the lady of Morency required, and went on to describe her efforts to learn from that lady about healing herbs.

He listened to them discuss the many and varied uses for swine-grass and wondered if Mary noticed that while every use she herself had for it was to treat digestion, every use Nan mentioned was to do with healing cuts and stopping bleeding. It was a strange circumstance, that he knew more about her than this woman who loved her so well.

When he finished with the woodcocks, he brought them in and found that Nan had removed the linen fillet from her hair. She was holding it out to Mary, who protested she must wash her hands first before touching it.

"To learn physicking from a great lady and stitching too," she marveled as she thrust her hands into a bowl of water and scrubbed vigorously with a cloth. "My own sister's daughter! She had fine looks but never such a fine manner as you have nor half the wit, and it's sure you never got neither from your father, may God assoil him."

Nan flinched at the words, staring at her aunt's back. She had not known her father was dead, it was clear. But just as quickly as the surprise had appeared, it was gone. She banished all feeling from that expressive face, casting a quick glance in Gryff's direction.

"Come, Aunt Mary, you will scrub your hands bloody and that is worse than any dirt." She crossed to take Mary's hands from the bowl and dried them with her own skirt, ignoring Mary's protests that she would ruin a gown so fine. "Sit you by the window so you have light to see."

The old woman did just that, holding the embroidered fillet so close to her eyes that her lashes nearly brushed against it. She sighed over it again and again, admiring the intricate detail, while her niece looked torn between pride in her work and embarrassment at being praised lavishly for so small a thing.

And so it went until the day was done. Nan cooked and cleaned as though it were her own house, so obviously comfortable here and yet made uncomfortable by her aunt's awe of her. Gryff would have left to find lodging for himself, afraid that Mary would ask him questions about his own life he was not prepared to answer, but both women seemed to expect him to stay. In any case, Nan kept him too busy. She bade him build a fire in the hearth and find mud to mix with straw so that he might repair a crumbled wall of the house.

It pleased him to do the work, which he would never have expected. It was evident Mary and her home had been neglected too long, and when the boy Edmer arrived it was just as evident that his mind was too feeble to be of much help to the old woman. He had brought a bit of cheese home, as promised, but lamented that he had forgotten to bring water and would have to go back to the well to fetch it – an almost nightly occurrence, it seemed. Gryff went with him, taking the mule and bringing back enough water and fuel to last days.

They ate the woodcocks and some porridge, a meal that Gryff thought modest but which they praised as bounteous beyond belief. When he curled on the floor in a corner to sleep, he found himself almost grateful for some of the hardships he had endured these last months. In his former life, he would have been appalled at all of this – the meager supper, the woodsmoke that stung his eyes, the hard earthen floor that served as his bed. But though he had never been inside a home so poor and squalid, he could see it now as a great blessing. It was far better, after all, than sleeping tied to a tree and wondering what villainy and brutality he would witness next.

✠ ✠ ✠

He had not slept more than an hour when he woke gently – not from a bad dream this time, but from the sound of their voices murmuring low. He knew he should make it obvious he was awake and could hear them. But he didn't because, as he had told Brother Clement countless times, he was neither saint nor monk.

"…any message must go through the priest just as yours did, asking after me," Mary was whispering. "So I did not answer, for then he'd know about her and bring his sour face to me and Edmer to preach Hell and damnation at us every day. And I could not think you would want your lady to know, and for shame I did not say it before so fine a guest as your Welshman."

"Tell me now," came Nan's voice. She spoke low, but did not whisper. When no answer came, she said, "I would know if she is dead, and no matter the shame of it, I would know the manner of her death."

"May God forgive me, but it were better that she died years ago than become what she is."

He could hear Nan's sharp intake of breath, and the painful hope in her voice when she asked, "She lives?"

He knew that hope, how it pierced the heart, the anguish it brought. He had clutched it to himself desperately for a time, and sometimes still felt it prowling in the forgotten corners of his heart. It was the Fiend's own torture, the terrible punishment for loving.

"Aye, she lives. In sin." Mary's whisper grew fainter, as though saying it aloud was another kind of sin. "She is become a bawd, Nan. A common whore herself and keeping a brothel full of them." She seemed to wait for some reaction, but she obviously did not know how long Nan could hold a silence. "It killed your father, it did."

"He killed himself with drink," came the swift reply. "And when he done it, he abandoned her to an evil fate. Haps he is redeemed now in death, if God is merciful. But I will not leave her redemption to chance."

"Oh sweet Nan, you were ever too good-hearted. Will you not understand? She don't want redemption, nor to be saved in any way. I begged her to come away and live with me here. But she said she would do as she pleased, and what pleased her was to open her legs for any man passing. She spat full in my face, do you hear?" There was another long pause. "You are so different from her that none would believe you were sisters."

It was a very long time until Nan's voice floated through the darkness, filled with a quiet conviction. "But we are. We are sisters."

After that there was no more talking. There was only a hard silence that settled over the room. He could taste the anger and sorrow that filled the air all the sleepless night.

1282

On Palm Sunday, Prince Llewellyn's brother Dafydd attacked an English stronghold, and yet another war was begun.

Gryff made the mistake of laughing when he first heard of it. Dafydd, of all people, to start an uprising. It seemed to him a farce that someone so like himself – loyal to the English crown, living among the Normans for so many years and from such a young age – would pretend to care about Welsh independence. Gryff said to Will that he thought it must be simple greed and maneuvering, that there must be some other motive than rebellion. Hadn't Dafydd once plotted to murder Llewellyn, in hopes of gaining his brother's lands and power? That old Welsh way of rival brothers. No one could seriously think such a man was committed to any cause but his own advancement.

But then the Welsh attacked more English castles, and Prince Llewellyn raised an army, and no one was laughing – least of all King Edward. Wales was in open and earnest rebellion.

"Who else has joined Llewellyn?" Gryff asked Will, who always knew every alliance, every political whisper. He knew as well exactly what Gryff was asking.

"Deheubarth."

Will did not say more, because that one word told him the only thing that mattered. If the southern realm of Deheubarth had joined Llewellyn's north in rebellion, his own family's fate was inevitable.

Gryff looked at the hawk's lure in his hands. He was repairing it, replacing feathers and attaching a stronger cord. Like the Welsh nobles, he thought: put the pieces together into the semblance of a bird that almost looked like it was flying free, but really it was only a target for the bird of prey. The hawk would strike it over and over, and one day soon it would fall to tattered pieces again.

"My father has joined the cause of Wales, then." The alliance between families was ancient, and still strong after the last uprising. His father always chose Llewellyn's fight over everything else.

"The Welsh have won many battles these past weeks. Many more than Edward would like."

"Ever do they win for a time, before they lose. And when they lose this time, what will be my father's punishment? Will he be forced to give his lands, or his other sons?"

Gryff might be reunited with his brothers after all these years if they too were made hostage. They would be fellow sacrifices to his father's politics.

But the look on Will's face put fear into him.

"It is not like the fighting of years past, Gryff. No more is it a mere nuisance to be tolerated by the king. Edward means to win at last, no matter the cost."

Gryff had no illusions about King Edward's skill at war, nor his capacity for ruthlessness. "My father will lose both, then. His sons and his lands."

"And his life." Will was only fifteen, but he spoke with a gravity and intelligence that belied it.

"Your brothers' lives too are forfeit, even young Owain, if they fight against the crown. There will be no treaties this time, nor any Welsh rulers great or small left to challenge Edward. He will conquer Wales entire, and has sworn to leave no treasonous Welshmen alive."

The blood had turned cold inside him as Will spoke. Strangely, he did not think of his brothers and their fate. It was the thought of Philip Walch and his sons, and what might happen to them, that brought a great despair into his heart. And others he remembered fondly – Madrun who brewed the mead, and Tuder who kept the hounds, and Father Ifor in his tiny village church.

They would be conquered entire. They would be ruled by Normans who despised them, thought them godless savages, and sought to stamp out all the ancient and most beloved Welsh ways.

"Aderinyth." He had to stop and clear his throat of emotion. It was rare for him to speak the name of his homeland. "It lies so deep within Wales that there is hope it will be spared the worst."

Will looked at him as though he could not believe he was so slow-witted. "And you are not deep within Wales, but here in the household of the king's brother. Think you that *you* will be spared, Gruffydd ab Iorwerth?" He pronounced the name like it was the most damning detail of all – because it was. "You are here as surety for your father's obedience, and he has joined a war against those who hold you."

Gryff wanted to scoff at this concern, but could not quite manage it.

"Edward will not want me dead, Will. I am a pawn." He pulled the new cord too tight on the lure and the seam in the leather was torn asunder. "I am meant to be used. He will use me, just as my father has used me."

Will nodded. He had that look he got sometimes, brow furrowed, lips pulled tight as he put his mind to work. He was too clever for one so young.

"I dread the day he has more use for your death than your life."

"Who? My father or my king?" Surely both could make good use of his death.

But Will disregarded this cynical query and said Gryff must increase his worth to the king. Advise the king's commanders on how best to fight against the Welsh, he said, and Gryff agreed. Remind the king that Gryff had sworn fealty to the crown, Will suggested – so he did. He sent messages to his father and his brothers, telling them they must submit to Edward, that they were traitors, that he condemned their actions and was shamed by them – and Will did his best to ensure everyone at court knew of these messages and sentiments.

All the while Gryff reminded himself it was true: he was ashamed; the Welsh should submit; rebellion was treason; Edward was destined to win.

And all the while, he and Will never spoke about the other truth – that his life was more valuable to a king he had barely met than it was to his own father.

Chapter Seven
1288

He dreamt he and his brothers had found the fairy in the lake. She stood at the edge of the water, lent-lilies and snowdrops in a carpet at her feet, with the mountains all around. She wore a coarse brown dress and Nan's face, a cloud of golden hair spilling free across her shoulders. They were waiting to see which of them she would name a king.

You must give the sword to one of us, said Rhodri, though Rhodri had never come with them to search for the fairy in real life.

But she had no sword, so she took the knife from her bodice. She held it in her outstretched hand, looking at each of them in turn. She was going to give it away to one of them, only because she had been asked. It sent a terrible dread through him. He knew it would mean disaster for her, and for him.

"*No.*"

It was barely more than a mumble as he jerked awake. He must have been restless in sleep, for she was already kneeling beside him. Her hand was on his shoulder, her face a little troubled as she looked down at him.

He swallowed down the dream fear and tried to speak naturally.

"Do I wake the house with my cries?" he asked.

She shook her head and lifted her eyes briefly to the window where light streamed in. After another day spent in labor to make her aunt's home more fit, he had slept the night through to full morning. They were to leave for Lincoln today.

He could still feel the mountains of his dream around him, smell the lake, taste the beginning of danger. His own hand came up to cover hers at his shoulder, and hold it there while he willed his muscles to unclench. They stayed that way for a quiet moment, tension draining from him while she waited patiently, radiating calm as his breath steadied.

He waited for her to pull her hand away. She didn't. His heart gave a sudden hard beat, a jolt that was not fear.

She was looking at his face. His mouth. Fixedly.

It was only a matter of turning his head to let his lips just barely touch her wrist. He waited for her to reach for a blade, but she remained still, watching him, fascinated. Her pulse sped up beneath his mouth. He did not dare even to breathe as her hand moved beneath his, turning over and moving closer. Haps it was yet another dream. It must be, the way her fingers curled against his jaw in a faint caress while he tasted the sweet skin inside her wrist.

She stared at the place where he kissed her as though entranced. Her fingers spread out against him, holding his face as his mouth opened over her pulse.

He thought he might die from the pleasure of seeing her lips part, of feeling the gentle rush of air escape her when he moved his tongue over her skin.

Five years. Five years since he had tasted a woman. And never one like her.

Her eyes met his, startling blue, and still she did not pull away or reach for a blade. She wanted this. The certainty of it caused his body to throb painfully, aching for more. He thought his breath must scorch her, that he would be burned to naught but ashes on the ground from this one touch.

In the same moment he began to reach for her, her aunt's voice called her name softly through the door. Nan jerked her hand away as though he had burned her in truth, her eyes turning to the door as she rose swiftly.

At the threshold she paused in the square of sunlight that fell into the house. She turned her head over her shoulder, in profile to him but not looking directly at him. A high color was fading from her cheeks.

"I would leave within the hour, if it please you, so we may enter Lincoln before night falls tomorrow."

The words were courteous, impersonal, as though there had been no touch between them. She stepped outside, leaving him alone with the aching memory of it, his mouth full of her heartbeat.

✠ ✠ ✠

To his amazement, Nan insisted on leaving the mule with her aunt. When Mary protested it as too generous, Nan only said the animal would be a hindrance to her in the journey ahead and that Mary did her a great service by keeping it. At least for a time, she said, for she was sure to come back.

"And until I do, your Edmer can go to the well and bring back more than enough for a day of cooking and washing and anything else besides," she said. He could also do as they had done yesterday, bringing rushes to the old woman who made woven mats and rush lights that could be sold at market – as she had used to do before her husband died. With one simple gesture, Nan gave them the means to better care for themselves.

It only made them yet more humble toward Nan, who was obviously uncomfortable with this deferential manner. She had changed back to the coarse gown yesterday, and replaced the linen fillet with a simple kerchief while she pounded grain in the mortar and her dog rousted out nests of mice. Nothing she did made her aunt look at her with less admiration, as though this lovely girl in a peasant's dress was a very great lady who condescended to serve them. And though they embraced tightly upon saying farewell, it was easy to see that there had been a disagreement between them.

"Don't go to her, Nan," he heard her aunt say. "She's naught but a slut, and unworthy of you."

Nan ignored this. She kissed her aunt on both cheeks and said, "You must send word to me if ever you need aught. So long as I live, I live in your debt. God bless you for it. God bless you."

With that, they set off down the road toward town. Gryff searched for a way to ask about her sister, but could not find words. In truth, he knew there were no words – she would only tell him if she wanted to, as with everything. He wanted to tell her that though she was not a great lady, she was better than most he had known and deserving of her aunt's admiration. But she would think he said it only in hopes of touching her again, so he bit his tongue.

It was market day in town, and she stopped at a stall to sell a bundle of belongings: her finer gown, the embroidered fillet, a shallow pan. Without the mule, she must reduce the baggage she carried. He would have liked to hear Nan haggle with the merchant over price, but the market at Wragby was as popular as had been promised and he found the press of people overwhelming. He felt like a falcon unhooded – too much to see, and everything that moved caught his eye and put him on guard, ready for attack.

He moved to where the crowd was thinner, and found a man who sold him a long leather strap that would allow him to carry the falcon's cage on his back.

What he wanted was a sword. He hadn't handled one since his days in Lancaster's household. It would make him a target for thieves on the road, though, and he did not have enough money for a decent one in any case. Long gone were his days of chivalry. He was no one now – in the muck, as she said. Useless in every way that mattered.

"She's a pretty one." A man with an impressive scar down the middle of his face was standing near. "Would like to get my hands on that, I would."

For a moment Gryff thought he meant the falcon. He glanced down at the cage he held, but then saw the man was looking at Nan. She had moved a little closer now, finished with her selling and examining the leather goods.

A part of him wanted to urge the man to try it and see what happened. But the irrational fear was creeping over him again, turning his limbs cold. The way the scarred man looked at her was too like Cuddy, the one of Baudry's men who had to be held back from raping every woman who crossed his path.

He told himself that nothing like that would happen here, in a crowded town square. Even if it did, she could more than defend herself from this man. Just as she could defend herself from a different man who now stepped too close to her side. It was one of the merchants who leaned in to speak to her, and she leaned away.

Now the scarred man beside him was saying she was a small bit of flesh but enough for the both of them. He was expecting Gryff to join in the leering and when he did not, he could sense the shift in the other man.

It was the swift calculation of how best to take advantage of someone weaker, the look of the well-practiced villain. How easy it was to recognize, after weeks of living surrounded by such men. How it filled him with this frozen panic.

Gryff kept his eyes on Nan. Even as the man beside her pulled the kerchief from her hair and reached for her, she appeared untroubled. Somehow she evaded the outstretched arm, the groping hand. There was no knife in her hand, only one of the long nails she carried in a pouch on her belt. Likely she could kill with it as easily as with a blade, and all while Gryff stood here useless, watching.

Then he felt a tug at his hand. The scarred man was trying to pull the falcon's cage from him. His other hand was reaching for Gryff's wrist.

One moment Gryff was wondering why her dog had appeared at his feet barking, and the next moment he was plowing into the man's chest, pulling the cage from his hand and throwing him to the ground.

It happened too fast to think, and then it felt too good to stop. He did not need a sword. He did not reach for any weapon. He used his fists, as he had dreamed of doing countless times, and relished the crack of bone, the feel of flesh giving way beneath the impact. It felt glorious. When the man stayed on the ground, Gryff used his feet – once, twice, and the third time it came to him that the man did not shout in protest anymore. There was only a feeble groaning.

Something – some dim memory of what his life used to be – made him stop before he beat the man senseless.

He was not a brute. He was not. He would not be.

He repeated it to himself as he caught his breath. Finally he looked up to find Nan was now standing by the falcon's cage, calmly watching him amid a mild chaos. Gradually he became aware that bystanders were arguing amongst themselves, over whether the constable should be called. The man who had been reaching for Nan was on the ground, clutching a foot that dripped blood. *More often she maims*, the knight of Morency had said, *a hand or a foot.*

"Go on then, get ye gone from here. It's a respectable man you've attacked." A townswoman with a basket full of onions jabbed a finger at Nan, scowling. "We'll not abide it. Be gone or you'll see a punishment."

Color flamed in Nan's face, but she did not move from the spot nor take her eyes from Gryff. With a tilt of her head she indicated the man he had beaten, and looked at Gryff with brows raised as though to ask if he was finished. He nodded, and she picked up the cage, snapped her fingers at the dog, and led the way out of town.

✠ ✠ ✠

They walked without speaking for hours. She followed a path that veered off the main road, as she had done before, and he wondered how she knew these byways. But he didn't ask. From the moment they had walked away from the market, he had been filled with a strange elation, a kind of relief that he did not question. His bonds had been cut nearly a fortnight ago, but only now did he truly feel his freedom.

It was likely a kind of terrible sin, to find some measure of joy only because he had beaten a man – even if the man was a thief who would steal Tiffin. But he was beyond caring about sin. It was not as real as this feeling, or the truth of this new life.

"I'm down in the muck with you, Bran," he grinned at the dog, who seemed every bit as cheerful.

Nan did not correct him to say the dog was named Fuss, which told him she was not so lighthearted. She had fixed the braces of blades to her forearms again as they left town, but he thought it was not her watchfulness that caused her mood. He too had injured a man – done more damage than she had, undoubtedly – yet only she had suffered censure for it. He remembered well how her cheeks had burned when the townswoman told her to be gone.

After many miles a soft rain began to fall, and they ducked under the canopy of trees to take cover. They found a clearing, with a broad outcropping of rock and a small pool of water fed by a stream. The leaves on the branches above were so thick that the droplets barely disturbed the pool, and Nan knelt to gather water into a leather flask. He unbuckled Tiffin's cage from his back and sat on a convenient stump to pull out the tiny loaf of dark bread that Mary had given him this morning as he said his farewell. *It's queer how quiet she's grown to be,* she had said to him with a nod toward Nan. *She were the most chattering girl.*

It was hard to imagine a chattering Nan, and even harder to realize that he would part ways with her soon. Their journey would end tomorrow. He should ask her everything he wanted to know now, before it was too late. He was debating whether to ask how she had learned to speak Welsh, or where she had learned her deadly skill, when she spoke.

"Why is it always me?" She was frowning down at her reflection in the pool, but glanced up at him briefly to see his confusion at her question. "There were other girls there, young and pretty. And smiling.

Some small as me, too. But it's me he come at. They always do."

It was an earnest question. He considered telling her that he had noticed no other fair maids at all. Few men would, with Nan there. That was no kind of answer, though. He took a bite of bread and studied her troubled face in profile. He could say it was the graceful line of her brow, or the perfect proportions of every feature in itself and all of them taken together, or how her skin seemed to glow with a delicate golden light. Or her eyes, so blue and so expressive that they would inspire every bard and troubadour who ever caught sight of her to sing of her beauty.

But in the end he swallowed and gave her the crude truth she asked for.

"Your mouth."

She turned a puzzled look to him, and he shrugged. He kept his eyes on the bread he held and spoke casually – or as casually as he could manage, when he thought of her mouth.

"God gave you the face of an angel, that stirs a man's breast and will cause his heart to ache with the beauty of it. But your mouth is the kind that moves a man to think of naught but hot sin. That mouth in that face…" He shrugged again and looked at her. "Is an uncommon allure."

Her eyes fell briefly to his hand holding the bread before she turned back to the pool. A crease appeared in her brow as she considered her reflection for a long moment. She let out a faint snort, either mockery or exasperation, before dragging her hand across the surface in a quick swipe and turning away.

Her practical air returned. From her bag she pulled a square of linen and a small jar and held it out to him. At his questioning look, she pointed down at his hand, where the knuckles were scraped and swollen from fighting. He recognized the jar from the priory; it held the salve she had used on the wounded knight. When he reached to take it from her, she pulled it back suddenly and said, "Is better you wash the wounds first."

Her voice held the slightest tremor, so unexpected and so revealing that he felt it shiver through him. He savored the sweet echo of it as he went to the water and did as she instructed.

This morning seemed a lifetime ago, but her touch had not been a dream, nor a hopeful imagining. There was a curiosity in her, a thread of desire. He had seen it. It was in her even now.

He turned back to her and walked carefully forward, ever wary. He knew he must not move too sudden, lest she feel trapped with the wall of stone at her back. Nor could he be too timid. He had spent years in being too timid, and he was free of that, too.

When he held his dripping hand out to her, she did not give him the jar as he expected, but patted the linen over his fingers to dry them. She attended his cuts as she attended to every task – brisk and sensible, efficient in her every move.

But after she finished and tied a strip of linen around his hand, she did not turn away. When he dared to brush his fingers across her cheek, she did not object. She did not move at all, except to swallow and wet her parted lips in a more provocative display than he'd seen in five long and lonely years.

It took every ounce of discipline he'd ever learned not to pull her to him and crush her against his heat. Instead he bent his neck to bring himself closer to her. He tipped her face up to look down at her mouth, the way her lashes lowered and her cheeks flushed pink, and her breath – oh God, how her breath caught, the unsteady rise and fall of her breast.

He waited an eternity, hot and hard and desperate, until she leaned forward into the slight space that separated them and brushed her lips softly across his. Then he gathered her face in his hands and kissed her, careful and coaxing, finding that thread of her desire and tugging at it, pulling her to him as her mouth opened and the sweetest sound came from her.

Silent Nan, making sounds of pleasure. Distant Nan, pressing close to him. She was the most intoxicating mixture of shy and eager, her hand pressing at the back of his neck to hold him to her, but her pliant mouth making no demands of him.

He wanted her to demand. He trailed his mouth down her throat, teeth scraping softly at her hot skin, pushing her a step backward until she leaned against the stone. Now her hand at his nape clutched harder, fingers twisting in his hair. Now her body arched gently up against his, her breath harsh at his ear. Now she demanded.

He came back to her mouth and waited there, holding himself back from the lips that were a breath away from his. His reward was her sigh, the hunger with which she kissed him, the boldness of her tongue exploring his mouth. His hands moved over her slight body beneath the coarse gown, over the braid that hung down her back. He pulled it apart, running his hands through her unbound hair at last, cool silk slipping between his fingers as she kissed him breathless.

It inflamed him, a blaze of lust that overwhelmed his senses. His knee pushed between her legs and he felt her body stiffen, her lips still. But she did not take her mouth away, so he took control of the kiss. An old lesson, easily remembered – how to seduce a willing woman, how to coax without words. The stiffness in her eased by degrees; it was a matter of moments until she was sighing again. He set a suggestive rhythm with his mouth, with his body. The thrust of his tongue against hers beat in time with the press of his hips. She seemed to melt under his hands, his mouth, so soft and yielding that he was mad with wanting her.

He did not know when it changed, or what exactly caused it. He only felt her mouth pull away with an effort – and it was the effort that mattered to him in the moment, so he moved his mouth to her throat, down to her collarbone. Her dress was modest, no way to reach the skin beneath it except to raise her skirt. When he had brought the hem as high as her knee, it dawned on him that her hands were not on him. He forced himself to pause, still tasting her throat, still pressed hard against her as he pulled back to look at her.

She had gone utterly still, her breath coming fast in shallow little huffs. She seemed impossibly fragile, as though she had grown smaller – because she had. She shrank from him.

She looked vulnerable. So small and vulnerable, like prey flushed from its hiding place and bared to the hunter. It called up the memory of her voice saying, *I was no more than a timid mouse. A mouse he wanted.*

He dropped his hands from her as though burned and stepped back. She looked at him, but for once there was no clear message in her face. She trembled all over, but he thought it was not fear. No more was it lust. Then his eyes found her hand, the knife clutched in fingers that shook, the first time he had ever seen her grip unsteady.

A protest hovered on his lips, a defense against the accusation she did not make. She had wanted it. She had kissed him.

And he had taken what she gave and more, not content with only a taste freely given. Her look damned him, made him one of those men in the king's hall who had made sport of her, who stole a touch and demanded her body, because they could.

He turned away, unable to bear the mixture of confusion and fear and courage swimming in her eyes. There was nowhere to go, but he strode away through the trees. He must go anywhere at all so that she did not look like this. Anywhere that he might forget the sight of her unsure hand trembling around her only defense.

Chapter Eight

She watched him disappear behind the trees at the edge of the clearing, her mouth bruised with kisses, her body burning. She wanted to call him back. She wanted to bury the knife between his shoulders.

She wanted to stop wanting him.

Her fingers would not let go of the knife, and yet she had no memory of taking it from her belt. To be sure, she had had no thought of using it in defense against him. That had not been in her mind at all. It was she who had kissed him, even knowing that her mouth made him think of hot sin. It was her body that asked for more. He only answered.

Why then – why did she feel like this?

Once, years ago, she had watched as a boy was pulled from a lake, gasping for air. *Don't you never go out so far in deep waters,* her mother had warned them as the boy coughed and wept.

Deep waters. This was how it felt to be saved from drowning, to have the suffocating waters recede and leave her dazed on the shore, struggling to learn how to breathe again.

Dim memories of her few nights as a wife had not prepared her for this. No more was she prepared to wonder why she had never felt this way with Oliver, who was kind and sweet and careful never to hurt her while slaking his lust. She did not want to think of Oliver at all, God forgive her.

She stared at the knife in her hand as though it held the answers to every question she had not dared to ask herself since she had cut the Welshman's bonds. He looked at her in lust, as many men did. Yet he was somehow different. Other men looked as though they would devour her whole and leave naught but crumbs on a plate. There was no room for herself in their lust. There was nothing to her but what they wanted to have.

Yet there was room for herself in his eyes. There was room for herself in his kiss – until there was not.

Fuss was whining at her in confusion. He cast a questioning look at where the Welshman had disappeared, then back at her. She gave him the signal to sit and he did, but he looked at her doubtfully.

"He'll come back, Fuss," she said, which only caused the dog to look at her more confused. He was not used to her voice. No one was used to her voice. She liked it that way. "His falcon is here. Nor will he leave it long."

She thought of how he had stopped himself from beating the thief too badly. She had expected the anger, but she had not expected the mercy. It was a rare quality in any man, whether lowborn or high. It was why she had not needed her knife. It was why he had walked away.

Slowly, she slid the blade back into its sheath and tried to return to plain, sensible thoughts. They should make camp here. There was an overhang of rock to protect them from rain, if it became strong in the night, and there was water. She should make a fire. She should bring out the pork pies she had bought at the market, her favorite, a treat for their last night together because it gave her joy to see him eat.

Instead she sat on the damp ground and called Fuss to her. He came readily, as though she were still herself, still the Nan he had always known. But he looked back again as though to follow the Welshman. "He don't need you, Fuss," she whispered, running a hand over his head, scratching his chin. "I do."

She knew who she was. She knew her place and her purpose. She had never doubted it, until now. One kiss, and everything was crumbling.

Fuss settled beside her, his little body curled against her leg, a heavy warmth that was as familiar as her own breath.

They would go to Lincoln. She would find her sister. The Welshman would part ways with her and find his new life, whatever it may be.

One kiss. She should regret it. She *did* regret it, even as she separated out the parts of it she wanted to keep. *Be selfish*, she reminded herself, and stored away the memory of the stirring in her belly when he moved against her, the pleasure of tasting him, the thrill of feeling what she'd only seen in others: desire.

It was the falcon that finally made her move. The Welshman always let it out of the cage and onto the perch as soon as they stopped. But this time she had distracted him from it, and she could not bear to think it might suffer for its confinement. He was forever fretting that the cage was too small as they journeyed, lowering the side of it so the bird might stretch its wings and carrying the falcon on his arm for hours at a time.

"Tiffany," she said, before she opened the cage. He always talked to it, murmuring in that soothing way. But Nan found words to be more useless than soothing, and so she could think of nothing to say beyond its name.

She knew enough not to be afraid, but was nervous of doing it any harm. If she had more courage, she would fashion a gauntlet and try to transfer the bird from the cage to the perch. Instead she lowered the bars as she had seen him do and watched as the falcon moved restlessly on the block. It was not hooded, and it looked at her with interest from eyes that were the same dark, dark brown as his.

They blinked at each other for a very long time while she turned her mind to her sister and what would happen. Somewhere just outside the walls of Lincoln, Aunt Mary had said. It should not be difficult to find. And that's what she would do. Find the place and circle over it and then swoop in, like she had seen the falcon do. Catch her sister and carry her away. Or dive and miss, as she had seen the falcon do even more often.

Would her sister be starving still? Would she look as the Welshman had looked, hungry and haunted and grateful to be found? Nan prayed not. But then she tried to imagine her sister fat and happy, content with her lot, and failed at that.

The only way was to be like the falcon: wait for the moment, react to the circumstance. Do not anticipate beforehand. Never forget that all is potential, until it is truth.

She knew the Welshman had returned by the way Fuss pricked up his ears in the same moment that the falcon's eye focused beyond her. Nan stood and moved away from the cage, never turning to face him. There was no way to know what was in her face, but she knew that she would not be able to hide her thoughts. Now the sun was going down and she had done naught but sit still, and that was telling enough.

She busied herself and watched surreptitiously as he set the perch in the soft ground, put on the gauntlet, and took up the bird. It did not escape her that he kept a careful distance from her while she built a small fire to warm the water. She washed the dirt of the day from her hands and feet, and he did not come near the water so that he might do the same. When she spread her square of waxed linen on the ground to make her bed, he moved far in the opposite direction – farther than he'd ever placed himself from her – and made his own bed there.

They seemed to prowl about each other like wary animals, and it gave her a deep and abiding satisfaction that he was just as cautious of her as she was of him. He was like so many of the men she had known from fine households, the way he had kissed her without an instant of hesitation, so sure of himself. So sure of her. After days of uncertainty, at last he had found his confidence again. And he found it by putting his hands on her, of course. A man who looked so appalled at Aunt Mary's house – while she was amazed to find Mary had a house at all – such a man took what he thought was his due, so long as nothing stopped him.

It was a good thing he was wary now. Let that be what he remembered of her, if he would remember anything at all.

There was still daylight enough but she smothered the embers of the fire without thinking and snapped her fingers for Fuss. When he did not come, she looked to see him seated by the Welshman. In the dog's mouth was the scrap of bread that must have dropped from the Welshman's hands when he had reached for her.

The sight of it reminded her they had not eaten this evening, and the realization shocked her as much as anything that had happened today. In her life, she had never once forgotten to eat so long as there was food to be had. Especially on this journey, when she ignored her usual appetite in favor of feeding him more.

Fuss looked reluctant to come to her, and he rarely ignored her beckoning. The dog was looking up at the Welshman, dropping the bit of bread at his feet, nosing his hand. She dared to raise her eyes to his face, to the features that were still sharp but no longer gaunt with desperate hunger. He looked back at her, and there was no arrogance in his expression, nor did she see the sullen resentment of a man rebuffed. There was only chagrin and, she thought, regret.

She turned away from the sight of it, and felt the kernel of anger in her dissolve a little.

The pork pies were each as large as her two hands together. She had bought three, and when she broke one in half so that they could share it all equally, she had to bite her tongue against apologizing that she had not put it on the fire to warm it. She set the portion on the stone next to him, avoiding his hands, and retreated to her own spot.

They ate in a silence that grew almost companionable as she watched him feed bits of his supper to her shamelessly groveling dog.

✠ ✠ ✠

"Will you take refreshment? Gladly will I ask my wife to provide a proper welcome."

The man named Elias stood just inside this well-furnished room of this large house, his clothes hanging off him, and spoke to Nan as though he could summon a feast with the snap of his fingers. But she had glimpsed the bareness of the house beyond this room, and the thinness of the young boy who had said Elias ben Joseph was his father and then brought them here.

"Nay, there is only the message to deliver and then will we leave you," she said, hoping it gave no offense. Her father always said the Jews had strange ways and she must be careful of them – not for fear of offending them, but because they might steal her away for dark purposes. From what she could see even as a child, though, they looked no different from everyone else in the town, save for the yellow badges they must wear. She reasoned they were like as anyone to be offended if their hospitality was rebuffed. "There is other business here in Lincoln we must attend before the day is done, and we cannot linger," she explained. "But if you would not be alone with me, you may call your wife."

He did not register any surprise at her bluntness, but only shook his head and gestured at his son to come into the room. Then, with an apology, he closed the door on the Welshman who was left to stand alone in the little entry.

She had come to Elias first because, of the people they sought in Lincoln, he was the only one she knew how to find with any certainty. But she had told the Welshman that the message she delivered was not for his ears, and he had not seemed to find it strange that she carried a secret message to a Jewish home.

Now she sifted through the few papers in her leather wallet and found the one marked with Elias' name. Truly, she only recognized the E at the beginning, but that was still a wonder to her. She wasn't nearly as accomplished as Aunt Mary thought, but she had learned to recognize some letters, if not whole words. She handed the paper to him and waited as he read it. She did not know what it said, but she could guess.

He took a long time to look at it. The color had left his face long before he finished it.

"There is more that is not written here?"

She nodded, and summoned up the words Sir Gerald had given her.

"I am to tell you that the king is like to do in England as was lately done in Gascony. For your safety and prosperity it is best to leave of your own accord, while it is still possible. And if you will come away, you have the protection of the lord of Darian as far as he is able to give it, even unto Basel." She twisted her fingers together, trying to remember all the words. "When the wine is next delivered, then may your family join the baggage train on its retreat, and have safe passage over land and sea. And…and that is the end of the message, though there be plainer words I am to give if they be needed."

Nan knew that Sir Gerald had meant for Elias's wife to be shielded from these more straightforward words, but she thought perhaps the child should not hear it either. The boy had stepped closer to Elias and held his hand now, staring at Nan with solemn eyes.

"Plainer words." Elias looked something between angry and frightened. "What are these plain words? That I am to abandon my home and my friends only for a rumor?" When Nan looked doubtfully at the boy, Elias urged her on. "My son is not shielded from these matters. Speak the message."

Nan looked at the way the boy's collarbone jutted out, and closed her eyes to recite. "The king has no more use for Jewish money now that Italian bankers serve him just as well, and as Christians. Remember you well the sorrows of your past, for they are like to be the sorrows of your future, do you stay. These words are kindly meant."

She looked away from the man and his son, and reminded herself she would not be playing messenger if Sir Gerald had not been injured, and the fault for that was her own. She worried that such weighty words would be dismissed because they came from an ignorant girl and not a knight of Morency. But it could not be helped, and at least she knew something of these past sorrows that threatened to return.

She had lived the first ten years of her life around Lincoln, though only rarely visiting the town itself, and grew up with the story of the eighteen Jews who were hanged because it was said they conspired to kill a Christian boy. Her father had believed in their guilt, but her mother and Aunt Mary had called him wrong. And she remembered when every Jew in England was arrested for coin-clipping – she had been working for the weaver, who lamented that such an unnecessary measure interrupted his trade.

"That great cathedral," said Elias, his voice bitter as he looked out the window. "When the earth shook its walls to dust, my grandfather gave money to help rebuild it, and knowledge too. The windows and the carvings – there is such decoration in it as shows my people were not always so reviled. And my grandfather's grandfather laid the stone for this house that I am told I must flee."

Nan nearly always kept her thoughts to herself, and easily, but it was an effort now to bite her tongue against saying he might sell this house and feed his son, and that he was a fool not to. Pride could not be eaten. It was none of her affair, though. This was the business and council of great lords, and she was only an accidental messenger.

"This is the message you send back with me?" she asked.

"Nay, I..." He looked down at his son, his hand on the boy's shoulder. "Give him my thanks. You may tell him I have heard his warnings and will consider his counsel."

She nodded, glad of the simplicity of it, and moved to the door. The Welshman waited patiently, the falcon's cage on his back and covered by his cloak. She should have agreed to refreshment for his sake, she realized belatedly. But he looked eager to be gone from here. He inquired of Elias of the friend he sought, a falconer who would have come from Lancaster five years ago, he said.

It was the first she had heard his voice since yesterday. Gone was his easy conversation with Fuss or his idle observations on the weather or landscape as they walked. She missed it. His silence and careful distance made her more aware of him every minute. His eyes never turned to her, and yet still she felt scorched by his look.

But they would part soon, and she would grow used to silence again.

It had been her intention to ask Elias where to find her sister, but in the end she did not. He said he knew the falconer they sought, a very good man, well-regarded by all. She did not want to ask him where to find a common whore who shared Nan's looks. Not in front of his son, in this house his grandfather's grandfather had built.

They took their leave of him, following his instruction to climb the street past the cathedral and then follow the lane behind the castle. They would find the falconer near the west gate. She watched the Welshman walk with ease up the steep street. He was strong now. There was no more need to journey at a slower pace and rest often, nor keep away from busy roads and crowded inns for his peace of mind. He flinched less and slept more. He was easier among people now.

He was recovered – not entirely, but enough that it would not pain her to leave him.

They reached the great cathedral and stopped to look at its grandeur. Seeing it from the road this morning had caused memories to rush in, the distant days of her girlhood when they would work in fields close enough to see it etched on the horizon. Bea had begged to come here when their mother was dying, sure their prayers would fly to God faster if said in such a place. Even from the outside, it seemed to soar straight into heaven. Though Nan had since seen many great castles and manors and churches, there still was nothing else like it.

"Will we go in?" The question slipped out of her, to her own surprise. "To give thanks for a safe journey. And it's a sight to behold, though you've seen such sights before, to be sure."

The Welshman blinked at her. He had been staring at the immense size of it, at the many pilgrims milling about, and the merchants hawking medals and trinkets.

"Never have I seen anything like this," he answered, looking again at the expanse of stone, his eyes following the spires up into the sky.

To think that he, who was so worldly, had never seen such a magnificent thing. It made her feel suddenly like she possessed a great wealth. It was different than the other things she had given him –

food and shelter, her protection and her words. Those were given because they were necessary for his survival, but this could be given only for joy.

She signaled to the Welshman that he should go ahead of her toward the cathedral. Some in the crowd cast a curious eye at the lump of the falcon's cage still beneath his cloak, and she meant to safeguard it from any mischief. Near the great arched door, she signaled Fuss to stay outside to wait, and they stepped inside.

It was only a few steps until the nave opened up before them, and she could not help but raise her eyes to it. They called it a ceiling but as a child she was sure it was heaven itself, the way it went on forever, the columns reaching up to meet graceful arches. Even now she was sure it was more than just mortar and stone and clever design, because to look at it made her spirit lift up and out of her. She could feel it leave her body and join the upward sweep of light. It made her feel tiny and mortal, and perfect and endless, all at once. It stole her breath away.

This was how she knew men were liars or fools when they called her beautiful – because this was beauty. This.

She only let herself look for the length of a long breath, before eagerly turning to watch the Welshman take it in. But to her amazement he was not looking up. He was still studying the carvings behind her. The enormous black stone font apparently fascinated him. She stepped close and he did not even notice, so she put a hand to his arm to draw his attention. He looked at her, startled, and she glanced at the nave, then back toward him.

His eyes followed her glance, and she watched his breath stop. He looked as she must, every time his falcon flew up into the endless heavens. Every time he murmured lovingly to it when it returned to him. Every time he stroked a fingertip through its feathers, a miracle of nature held easily on his wrist, looking at him from ancient eyes and trusting him above all else.

Now his face turned up so far that the dark hair fell away from the scar by his ear, exposing the patch of shiny skin. His features were a little like the falcon's – dark eyes under a heavy brow and sharp cheekbones – but his full mouth was a soft contradiction to that. It turned up naturally at the corners, giving him an air of good humor. Now his lips parted as he stared in awe, and the air rushed out of him in a soft sigh.

He stepped forward, still looking up, dazed by the sight, into a pool of color caused by the daylight coming through stained glass.

"It is more beautiful than I could have dreamed," he said.

"Aye, it is," she said softly. Unnecessary words. "It is beautiful."

She blinked, and turned her face away from him and back up to the soaring heavens.

They made their way slowly around the nave, following in the wake of a sea of pilgrims, and said their prayers of thanksgiving. Soon after, they left and found the lane that led around the castle and toward the west gate, where lived the falconer.

At the Welshman's bidding, a boy outside the mews ran in to call his master. The man who emerged was handsome, with rugged features and deep brown skin, and dressed so well he might easily be a lord. Nan suppressed her urge to bend her knee in courtesy and offer to fetch him ale.

He did not even see her. He only saw the Welshman and stopped dead, staring at him.

"Gryff?" He said it like it was an unthinkable word. He looked the Welshman up and down, and his eyes filled. "Do I dream?"

The Welshman stepped forward and put a hand to his shoulder, then embraced him like a brother.

"Hal," he said, his voice choked with happy tears.

He kissed the falconer's cheek as they gripped each other, crying and laughing, rejoicing to find one another.

It was such a sight that Nan felt her own eyes prick with tears, overwhelmed by too much beauty in one afternoon.

1283

He stood, dazed and despairing, in a corner of the hawk-house with Hal's father. Moris Hartwin had become like a true father to him over the years, and seemed perfectly pleased to treat Gryff like his own son. It was he who had heard the ominous whispers between lords as they hunted that morning and repeated them now to Gryff.

"It can only bode ill." Gryff had said it at least a dozen times now. Every debate and every imagining – every path came back to this. "To hope it is for my safekeeping is senseless."

Prince Llewellyn was dead. Gryff had learned it two weeks ago and was still surprised at how it grieved him. The prince had been such a large and looming figure in his life, and now he was no more. But the uprising did not end with Llewellyn's death. The fight against England continued and, predictably, some of the Welsh nobles began to turn on each other now that hope was fading. They traded their loyalty away to the king for English titles and promises of continued wealth.

Those few Welsh who stayed true to the fight followed Llewellyn's brother Dafydd now. Gryff had sent yet another message to his father and brothers, warning them that the king's wrath would be unlike any they had yet known if they dared to follow Dafydd. He had begged them to see the sense in making peace now while the king might still reward them for it. If they waited too long and fought to the bitter end, they would hang.

His only reply was the news yesterday that his father led a fresh attack on the king's army.

And today Gryff learned through whispers that he was to be taken from Lancaster's household at last, to be carried for reasons unknown to an unnamed place. It filled his mind with dark portents.

"Know you what Edward intends for Llewellyn's daughter?" he asked Moris. "Will has said the king is resolved that she will never marry nor live free. She is a babe in arms, born only months ago and damned because of her father. Already they plan prisons for the sons of any Welshmen who have led the fight against Edward. The fathers will hang and their children be made captive for life."

Moris rubbed a hand over his face. He had begun to look old in this last year.

"We cannot know any of it for truth. It is yet only rumor and intention."

In better times, Gryff would have laughed at this optimism. Now he only pulled his cloak tighter around himself, shivering in the January freeze. Hal often said that his father was too good, always expecting reason and justice.

"When they come for me, then will we know it as truth."

"Cannot William discover what is planned for you?"

Will was at court, and if he knew anything he would never trust such intelligence to a letter – if he would share it at all. Of late Will had grown closemouthed and even more cunning. He valued his place at court and in the king's trust highly. Mayhap more highly than any friendship.

"Did he know of it and wish to warn me, he would have done it already," Gryff answered, feeling his heart sink further. It was the first time he admitted to himself that he did not feel sure of Will, who was no longer a lonely boy hoping to make a friend. Will was in line to be a great Marcher lord and, as such, would be nearly as powerful as the king himself. Now more than ever, as powers shifted, a Marcher lord could not be trusted to stay loyal to a powerless friend.

"They say the king speaks of such bloody vengeance against the Welsh that any who think to defy him will quake in terror. If I am suspect–"

"But you are not!" Moris was insistent.

This much was true. Gryff had spent nearly a year in demonstrating that his loyalty was to Edward and not to Wales.

"My blood is suspect," he said bluntly. There was no hope that the king would forget that he was Welsh, and that his father was even now laying siege to a Norman castle. Gryff had to admit it was a most efficient way to end all resistance to Edward's rule: stamp out the bloodline of every man who fought against it. "I tell you true, if I knew a way to escape these walls, I would fly far from here. I would flee to somewhere safe, though I know not where that might be."

"Haps you should," came Moris's unexpected reply. "If it is your life in the balance, you should."

Gryff blinked at him, this man who cared for him like a father and who rarely spoke with such a dire tone. To flee was unthinkable, an irrevocable decision that would likely damn him in the king's eyes. Before he could say so, there was a noise, the sound of someone entering at the far end of the hawk-house.

"Say nothing to Hal of this." Moris spoke low and urgent. "He can say in truth he knew naught, do you choose to flee."

It seemed absurd even to think it. He would have said something to Hal despite Moris's warning, but he did not want to burden his friend with so much grim news. It was easier to curse the cold and talk about which birds should be flown on tomorrow's hunt. It was easier to forget that no matter what he might choose, his days here were numbered.

Gryff spent every moment of that day expecting the king's men to carry him away and, now that the seed of the idea was planted, he passed a sleepless night considering the possibility of fleeing. To France, perhaps, or further. First he would have to find a way to escape this fortress filled with men loyal to the king, and that was a seemingly insurmountable obstacle.

But then he realized it might not be so difficult. He had lived here for so long and was such a part of the household that he had all but forgotten, until recently, that he was a hostage. And everyone else here, including the household guard, had grown just as relaxed in their attitude toward him. Still he thought of no way it could be done. Outside these walls the only people he knew were his Welsh kin, and to go to them was certain death. He had no horse, no coin, no place to go.

In the morning, it all seemed like the most desperate kind of fantasy. He put it out of his mind and tried instead to dismiss the growing dread. He tried to tell himself that there was no noose tightening around his neck, that the king would let him live in peace and free once the war was done.

Then the message from Will came, a whisper from a courtier as he passed in the hall that very afternoon. "Be on your guard. Your bastard brother thinks the time is ripe to make himself the only living heir."

The man was gone before Gryff could ask if this meant his trueborn brothers were dead.

In the hawk-house he told Moris that perhaps there was naught to be lost if he fled for his life. If Rhodri did not kill him, the king was like to throw him in a tower.

Moris nodded somberly and said he knew a place. It was not as far as France, but in time Gryff might be able to make his way out of England to certain safety. Until then, it was simple enough to smuggle him out hidden beneath the empty barrels that would be delivered to Monmouth tomorrow. And there, said Moris, was a friend who would lead Gryff in secret away from this place he had come to think of as a home.

He was to go to a Brother Clement, who tended the hawks at an abbey deep in the wilds. It was far from Wales and Windsor and anywhere kings or murder-minded bastard brothers might find him.

Chapter Nine

1288

"By the saints, look at her. She is a beauty."

They had progressed as far as the mews, where Gryff took Tiffin from her cage. Hal looked the falcon over while Gryff breathed in the smell of the place, awash in memories. He had not felt so content since he had left Lancaster's household.

"You have not known her weight at all since the Epiphany?"

"Nay, we have been forced to live wild and her diet has been whatever could be hunted in the winter woods. It has been a little easier these last weeks, now spring is come, God be praised."

"She seems in perfect health." Hal kept his eyes on the bird but put a hand to Gryff's shoulder again, squeezing. "It's in his blood, little Tiffany," he said with a confidential air. "There are few who could care for you so well."

Gryff tensed, suddenly remembering they were not alone. He caught Hal's eye and gave a meaningful glance in Nan's direction, muttering, "There are fewer still who know aught of my blood."

Seeing Hal was the only thing that could have made him forget Nan for whole minutes. His friend had as yet taken no notice of her at all. She hung back, watching them silently from the doorway as though hesitant to come inside.

Hal only gave the barest nod of understanding to Gryff, his brows flicked upward in curiosity. He turned to see Nan framed in the doorway and his brows rose further. Even with the late afternoon light behind her and her face shadowed, she was so comely that a man could do little more than stare.

Gryff introduced her as a servant of Morency, and said only that they had met on the road and were recently come from Wragby. Let the full story be told later, when he had time to explain all of his strange journey over these last five years.

When Hal said he was pleased to offer her his hospitality, Nan shook her head and spoke.

"I will leave you now, but first I would ask if you know the woman I seek. She is…" Nan faltered for only an instant. Her eyes had been lowered in an unusually deferential manner, but now she met Hal's gaze. "I am told she is a common whore, mayhap a bawd, and lives just outside the walls of Lincoln. Her name was once Beatrice, though she may be called different now, and her hair is like mine."

In spite of the distance between them, Gryff could feel her tension. It radiated off her, her jaw clenched tight as she blinked at Hal, expectant. He did not know what she imagined the answer might be, but he saw she was bracing herself for it.

"Her hair?" echoed Hal, politely confused.

She had put up her hood when they had entered the church, and now she pushed it back from her face. Beneath it, the plain blue kerchief only showed her hair at the edges, so she reached over her shoulder to untuck the cloth and pull a sheaf forward. It fell shining to her waist, little ripples of golden silk that flowed over her breast to her belt. Gryff could still feel it between his fingers, cool and soft, the first touch he had stolen from her.

"Bettie," said Hal immediately. "She is called Bargate Bettie." He was looking at Nan a little doubtfully, a little curiously. "She is a bawd, aye, and her place is south of Bargate bridge."

She nodded and tucked her hair behind her, pulling the hood back up. None of the tension had left her. Gryff saw her snap her fingers for Fuss before she remembered that the dog, still wary of birds, had not followed her inside the mews. In the moment that she paused, it struck him that she would leave now. Without a word, she would leave him.

The elation of finding Hal was swept aside, replaced by a formless fear. No more would he find her by his side when the memories froze him, or stole his sleep. Tomorrow he would wake to the dangerous world again – and she would not be there to steady him with her quiet acceptance of that danger, her acceptance of him. He might never hear her silence again.

He tried to move his tongue to thank her, but the words would not come. Mere thanks were inadequate. *You saved me*, he wanted to say. So much had she done for him – and what had he done for her in return, but steal touches and cause her to shrink from him?

"It is unwise to go there now." Hal spoke emphatically, stopping her just as she was turning to go. "It is no place for decent women to wander, if they would be safe from lecherous rogues."

"That's no concern to me," she assured him.

Hal scoffed at this, incredulous, and Nan looked to Gryff, her eyes meeting his directly for the first time since he had kissed her. It startled him, but he did not shy from it. His friend looked at her and saw only her slight stature, her youth and her beauty. Hal did not know how much more there was to her.

"She will be safe," said Gryff, holding her steady blue gaze. He wanted to put everything into his look, all the things he did not know how to say – apologies and thanks and hopes that they would meet again – but he was not as eloquent with his silence as she was. He only looked for as long as he could into the blue that burned him.

"It will be full dark soon, and it is far," Hal protested. He was adamant. "Nor will Bettie have time to greet you at the hour when her trade is most brisk. Come, I beg you will have sense. In the morning I will take you to her. Never will my wife forgive me, do I let you go to such a place alone."

A hint of doubt came into Nan's face. She glanced over her shoulder to see the setting sun – and then down to find her dog sprawled in the dirt outside, chin on his paws, perfectly content. She seemed to consider for a long time before giving a reluctant nod.

Hal beamed. Gryff tried not to, and then turned to ask his friend when he had acquired a wife.

✠ ✠ ✠

"Monks!" Hal had shouted with laughter at first, but by now he had settled into intermittent bursts of chuckling. If it weren't for the child sprawled on his chest, almost asleep at last, he probably would still be howling. "Five years with monks – and you tell me they were the kind who stayed true to their vows! I am full amazed you have lived through it."

Gryff couldn't help laughing a little himself, largely because of the sleepy child whose face pulled into a reflexive grin, eyes still closed, in response to her father's humor. She was barely a year old, and her brother born only two months ago. Hal had lived a very different life for these last five years than had Gryff.

"The vow of chastity they kept, it's true, but had they kept a perfect poverty I think me I would have perished long ago. The abbot loved his hawking too well, and I thank God for it. It is how your father knew Brother Clement, and why I was taken in."

"He never spoke of it." Hal's hand covered the little girl's back, gently patting, urging her to sleep. "Never did he breathe a word of your flight, nor did he betray that he knew aught of where you had gone. Not even when Lancaster questioned him. In his last hour he whispered to me that you were safe, but no more than that."

Moris had died a year ago, a fact that came out as they had sat down for a meal with Hal's wife and children. The rare letters sent to Brother Clement were the source of the few precious scraps of information that had come to Gryff over the years in hiding, and the last had said that Hal's father was ailing. It struck him that the letter was turned to ashes now. So was the one that had informed him that Hal had gone to Lincoln, and the one that announced his own father was dead, and his brothers. The letter that described the execution of the last Welsh rebel Dafydd and the imprisonment of his sons – that too had been eaten by flame.

Hal glanced toward the stairs. His wife had disappeared there with the baby, saying she would return to see to their comfort as soon as the boy was fed and sleeping. But Hal said she was like to fall asleep herself, tired and overworked since they had found no replacement for the maidservant who had recently left them. Nan was upstairs too, obviously astounded she would be given a bed and an entire room all to herself for the night.

Now that he and Hal were alone, they could speak more freely.

"He feared for you, Hal, else I would have bid you farewell ere I ran away." He looked at Hal's thumb brushing against his daughter's curls. "If I have brought danger to you by coming here, he will haunt me."

"Nay," said Hal. "Never would he fault you for coming to me. Nor do I believe you put me in peril."

"Think you there is no danger to me from the king?" The question came out of him as half-challenge, half-hope.

"I know little of the king except which birds he cares to fly when he comes to Lincoln. But I have heard of no reward offered for you, and that has been some little comfort. You did well to come here now, when the season is done and the birds put up for the moult."

They both knew Gryff must decide what to do before the season began again. Hal was as excellent a falconer as his father had been, and kept a mews favored by the king himself. But a falconer was a servant, not a confidant, and so Gryff could not expect his friend to know all the tidings of court and king.

"Have you seen aught of Will these five years past?"

"He writes often to ask advice of me for his birds, though his own falconer has skill the equal of mine." Hal's face split into a smile. "He is nothing like he was as a boy, except for that."

Gryff smiled to remember it. "Still looking for a fast friend, you mean?"

"One friend in particular. He hides it well, but from the first he has tried to find you." Hal's smile faded into thoughtfulness as he leaned back. "It is slyly done, the way he seeks information of you from me. He came with the king last year on the hunt, and said to me in secret that should you ever need him, you may still count him as friend."

It should have been a relief to hear, but he knew Will too well – and he knew the king's court even better. Gone was the guileless boy he had first met all those years ago. In his place was a Marcher lord, and a favorite of the king. Gryff rubbed a hand over his face.

"And do you believe he can be trusted?" he asked.

His friend looked into the embers of the dwindling fire, considering. The child in his arms had fallen to sleep at last.

"You know Will. He is so cunning I cannot say with certainty. But as to my belief – aye, I think he yet loves you like a brother and would not betray you." He looked up at Gryff. "Never does he miss a chance to speak ill of your bastard brother. I can think of no reason for it, save that Will hates him for your sake."

This had the effect of simultaneously causing a wave of affection for Will and a small shock to remember Rhodri, whom he had put out of his mind almost entirely. For five years, life had been simple, the days orderly and free of intrigue. Now everything became complicated again, only because of the blood that ran in his veins. It made his head ache, to consider all of the machinations, the wheels set in motion after he had run away.

He did not want to think of any of it. He only wanted one thing.

"And if I… Think you I can go home?"

He knew it was how he said the word – *home* – that made his friend's hand press gently on the sleeping child, holding her closer. Gryff would have said more, but there was a sound from the stair.

It was the dog, and a moment behind it came Nan. Her hair was in its braid again, her rough dress the same she had worn for most of their journey. Still the sight of her made him catch his breath. She was like a flame that had escaped the candle.

Her gaze moved over the scene of the two of them beside the hearth, the child dozing on Hal's chest. She had said very little all evening, yet her silence never felt rude. Now she murmured good eve to them and inclined her head toward the rear door as though asking where it led and if she might go through it.

"The yard is empty," said Hal, understanding her easily. "It is only bare dirt, but enough space to train the hawks to lure. You are welcome to exercise your dog there, so long as he leaves no foulness behind as token."

She nodded, and beckoned the dog to follow her as she walked to the door. She held a lamp, and the light glanced off the blades that were now strapped to her forearm again. Gryff wondered if she did not trust this house, or him, or if it was only that it was a new and strange place and she felt better to be armed.

After she had gone through the door, Hal spoke with a knowing smile in his voice.

"No common lanner, I think." Hal's words flooded Gryff with memory, the lost frivolity of their youth. This was how they had used to speak of ladies and maidens, long ago in that other life, comparing their looks and temperaments to birds of prey. "I would say merlin for her size, or haps a hobby for her beauty."

Gryff looked at the sleeping child in his friend's arms. It was hard to believe that they had ever been so callous and carefree. "She is neither falcon nor hawk."

"Oh?" Hal's brows shot up, and he looked at Gryff with a new interest. "Nor is my wife, and she was the first woman of whom I ever said that. It is why I made her my wife."

It took a moment until Gryff could laugh at the words, and the implication. He did not know how to explain to Hal that this opinion was not born of any special feeling for Nan, but the simple fact of her. Any man who thought he could so easily know her was a fool. She was like the falcon who killed with a glancing force, and also like the hawk who clutched the prey close to kill it – and yet she was like neither, for she did not seek out quarry nor come to a master's call. She was sharp-witted and beautiful and deadly and kind, and there was no other creature like her.

From the yard where she had gone there came a faint sound, a soft thudding that repeated at intervals. Hal heard it too and seemed just as confused by it, so Gryff went to the small window that looked out over the space. He lifted the curtain that kept out the night air and saw only the lamp she had carried. It was set down on the packed earth in a far corner of the yard, and neither she nor the dog were anywhere to been seen.

Then a blade landed at the edge of the circle of light, the tip buried in the dirt. It was one of the short blades she carried on her arm, and now he saw the others that were planted in the ground. Another landed as he watched, and he realized it landed there by design – she was aiming to make a circle, marking the ring of light around the lamp. She was practicing her art.

"What is it?" asked Hal from his place by the hearth, and Gryff did not know how to answer. He simply made a beckoning gesture and Hal slowly raised himself, the child limp against his chest, and came to the window.

Gryff had not yet told him about his time with Baudry and the thieves, nor of Nan's part in saving him. It had seemed too outlandish a tale to tell, seated at a table with Hal's family while Nan ate more than he had ever seen her eat. He thought he would be able to speak of it to Hal, and soon – but not quite yet.

Now he moved to make room for his friend to look out the window, and watched the astonishment come into his face as the blades flew out of the darkness. When eight short blades ringed the lamplight, four more were thrown to land within an inch of the lamp itself, on four sides. The plain eating knife that hung at her belt came first, and then the dagger from the sheath at her back. The long dagger she carried in her boot landed on the far side of the lamp, and on the side nearest to them was a knife he had never seen – silver, small, almost dainty. He wondered if it was the one kept in her bodice.

She came forward out of the darkness and stooped to pull the blades from the ground, intent on her work, never noticing they watched her. Or perhaps she noticed and did not care. She moved the lamp farther back, against the wall that enclosed the yard, laid her kerchief on the ground before it, and walked back into the darkness.

"A sparrowhawk, then." Hal was grinning, disbelief and delight in his face as the blades began to fly through the air again. And though she was no bird, Gryff could not disagree with the assessment. Sparrowhawks were deadly on any terrain, effective and efficient and full of surprises.

This time she used the kerchief as target, surrounding it on all sides. Hal asked him if she had learned the skill from Morency himself and Gryff answered that he did not know, nor did he care to ask. The lord of Morency was a favorite of the king, and the lady of Morency was Will's sister. It was easy to say too much to Nan, to reveal enough of himself to her that she might learn who he was, and one day speak of him to those she served. They were members of a world that might yet seek to imprison or kill him, so he did not speak to her of them.

When she emerged from the darkness again to pull her knives from the ground, Hal called out softly to her. She stiffened, but did not startle. She must have known they watched.

"You need not throw only into the dirt. That wooden post there, and the lintel. You may throw where you like." She looked doubtful, timid, her eyes roaming around the yard. "In faith, there is naught you can damage. Come, I will be glad of the diversion."

She seemed to take it to heart, and spent the next hour in a display of such skill that it amazed him anew. She threw the knives into the post, a straight line from top to bottom, then a double line along the side, then whatever pattern Hal suggested. She threw the nails, too, from the bag she carried, filling in the spaces between the blades and never striking metal upon metal.

When they asked if she could hit a target unseen she brought the lamp to her corner of the yard, leaving the post in darkness, and threw. It was a sight to behold. The dog at her feet, she looked ahead into the blackness and drew her knives, one after the other, methodical and sure. Some she threw with her left hand and some with her right, some by the handle and others by the tip of the blade. Every one of them landed with a thump, so it was not a surprise when she went forward with the lamp to reveal the post full of knives – but it was a surprise to see the short blades in a circle, the longer blades arranged in a square within it, and one nail at the center.

"She must have learned from Morency," he said to Hal, observing the tiny prideful smile she was trying to suppress. "If not the skill, then the taste for spectacle."

Hal smiled. "Is a vanity well earned." He hefted the child up on his chest and said, "My arms will take no more, and the morning will come soon enough. I'll bid you good night."

He called softly out to Nan to thank her for the show and retreated up the stairs with his own lamp, leaving Gryff with only the soft glow from the grate in the hearth. He stayed at the window for a time, watching her throw blades into the post, wondering if she would ever tire of it.

Eventually it began to feel wrong, as though it were too intimate an act to watch her in silence from afar. He retreated to the broad bench by the hearth that was to be his bed for the night, pulled his cloak over himself, and tried to fall asleep to the sound of the knives hitting the wood.

But he kept hearing the wounded knight at the priory, warning him not to look at her in lust – a warning she had silently echoed, and still he had not heeded. All he could see when he closed his eyes was her shrinking from his touch, blade in hand. All he could feel was the curl of shame it brought him, mingled in with the memory of her mouth open to his, the feel of his knee parting her thighs, the raw pleasure of thrusting against her.

The only indication that she had finished her practice was the silence that came from the yard. He thought he heard her step inside, but could not be sure – she had extinguished the lamp and all was darkness. The night settled around him, and it was not as unfriendly as it had been only a week ago.

"Will you stay in Lincoln?"

She whispered it, low enough that it would not wake him if he slept. He opened his eyes to the gentle glow in the hearth, knowing she could see at least the outline of him. It was the first time she had asked him anything of his life.

"Nor have I decided what I will do." He could not stay with Hal forever, much as he might like to. "I have nowhere else to go."

"Your home," she said, switching to Welsh, surprising him. "Will you not return there, to ease the hiraeth in you?"

He closed his eyes against the word. It was like one of her blades, thrown with casual precision straight to his heart. "What know you of hiraeth?"

He expected the silence that followed, because it was so often her response to his questions. But after a moment, she spoke again.

"I know how you spoke of that place. I know hiraeth is what fills the distance between where you stand and where lives your heart."

Her dog came to him out of the darkness, pushing at his hand, asking to be caressed. He moved his fingers across the soft fur as the ache spread through him. She made it sound so simple. "To return there now… Is a perilous thing, for a Welshman to travel roads made by an English king."

"The roads made by kings are not the only paths a man may follow."

He considered that. It seemed to him every step he had taken in his life was determined by the king. If not for Edward, he would never have left Wales, nor fled into the wilds. Nor would he have come to Lincoln, where dwelled the one friend he could trust with his life.

"And you?" he asked the darkness. "Will you stay with your sister, now you have found her?"

The darkness did not answer him. He could almost feel her thinking, deciding what words to give him. She was so self-contained, the boundaries around her person and her spirit so sharply drawn, never giving more of herself than she wanted. But he thought he could feel a thread of her come free, a tendril of her closely guarded self wending its way toward him through the dark night.

"I am no whore. Nor do I wish to be made one."

Her voice was soft, her words deliberate. He turned his eyes to the hearth, the curl of shame spiraling through him, and looked a long time at the embers and the ashes. The words he wanted were not to be found there, or anywhere. Tomorrow she would walk out of his life, and he would likely never see her again.

Her dog moved under his hand, going to the stair, following her out of the room. It loosened his tongue at last.

"Never can I repay my debt to you, for saving my life." He stared hard at the dim glow. His wretched life. "That I returned your goodness and charity with dishonor – I will repent it to my grave."

It seemed forever that he lay there with nothing but the vivid memory of her hands peeling a turnip, her voice telling him how a serving girl was treated by powerful men. So few words had she ever spoken to him, and he had disregarded them when it mattered most.

She did not seek to reassure him, or grant him absolution. But her quiet voice reached out to him through the night to say, "There is no debt between us. Sleep easy, Welshman. Gruffydd."

Then she was gone, and he was left in the dark with the sound of his name in her mouth.

CHAPTER TEN

In the morning she told the kind falconer there was no need to hurry, that she would wait while he attended his duties. In truth she need not wait for him at all, now that she knew where to find her sister. She told herself that she was weary from an almost sleepless night, that she preferred to have the falconer with her – a man of consequence, thoroughly respected and respectable – when she walked into her sister's world.

She told herself many things, and none were the truth. It was not the rain that made her pause, nor the pleasurable sight of the Welshman in the yard training one of the falconer's birds to a lure. It was dread at what she might find.

Never would she have believed that she would pause at this last step toward her sister. It was not that she was a whore – many times she had thought Bea might have been forced to prostitute herself. In some ways, it was the best she could have hoped for, the least evil of many fates that could befall a girl of her station. Not starving or dead, just a common whore.

Now she could see that she had always imagined saving her sister. That's what had been in her mind, that she would find Bea and carry her away somewhere safe. It's why she had gone looking for her in the first place. But if what Aunt Mary said was true, then Bea did not need to be saved. There was no great urgency in the task.

So Nan hesitated, agreeing to wait until morning, delaying departure, nervous of what she might find. Afraid there was no more of her little Bea, and she must learn to love this Bargate Bettie. But no matter her fears, the day would not wait.

It was midmorning when they crossed the bridge amid a crowd of people and carts and animals. The falconer had said there was a small market just beyond the bridge, near to where her sister could be found, and he had some business there. The Welshman came too, and she felt the tug of his attention with every step. It had been her constant companion these many days, from the moment he had first seen her, and she would be free of it soon. It should make her glad. It should be a relief.

At least she need not be burdened with worry for him, so changed was he in the presence of his friend. It seemed to her as if he had found a lost piece of himself in the moment his friend had said his name. If he had regained his confidence as they left Wragby, now he had found his full ease and comfort. He had come back to himself. As they passed through this market, among all these people and their noise, he did not flinch or stare or shrink. He was well. He would be well.

At the edge of the crowd she paused to look at the few buildings ahead, along this road that stretched from Lincoln to London. It had the look of the sort of place where common whores did their trade, where she was like to find her sister. Suddenly she was remembering their mother. Her thin face rose up in Nan's mind, how she looked in those last hours. *Care for your sister and brother,* she had said. Oh, how Nan had failed at that.

A sharp tug at her arm caused her blood to race, her hand to jerk out the knife and brandish it too quickly. It had been years since she had last been taken by surprise, and in a crowd at that. She wheeled around to find the shocked face of a young woman peering at her. Ruddy cheeks and yellow hair and wide-set, bright blue eyes that looked a little wild.

"Nan?"

She felt a tickle of recognition. Her body seemed to know before her mind did, her fingers going slack and her knife falling to the ground. Then all at once she was flooded with certainty.

"Bea." She blinked up at her. Up. At her little sister. "Little Bea."

She watched her sister shake her head in disbelief. "Nan. You're Nan."

She nodded. All of her felt numb. She thought she might never move from this spot. But even as she thought it they were embracing, a fierce and desperate clinging to one another. There was nothing else left in the world but her arms wrapped tight around her sister. Her sister who should be dead. Her sister who was tall and sturdy and grown to womanhood against all odds.

"Look at you." Bea pulled back a little to look into her face, knocking Nan's hood down, touching her hair. "You're the spit of her, but in full health. God forgive me but I forgot her face until I seen you."

Nan grasped her sister's shoulders, frantically looking her up and down. Arms and legs, her body whole and sound, no illness or injury evident. She felt the hot rush of tears tumbling down her face.

"Look at the flesh on you." She was sobbing now. Anyone would think it a tragedy, the way she wept, when it was the best thing she had ever seen. She gripped Bea's arms, strong and healthy and perfect. "You're not starved. I prayed for it." There was no stopping the tears, no hope of speaking sensibly. "I prayed and prayed."

Bea shook her head, her face screwing up in that way she had when she did not want to weep. Nan thought her heart might burst at the sight of it, so familiar and so heartbreaking. She dragged a sleeve across her own face to wipe the tears away even as more tumbled down, then wrapped her arms around her sister again. They were a spectacle in the street and her knees might fail her at any moment and leave her in the dirt – and she did not care at all.

"I'm here now, Little Bea." She spoke into her sister's ear, fierce and certain. "I'm here, and there's no one can take me away from you, not never again."

✠ ✠ ✠

They were in the common room that served as kitchen when she began to understand that the uncomplicated joy would be a fleeting thing, never to return. Still, she was content with her journey's end as she sat in this house that Bea managed.

Not Bea, she reminded herself over and over again – it was Bargate Bettie who ran this place. And she was struggling to understand Nan's life.

"I serve the lord *and* the lady, however they should need me," Nan explained. Some of the women who lived here had come for their meal, and Nan did not like to speak of the business of Morency where they could hear it.

Bea gave a knowing grin.

"We've been known to serve lords too, but never their ladies. Is he a kind one, then? He must be, to let you leave his bed and come here. But for all that you look well, I see more bone than flesh on you."

She pushed another of the small loaves across the table to Nan, who was mortified by this assumption – less for herself than for Morency. Nan's place there was strange enough, even without her humble birth, and defied simple explanation. She should not have tried to tell it so soon without considering her words. Her sister had never served in castle or manor, nor had she much knowledge of great lords and ladies, so she was only guessing the best she knew how. That didn't save Nan from feeling the affront.

"Morency is ruled well by Lord Ranulf. He's a good knight and true. Nor would he never dishonor his lady, and there are few enough lords I can say that about."

She would have said more but she was distracted by a young girl who stood at her elbow, trying to get her attention without interrupting. It reminded Nan of herself when she was that age – perhaps ten years or so, the same age as when her father traded her to the weaver for a handful of coins. But this girl, with her black hair and eagerness to please, was not starved or dirty. She held out Nan's knife, the one that had dropped to the ground when she saw Bea.

Nan took it and thanked the girl, but the knife prompted more questions from her sister. She spent the rest of the afternoon explaining that she had learned the knives for defense, never saying it was Lady Gwenllian who had taught her. Instead, she told how she served Gwenllian in the herb-house, and with needle and thread, and many other household duties. Those women who stayed and listened seemed as overly impressed as Aunt Mary had been.

But Bea only seemed a little amused.

"It's no astonishment to me, making yourself the favorite of a great lady." She laughed in a way that was a little mocking, the barbed tease of a true sibling. "You always did love to be a good girl."

Nan looked down at her hands where they were folded neatly in her lap, withstanding the wave of memory. She had not forgotten all their sisterly bickering when they were girls, but she had forgotten that this was ever the chief complaint. She hadn't understood her sister's resentment then, and she didn't understand it now. Why should she not want to be good?

"And *you* loved to take all the butter, and then pretend I ate your share."

For the barest instant it was like they were children again – she saw the angry denial rising up in

Bea's face, and felt her own protest forming. But then Bea's face softened and her mouth quirked up. In a blink it was gone and they were grown again, looking back on that life together.

"It was rare enough there was butter to fight over, nor even bread to put it on. It's no wonder you're a little thing, and all bones."

"Not for lack of eating." Nan smiled. "Lady Gwenllian, she says I'll never eat enough to make up for the years my belly was empty, but I may as well try."

Bea pushed the last scrap of the loaf at her again, then turned to send the other women off to their duties. The youngest girl who had retrieved Nan's knife was too young to do the work of the older women, and her role was to clean and fetch and serve. Nan tried not to think how one day she'd likely become a whore like the rest of them. Not for the first time, she said a silent prayer of thanks for Aunt Mary. If her aunt had not insisted on finding Nan a good place to serve, there was no knowing what might have become of her.

When all the others were gone and she was left alone with her sister again, she asked one of the harder questions.

"Did our father do well by you with the money he gained from selling me off?"

The weaver had paid the equivalent of six years' wages to take her into service. Nan had gone gladly, knowing the coin was meant to feed her sister. It had seemed a fortune to her, and an even greater fortune that she'd gone to live and work in a place where her own belly did not grumble and ache every day.

"He bought me shoes." Bea smiled fondly, remembering. Then a hardness came into her face. "But you must know he drank it, no matter that he tried to do right. It was Mary who wrested a few coins from him and gave it to the miller so he would put aside a bit of something for me every day."

That was the best that could be hoped for, from their father. He had never been the same after that terrible year when their mother died. Nan counted it a blessing he was only weak and useless, and not cruel. She listened to her sister tell the story of what had happened after Nan was gone. It was all just trying to find work in the fields where they could, as they'd always done – but now their father drank even more, and there was little work to be had. After a few years, Bea had found a kindly alewife who had given her a place to sleep and enough work to keep her in one place.

"Then I took up with the candlemaker's son and we run off here to Lincoln. I went round to the shops once to ask after you, but you weren't nowhere to be found."

By that time, Nan calculated, the weaver had died and she had been sent to Chester – or maybe on to Rhuddlan to serve in the king's hall. If things had happened differently, if a depraved lord had not sent her life in a new direction or if she had thought to go looking for Bea sooner, then it might all be different now. She might have kept her sister from resorting to this whore's life.

She listened as Bea went on to describe how she fell out with the candlemaker's son and found a mason who was happy to pay her for what she'd previously given for free. Then there were more men who paid, including a priest who was her best customer. "I still warm his bed sometimes, when he is lonely for me. Fergus don't mind it."

Fergus was the man she had met a few summers ago, and he had told her she had a good head for business. This was his place, an inn where a few whores had already been plying their trade when he met Bea and invited her to come here and make a proper business of it. She had brought in more women – seven in total now, and always more wanting to come work here where they were sure to find a safe and prosperous place.

As her sister spoke, Nan felt an increasing sadness. It was not that Bea was a whore and a bawd, nor even that she seemed proud of it. Aunt Mary judged it foul and sinful, but Nan could not think so harshly of anyone who turned to whoring. It was only one of many necessary evils for the poor and the lowly. It was to be avoided if at all possible, of course, but when you had no name and no real home, no notion of where your next meal might come from, then it was no easy thing to avoid. For the whole of her own life she had barely escaped it. Sometimes she even thought her brief marriage to Oliver was not much different, for she had always known she must give herself to some man if she was to have any hope of surviving.

Her sadness came from the discovery of how different she was from her sister, who did not seem as if she had tried very hard to avoid this life, nor did she mind it so much. In this way, it was as Aunt Mary had said: they were so different that none would believe they were sisters. Nan could not imagine ever being happy to bare her body to a strange man – to many men – and let him do what he will. Even before that terrible lustful lord had made it seem a terror to her, she had been that way.

But Bea was different. Bea was Bargate Bettie, a thriving bawd even at this young age. And there was more as the day went on that made Nan feel more alone than she had expected to, if she ever found her sister.

Even while she was glad Bea was not a timid little thing, she was loud and brash in a way that grated on Nan's nerves. Her man Fergus arrived, and though Nan had known worse men by far, she could find nothing pleasing about him. His wit was slow and stupid, and he stank as though he'd not washed in a month. Even had he not looked over Nan with lascivious eyes when her sister's back was turned, she would have thought him unworthy of Bea. Yet her sister clearly loved him well.

Most disagreeable of all were the little things Bea said from time to time that made Nan feel an unaccountable shame. When asked, she described the comfits she had tasted for the first and only time at Morency last year – only to have Bea sniff and say, "Well, it's a fair fine life you lead." And Nan thought to tell her sister about her best friend at Morency, but when she said Robin was the son of a minor lord, Bea asked if she had any friends who were not gentry.

Nan turned her face down at this, hoping to hide how her sister's resentful tone wounded her. It was not envy of her life, she thought, but just a different flavor of the same sentiment she had felt from Aunt Mary. She had no words for it, but she knew it was a way of letting her know that she was not like them. That she did not belong in their world, at least not for longer than a visit.

But where did she belong, if not with the last of her family? Unbidden, the Welshman came to her mind, and the way he talked of his home. It was lost forever because even if he stood on the same soil again, too much had changed. The home he remembered – the place and people and feeling – was gone, and he was doomed to long for something that he could never have again.

As evening came on, the house became busy with the comings and goings of customers. Bea must attend to business now, and she called for the little black-haired girl to take Nan to a room for the night. "It ain't as grand as you are used to, I'm sure," she said, again with that faintly hostile air, "but it's away from the grunting and the sweating, and there's enough room to stretch your legs out."

There wasn't room for much more than that, but Nan was glad of this small space where she could close the door against the sounds of the brothel. Because she could not sleep, she thought over the long day, amazed that it had begun in the home of the friendly falconer.

She had not even said a farewell to the Welshman. The joy of finding Bea had wiped out all thought of him. Now she remembered the outline of his face against the glowing grate as he reproached himself for repaying her charity with dishonor.

It was the first time a man had ever said anything like that to her. There were men aplenty who had taken more than she wanted to give, but this was the only one who was sorry for it.

Sleep would not come to her, weary as she was. There was too much to consider. She spent long hours contemplating the vast distance between the sister she had sought and the sister she had found. It seemed impossible to bridge the space between them, until the door of her room opened and Bea was there. She came in quietly as Nan admonished Fuss to silence, and slipped under the blanket to lie next to Nan in the dark.

"Do you think of him still?" she whispered, and Nan could hear tears in her voice. There was no question who she was talking about. "I think of him most days."

Her hand found her sister's and their fingers intertwined.

"Aye, how could I not?" She felt her own tears leaking out but, as she had when Bea was just a little girl, she did her best to hide them. "I promised her to look after you both."

"There weren't no way to save him, Nan. I've thought of it over and over. He were too little for anything but a wet nurse, and us with no way to pay one, and starving ourselves."

She felt Bea's face press into her shoulder. This was the inescapable truth of sisters, of siblings. No matter how different they were, no matter how far apart life took them, there was no one else who shared these memories. The same early sorrows filled their hearts, and the same joys. When they slept, the same places and faces appeared in their dreams. Only the two of them remembered the brother they had

had for a little while, and only they could whisper his memory between them.

"It's like I told you, little Bea. He's our own angel in heaven now, for how could he be anywhere else."

"I hope it's so."

"It is," she insisted, suddenly more sure of it than ever. "How else can we both still be alive, and doing as well as we are? We've had more than our share of good fortune. It's him looking out for us."

She felt Bea's arm wrap around her waist, strong and full of life, holding her close as they had used to do when they were girls.

Her sister. She had found her sister. It was all she had wanted, and here it was, holding her in the dark and sorrowful night.

Chapter Eleven

He woke at dawn with the image of Brother Clement lingering in his mind and dread choking him. But when Gryff turned his face into the bed linens, he remembered where he was. He remembered that she had slept in this bed, and that gave him a kind of comfort, as though a part of her remained here in his friend's home.

Her words came to him, as they always did now in these moments of dread. She had insisted it was a mistake to hide from memory, and already he had learned she was right. He made himself open his eyes and listen to the distant sounds of the waking house while he carefully summoned his last memory of Brother Clement. Somehow the sound of Hal's child crying downstairs made it more bearable.

When the dread had subsided, he took himself down to the main room to find Hal's daughter smeared with porridge and smiling broadly at him. At the sight of it, all the melancholy in him vanished as though by magic. He suddenly felt himself the most fortunate man in Christendom. Only weeks ago he'd had nothing but a pair of birds, a belly full of hunger, and certain death breathing at his neck. Now he had choices he might make, and a fast friend, and the agreeable sight of a smiling child to greet him.

Hal's wife Sara was intercepting the little girl on her way to Gryff, holding the baby boy in one arm and attempting to wipe the girl clean with the other. Gryff laughed at the sticky hands reaching up at him, which delighted the girl so much she squealed and stamped her feet.

"God save, is there any maiden you will not woo?" Hal came from the yard and scooped his daughter up, wiping her hands and face clean. "Beware your heart, little one," he said to his daughter. "He is too old for you."

The instant Hal let the girl go, she came straight at Gryff, who lifted her off the ground. "Too old," he affirmed to her shining face. "And unworthy of a maid who is born of the line of Sir Morien himself."

It was an ancestral claim that had been invented as a jest when they were boys, but Gryff had not expected Hal's wife to laugh quite so much. Patting the baby on the back, she said, "Those were some of his first words to me, that he is descended from Sir Morien himself! As though I would surrender my virtue sooner if I could imagine him a knight of the round table. Did it work on many maidens when he was young?"

Gryff opened his mouth to answer, but his friend gave him a look that stopped his words. Then he could only laugh as Hal went down on his knee with hand over heart and declared to his deeply amused wife there were no maidens before her – or if there were, she had eclipsed them all in his first sight of her – and many other extravagant compliments. He ended by begging her to give him a token he might wear as favor while he raked out the mews.

She gave him the porridge-soaked cloth and a kiss, and sent him on his way with a teasing, "Off on your quest, then, Sir Morien."

Gryff felt an absurd moment of disappointment, as he had when they were boys, that it was only a jest. It had been his own invention, but he had always secretly told himself it was true – or at least that it could be true. He had liked to think that Hal was Welsh too, and both of them descended from Arthur's knights. He still liked to think it.

In the mews, they fed Tiffin handsomely. The sooner she put on weight, the sooner her feathers would begin to moult. Then, months from now, she would be ready to hunt again.

And during all those months, Hal would be here with his laughing wife and growing children.

"I do not dare to stay here, Hal. Not even for the coming summer months." He looked up and down the row of perches, valuable birds whose owners might come at any time, any minute, to see their hawks. Most were Norman lords, and some might easily know Gryff on sight. He could risk himself, but he could not risk Hal and his family. "Naught has changed in five years – or all has changed, and I cannot know it."

Hal paused in cutting the meat he was preparing to feed an impatient goshawk. "Where will you go?"

It had been in his mind, but he had not truly thought of it. Now the choices were clear. "There are two paths, I think. To Edward's court, and beg his mercy. Or to flee again, to France." He paused. "Or Aderinyth."

"Will we pass the day in debating the merits of each path," Hal asked mildly, "or will you tell me now that you go to Aderinyth?"

Gryff stopped breathing for an instant, transported back to another mews, another time, another man who knew him so well. He let his breath out in a long sigh. "By God, you are like your father."

Hal smiled at this, almost as if he had expected it. "Nay, my father would have your journey planned already and send you forth without delay. I have not his wit nor his foresight."

"Yet you know I think to go home, though there be naught for me there and no good reason in favor of it."

Hal fed the last bit to the goshawk and wiped his hands clean. He spread them out before him as he faced Gryff, as though the answer were evident.

"Ten years have I known you and called you friend, Gryff. Ever have you sworn that you have no love nor duty to that place, but the lie is in your face each time you speak of it." He shrugged. "It is your place. They are your people. You cannot say there is naught there for you."

There might be nothing left but the hills and the mists. All over Wales, Edward was tearing down the old and building enormous new castles. He was discarding laws and destroying customs. Gryff was afraid to know what he was doing to the people.

"Were I to go there, I could never again lay claim to my name or family, lest Edward hear of it. Better that I am thought dead or in exile forever, and I live out my days as any common Welshman." He laughed a little, unexpectedly cheered by the thought. "I have played that game well enough these five years past, and have found it rare pleasing."

Hal handed him a broom and invited him to begin this commoner's life now by sweeping out the gravel. Gryff did it gladly, all the while remembering that long-ago day when he had ridden away from his home, and how he had never thought to be away for so long. How certain he had been, as a boy, that he belonged there and would return. How he had spent years trying to forget that certainty, and how right it felt to have it again.

✠ ✠ ✠

The kitchen kept by Bargate Bettie was not used much for cooking meals. Most food was brought from the cookshop across the way and Bettie herself saw no need to hire a cook when the customers did not come here to eat. But there was a fine, broad hearth in the kitchen and Nan never could stand to be useless, so she spent her time making barley bread and pottage and other simple things that could be easily managed with little help. Today it was a fish stew.

She had always felt most at home in a kitchen. Even at Morency, where she had no business among the pots and the platters, she found reasons to visit often. Kitchens were always warm and rarely still, and they all felt familiar as no other place ever did.

Over the last few days she had learned the rhythms of this house, of the women who worked here and the men who came at all times of day and night. She had not known what to expect of a brothel, but in many ways it reminded her of any other kind of serving work: few of the workers were enthusiastic about doing it, but it must be done every day. It was a clean house and all the women were kept fed, warm, and healthy. Bargate Bettie had standards, as she regularly emphasized to Nan.

"I've brought the wine."

Little Cecilia had crept in the door, and would surely slip away almost as silently. The youngest member of the brothel seemed to like helping Nan, but had taken to vanishing any time Bea might be near. There had obviously been some disagreement between her sister and the girl, one of the many mysterious dynamics here that Nan tried to disregard. It was her sister's business, and Nan had no intention of becoming a permanent part of the household.

She smiled her thanks at the girl and poured the wine into the pot. When she turned back around, Cecilia was gone. A moment later, Bea appeared.

"We'll be fair spoiled, do you keep on like this." Her sister took a long and appreciative sniff of the kitchen air. "Fergus had thought to make this a proper inn, but I said to him it were better to make use of my whoring than my cooking, as I had plenty of one and none of the other."

Nan stirred the pot silently for a moment, her back to her sister. Being here, she often thought of the inn that she and Oliver had planned to run. It was going to be their future. Funny, how easy that had been to forget for so many years.

She could tell Bea about it now. Just open her mouth and say she had a husband once, and his name was Oliver, and he had wanted to keep an inn but then he was killed.

"You can learn cooking," she said instead. She tried, but could not stop herself from adding, "I could find a place for you in the kitchen at Morency, or in the –"

"Oh, when will you stop," came the predictable interruption in Bea's gently irritated voice. "I don't want no place at your Morency, nor serving any lord or lady."

"It need not be Morency. I will find a place for you somewhere, and respectable work. Only come away from here, Bea."

This had become her constant refrain, her reason for staying. She did not want her sister to remain in this life. Yesterday they had argued about it, with Bea saying that her immortal soul was her own business and Nan had no right to judge her – and Nan protesting that it had naught to do with sin or judgement. Why would anyone want to live this life unless they must? It was hard and filthy and reviled, and Bea did not have to do it anymore now that Nan could help.

But saying so only made Bea turn cold, as though Nan only said these things to boast of the high and mighty people she knew.

"Just as well could you stay here and I find a place for you. I've got men asking after you already, did you know they call you the Bargate Beauty?" Bea let out a laugh of genuine amusement before subsiding into thoughtfulness. "I'd have you making twice the coin with half the work, and all of it on your back. An easy life, Nan, if you want it."

There was a gleam in her eye that was more than amusement. She meant it. Every word. And for a moment – just a fleeting moment, no longer than the beat of an eyelash – Nan fought down an impulse to pick up the nearest blade and send it into the wall an inch from her sister's head. That would stop her words.

The impulse faded quickly, but the anger behind it did not. It showed in her face along with all her disgust, for she had no hope of hiding it. She turned her back to Bea again and picked up the long spoon with a shaking hand. It had been years since the anger had come on her so swift and strong.

When Nan had begun to tell how she had dodged the groping hands of lustful men in the king's hall, her sister had laughed like it was a fine story. Nan had gone on to tell about the time one had caught her, how he had yanked her dress down to drool on her bared breasts but was too blessedly drunk to do more than that before he was snoring. Bea had shrugged and called her fortunate.

After that, Nan stopped trying to tell the important things. Silence served her better. It had for many years.

Now she took her time pulling the pot off the coals. There was a hard knot forming in her, a fist closing. She might love her sister, but she could not give all of herself to someone who could laugh at her past torments, and ask her to make a living on her back.

"Our mother never wanted that for either of us," she said calmly. She stirred the stew, knowing she must taste it to see what seasoning it wanted but having no appetite for the task. A memory came to her, and tugged her lips into a smile. It was better when they talked about the old things. "Do you remember what she did when the bee stung you?"

Bea shook her head sadly. "I don't remember nothing of her. Just her shouting as the baby came, and then she was gone."

"It stung your hand, and you cried and cried. She put honey on it."

"And… and she said honey was the cure for a bee's hurt." She looked at Nan, startled, her face brightening. She loved these crumbs of memory. "I do remember! A cure for Bea's hurt. She was clever, wasn't she?"

Nan smiled. "Clever enough. You stuffed your hand in your mouth to suck off the honey, and we heard no more of your wailing. Well, until the next time you wanted honey."

They laughed, and tried to remember more things together, more bits of shared life to stitch them closer to each other.

Chapter Twelve

That night in the small room, Nan sent one blade after another into a head of cabbage. She was careful to throw gently and aim precisely, so that it was not cut to pieces and ruined. The Welshman and his friend had watched her like she had some kind of wondrous magic at her fingertips, but there was no more to it than what they saw with their own eyes: endless practice and repetition.

She was tempted to pull out the memory of his kiss, to hold it in her hand like a jewel and turn it this way and that so she might see every angle of it. In this house she was surrounded by lust, easy and comfortable, as ordinary as cabbage. It seemed to have nothing to do with her, until a stray sound of passion would drift to her in the night and she remembered his body pressing into hers, the stirring in her belly, the taste of his tongue.

But that was too much to contemplate now, when there were so many other things crowding her mind. She turned her attention to the target, and threw. She used the short blades from her arm brace, as she always did when she must pick apart a complicated knot inside her head.

A blade landed to one side of the jutting stem, and she considered her sister's age. Bea was young enough; she might change. Another blade landed above the stem, and Nan thought of how she could not stand to stay in this house much longer, if men would think her body was for sale. Two more blades landed, two more doubts: she should have started looking for her sister sooner, she should not leave her here.

She retrieved the blades, running her fingertips over the letter stamped into each. What would her lady advise her to do? What would she say of Bargate Bettie and the business she did? Nan snorted to herself at the thought, and threw again. No matter how wise and shrewd, great ladies did not know starvation, nor what it meant to have no name and no protection in an unforgiving world.

When the stem had been cut out of the cabbage, she heard Fuss make a faint sound that was not quite a bark – his way of announcing a friend had arrived. She turned and saw the girl Cecilia just outside her door, obviously trying to hide in the shadows. Nan gestured her into the room, then slipped the blades back into the brace. The girl watched the flash of metal.

"Can you teach me?" she asked.

Nan began to nod, then stopped. What if she did not stay here? There was only so much that could be learned from a teacher. Most of it was just constant practice, and the girl had little time for that among all her duties. Still, there were things she should be taught – that every girl should be taught. Her mind flew back to the hours spent with Gwenllian, all the learning that came before the knives, lessons in how to escape a man's hold.

"Do the men grab for you?" she asked.

Cecilia only looked at her with round eyes, as though afraid to answer. She stepped closer and whispered, "She says I must start earning my keep." She had begun to weep, red face and wet cheeks. "I'm to let them grab me."

Nan knelt down to look her in the eye. "Who?" she asked. "Who is it says that?"

"Bettie," said the child.

Nan found a mostly clean square of linen and gave it to the girl so she could dry her tears. "She only means to say you must keep the floors clean, and run to the cookshop." She pushed the hair off Cecilia's face. "Is true you must earn your keep, and so must we all. But you're not to serve the men." *Yet*, she might have said, but did not like to think of it.

Cecilia just shook her head, her tears slowed but not stopped, and touched her fingers to the blades on Nan's arm. They stayed that way in silence while Nan considered giving the girl a knife, just to help her feel safe. She must be taught a defense, if the men were grabbing for her.

Fuss barked suddenly and loud, and she looked up to see one of the women at the door. It was the one with the red hair, Rosamund. They called her Rosy, and she was more girl than woman.

"Come, Cissy, you cannot hide every night." She said it kindly from her place at the door, casting a worried glance at Fuss. "He's waiting now, best to get it over with quick."

Nan looked between the two girls, her breath speeding up. The little girl was gripping Nan's skirt now, refusing to look up. A nervous impatience radiated off the older girl.

"Who is it that waits," Nan asked, "and what is it he wants from her?"

There was an edge in her voice, and the girl named Rosy would not meet her eye as she stammered an answer. It was a jumble of words that seemed to say there was a man who visited the brothel regularly, well-known to be a good sort unless he drank too much. He had arrived not long ago and waited in her room for Cecilia. "Bettie said as I'm to take her to him straightaway when he visits," she said. "But it's four times now that he's come asking for her only to find she's hiding away."

So it was Rosy who had told the little girl she must let the men grab her. It could be she wanted to harm Cecilia out of spite, but Nan saw no obvious malice in her. It was more likely she had simply misunderstood.

"Nay, you've heard it wrong." Nan let her hand rest on Cecilia's hair in a calming gesture. Both girls had that nervous look she knew well, afraid of the trouble that might come of neglecting their work. "Ye are both mistaken."

They had only to find Bea and let her say it outright, to end the confusion. She had to promise Cecilia she'd let no harm come to her before the girl took her hand and came along. Nan was watchful as they made their way, tensing at every sound, wary in this house full of lustful men. She realized she had no notion where she might find her sister at this time of night, but Rosy led the way to the room opposite the kitchen. The door to the street was there, and Bea leaned against the frame, looking out toward the tavern across the way.

When she turned and saw them, she frowned in confusion.

"What's amiss? Rosy, one or the both of ye should be with him – or did he take to drinking?"

Rosy cast an anxious glance at Nan before speaking. "Cissy don't want to go to him."

Nan waited for her sister to show more confusion – to ask what she was on about, and wonder why Cecilia was anywhere but her own bed at this hour. Instead, Bea gave a sigh like she was working to control her temper, and rolled her eyes to the heavens as though asking for patience.

"And so you leave him alone and disturb my sister with what ain't her business?" She gave Nan an apologetic look before bending over little Cecilia and speaking with a tone of great forbearance. "Now, you cannot dodge forever, ungrateful girl, and so I have said to you for weeks now."

She went on like that, asking if Cecilia did not like to eat? And would she like to be on the street? And had not Bea given her time to ease into things, and chosen a pleasant man for the deed so she need not be so afraid?

It seemed to take a very long time before Nan's mind could truly comprehend what was happening. It was impossible. She could not believe she was hearing it. She could not believe it was her sister saying it.

"Beatrice." It was their mother's scolding voice that came out of Nan, startling them both. It hung in the air while she stared at her sister, bewildered. "She's a child."

Bea lifted her brows at that. "Aye, a child that's been fed every day for months, to say naught of the clothes on her back and the fire that warms her. There's them that like em young, Nan, though few are decent enough to be let near a young girl."

"Decent?" Nan struggled to understand the words, to match them up with her sister's nonchalance. Her hand tightened on the girl's shoulder. "She's but a *child*. And frightened. There's naught decent in it."

Bea's face closed up, that sour look that said she thought Nan was boasting. It confounded Nan even further – how was anything she had said boastful?

"As bad as Aunt Mary, you are, sitting in judgement of me. You know naught of it," she sneered. She set her hands on her hips and glared a moment before taking a calming breath and returning to a more reasoning tone. She barely contained her impatience as she explained. "Never would I do as other bawds are known to, Nan. No girl can say as I ever let a man force himself on her to steal her virtue, so that she must turn whore. I can name you ten girls now who come to this life that way, and their stories would fair break your heart. I wouldn't never be as cruel as that. It's her choice, and she'll go freely to him without I force her."

When Nan found herself unable to muster her voice to respond, Rosy spoke. She was just at Nan's elbow, but it seemed almost as though her words came from a great distance, in a tiny voice.

"That much is true. If another bawd takes Cissy, it's sure to happen just like that."

But Nan could only stare at Bea, who so clearly thought she was being reasonable. Did she truly not see?

"You force her to choose between whoring and starving," Nan said, measured and clear, willing her sister to comprehend. "It's no kind of choice, and it's all manner of cruel."

It was appalling, the way Bea scoffed and rolled her eyes. Like they were fighting over who had eaten all the butter and lied about it. Nan looked down at the girl's bent head, felt her thin shoulder trembling under her hand.

"Bea." She waited for her sister to look her in the eye. "She's no older than I was, when he sold me off." Nan could still see the man she had almost been given to, so eager to have her that Aunt Mary had shamed their father for considering it. "Only think of it, if I had been forced so young."

"And what if you had? It's only the way of things," Bea shrugged.

"Hear yourself! You cannot mean it."

"I do mean it," she snapped. "You would have done your duty and been no worse for it."

The words hit Nan like a stinging slap to the face. It woke her just as a slap would, and she stared at her sister with clear eyes for the first time.

Bargate Bettie was not just a mask that Bea put on when needed. This was who she truly was. This was what she truly believed. And it seemed to open a great chasm at Nan's feet, a hole in the earth that threatened to swallow her.

Nearly all of Nan's life, over and over again, lecherous men had reached for her. And over and over again, good and kind people – women, always women – had protected her, or tried to. It was one of the few unambiguous truths she had learned: there were the kind of people who would sell a girl to a lecherous man, and there were those who would object to it. Everyone in the world was sorted to one side or the other of that great dividing line.

She had never thought – not once, in all the time she had searched – that her sister would be on the wrong side of it.

Love for her little Bea swelled up in her, filling her throat with a tenderness, and at the same moment she felt something crack within her. It was like a frozen branch in winter, splintering in her chest.

When Bea reached to take the girl's arm, Nan stepped forward to put herself between them.

"She won't be going to him tonight, Bea."

She said it calm, and then did not know what else to say. Words were useless. They only ever said what was already obvious, or confused everything more. Her mouth was weary with speaking. All of her was weary, and cold, and broken.

Behind her, the child that her sister would make a whore huddled close to Nan's back.

"I'll go to him," came the placating voice of red-headed Rosy. "He'll be getting impatient."

"And you've a business to run," Nan said, her eyes never leaving her sister's.

Bea looked as if she would protest, but there were two men stumbling in the door now, happily drunk and asking Bargate Bettie which of the whores had time for them tonight. When she turned to greet them, Nan took Cecilia's hand and went swiftly back up the stairs and to the little corner room.

She barred the door and sat on the floor. She stared at the lamp flame until it blinded her, wishing it could blot out the knowledge of her sister's treachery.

Chapter Thirteen

When asked if she had nowhere else to go, little Cecilia said she was orphaned. She came from a village not far from Lincoln, but there had been no one to take her in when her mother died. She had come to town to look for work, and found it here in the brothel. Nan sat silently through the child's explanations that she knew she should be grateful, and was. Bettie kept a good house and never beat her, and she didn't want to be disobedient. She was sorry, she said. Over and over again, she said she was sorry that she was too frightened to do her duty, until Nan could bear it no more.

"Don't you never be sorry for it." She was surprised by the sob that almost escaped her. She felt scraped-out and hollow, incapable of so much feeling. "Don't you never let no one say it's your duty. Nor will I let it be your fate."

She bade the girl lie down and sleep now, and sent Fuss to curl up beside her. She had to look away from them, because the sight almost caused the sob inside her to come loose again. When asked if she wanted Nan to find her a new place, somewhere she might do hard but respectable work, Cecilia had readily agreed.

Nan stared at the battered door of the room for hours, trying to think of a suitable place that would accept the child. Somewhere safe and protected. But every thought skittered away from her, impossible to hold on to. Her mind was a wasteland. There was only this door and the night. There was only waiting for the morn, when she must open the door to face her sister.

A footfall made her heart jump. She drew her dagger and looked quickly to Fuss, who was so deep in sleep he did not even twitch when a soft voice called, "Do you wake?"

She stretched out a staying hand in Fuss' direction in case he should wake, and opened the door a crack. It was Rosy, her red hair reflecting the light from the candle she held.

"Will you be staying with Cissy, then?" she whispered with a glance toward the pallet where the girl lay. "Only the tanner – him as has been wanting her – he went off to the tavern. He was cursing all the way and saying he will return for what he was promised."

Nan nodded, and wondered if she should say anything more about her plans, what little she had of them. It was so strange, to be looked at in this way by these girls – as though she knew what to do, or had any kind of authority.

From her memory rose a vision of the woman who had put herself between Nan and that lustful lord so long ago, how she stood so proud and tall and unyielding. And then she thought of her lady, burning with conviction and radiating power as she carried Nan away to safety. They had seemed avenging angels to her, the women who had saved her. Had they felt this way, deep inside? Uncertain and fearful and small?

"She's a good girl," said Rosy, her eyes on the sleeping child. "It's not a bad place here, truly. But I do remember well how I had dreams of escaping this life once. It's a hard thing for a girl to accustom herself to."

Nan looked at this young woman who looked no more than sixteen years old, who was already so jaded and yet still wistful. "Where did you dream you would go," she asked, "if ever you escaped?"

"To the sisters of the Magdalene," she replied promptly. "I will go someday, if ever I find a way to manage it."

A convent. It might be a solution, if there were no other way.

Nan pulled her inside the room so they could speak in the assurance that none would hear them. She questioned the girl, and learned how as a child Rosy had hoped to live with Benedictine sisters. But having no dowry to give the Church, she fell into working life instead, and then into a whore's life a year ago. She had never intended to stray so far from decency, she said, but then no one did. There were few options when circumstances were dire.

All the while she spoke, Nan looked between these two girls and thanked God, over and over again. Good fortune and unexpected kindness and unearned mercy, that's all that had kept her from a place like this. She was painfully aware that the only real difference between her and her sister was their luck.

That was what she had told herself these last few days. Now she knew there was something more than circumstance, something fundamental in their natures. *You are so different none would believe you were sisters,* Aunt Mary had said. She had tried to warn her, but Nan had not wanted to believe it. She still did not want to believe it.

But what she wanted did not matter. It did not matter at all.

"If you would leave this house and this life," she heard herself say, "I will see you safe away. But it must be now, when morning comes."

Rosy sat up straight from her slump against the wall, near to dozing off. "But…I've nowhere to go, nor coin to give the sisters to take me in. And there are the customers, Bettie won't want me going off with no warn–"

"I will see you safe away from here." She looked the girl straight in the eye. She spoke it as an oath, a vow between them, certain and steady and true. "I will let no evil befall you."

As the words fell from her lips, she was suddenly sure of herself and her course again. If only just for a day, she would take these lives under her protection. The enormity of it pressed on her. This was the debt she owed, one that she would happily repay a thousand times over. But now she understood, as the girl stared at her with hopeful eyes, how heavy was the weight of a life, a soul. Two of them.

She saw the moment when Rosy believed her, the threshold where doubt dissolved into certainty.

The girl nodded and said, "I will take these hours to think on it, then."

They turned down the lamp and sat in silence, waiting for the dawn.

Nan listened to the girls' fragile breath in the dark, and took her time with her prayers. She asked God to bless and care for those who had protected her when she was vulnerable. She began, as she always did, with her Aunt Mary who had shouted that she'd not let Nan be sold to a filthy lecher. She ended with Gwenllian, her teacher and friend, who had given her the gift of knowing how to protect herself.

She held the vision of Gwenllian in her mind, the first time she'd ever seen her with blade in hand – so beautiful and fierce – as daylight filtered into the little room. Fuss was looking at her, expectant, and little Cecilia opened her eyes.

"We leave now," Nan said, and turned to Rosy. "Do you join us?"

At the girl's nod, she stood and gathered her few possessions. At her belt she tied the purse of nails, strings loosened so she might reach them easily if needed. Every blade was put into place – at the front of her belt, in the back, her boot, her garter, the braces on her arms. Her fingers pressed briefly against the dagger in her bodice, her heart's protection, and she prayed today would not be the day she must draw it.

They need only walk out. The house typically did not rouse until midmorning, and all was quiet at this early hour. Still, she felt a foreboding that caused her to clutch hard at the small bag of belongings over her shoulder while she rested a hand on the knife at her belt. When she asked the girls if there was aught they would take with them, only Rosy nodded and said she would gather her cloak from her room.

Just as they neared the end of the corridor, Fuss let out a bark. He had followed Rosy around the corner into her room and now there were voices shouting, all while Fuss made enough noise to wake the dead.

In an instant, Nan had a blade in one hand and a nail in the other. She pulled little Cecilia around the corner with her by instinct, not wanting to let the girl out of her sight. The smell that greeted her told her it was the tanner come back, as promised. In the room she saw him – a tall, thin man shouting drunkenly as he fell onto a small bed. Then she saw a flame of red hair flick out from beneath him and heard Rosy cry out.

Nan only made the nail graze his ear because she did not want him to keel over onto the girl. When he reached up to clap a hand to the side of his bleeding head, Rosy darted out. She was clutching her cloak to her, and she wasted no time getting away from him. But he snatched at her dress and yanked her back, so Nan stepped forward and drew her blade across the back of his leg, just above the knee, to sever the sinew. He dropped like a stone.

"Fuss!" she said sharply, with a stamp of her foot, and he settled down to a growl. The drunken man was howling, though, and the girls were staring at the blood, so there was no hope of a quiet exit now.

She would feel no guilt for crippling a man who would bed a child, but it meant that trouble was more likely to follow them. They must move swiftly now and without hesitation, for she was a stranger in this town and the might of Morency was far away.

She hastily slung her bag crossways over Rosy's shoulder, so she could move unencumbered. After a bare instant of thought, she chose the dagger from the back of her belt to put in the older girl's hand, then pulled the small silver knife from the garter at her knee to give to the younger girl.

There were voices in the corridor now, moving toward them. The drunken man on the bed was trying to rise and come at her but his leg collapsed beneath him. His bellow followed them as they moved past sleepy women emerging from their rooms, and down the stairs until they reached the place where she had left Bea last night.

Her sister was not there, but her man Fergus was. He was rising from a bench by the door, the noise having woken him, scowling in confusion at the stairs.

"What's amiss?" he asked, looking from Nan to the girls beside her.

Nan let silence serve, as she ever did, but Rosy offered, "Someone's done the tanner a terrible hurt." She did not even pause in her step as she said it, the clever girl. Fergus ran to the stairs and they exited the house, stepping into a gray morning.

There. They were out. They paused outside the door while, at Nan's bidding, Rosy put on her cloak and pulled the hood up to hide her bright hair. The small market up the street was only just beginning to stir, and there were few people to witness them leaving the brothel. She was leading them in the direction of the market, back toward the walls of Lincoln, when she heard her name.

"Nan! Nan!"

There was a desperation in it, a panicked fear that Nan could not ignore. She turned around to face her sister, and felt a similar terror rising in her breast, scrabbling like a frantic animal to get out.

She had been taught how to fight despite fear, how to find and keep her balance through it. *You will fear no man,* Gwenllian had promised. *They will fear you.* So she had said and so it was, but nothing a man could threaten was like this.

Bea was red-faced and running, relief washing over her features when she reached Nan.

"There's no hurt on you? Oh, I'll take the hide off Fergus for letting him in after so much drink, falling asleep at the door, the great useless lump. Tell me it's none of your blood I seen back there."

She was running her hands over Nan's shoulders and arms, patting her gently as she looked for injury. Nan only shook her head wordlessly. Gradually, a crease of confusion appeared in Bea's brow. She looked at the girls, then back at Nan.

"Where do you go, Nan?"

They looked at each other a long moment, Nan breathing unevenly and Bea not breathing at all. She thought of their mother. *Look after your brother and sister.*

"I take Cecilia to find different work," she said simply. "And Rosy would come too."

Bea's brows raised in surprise and skepticism. Her hands dropped from Nan's shoulders and she shook her head, rejecting it. She spoke past Nan, to the girls. "And who will pay what ye owe? It's another year for you, Rosy, and three for you, Cissy. Nor do I know what they've told you, Nan, but –"

"There is naught they could say to stop me taking them from here, when they do not wish to stay."

Her sister's expression soured at this, eyes narrowing. Some of the women were at the door of the brothel, peering out at them. Fergus appeared too, starting up the street toward them slowly, and more people coming to the market now. Bea set her hands on her hips, her face hard as she looked at Nan.

"Oh, you are so *good*, are you not? Better than me and better than a whore's life, and you think they are so much better too!" She gestured a hand toward the girls. "And who cared for them before you came along, eh? It's me that feeds them, and me that puts the clothes on their backs and gives them beds to sleep in, or they'd be in the street. What have you to say to that?"

Nan had nothing to say to it. Or perhaps she had too much to say, all of it tangled and throbbing at the back of her throat. Words were so useless. They never managed to say anything that mattered, no matter how many were heaped on top of each other.

"Their debt will be paid," she finally choked out. "I will send it to you."

"Send it?" Bea's combative pose wavered, her face softening in uncertainty. "You…you'll not return?"

Fuss was growling. A cart had stopped just behind Bea on its way to the market, the owner watching them curiously. Nan could see a tiny hole starting at the seam of Bea's bodice, and imagined taking a needle and thread to it. Three quick stitches and it would be mended, good as new. Until it frayed again.

She looked in her sister's eyes – a look with no beginning or end, full of the deep recognition that only came with family – and they knew. They both knew she would never return, and they both knew why.

"Fare you well, little Bea," she said barely above a whisper. The memory of her sister's arm tightened around her, the feel of her face pressed against her as she wept in the night.

"Nan," she began, but then there was a noise behind her and Nan turned to see Fergus reaching for Cecilia. He was telling her she would not be going anywhere as he caught her around the waist.

The nail went into his shoe, just enough to nick the side of his foot. It was what she did to poachers or anyone she did not wish to truly harm; it was meant to startle and to serve as warning. He only cried out and looked down, but did not let the girl go. Nan pulled a blade from her arm brace and in one uninterrupted motion, she let it fly, the tip of it slicing open his shoulder on its way to the ground. Another warning, because she did not want to kill a man in the street where everyone watched. The next would land true if he did not let go, no matter the consequence, but as she drew it he cried out again and dropped the girl.

Little Cecilia held the silver knife in her fist, eyes wide but determined as she backed away from him. She had pricked his hand well enough to draw blood, and now Bea was shrieking, cursing the girl, an ugly look on her face as she strode forward with hand outstretched to grab the child.

The blade caught her sister's sleeve, aimed precisely to land in the two inches of loose fabric near the elbow, and pinned her arm to the wagon next to her. It halted Bea in her tracks, stopped her cursing with a gasp as she looked bewildered at her suddenly immobilized arm. *Arrogant flourish*, Gwenllian would call it, but Lord Ranulf would smile with approval and say arrogance could prove useful in a fight. And so it had.

Nan picked up the blade that had dropped to the dirt and held it tight between her fingers. She would leave the other behind in the wagon, a memento for her sister. They must go and quickly. More people were in the street now, gawking, and there was the man inside the brothel who might any moment call the law on her.

She looked to the girls and gave a jerk of her chin, and they moved readily in the direction of the market. Her sister's shouting followed them.

"Nan! Nan! Will you leave me again?" There was such anger in it, and such despair. Bea let out a sob that would wrench the hardest heart. "Have you only come to show me how well you've done, and now you're finished with me? You said there's no one can never take you away from me again. Nan!"

She turned and saw Bea ripping her sleeve in an attempt to free it, cheeks wet with tears. Disgust and love and rage rose up at the sight, a wave that threatened to drown her.

"I searched for you!" It burst from her, filled with a fury that could no longer be confined to the path of a blade. There was a burning in her lungs, a sharp and painful ache that formed itself into words. "I searched *years* for you. I prayed and I hoped and I found you, and I swore to myself there is naught I would not do for you, *naught*." Already her throat was raw.

"Nan –"

"And you would make a whore of a child! You would let her starve did she not obey, though she cries out in terror of it. *Starve*." She would not weep. She must keep her eyes dry and clear, so her aim stayed true if she must fight. "Foul and corrupt. That is what you are become. That is who you are."

Bea clutched her torn sleeve and stared at her, tears trickling down, jaw working angrily.

"And I am your sister," she said. "I am that, too."

Nan looked at the face so like her own, the only other person left on earth with their father's eyes and their mother's smile.

"Nay," she answered. "You are Bargate Bettie. And she is no sister of mine."

She turned away. They might have been children again, so much was it like the last time she had left her family. Just as then, she walked away with purpose and a heavy heart. Like then, the sound of her sister's weeping followed her.

But this time she did not look back. This time, she did not want to.

Chapter Fourteen

They were in the yard training a newly arrived falcon when Hal was called to greet a visitor. Gryff wondered whether to hide himself in the mews in case it was a courtier who might recognize him, but in the end he only pulled up his hood and retreated to a far corner of the yard. It proved to be unnecessary, though, because Hal reappeared within moments.

"Come," he said, and gestured Gryff to follow him to the front of the house. He had beckoned his wife as well, her arms free of the children that slept every day at midmorning.

He did not know what to expect, but he would never have thought to see Nan there, her head bowed and eyes on the ground – a vision that sent happiness flooding through him. He barely had time to register it before her dog was bounding at him, barking joyously and turning circles, jumping up to greet him. Gryff knelt, unable to stifle the smile that took over his face as he scratched the dog's head. She had returned. She was not lost to him forever.

"There you are, mighty Bran," he said, laughing. The dog whined and danced in answer. "Mighty Fuss, I mean to say. Did you miss me?"

He was waiting for Nan to silence the dog, as she ever did when it was too loud for too long. When she did not, he looked to find her eyes on him, a bright blue shock that traveled along his spine. Her look lingered just long enough for him to see something was different in her. Something had happened.

But then she looked away and he noticed the small figure just behind her, a very young girl with muddied feet and a threadbare dress. Nan gestured the girl forward and said, "This is Cecilia."

"It's Erma," the child said with a sheepish look upward at Nan. "Bettie thought it too plain. She made me be Cecilia instead." The stricken look on Nan's face dismayed the girl, and she hastily said, "But I will be Cecilia, I don't mind it."

Gryff resisted a sudden and powerful urge to step forward and enfold Nan in an embrace. She looked so bewildered, like a child who had discovered she was lost in a dark wood. He bit his tongue against demanding to know what had happened, all his happiness at seeing her swallowed up in concern. But as he watched, she seemed to come to herself again. She looked down at the dog that had returned to her side, blinked, and shook her head slightly as though to clear it.

"Erma, then." She turned back to Hal and his wife, adopting her most deferential manner. "She looks for work, and I did remember as how you are without a maidservant."

The girl stepped forward at this and launched into a brief and practiced speech, detailing her experience in housework, her willingness to learn how to care for children, her prodigious skill in soapmaking, and her recently acquired but scant knowledge of cooking. As she spoke, Gryff noticed another, older girl standing at the edge of the street as though awaiting permission to come any closer.

After establishing the child had no family and wanted no more than room and board as payment, Hal agreed to take her on – though he insisted she would have a penny every week for her work. The girl smiled in relief, but Nan set a staying hand on her shoulder and looked to Hal's wife. Only when she nodded did Nan seem reassured, and spoke again, her words practiced and formal.

"I go now to the priory at Broadholme," she said, "and it's there I'll ask you to send her if ever ye wish her gone from your household for any reason. I hold myself responsible for her until she is grown, and I would not have her cast into the street if she does not please you."

When Hal assured her that, if needed, he would do as she asked, she nodded and lifted her hand from the child's shoulder. She looked so very tired. She also looked like she was preparing to leave now, this very minute.

"Where is it?" Gryff asked. "The priory?"

"To the west, and not far," said Hal, when Nan did not answer. "It is easily reached by nightfall, even do you stop and eat with us. Will you not share our meal, as thanks for delivering a servant so sorely needed?"

Gryff could hear the warm persuasion in his friend's voice, learned from his father. As hard to resist as it was, Nan did not readily agree. She seemed to consider it a moment, glancing over her shoulder to the girl who stood in the street. Gryff prayed for the heavy clouds to open up and make the prospect of travel more dismal.

"If you take me in your home even for an hour," she said quietly, "you must take also a whore who travels with me, and the risk that follows me for certain troubles I have lately caused. I know you cannot welcome either of those things."

Her face burned now, a flush along her cheeks and neck that spoke her shame as she kept her eyes downcast. Gryff did not want to look away from her even for an instant, but he made himself. He turned to Hal, only to see his friend had already decided.

"There will not come an hour when you are not welcome here, no matter who or what accompanies you," Hal answered, just as quietly. "I thought my friend lost to me forever. And so he would be, without you."

Her eyes came up at that, a startled look that landed on Gryff. He had told Hal some of it – how the villains had held him and what had happened when they attacked her party on the road. It was only the barest facts with few details, just enough to explain these last few months of his life. He had not said a word to his friend about the depth of his gratitude to Nan. There was no need.

She turned back to Hal and seemed to consider his offer.

"I would not wish to return your welcome with misfortune." She looked squarely at him and took a deep breath before speaking bluntly. "I've done a grave injury to a man, because he would hold a girl when she wished to escape. He may come after me – or as he cannot walk, he'll send the sheriff after me. And then you'll be found to have me at your table, and a whore too. It's better I leave Lincoln without delay than I bring such disrepute to your good name."

"Was the hue and cry sent up against you?" asked Hal.

"Nay. But nor did I leave that place quietly."

At this, the little girl spoke up. "Bettie don't call on the watchmen, and she told us we was never to do it," said the child, eager to explain. "The tanner will have to go himself, when he is sober and able to stand on one leg."

While Gryff entered into wild speculation about what might have transpired, Hal only smiled at the little girl and gestured to the hooded figure who stood at the edge of the street, beckoning her to come closer. He acted as though the matter had been settled.

"You are weary, and is better you take your ease now and journey to the priory when you are refreshed." He spoke to Nan but was already turning toward the house, indicating they should all follow. "And will you deny us the story of this tanner who cannot yet stand on one leg?"

He and his wife led the girls forward into the house, the distant wail of one of their children signaling a return to order and routine.

Gryff stood looking at Nan, waiting as expectantly as her dog. She had that bewildered look again, softened only slightly by a vague relief. He thought of the moment when she had turned to him among the trees, when he had been frozen in fear at the mere twitch of a hare in the brush, and she had called him to his senses with only his name and a touch.

But his touch would not calm her. He could only wait for her to see him, and then withstand the searching look she gave him. It reached inside of him, seeking the answer to something he could not guess. She was so skilled at communicating silently, putting whatever she wanted to convey into her expression. But now he could not decipher what she meant to say, or what she wanted. It was only him – everything in her intensely focused on him for an endless, heart-stopping moment.

Then she blinked, and became only a weary woman. She looked so fragile that she might blow away with the wind.

"Nan," he said, and watched her fight off sudden tears. It was only an instant, so quickly come and gone that he would not have noticed if she had not been looking in his eyes. But it had been there, and she had let him see it.

✠ ✠ ✠

Nan said a silent prayer of thanks to the Virgin that the goodwife of this house was not unkind. She had warned little Cecilia – little Erma, that was – that they could not be assured of a warm welcome at this or any respectable establishment, when they came from a brothel. But the girl was so excited at the idea of working for a family, instead of living in a convent, that Nan knew she must try. Though it left her open to the scorn of her betters, she decided she must at least begin here, in hopes that if the falconer turned the girl away he might suggest other places to look for work in town.

She had not dared to hope for this much generosity. It was obvious to Nan that the goodwife was not happy to welcome a prostitute into her home even for the length of a meal, but she hid her distaste for Rosy and treated the little girl no differently for having served in a brothel. If there was a slight coolness in her demeanor toward Nan it was only to be expected, and it did not prevent her from offering a private place for the girls to bathe themselves.

Nan and Rosy carried the bathing tub and stool up to the room where she had slept on her last visit. There was a cake of good, soft soap in her bag, and she bade Rosy to wash the younger girl clean with it, using the water on hand while Nan went to the well to gather more. She left to find another bucket, the sound of Rosy's voice following her. "There, Cissy," she soothed the overeager child. "It will take no time at all and your new mistress will have you clean before you're sleeping by her fire."

The Welshman had retreated to the mews, which meant his eyes did not follow Nan as she moved silently through the house. She was conscious of his regard every moment, as though it mattered more than any of the other things pressing on her heart. It was because he had been with her at Aunt Mary's, she decided. He had glimpsed these bits of her life that were unfathomable to anyone else who knew her. That was the only reason she felt the urge to lean into his warmth. She should return to Morency, where she might find comfort in her friends.

But the thought of it filled her with a horrible, unexpected dread. She carried the heavy buckets up the stair, dropped the heated stones into the water, and tried not to think of it as she lathered Rosy's coppery hair. All of Morency knew she had left in search of her sister. They all awaited her news, and what could she tell them?

She poured the water to rinse Rosy's hair just as they were called to come to table. Downstairs, she looked at the two girls with damp hair and freshly scrubbed skin, at the babies delighted with the new faces in their midst, at the steaming bowls of pottage – and she could not bear to sit among them. Though it was a lie, she said she was not hungry and then avoided the Welshman's gaze as she went to gather more water.

In the little room, she set Fuss to watch the door and stripped to her skin as the hot stones gave their warmth to the water. There was only the dagger over her heart left on her, hanging between her meager breasts on the worn leather thong. She scoured every inch of herself, removing every last trace of her sister's foul world. Her hose and linen undertunic were plunged into the water, and she searched out the harsher soap in the depths of her bag so that she could make it all come perfectly clean.

Sitting naked on the stool in the tub, dirty water to her ankles, arms and shoulders aching from the work, she made herself imagine returning to Morency.

She tried to speak it aloud as she must say it to her friends.

"My sister lives. She is a bawd." That was easy enough. It was harder to say, "I will have naught to do with her," but not impossible. And then: "She sees no evil in forcing a child to whore."

Her mouth pressed hard against her arm on the last words. It was the truth, and it felt like poison on her lips. It was the worst part of all, that Bea saw no wrong in it; the way she had looked at Nan as though she were being prudish and unreasonable. *She don't want redemption,* Aunt Mary had said, but it was worse than that: she saw nothing that need be redeemed.

Nan looked at the wet linen draped over the edge of the tub. It should be set in front of the fire to dry, but she could not make herself rise to do it. She could only sit and shiver, and wonder what to do with herself. Morency had been her home these four years, a comfort and a haven. All her time there had been spent in study – in making herself better, safer, stronger – always in anticipation of finding her sister. Always with the aim of giving them both a better life than the one they had been born to.

And this was what it had come to. All that preparation and planning, to end like this. The thought of returning to the place where all her hopes had lived… It was unbearable.

She might go to her Aunt Mary instead, and perhaps it was her duty to do so. But the idea made her clutch her arms about herself in misery. She did not belong there. Her aunt had all but said it with her extreme humility, the same thing that Bea had flung at her as accusation – *better than.*

It did not matter that Nan did not think herself better. Aunt Mary did, and she would forever put a distance between them, a buffer of admiration that only made Nan feel shut out, a stranger to her own family.

Long ago, when she had been so hurt and hopeless, the only place she felt she would ever belong was in the kitchen at her lady's manor. And then in her lady's solar, where quiet words passed between them and every shameful thing was accepted with compassion.

What she would not give to be there now. It was so far away that it almost felt like part of a fable, impossible to reach, the whole breadth of England between this place and that one. She imagined it – the manor at Dinwen, the wide hearth in the kitchen and the peace of the lord and lady's chamber. The ground would be covered in bluebells now, the kitchen garden newly planted, perhaps even a tree chosen to become the May pole already. And her lady would be there, full of wisdom and comfort and silent understanding.

It was far, but so was Morency. And what did distance matter? There was nowhere else she could imagine herself, and nowhere else she wanted to be. She would go.

As soon as her mind settled on it, a great exhaustion washed over her. Now she could sleep. She did not even care that it was daylight, and she had never in full health been idle while the sun was in the sky. She pulled the dress over her head, almost welcoming the scratch of the coarse wool against her naked skin. She fastened the belt over it so that she would have her blades at hand. She ignored common sense, leaving her linen dripping on the tub and her hair wet, and lay down on the bed under her cloak.

Fuss came to sit just below where she lay her head, wanting to be near her but knowing better than to jump onto the mattress.

"You will like Wales, Fuss," she mumbled as she allowed herself to drift to sleep.

✠ ✠ ✠

Long after the sun had set and the household was settled to sleep, Gryff found her in the yard where only a few nights ago she had entertained them with her skill. It was the silence that had called him to her, for there was no sound of blades landing. She stood in the night, illuminated by the lamp set midway between her and the post. There was a dagger in her hand but she only held it indifferently as she stared at the post with a blank look.

"Nan," he said, but she made no acknowledgement of him. Not even a glance in his direction.

She had slept all afternoon, so late that they must stay the night and go to the priory in the morning. The girl called Rosy fretted Nan would make herself ill by sleeping with wet hair and refusing her supper. Both girls treated her with a telling mixture of awe and affection. When asked while she slept of what had happened at the brothel, they said only that they had wished to leave, and Nan had sworn she would carry them safely away. The tanner was drunk and deserved what he got – that was all they would say when pressed for the story.

Still, Hal had thought it best to be cautious. If the man had died, or even were the injury grave enough, it might mean death for whoever had done it.

Now Gryff gave the news to her silent profile.

"The boy who works in the mews here." It came out in Welsh, and he did not question why. "He was sent to the market at Bargate today. There he learned the story of a tanner who drank so much that he did nearly cut his own leg from his body."

Her head angled slightly in his direction, her eyes on the ground.

"Verily he must be drunk still, to tell such an outlandish tale."

It surprised him anew, to hear how refined was her voice when she spoke in Welsh.

"Nay, he does not tell it. It is Bargate Bettie who has said she saw it herself. She has given the constable the names of witnesses who have sworn the same. There will be no search, for there has been no crime."

She was so completely still that he almost believed time had stopped. Not a breath, not a twitch, nothing but the statue of a woman who possessed every feature praised in countless ballads. How many times had he heard troubadours sing of this ideal beauty – the long golden hair, the sparkling blue eyes, the fair face and delicate form? And the silence, of course. The songs never hinted that there could be more, that there were entire worlds within her that went unsung, that the look of her was the least of her.

At last she blinked, and turned her face up to the night sky. He could not tell if it pleased her or pained her, this news that Bettie lied to keep her safe. But he remembered her joy and relief when she was reunited with her sister, and there was none of that in her now.

The sound of the blade hitting the wood startled a gasp from him. She was so fast that he had not seen her move, and had barely registered the passing flash of metal in the lamplight. The dagger was at a steep upward angle, the tip buried lightly at the edge of the post. It dangled for an instant before falling to the ground.

She looked at the splinter in the wood caused by her imperfect throw. Now there was fury in her, together with grief. It seemed to him that she was spilling free, the strict boundary he had perceived around her spirit dissolved, all the feeling within her suffusing the night air.

"You spoke of your brothers." Her voice was tattered, raw. "The boyhood you shared with them, the games you played, the hills and the…" She trailed off for a moment, and he tried in vain to remember all the things he had said. "Were you all so like unto each other? Did you never feel as a stranger set down in your family – or that one of them was the stranger, and so different that you must disavow him?"

He could almost feel his father's eyes on him in the dark. Gryff had always been the one who was different, preferring Norman ways, content to call Edward his king. But he had never been disavowed.

"My father had a bastard son," he said to her. "I called him brother until he tried to kill me."

She looked at him then, a tender pity in her face amidst the shock. How strange it was, to be reminded that a murderous brother was not an ordinary thing.

He lifted his shoulder a little, and the corner of his mouth, an apology for the inadequacy of his answer.

"Greed makes monsters of men. And of women too."

He felt her look move over his face like a touch. It caused the edges of his scar to prickle in awareness, the patch of burnt skin that would never let him forget. Her gaze fell away and she nodded, almost to herself.

She walked forward to pick up the knife, and he set a loaf on the bench before turning to go back into the house. When her voice came again, he stiffened in surprise.

"I journey to Wales," she said. "On the morrow I will deliver the girl to the priory, and then take the road west."

She waited for him to say something, but he could not. Only Hal knew his intention. There was no way she could have known he had planned to go, to try to find his way home.

"I need not travel the roads made by an English king, Welshman," she offered. "Will you come?"

He swallowed, an exhilaration gripping his heart.

"I will."

He left her, but went to the small window to look out. He watched her discover the bread he had left, her expression softening at the sight of it. She lifted it to her face, inhaling deeply. The sound of her barely whispered thanks reached out to find him, curling around him in the night.

Chapter Fifteen

There was a texture to silence, different qualities and sensations to it, uses for it he would never have guessed if he did not put his own reactions aside and consider, instead, why she so rarely spoke. He had begun to understand it as they were preparing to leave Lincoln. She had stood before Hal with a small purse of coins in her hand and asked how she might have it safely conveyed to Bargate Bettie.

"I will see that it is done," said Hal.

She nodded, satisfied, and handed over the coins. "I would have her told this is payment for the debt owed to her, so there's no need to come looking for them that owed it."

"Is there no other message you would send?" asked Hal, who had seen her embrace Bettie and weep with happiness to find her. His voice held a faint concern, an incredulity that she intended such a cold exchange as her parting with her sister.

Instead of shaking her head, or answering no, Nan only let her silence speak. There was something in it, in the way she stood still and did not raise her eyes to Hal, that was a clear rebuke. It was a silence calculated to silence *him*, to make him understand that whatever was between the sisters was not his to question, that she would not have any words put in her mouth or forced from her lips. She had nothing more to say to her sister, and his judgment on that was not welcome.

She would never say these things aloud, because she was too aware of her station in relation to Hal and too grateful to him for his hospitality. But she achieved the same thing by saying nothing at all for exactly the right length of time, before thanking him most humbly for his aid.

Moments later, as Gryff said his farewell to his friend, she seemed to disappear entirely. It was only later that he reflected on how she had cloaked herself in silence to give the illusion she was not there at all. In fact she had been near enough to hear his promise to send word from Aderinyth when he was settled there, so that Hal might send Tiffin to him. Nan had stood in plain sight, but the quality of her silence made him forget she was there, and so he had said the name of his home. He had not meant to let her hear it until she must.

At the priory, he watched her carefully put words and silence together in just the right way to gain an audience with the prioress. The sister who had greeted them looked severely at her and the redheaded girl, instructing them to apply to the almoner after the nones prayer, like they were common beggars. Gryff had stepped forward, prepared to use a less humble approach so that they would be heard, but there was no need. A meek Nan said, "We will gladly do as you say, if the prioress wants us to wait." She pulled a folded piece of parchment from the wallet at her belt and waited in silence while the sister glanced at it, sucked in her breath, and ushered them inside.

It must be something that showed she was from Morency, to have commanded such immediate respect. And yet Nan had not said the name, nor seemed at all boastful or proud of her connection. She was a mute supplicant who let the paper speak for her, and it was an attitude that served her well. The prioress granted her a private meeting, accepted the girl into the priory, and sent Nan on her way with provisions and wishes for a safe journey.

Now as they made their way west he let the silence grow between them, acquiescing to it every day, feeling himself bound to her more and more because they shared it together. He did not try to fill it, as he had felt compelled to do when they journeyed before.

Instead he decided to ask her one thing every day, one carefully chosen query. He passed the hours in stealing glances at her, trying to forget the feel of her breath against his lips, and deciding what question he would put to her.

"Where in Wales do you go?" he had asked at the end of the first day.

"Well north of Aderinyth," she answered, after only a little pause.

He waited, watching her, resisting the urge to press for a more specific answer. This was the more common use of silence, more familiar to him – to allow the weight of it to force a response. No matter how reluctant to talk, the natural aversion to silence could so easily coax words from anyone. Maybe even her.

He could feel the tension rise in her, see the way her jaw clenched against saying more as she avoided his eyes. It was a relief to know she was not immune. But then she looked up, and that was the end of his relief.

Her gaze landed on his mouth, at first by chance and then resting there too long to be accidental. Her own lips parted as she stared at his, and fire shot through his veins. It seemed to last forever, long enough for him to wonder if she did it intentionally – to hope against hope it was intentional – as his blood pounded and his mouth remembered the feel of hers, hot and pliant, delicious.

And then she blinked, ending it. She turned her face down to search through her bag, but could not hide the delicate pink that suffused her cheeks or the way her hands fumbled, unusually clumsy as she set out the food. The knowledge that it affected her sent lust coursing through him.

She must know what her look did to a man. What it did to him. He told himself it was just a moment. A strange moment where she remembered their kiss and perhaps did not entirely regret it. That was all, and he should be glad she blushed at the memory instead of gutting him.

The next day she paused in the afternoon to look in the direction of the main road. They kept it in sight but did not travel on it. By an unspoken agreement, they had again skirted villages and slept under the trees instead of finding an inn or guest house. It was safer for him, of course, to avoid as many people as possible, but he had expected her to prefer the company of other travelers.

But then he remembered how she had looked when she had asked why men always came at her, and he understood why she did not suggest joining a larger party. To travel alone was better for them both, even if it meant he would spend the nights listening to her sleeping breath, remembering her look, burning for her.

Now she led them further away from the road, decisive in her steps. They walked a narrow, barely visible path, wading through flax growing at the edge of a field until they reached a river. This must be the route Hal had suggested – they should follow the river north before striking west, to avoid a forest notorious for its outlaws. But Hal had directed them to find the river flowing through a village much farther down the main road.

This was undoubtedly the river he meant, and it baffled Gryff that she had so easily found it despite her disregard for the instruction given.

"How knew you the path was there, and that it leads to the river? Do you know this place?"

He had broken the silence without thinking, without first considering whether he should spend words on it. She seemed surprised at the question, but did not lift her eyes to his face.

"I may have known it, when I were a babe." She shrugged, uncertain. "But nay, I do not recognize it."

That was all the answer he was likely to get, and he spent several minutes walking beside her, trying to decipher the meaning of this particular silence. She did not seem angry that he had asked it, nor did she have the air of hiding something from him. He thought it was born instead of a simple disinclination to speak at length on something she thought insignificant.

But then she spoke again, and he saw it was only that she had been looking for words to explain.

"There are always other ways." She still did not look at him. "The king makes roads, and the Church, and lords and towns – them that have authority, they make roads so you will go the way they tell you to go. But there are some as would choose their own way, and make a path that suits them. Like how a bird will fly direct across the sky, and pay no mind to the roads men build."

"A bird sees all paths from above, but you are no bird," he observed. "How did you know the way?"

She frowned a little. "It's only sense. We are far from any market town here, and for as many as must lead their cattle along the main road, there must be a path to take them to water. And so I kept my eyes open until I seen a little dirt track, and it goes past the fields and toward these trees that are like to grow near water."

He looked back at where they had come from and wondered aloud, "How is it that I saw naught?"

She made no answer, and when he turned back he found her eyes on him. She looked away quickly, but he could feel the heat of it on his skin, a fire along his throat and jaw where her gaze had been fixed.

The bloom of color across her cheek told him it was not his imagination. The way she kept her eyes down as she resumed walking just a touch too quickly said more than words ever could.

"You've not needed to see it," she said finally, in a hushed voice. There was something awkward in it, something like embarrassment. "It's the lowly who must search out hidden ways, and stray from the path set out for them, to survive."

If he were daring, he would ask if she meant her sister or herself when she spoke of straying from paths. But he did not, because he only wanted her unease to pass. Whether it was because she had met Hal or because she had a sister who shamed her, she seemed to be more conscious of how he was not as lowborn as she. It was another reason to be glad they journeyed alone and avoided civilization. They traveled the same path now, and it was not the one the world had set out for either of them.

"I am in the muck now, as you said to me." He smiled to put her at ease, even as he felt her silence descending on them again. "Before this journey is done, I think me I will have learned very well how to search out secret ways."

After that, the quiet between them was comfortable again – or as comfortable as it could be, when he spent every moment remembering her eyes on him, wondering what would happen if he ever dared to touch her again. He did not let himself think beyond that, but it was enough to fill his mind for hours. He imagined brushing his hand against hers, and how she might tremble as she had before. He allowed himself the fantasy of putting his fingertips to the inside of her wrist, where he had put his mouth days ago, and feeling her pulse leap with excitement.

They were innocent enough thoughts as she walked silently beside him, but at night his dreams took them further, until he was sure he would roast in hell for the sins he committed in his sleep.

At the end of the day she washed the dirt from herself as she always did, lifting her hem to bare her feet, her ankles, her calves to the water. Wet skin, just within his reach. The firelight played against her throat as she bent over the flames and his mouth watered, remembering the taste of her, the feel of his tongue sliding over her neck.

It was madness. He had been a fool to think he should travel alone with her for days, for weeks. He would go mad.

The next day he ignored the tendril of hair that had escaped her kerchief, and the look of her mouth when she gave a soft smile to her dog, and the faint scent of her that might only be his hopeful imagination. Instead he made himself look at the blades ranged along her forearms. They were short, small, deadly – like her. He thought they must have been made specially for her. The letter E was stamped into the metal at the base of each one, and he considered asking her what the meaning of it was, as his query for the day. Or perhaps why one was missing.

But the rain came down before he could ask anything, a light smattering that turned into a downpour just as they were preparing to light a fire and eat their evening meal. There was no easy place to shelter here beside the river, but they had passed a small building not long before stopping, an empty cowshed at the far edge of a field. Now they gathered their things and ran to it.

It was empty because it was half in ruins. There was still some of the roof overhead, thatching that needed repair but held out the rain in one corner. Gryff looked around and saw nothing but beaten earth, blessedly dry where they stood – a patch large enough to build a fire.

He watched Fuss shake the rain off and imitated him, shaking his head, wiping his hands over his face and through his wet hair. When he turned to her all he could see was how the rain-splattered dress showed the outline of her legs more clearly. The edge of linen beneath it clung to the skin at her collarbone, droplets chasing each other down her chest.

He knew he was staring. He could not seem to tear his eyes away from that pale crescent moon of flesh showing through the soaked linen. When he finally did, it was to find her looking at his mouth again. He held his breath as she moved her eyes restlessly, glancing over the floor and the dog and the walls but always returning to him.

Instinct made him walk to her, slowly, prepared with every step to halt. She only watched him as he came closer, her eyes trained at the base of his throat as he advanced. He stopped inches before her, the slightest bit too close, near enough to just barely feel the heat that rose from her body.

He reached very carefully to take the bag from her hand. There was a stiffness in her, a quivering tension, but she did not move away from him. He spoke softly, as though sharing a secret.

"Would you have me build a fire?"

She swallowed, and nodded. He reached behind her with slow and controlled movements, attuned to her every breath, and pulled her cloak forward over her shoulders. He drew the edges together over her chest to cover her fully, hiding the sight of her damp skin, savoring the little shiver that came from her.

Then he stepped away and built the fire, not regretting that he had spent his day's words on such a mundane question, preparing himself for another torturous night of unfulfilled lust.

Chapter Sixteen

Nan's habit was to wait, hidden in the dark, watching for an hour after the sun had set to be sure no villain lay in wait to attack them in the night. It was long past an hour, and she could hardly see anything for the steady stream of water that ran off the eaves. Still she stood and listened to the rain fall as she tried to forget the heat that rose off his body, the huskiness of his voice offering to light a fire.

She was pressed against the outside wall of the cowshed in the narrow strip of dryness, afraid to ask herself why she had invited him to journey with her. It was not like her to do so. But then again she no longer knew herself at all. It had started from the moment he kissed her, this unravelling. Perhaps even before, from when she first saw him starving at the side of the road.

She had always known who she was, sure of her place and her purpose. But now she could not say she was sure of anything. No more was her purpose to save her sister from imagined suffering. No more did she shun the idea of a man's touch – of this man's touch. She felt weightless, untethered from the life she knew, from all her ideas of how she should be.

Fuss was curled near the door, looking out at her from a nest of waxed cloth. The Welshman had put it there, not needing it himself when the floor was dry and knowing that Fuss must always dig at something to make a bed for himself. He had smiled as the dog pawed at it, that warm smile that made her heart glow, so she had looked away – only to steal a glimpse of his body under the cloak, the firelight filtering through the linen tunic to show his form clearly.

As well cut out her eyes as lie to herself. She wanted him, that was the truth of it. She should not. Better to want something that would not risk her body and her heart, that had no dire consequences. Better to want something that was easy, for once.

She slipped inside the shed and saw him lying in the faint glow of the tiny lamp. She had left it burning in hopes it would prevent her stumbling over him in the dark. His breath was slow and even, but she knew he did not sleep. He never slept until she returned from her vigil.

A divided mind, a divided conscience. She wanted him. She should not. It was foolish. It was tempting.

Be selfish, came the whispered answer of her heart.

The stout branches against the wall where she had spread her dress and his tunic to dry, damp hose laid atop it all, took up nearly half the dry space available. She took off her belt and set it beside the arm braces, then held her cloak close over her linen shift as she stood over him.

He looked up at her, calm and waiting, all that unending patience in his eyes. When she knelt beside him, he did not startle. When she tugged at the cloak laid over him like a blanket, his breath caught – but he stayed still.

Beneath the cloak was the warmth of his flesh, the beat of his heart accelerating as her fingertips moved over his chest, an exploration and a question. What a strange thing, to want a man so badly. To want him to want her. To see that he wanted this, and be glad.

She sensed his intention to reach for her, so she leaned back from him to prevent it. Immediately, she felt the intention fade. It was…different, unexpected, a relief. This was new to her, how he did not impose his will in any way, ceding everything to her. All she had known of coupling beyond the hated groping of strange men was what her husband had done to her. And though he had been careful and kind, her only role for those few nights they had been together was to lay pliant beneath him until it was finished.

That was not what she wanted with the Welshman. She wanted things she could not name. She wanted his kisses and his touch, but she did not want her desire to be drowned by his.

Her hand slid over the rapid pulse at the base of his neck and then under the linen, over his heart. She marveled at the feel of the soft hair against her fingers as she put her lips to his. It was as she remembered it – better than the memory, the way his mouth opened hot and inviting, the way her tongue knew now how to taste him while her hands moved over him. The same liquid excitement ran through her as before, the same prick of pleasure at the tips of her breasts, the same urgent need to press her body against him.

Now his hands drifted up to untie her cloak and move into her hair, pulling the strands of her braid free as she let her cloak fall away. It left only the thin layers of linen between them, a realization that was at once exhilarating and unnerving. She deepened the kiss, reveling in the harshness of his breath against her cheek, the feel of his hands in her hair, his body laid out beneath her.

He did naught but touch her hair, her cheek, and kiss her. All the while, she let her hands move over him. The hollows caused by hunger were gone, leaving only lean muscle. Never would she have thought to take pleasure in a man's body like this, to touch it and explore, to learn the curves and lines of his flesh while he lay still. It made her want the soft and hidden places of him. She tugged his linen tunic upward, then pulled loose the ties of his braies and smoothed a palm over his bared hip.

A shot of raw and carnal pleasure raced through her when he responded with a gasp, his fingers tightening against her scalp. His excitement ignited her blood. Never had she felt anything like it, and her teeth raked against his lips, hungry for him, craving more. Then his hand was at her breast, a firm stroke, a squeeze of her flesh while he held her mouth pressed hard to his and the knife was in her hand as she jerked away.

She hovered over him, ragged breaths, body still feverish and wanting him even as she held the blade to his breast. The knife – she had drawn it almost without conscious thought, muscle and bone reacting to threat.

She would not hurt him. She never would. Only he must not grab at her like that, so sudden and controlling.

He was holding his breath, his whole body tensed. She could feel the confusion in him beneath the alarm. The dagger between her breasts remained, hanging heavy inside the linen. It was the little silver knife from her garter she had pulled, one that he probably did not even know she wore. She waited until his eyes moved from the gleam of metal to her face, and then tried to conjure words to answer his look, to explain.

But she did not have to. He seemed to understand without words. He held her gaze and took his hands away from her hair, her body, a slow retreat until they rested at his sides. He lay there prone, undefended, an offering. His eyes moved to her mouth, a hungry look that beckoned her to kiss him again. And she wanted to, more than she wanted to try to explain anything. She bent down to his lips, inviting the warm thrust of his tongue, keeping the blade in her grip but moving it away from him as she stroked her other hand over his hip again.

She pushed the linen away to bare all his body to her touch, her look. The curve of muscle on his chest fascinated her, the plane of his abdomen, the hard flesh jutting out at her from the join of his legs. She touched him in gentle exploration, marveling at the feel of him, solid and warm. When her fingertips scraped across his nipple, he let out a harsh breath that thrilled her. Her hand moved along the curve of his inner thigh, soft and vulnerable, and she could feel how he held himself taut, all the power and desire in him restrained, held in check. For her.

It aroused her, sent heat through her until she almost could not bear it. She guided his hand to her breast and sighed to feel the same touch that had frightened her only moments ago. What a mystery it was, all of it – how it satisfied but stoked the flame higher, how it made her want to lean down and put her mouth to his chest, his belly, run her tongue across his skin while he fondled her.

When her fingers curved around his cock, he gasped again and jerked as though touched by fire. A groan of pleasure came from him and seemed to echo all through her. It must be a sin to delight in it so much, this feeling of holding all his lust in the palm of her hand, to stroke the length of him and hope to hear his gasp again. He gripped her wrist, hard, stilling her hand as air hissed through his teeth.

She looked up at him and watched his throat work to gulp air. It only made her want him more.

"God save," he gasped, his voice strained to the breaking point. "I cannot… You must stop, or I…."

She slackened her hold but did not take her hand away. She leaned closer, pressing her breast into his hand and her lips close to his ear. "I want you to."

Her mouth pressed along his jaw and then his lips. She pulled back so that he might see her face and know she understood that he would spill his seed, and she wanted it. His eyes fixed on hers, dazed, and she knew at last a little of what it meant to wield beauty like power. She had always rejected it, knowing the beauty they said she possessed could be used in that way. But the way men looked at her never made her feel powerful; it only frightened her. Until now.

His palm circled hers around him, guiding her in a firm stroke of his flesh. His other hand grasped her breast tighter, pressing the stiff tip between thumb and forefinger, pulling a sound of lust from her. She felt him grow impossibly harder as her hand moved with his, rhythmically, the excitement in him building to a frenzy. His hips lifted – a powerful thrust as an animal groan rose from the back of his throat. She put her mouth on his to catch it, her hand moving on him as he convulsed beneath her.

When he lay still, panting, she savored his mouth, dimly amazed at herself. She felt wild and reckless. Ravenous. She only pulled back from him when his hand slipped off her breast and moved to pull the linen over his head. He wiped it across his belly, cleaning himself, his eyes refusing to meet hers.

She did not have room for shame in her. Not now, when there was still so much desire. A melting heat had settled between her legs, and all her skin felt alive and aching for him. She did not know what to do with it if he would not look at her. The blade was still in her fist – it seemed impossible to let it go when she was so exposed – but with her other hand, she brought his touch back to the ache at her breast and waited.

He turned his face to her then, rising up on his elbow. When he brought his mouth to her breast over the linen, her whimper made him clutch her tightly. She shifted to bring her leg over him, rucking up her shift to her hips to straddle him as he sucked at her, fingers twisting in his hair. Already she could feel his manhood stirring again, a gentle pressure on the inside of her thigh that she could not help but rub against.

She grew frantic as his mouth moved on her breast, her throat, his hands brushing leisurely up and down her sides atop the linen. Her hips rocked against him and found pleasure there, a discovery that left her breathless. She slid herself along the length of him, the cleft between her legs gliding across the same path her hand had taken earlier, and felt his moan vibrate through her. God save, she had not thought it could be like this, that her body could feel such things.

It was what she wanted, what her body pleaded of her, when she pulled back and fitted him inside her, hard and hot. She almost sobbed with the pleasure of it. Then his hand came forward to touch her in the place that stole her breath and she bucked against him, uncontrollable waves of sensation that blotted out everything but the feel of him as the pleasure burst inside her. It went on and on, and she groaned as he had done – as he did again now, his hands gripping hard at her hips as he thrust up into her.

The lamp had died out when she came to herself again. His breath was a harsh panting against her neck, her knees around his hips, the rain still falling.

She felt even more untethered from her life, floating free, holding onto him in the blackness. The strong beat of his heart seemed the center of the world. He was a soft place, one where she might at last rest her head and feel safe.

✠ ✠ ✠

The early morning light was flooding the ruined shed when he woke, naked and alone. His cloak was tucked around him securely, though his last memory was of her body covering his, her cloak spread over them both as he savored the feel of her and thought he could not possibly sleep. Obviously he could.

When he sat up, he saw he was not alone. Fuss was keeping watch by the door, and gave a single bark before running forward to bid Gryff good morn. Relief surged through him at the sight. There was no sign of her at all – the lamp, her clothes, her bag were all gone – but if her dog was here, then she could not be far.

Beside him was his flask of water and two oatcakes set atop his folded tunic. He dressed quickly, though he could not find his linen, and slipped the food into his bag before setting off to find her. Fuss bounded ahead to where she knelt on the ground not far away. Her hair caught all the morning light, a flare of gold against the green.

He approached slowly, wary of startling her from behind until he realized this was the dog's purpose: to watch over him, to alert her to his movements, perhaps even to safeguard him when she was not there. Her arms and shoulders were working at something, some task on the ground, and she did not pause as he stepped near.

It was his linen. She had it stretched across a broad stone, rubbing soap into it. As he watched, she lifted her flask of water and rinsed it, washing all the foulness away. She folded it into a square and carefully pressed the water out, all her movements practiced and sure.

When she stood and held it out to him, she did not look directly at him. He thought of the food and clothes left beside him, how she had spent her morning attending to his needs as he slept.

"You are not my servant," he said roughly, as he took it from her. "Nor would I have you act as one."

"I am accustomed," she answered with an air of apology. "Some are born to serve."

So well was he learning her silences that he knew the stiffness in her was not a rejection of him. It was uncertainty, the strangeness of returning to a life of daylight together when they had shared the night. She turned to practical things and tried to make the day ordinary, as though the entire world had not changed.

"Nan –"

"There's little food left and no town near," she said quickly, a frown of determination between her brows. "We must hunt today."

But she did not move from where she stood. He lifted a hand to push the loose strands of hair from her cheek and rested his palm there, cradling her face. "Nan," he said again, soft.

Her hand came up to curve around his wrist. She turned her face and pressed her lips to his palm, holding him there. "Welshman," she whispered against his skin. Sunlight fell on her face, illuminating the curve of her mouth as she smiled.

Chapter Seventeen

They drifted westward, and she found relief in having no driving purpose beyond finding nourishment and shelter every day, wandering in the direction of Wales, and simply being with him. No more did she resist looking at him, or standing near to him, or touching him. No more did she resist speaking when she might normally have bitten back words.

She had felt him surrendering to her silence before, and that was wonder enough. But now he adjusted himself to it, allowed room for it without impatiently waiting for her to speak again. It was part of her, and so he did not shove it to the side or disregard its importance.

It was the same as when she touched him, or he touched her – or even when they did not touch at all. She felt in him, always, this allowance for her desires, for what she wanted and did not want. He accommodated her and she, who had grown accustomed to living in service of other people and other purposes, found it more pleasing than she could ever have imagined.

"How do you come to speak Welsh?" he asked her one day.

She had just given a command to Fuss in words instead of using their signals, because her hands were busy stoking the fire and stirring the soup. Fuss had been trained with Welsh, as she had been. It had seemed natural to her when he was a pup.

"Those who taught me the blades did use the Welsh language in their training at Morency," she answered, and hoped he would not ask more. Lady Gwenllian had been her true teacher, though others had trained with her, including Lord Ranulf, hard as it was for him to do. But a highborn lady should not have such skills. To say the secret to anyone – even one she trusted well – felt too much like betrayal. So too would it feel like betrayal to deny Gwenllian and say someone else had taught her. And to lie to him would make her feel wretched, so she hoped he would not ask.

He did not. He seemed almost to shy away from it, and she knew it was the mention of Morency that restrained him. Like her, he did not want reminders of the world. They were outside of everything here. There were no masters, no family, no duty – there was only each other.

There would be time enough for the world and all its cares when they reached the end of their journey. Until then she would live only for the day, for the moments when she caught the soft look he gave her, or could watch as he patiently worked thistles out of Fuss' fur while murmuring soft and soothing things, so careful and attentive that she almost could not breathe for the tenderness that swelled in her at the sight.

She lived too for the nights, for the shadows that moved across his skin until the lamp flickered out, and the delights they discovered together in the dark. The way he touched her was a revelation – like it was a privilege, like there was no response her body could give that would ever be wrong. Some part of her could not quite wholly believe in it and stayed always wary, a corner of her mind alert to danger, a hand that would not let go the blade. But all that mattered was the pleasure of the moment, with no yesterday and no tomorrow. Everything felt far away. Only he felt real.

One evening as the sun went down, it lit up the sky in shades of glowing russet and copper. They sat and watched it together. She turned to look at the color reflected on his face, the shining patch of scarred skin turned amber by the light of sunset. She thought of the first time she had touched him there, when he had cried out in his sleep. *In my dreams I burn and burn*, he had said.

"Do you still dream of burning?" she asked, because she might never know if she did not ask him. Some things were worth putting into words.

He did not seem surprised by the question.

"Is rare now, and when I do dream it, I know it is a dream." His eyes were on the blaze at the horizon, his voice soft. "And then I wake, and you are there."

She bit her lips together, the now familiar tenderness swelling inside her. She reached a hand up to the scar, a soft caress that traced it back behind his ear. When she leaned forward and pressed her lips to the place, he slipped an arm around her and she felt it again – the same thing she had felt from him many times since she had made herself his lover. He wanted something more, but held the urge in check while he considered if she wanted the same, assessing her body's reaction to find an answer.

This time he wanted to pull her into his lap, and she did not want that. She could tell this was his urge for the same reason she did not want it: because she had been pulled into the laps of countless men when she had not been fast enough to dodge their grasp. She could not like it, no matter the man who did it. But she did want to be nearer to him, so she squeezed his hand at her waist and kissed his lips. Then she slipped behind him, her knees on either side of him so he could lean back on her. They watched the sun melt from the sky as he held her hands to his chest and she felt the soft tickle of his hair against her cheek.

In moments like this, she did not ever want to reach Wales. She never said it aloud, for fear he would think she did not care if he never went home. In truth she wanted nothing more than that, for him to reach the place he yearned for. If there could be some way to give him his home while keeping the world at bay, she thought she might sell her soul to know it. But that was impossible, so she must be content with their leisurely pace on the journey.

One morning she woke to the feel of cool air on her bare skin. Her eyes snapped open, wary of danger until she remembered that last night in the dark, he had taken off her shift. She had wanted it, wanted the feel of his skin on hers, his body hot all along her back while she guided his hands over her and he thrust inside her. But she had, for warmth and modesty's sake, always put her shift back on before succumbing to sleep. Until now.

The cloak only half covered her and his eyes were fixed on the place between her breasts. The dagger that normally hung there had shifted and exposed the scar. Scars.

It was the first he was seeing it, and in the harsh morning light. The thin lines showed clearly where her flesh had been cut. Now his eyes came to hers and she only looked at him, her jaw tight, a look that told him he could satisfy his curiosity and push the cloak away from her hip. He did.

It was an uglier scar there, where she had been burned. She knew he had felt it already, whenever his hands had grasped her hips, or caressed her in the dark. Now he saw it, and she watched his face twist with feeling. He looked up at her, his brows knitted together with confusion and a little anger. It was a look that asked what had happened, why this had been done to her – for it was obvious that it had been done deliberately.

"Did you think he went away docile, after I ruined his sport and withered his cock?" she asked, her voice flat. It angered her suddenly, irrationally, that he dared to be surprised or appalled at this. What a luxury, to be able to believe in the honor of men. "His anger must go somewhere. Water rolls down a hill, men's anger falls on women. It's the way of the world."

Fool, she wanted to say at the end of it, but clamped her jaw against it. She sat up. In the soft sound of his breath she could hear that infinite patience of his, steady and calm, the way he waited for the falcon in its flight. It was not a helpless or hapless state, this patient waiting of his. He was there within it, unmovable. He would not advance unless invited, but nor would he yield his place, or himself, only because of her mood.

"You said naught of this, when you told me what happened." It was not so much accusation as it was bewilderment. "Yet you did teach me it must be put into words. Can you not speak of it?"

She almost scoffed. Not speak of it? She had spoken of it countless times, and she did not care to speak of it again to satisfy his curiosity about the details. They cut her, they burned her, she lived. It was simple enough to understand. She stood and reached for her shift, pretending it did not affect her to stand naked before him, scrawny and small and marked with ugly scars.

"I tell what I want to tell and not a word more." She gestured to the places she was marked. "Talking won't tell you no more than you can see with your own eyes, will it."

She turned away and pulled her linen over her head and then her dress. Fuss sprang up from his place beside the trees that hid this tiny clearing, eager to see where the day would take them. She fastened her belt with the blades in it around her waist, and pulled on her boots without her hose.

There was the long, elegant dagger for her boot, but she did not slip it in at the ankle. She held it close like a talisman, bundled her hose and the braces of knives into her cloak, and said, "I'll go gather more water."

She did it every morning, but never announced it. She could feel the meaning of it fall on him, that he was not welcome to follow her. It was all she could do to remember to take the flask.

At the stream she knelt and put a hand into the water, wishing it was colder. Cold enough to shock and numb, to freeze the hot tears that seemed ready to spill. It was not fair. The world and all its ugliness had intruded on this soft place they had built between them. And it was she who had carried it in, written on her flesh.

The memory of it had long ago lost its sting. What had happened was a fact no more or less shameful to her than that she had scrubbed floors and served ale. But it was a reminder of who she was and had always been. A reminder that she was from a different world, a worse world, than him. Whatever misfortune had taken him from his home and put him at the mercy of villains was only temporary. That was not his true fate.

The long dagger was still clutched to her breast, pressed against the other blade that hung from her neck beneath the linen. She said her usual prayer of thanksgiving with a little more fervor, put on her hose, then pressed her lips to the dagger before slipping it into her boot. It soothed her, to have it where it belonged.

She watched sunlight play on the water while Fuss dug at the ground, covering himself in dirt as he tried to reach the center of some creature's burrow. They would come to the end of this forest soon. Chesterfield could not be more than half a day's journey from here. They must go to the market there, to buy provisions and avoid poaching any more. But after that, Wales was days away. More than a week, even did they not dawdle.

She began a new prayer, that they might somehow hold the world back, or that they would find a way to fit this fragile bliss into the reality that awaited them. She closed her eyes and silently pleaded that she would not have to let him go. Not him too. Not yet.

When she opened her eyes, he had appeared. Down the stream a little, he stood with his back to her. She rose and went to him, Fuss running ahead as always. He had her purse of nails, and the little silver knife that she had left behind in their bed. The sight of it troubled her. She did not like to think of how much she needed it, how her fingers would not let it go in the night even as he held her.

There was an old stump of wood he aimed at, throwing one nail after another at it. Few of them stuck, though he threw with great force. He only paused for the briefest moment when Fuss settled at his feet, then threw again.

"You could kill him," he said when the nails were spent. He held the little silver knife in his palm. "Why do you not seek revenge?"

An impossible question. As well ask why she did not drain the seas after the destruction of a tempest. She looked at his thumb rubbing across the grip, interrupting the light that gleamed on metal.

"Would it erase the scars from me, or the memories I bear?" She barely noticed it came out in Welsh. "Would it raise Oliver from the dead?"

He shook his head. "Nay. But I cannot understand how you have no hate in your heart."

She almost laughed at that. No hate.

"There is enough hate in my heart to burn down the world entire." Her voice shook, her throat ached from the effort required not to scream it. She looked at his profile and gathered the rough fabric of her dress tight into her fists until her fingers grew numb. "But you are in the world," she said. "You are in my heart."

He turned to her and she felt naked again. She meant to say they must go to the market today, that he would never reach his home if they wasted days in wandering.

Instead, she stepped forward into her fear and kissed him, because he made her greedy and fearless. He made everything new and beautiful. She had no care for the market, or the road that awaited them, or their journey's end. She only cared for him, and so they stayed there all through the day and night.

✠ ✠ ✠

He had begun to imagine Nan in his mother's solar, looking out over the valley below, framed by the carved stone of the window and the hills beyond. But then he reminded himself that the stone was probably rubble now and even if it weren't, he could never go there again.

As they moved westward, she became more real than his memories – of the thieves, the abbey, the years spent as hostage. Only Aderinyth seemed as vivid as she was, as important. His mind kept serving up images of her there, with him. He saw her on the mountain path that led to the most hidden nest of white gyrfalcons. He imagined her listening intently to Philip Walch, who would love her like a daughter. He knew with a certainty she would never sneer at the place or the people, and that she would look at the mountains in the same way she had looked at the ceiling of the cathedral.

He knew he wanted her there, but was afraid to ask for it.

"I've no coin," she announced as they entered Chesterfield. The way she said it and the set of her mouth told him that the money she had sent to her sister was the last she had. "I must earn some while we are here."

His assertion that she need not do so, as he still had a little left from the long-ago sale of the hawk, was politely disregarded. He watched her eyes light up at the sight of an old man selling meat pies, then was amused to hear her quiz the man on his method of cooking them. It seemed to meet her approval in the end, and she said she would return to buy some once she had found a place to sell one of her knives.

Gryff saw her touch one of the blades on her forearm. He had seen her touch them in moments of idleness, her fingertips rubbing over the letter stamped at the base when she was lost in thought. She cherished them, and she had already lost one on this journey.

"Would you trade a pie for entertainment?" he asked the old man suddenly.

That was how they found themselves, an hour later, with a crowd of onlookers placing bets on what the fair maiden could hit with her knife. She did not like it as much as she had when she'd shown her skill in the privacy of Hal's yard, but she did not object. Gryff was careful to stay close to her, gathering all her winnings into a basket he bought for the purpose. He kept it in easy view so that she might say when she had enough.

In the end, there was a small pile of coins, food enough to last them a week, and a few too many admirers for her comfort, or his. Only one man was fool enough to reach out for her as she walked away, his voice urging her to stay while his eyes held a greedy, lecherous look. Gryff moved swiftly between them and stamped his boot on the man's foot. His own hands were full, but he would drop everything if he must and take up the knife at his belt. He did not need to do more than look at him for a long, hard moment before the man slunk away.

"Will you teach me that?" asked Nan as they walked away from the market. She had pulled a meat pie from the basket and was licking the juice of it from her lips.

"Teach what?" he asked, attempting to tear his attention from her lips. He seemed to spend most of his days pleasantly distracted by the sight of her mouth, and his nights more than distracted by the feel of it.

"The way you looked at him." She said it with her mouth full, and swallowed before continuing. "You looked like the king himself, and would throw him in a tower or have his head on a pike. But it's calm-like, not full of temper."

His father had had that look, and his grandfather too – *the eye of Arawn*, they called it in his family, likening their belligerent pride to the pagan god of the Welsh underworld, gathering souls with a glance. He almost said as much to her, almost told her how the bard had stood beside the great open hearth and sung the legend of Arawn, how his brother Owain had loved it best of all the poems, how Gryff was the only one of his brothers who did not quail when their father gave that fabled look.

He did not say any of it. They were dead. He could never be that person again.

He knew she thought him a falconer, like Hal, employed by some wealthy household before misfortune landed him here. There was no reason to tell her otherwise. It was the only thing he would be, from now on. Just a simple falconer, and not even one of great status such as Hal was.

"Can it not be taught, Welshman?" she asked with a grin, before taking another bite of her meal.

She never called him by his name. To her he was only Welshman, and each time she said it, his heart felt lighter. A simple Welshman, safe from anyone who would throw him in a tower.

"I think me your defenses are more use than any look," he assured her. "The sight of your blade is enough to drive away all but the most witless."

They gave a coin to a man who let them shelter for the night in a loft above his granary and Gryff counted himself witless when she bared her body to him, wrapped her legs around him, but would not set down her blade. Her fist stayed closed on the silver knife, though it stayed in its sheath and she never held it to him after that first night. He had begun to dream of the day she would let it go, and take off the dagger that hung from her neck as well. It became entwined with the vision of her in Aderinyth, as though he need only to bring her there and her doubt and distrust would melt away.

In the morning, they made their way to the crossroads outside of town. They could continue west through the rolling hills and dales and reach Wales in as little as a week. Or they could follow the southern road, travel much farther, moving southwest until they crossed into Wales closer to his home.

He still did not know where she intended to go – only that it was north of Aderinyth, and so the western path was hers, the shorter path. He could ask her destination, but somehow the words would not pass his lips. They stood at the crossroads without speaking, the heavy basket of provisions slung over his shoulder.

He would follow her, to wherever she journeyed. He could make his way to Aderinyth from there. Without her, if he must.

"Will we go south now, or later?" she asked.

In all their journeying, she had never asked him this. She only chose the road silently, leading him by hidden ways to where he wished to go. Now she stood very still, her eyes trained on the ground, a delicate color high on her cheeks.

"South?" he echoed.

"To Aderinyth. There is coin enough to last the journey now. If you want… If you would have me come there."

He dropped the basket and kissed her, relishing the sound of satisfaction and relief that came from her. He remembered himself in time to keep from devouring her right there. She was so fierce that he forgot sometimes how small she was, how easy it was to overwhelm her slight form. But now she kissed him back, her hands holding his face.

"Home," he said, smiling against her lips. "Aye, I would have you there."

Chapter Eighteen

He knew such joy could not last forever, but he never expected it to falter before nightfall, nor shatter within a day.

They did not journey far from Chesterfield, but found a place off the southern road long before night fell. At his request, she showed him how to throw his eating knife. He had asked mostly because he wanted to hear her voice more, and thought she must speak to instruct him. He was right.

"My wrist," she said, as his hand moved slowly down her forearm. He stood behind her as she took aim at a tree only a few paces away. "It's my wrist you're to feel as I throw, not the rest of me."

She was half-amused, half-exasperated. She took the study seriously and expected the same of him. He put his fingers lightly around her wrist and felt it as she threw – a sharp snap, very contained, that he thought would take a thousand hours of study to learn.

Three times she threw, instructing him to watch not the knife but her arm and how it moved. It was not a graceful movement, nor was it graceless. It was powerful and swift and smooth. It was as beautiful as she was.

When she brought the knife back from where it had landed in the tree, she gave it to him and stood behind him. She put her hand on his so she could guide it in its aim and stood on her toes, her breath against his ear.

"The feel of it as it leaves your hand – take note of it," she said. "You'll know if you've done right by how it feels."

He threw. It didn't feel like anything as it left his hand, but obviously he'd done it wrong. It hit the tree far off center and fell to the ground. She kissed the back of his neck lightly, causing a flare in his groin as she went to retrieve the knife. He was suddenly far less interested in his aim.

She had just handed the knife to him, looking at him with invitation in her eyes when Fuss came bursting through the tall grass between the rocks that hid them from the main road. The dog was barking frantically, but Nan did not seem alarmed. She stood still, her own dagger drawn in reflex, looking slightly disbelieving while Fuss ran a circle around her and then bounded back through the grass, barking all the while.

"Nan?" he asked, gripping the knife.

When a tall youth strode into the clearing, Nan rushed at him. The dagger fell to the ground as she jumped up to embrace him. Her arms were around him, and he hugged her tight, swung her around as a smile brighter than any Gryff had ever seen lit up her face. He blinked at it, adjusting to the plain fact that there was no danger here.

"What fortune is this?" cried the youth. Not truly a boy, but only barely a man. He was tall and fair and full of joy. He planted an exuberant kiss on her cheek, and then another and another. Gryff waited for her to pull a blade and gut him, but she only kept hold of him and, incredibly, buried her face in his neck.

"Who journeys with you, Nan, or will I have to discover his name myself?"

His voice matched his clothes: wealthy and noble. He could have come straight from the king's court, this handsome boy who was allowed to squeeze her tight in his arms and pick her up without warning. She did not shy from his touch, or stiffen, or require any careful approach.

Gryff felt his heart shrivel with envy. Then he heard her reply, a soft murmur against the stranger's cheek.

"He's my Welshman."

She pulled back, and the boy put her down but did not let go. She turned to Gryff, smiling shyly now.

"This is Robin," she said. "Robin Manton."

✠ ✠ ✠

Gryff thought most men would find it difficult to dislike Robin Manton. He was warm and courteous, never brash or boastful, and eager to please. Fuss adored him as much as Nan clearly did, which spoke well to his character and made Gryff exceptionally churlish.

Robin's horse, a fat and docile rouncey, was brought behind the tall stones that hid them from the road. Robin was coming from a tournament and had stopped in Chesterfield this afternoon, planning to carry on his journey after a good meal. "But a man at the market did say the fairest maid he had ever seen paid for her supper with her knives, only yesterday." He smiled broadly. "In faith, I knew it must be you even before he told me you split a reed at forty paces."

He had ridden south, reasoning she was headed for Morency and wondering why she was so far from Lincoln. Fuss, who had been keeping guard over their hiding spot, saw Robin on the road below, ran to greet him, and now they must share their evening with this boy who sat so close to Nan that their knees touched. Gryff attempted to glare his disapproval at the dog for this betrayal, but Fuss was too busy staring worshipfully at the newcomer.

"But wherefore do you wander so far from Lincoln?" Robin asked her, with a sidelong glance toward Gryff. "What of your travels to Wragby and your business there? And where is Sir Gerald?"

"Injured by knaves who attacked halfway to Lincoln, and I must leave him to heal at a priory."

She said nothing about having met Gryff, nothing about her aunt or her sister, nothing about why she was here instead of on the road between Lincoln and Morency. Instead of pressing for answers, a perplexed Robin only looked at her intently, observing her stillness and her downcast eyes for a long moment. Gryff held his breath and prayed the boy would not ask what had happened at Lincoln.

Anyone could see she did not want to speak of it. All the sweet contentment that had been in her for days was draining away as she sat silent in the face of his curiosity.

Gryff opened his mouth, prepared to say anything to deflect the questions, but Robin moved. He simply touched the back of Nan's hand, barely a brush of his fingertip, to draw her attention. When she met his eyes, he gave the ghost of a nod. His voice was light as he asked, "You have sent word to Morency that you will be delayed in your return?"

This casual change of subject endeared him to Gryff. He would think of what it meant later, that this boy could understand her silence and communicate without words. Right now he was only relieved to see the tension leave Nan.

"Aye, I asked the prioress at Broadholme to send word." She looked at Gryff, a faint smile briefly chasing across her face. "But now I'll be going another place, and should send a new message."

Gryff smiled back at her, vaguely wondering how it was that a servant had such freedom in where she may go and how long she may be away from her duties. He might have asked, but Robin burst into a fresh grin of delight and said, "You must come to the manor at Whitting with me, then! Is but a few hours from here on foot, a message can be sent from there."

"Whitting?" Gryff asked sharply. "Whose manor is that?"

"It is one of Uncle Rob's holdings," the boy said to Nan, who looked delighted at this news. He explained to Gryff, "My uncle is Robert de Lascaux, the lord of Darian."

He kept explaining, saying it wasn't truly his uncle but a friend of his father's who was dear enough to be family, while Gryff ran the names through his memory. He could not recall a lordship of Darian at all, which meant it must be a small place and a very minor lord. The name de Lascaux meant little to him, unless this uncle was related to the man who commanded a force in the Aquitaine – and if he was, Gryff could not remember ever meeting that man or anyone of that family. He was sure he had never heard of Whitting.

"You must come! There will be soft beds for you both, and a hot bath," Robin said, his eyes dancing with excitement. "And if the time is right I think me there may be something even *better* than all that. Better even than pork pies," he assured Nan. "Though I know you will say there is naught can be better than a good pork pie."

To Gryff's intense gratification, Nan looked at him briefly before blushing prettily and saying perhaps they would go to Whitting tomorrow, but for now they should eat something. She busied herself in searching through the basket for the best offerings, while Gryff felt the boy's curious eyes on him.

As the evening wore on, it became plain that these two knew each other from Morency, that Robin was squire to its lord. Gryff would have asked him more, including why a squire went to tourney without his lord, but he was afraid of saying too much and revealing his familiarity with that world. Instead they spoke of hawking, a subject about which Robin was almost as passionate as the sword. It was a safe topic, except for the moment when the boy said his father had once owned a peregrine of Aderinyth, the best-trained bird he'd ever seen.

Gryff could feel Nan look at him when the word was spoken. When Gryff only replied that it was well known that the best falcons and falconers came from Aderinyth, she no doubt took it as modesty. Perhaps he need not hide it. There was nothing wrong with being a common man from Aderinyth, after all, and this boy would only know him as that.

The light was failing, and Robin was saying he must stay awake and keep guard because of the horse. Nan insisted they must take it in turns, that he would take the first watch and must wake her halfway through the night so she may take the second.

"How easily you command me! You peck at me as a wife pecks at her husband," Robin teased her with a laugh. He turned to Gryff like it was a fine jest. "She could be my wife, you know. I asked her years ago and she refused me. My heart yet bears the wound." He turned back to Nan with a wide grin. "You may still say yes, Nan, never will I disclaim the offer."

"You were a boy. And I know my place, even do you not know your own." She was cleaning the mud from her boots, and did not look up from her task. She did not laugh. "You'll find a good lady soon enough, worthy of your name and estate."

After that, he bid Gryff good night and went to keep watch by his horse. Nan went with him, and Gryff could hear their whispering at the edge of the clearing for what felt like hours. He could make out no words, but it was her voice as much as his. It seemed to go on and on, more than she had ever spoken to Gryff. He tried not to think of the dagger she wore over her heart, and how the symbol on it looked very much like the letter R.

He lay awake and reminded himself that they had made no promises to each other, spoken no vows. They had barely spoken at all, and it had not seemed to matter until now. But it did matter – of course it did – that before he had ever met her, she had had a life and a purpose, people she cared for. So many things she must leave behind if she were to come with him to Wales. For himself, he left little behind but danger. And there was little that would greet him – no family, no lands, no name he could claim.

She came to him finally, a quiet and careful step, and knelt beside him.

"I must go with Robin to the manor tomorrow," she said low. "Will you come? We need not stay the night there." She spoke Welsh, but he did not answer. Her hand brushed against his shoulder and rested there. "I know you wake, Welshman."

He tried to imagine watching her walk away with the handsome, smiling Robin, disappearing into a manor while he waited sullenly to see if she returned to him.

"I will go whither you go," he said at last. "If you do truly want me with you."

Her hand moved to cup his throat, her thumb stroking his jaw for a long moment of silence.

"Robin is my bosom friend, since he was a child. He is like a brother to me. You need not fear I have any secret desire for him."

He wanted to pull her down onto him, to feel her hair spill free between their naked bodies and kiss her, make her gasp with pleasure until she forgot everything but him. He hated that he could not.

"And if he has a secret desire for you?"

"He does not." There was laughter behind her words, as though she found the idea absurd. But she sensed his doubt. She spread her fingers over his cheek as she leaned over him and said, "Think you I would not if know he lusted me? Think you I could be easy with him if he did? Have sense, Welshman."

Like a fog lifting, the doubt left him. Never would she be so free with Robin – embracing him, allowing his nearness, smiling as he greeted her with kisses – if there was even the chance he felt more than brotherly toward her. She whispered a good night and brushed her lips softly against Gryff's before retreating to sleep a short distance from him.

Somehow he slept, and in the morning they walked to Whitting. It was only two hours, and Gryff might have forgotten to worry about what awaited them there if not for Robin, whose every manner suggested anticipation of a great surprise. *Something even better than pork pie*, he had said last night, and Gryff could not fathom what it might be.

Nan had obviously told Robin last night, as part of their whispering, that Gryff came from Aderinyth. When Robin asked why he had not said so, Gryff only shrugged and said he had been a boy when last he had seen the place. They spoke of falconry in yet more detail for the short journey, and Gryff felt his dislike for Robin Manton dissolve almost completely.

They reached the manor long before midday. It was not a large place, but very well kept with a good number of buildings in excellent repair. The prosperous manor of an inconsequential lord, he thought, until he saw the dovecote, and the very fine palfreys in the stables. Gryff pulled his hood up, wary.

"Good fortune is with us again, Nan."

Robin was smiling at her as he handed his rouncey over to a boy who had run from the stables. Nan raised her eyebrows at him in question as they walked toward the hall. Just as they reached it, a man stepped out, his face full of surprise and pleasure. Fuss immediately ran to him, yelping happily.

Robin cried, "Uncle Rob!" and threw his arms around him in greeting.

This, apparently, was the surprise. Gryff felt only relief that he did not recognize the man. He was older, with gray hair at his temples and deep lines of laughter around his eyes. He and Robin were alike in their warm and cheerful demeanor, obvious at a glance.

"There's our Nan," said Lord Robert with gentle satisfaction, when he broke free of Robin's embrace.

He looked down at her where she had sunk into a deep courtesy before him, her head bowed. There was a fond smile on his face as he stepped close and gave her a chuck under the chin. It was a fatherly gesture, far too familiar to be an ordinary exchange between lord and servant girl. Gryff's confusion at it changed to amazement when Nan raised her face. She flushed with pleasure and looked at Lord Robert with a shy kind of delight, as though she not only did not mind that he touched her uninvited, but hoped he might do it again.

"You've been to Lincoln?" he asked her, and she nodded. "The message?"

"I have delivered it, my lord." She glanced quickly in Robin's direction, and then at Gryff, clearly indicating she had more to say when they might be more private.

"There will be time enough for tales after I greet your guest," he said.

He turned to Gryff, who realized belatedly that he should bow. It was far more restrained than Nan's show of deference, and in any case Lord Robert disregarded it in favor of an outthrust arm, a firm shake of his hand when Robin gave his name and said he was Welsh.

"It will be Gruffydd, then." Lord Robert smiled at him like an old friend. "Though I will call you Gryff, do you prefer it. Well met, and my lady wife will be most glad to greet you."

Nan gave a sharp intake of breath and looked at Lord Robert with an eager hope. "Aye," he grinned, and Robin laughed. "You will find her in the solar above."

He nodded to a stair, and Nan fairly ran to it, so fast was her step. They followed more slowly in her wake, with Robin telling of how he had met Nan on the road and hoped Lord Robert would be at Whitting but could not be sure, and so left it to be a surprise. Gryff knew they would ask how he and Nan had met, why he was with her, and he tried to think of some simple explanation for it. These people seemed as family to her, strangely as protective of a servant as they would be of a daughter and sister. They would not simply accept that he traveled alone with her.

They reached the solar, stepping inside just as Lord Robert was saying that his lady wife was Welsh too, and that his new lordship of Darian was in Wales – information that came too suddenly and too fast, and all at the same moment that Gryff saw the face of this lady wife. His heart stopped. Everything stopped.

Lady Eluned. Will's mother. God help him, she would know him at a glance.

Quickly, he pulled his hood closer, letting it hang as far down as he could manage, angling his face away from her. He forced himself to breathe slowly and said a silent prayer that she would not see him, not recognize him.

He had been barely fourteen when she had come to visit her son and spent an afternoon in conversation with him and Gryff. There were as many years on his face as hers, he reasoned, and a scar, and he had the advantage of having been a forgettable boy while she was as great and formidable a lady then as she was now.

If Will's father was dead, then she must have remarried this Lord Robert. A new lordship of Darian in Wales – he had heard this was what Edward had done with the conquered land, parceling it out to favorites. It was true to Lady Eluned's nature, to keep herself in power and wealth by marrying a man who had been granted Welsh lands. And somehow she had come to know Nan, whose hand she clasped tight in fond greeting, a palm cupping her cheek, affectionate as a mother. She did not look in Gryff's direction, so focused was she on Nan.

And Nan… Nan was giving her such a look that it stunned him. It reminded him of when she had seen her sister, all the joy and relief and love, but with something more. Respect and reverence. He thought of her face in the glow of firelight, a half-peeled turnip in her hands as she said, *A great lady saved me.*

This was the lady. Lady Eluned had saved her. Of all people, Lady Eluned.

He drifted slowly backward, praying he might inch his way out of the room before being noticed, as they conversed with perfect ease of ordinary things. Yes, Nan had been to Lincoln, and her tone forbade speaking of it any further as Gryff stole a glance at the other ladies in the room. He thought he recognized one, and pulled his hood even closer. Lady Eluned was explaining that they had journeyed out of Wales to do business at court and had only lately come to Whitting, while Gryff took a small step backward, almost stepping on Fuss.

Their voices went on, a gentle rise and fall as he prayed for a quiet and unseen escape from this pleasant lion's den. Word had come from Morency that Sir Gerald was healing well; the prioress at Broadholme sent greetings to Lady Eluned who was a patroness of the order; they had worried for Nan when they received word of the attack that had injured Sir Gerald. All the while, Gryff kept his head down and made his way to the door, inch by slow inch.

He was at the threshold when he heard Lady Eluned raise her voice a little to say, "But now you must tell us, Nan, how it is you have found a prince in your travels."

His stomach dropped. He froze, not even breathing, and turned his eyes up to look at Lady Eluned.

She watched him steadily, perfectly composed. She glanced at Nan's puzzled face, and raised her eyebrows in polite surprise. "Did you not know?"

Nan blinked at her, uncomprehending, then turned to Gryff for explanation. He could say nothing. He could only wait for Eluned to say it.

"I see I must introduce you."

They were all looking at him now, everyone in the room. He pushed his hood back, because there was no use in hiding. A feeling of unreality came over him as Eluned's eyes fixed on him and proclaimed his name.

"This is Gruffydd ab Iorwerth ap Cynan Goch, the last Prince of Aderinyth." Her eyes never left his, not for one syllable of it. "This is Nan," she said to him, infinite power in the way her hand settled lightly on Nan's shoulder. "And she is under my protection."

Chapter Nineteen

Nan was staring at him, dazed.

"Prince?" she echoed, as though she had never heard the word before.

"Tywysog Aderinyth," Lady Eluned supplied, giving the word in Welsh as though that would clarify the matter. Her hand never left Nan's shoulder and her eyes never left Gryff until she said, "Forgive me, my lord," and sank into a very deep courtesy.

"Nan," he began, and stopped. He did not know how to continue. She looked bewildered at Lady Eluned's show of deference, then looked back at him with disbelief.

"All have believed you dead these five years, Prince Gruffydd," Lady Eluned informed him when she rose. "All but my son." She clasped her hands lightly before her and turned her eyes to her lord husband for a brief moment. The ladies who had been embroidering near the window until they had heard the word prince now stood gawking at him, and she addressed them. "We wish to be private. Go now.

You will say naught of what you have heard here, or I will know of it."

Nan flinched a little at the words, and looked as though she took them as a command for herself. She had even lifted her foot in preparation to walk away, but Lady Eluned's hand came gently to her shoulder again. Protection. Nan was under Lady Eluned's protection.

"The abbey was your hiding place," said Robin in a voice of discovery when the other ladies had gone. "The abbey in the wilds that burned."

"I feared for my life." He said it to Nan, who was staring somewhere in the vicinity of his chest. "I feared Edward would imprison me." He saw confusion crease her brow at the name, and said, "King Edward."

Lord Robert spoke somewhere behind him. "It was not an unreasonable fear. But how came you to know Nan?"

Beauty and blood, a hundred miles and more from this place. He could still see her cutting the rope that bound him, handing him bread. "She saved my life," he said, still looking only at her. "You saved me."

"The thieves that attacked on the road out of Morency, when Sir Gerald was injured," Robin dutifully explained to the others. Nan had apparently told him everything last night. "They captured him when the abbey burned."

"What fortune that you were spared, and could hide your identity for a journey the breadth of England," observed Lady Eluned. There seemed to be a barely restrained anger in her, pulling her voice tight.

"If not the king, my bastard brother would see me dead." He must explain it. If only Nan would turn her eyes up to him. "I must be a nameless Welshman, to live."

They all seemed frozen in place, waiting for something – waiting for Nan, to do or say anything. But she was as still and silent as stone.

Lady Eluned let out a breath, too emphatic to be a sigh, and said, "We must discuss what is to be done. Sit you down, my lords, and I will call for refreshment."

As though she had been waiting for the words, Nan dipped her knee quickly and whispered, "I will see to it, my lady." She fled from the room, as swiftly as she had run to it only minutes ago.

Gryff stared at the door where she had disappeared, wanting to go after her but knowing he must not. He knew every line of her body, every wordless sign that told him she did not want him to follow. Later, he would find her and explain. It was only a name. It meant nothing. So long as it did not kill him, it was only an inconvenient name.

"Robin." Lord Robert's voice was low. "Be sure we are not disturbed here. And go to her."

Gryff watched Robin leave, fighting against the jealousy that sprang up to know her friend would be welcome when he was not. But that could not matter now. He forced his attention back to this moment – this dangerous moment when he stood under the roof of two of the highest nobles of King Edward's court, and they knew who he was. It was an unwelcome feeling, to slip back into the role of hostage prince and face all the political maneuverings that must go with it. But he must, if he was to survive.

Instinct told him that Lady Eluned's opinion mattered more in this. His father had known her a little and had believed she was deeply sympathetic to the Welsh cause, that she despised King Edward. But Gryff's father was forever looking for allies. Will had said his mother was proud to be Welsh, but was loyal to the king.

Gryff finally turned to face her, and found her looking at him with outrage.

"You *fool*," she seethed. Her fury filled the room, so forceful that he almost took a step back. "You have bedded her."

He grit his teeth and glared at her, equally outraged at this presumption. The gall of her, as though she had any right to know his intimate affairs. But she did not quail beneath his look as any other mere mortal would.

"Do you deny it?" she snapped.

He stood to his full height and curled his lip in scorn as he looked down at her. "How do you dare to –"

"Oh I dare, my lord prince, for I do not say lightly that she is under my protection." Her color was high, her fists clenched. "Knowing the king would wish every royal Welsh line ended, knowing your own brother would murder you in hopes of your inheritance, *still* you took her to your bed." Her voice had risen almost to a shout, her scorn easily outpacing his. She looked as though she might strike him. "What think you such a king or such a brother would do if you have put a babe in her belly? If your life is forfeit, what then is the life of your child or of the woman who bears it? They would hold her life as nothing, you *fool*."

Now she was shouting, and it was the only reason he could hear her above the rush of blood in his ears. The words seemed to cut into him, sharpened by undeniable truth. God forgive him. He had not thought of it. Not once.

"Even believing the king would see you and all your line wiped from the earth, you could not control yourself," she spat. "I say it is a murderous lust in you, my lord, for you have risked her very life only for your pleasure. Did you not think even *once* of the consequence? Rhodri would put her to the sword as you watch, did he think she might carry your son, he would not suffer her to live –"

She stopped abruptly. Her husband had come to stand near to her and put his fingers lightly on her wrist. Only that soft, discreet touch, and the whisper of her name, and she halted her tirade. Her breath came fast, her jaw clamped tight as she tore her angry gaze from Gryff and looked to Lord Robert.

"Young love is heedless," he said, his voice as gentle as his touch as he looked steadily at her. "Nor has it any care for danger, nor any thought of death. Surely we must forgive the recklessness of young lovers."

Her face softened, the fury fading as he spoke. They looked at each other a long moment, his hand on her sleeve, before she nodded in assent. She stepped back and turned away to the window, but not before raking another scathing glance across Gryff.

Now Lord Robert stood alone before him and he felt like a boy again, back in his earliest years when his father's silent disapproval was so unbearable he would rather die than endure it. The shame seemed to suffocate him. But the shame was nothing to the horror of thinking that Nan might bear his child and be hunted for it. That he may have cursed her to his own fate – it was torment beyond anything the king might do to him.

"Sit you down." Lord Robert nodded to a bench near the hearth. When Gryff did not move, he said, "You look as if you will fall over do you not sit, boy, I will carry you there if I must."

His words acted as a bracing slap in the face. *Boy*, he said – not prince, not lord – and spoke to him as a child. The light contempt and lack of deference was so typically Norman that it had long since ceased to offend. It almost made him nostalgic. He sat.

"In faith, you may be thankful we know you did not force her. Any man who had tried would not yet have all his limbs." He said it as he walked to a table in the corner where there were cups and wine. He poured as he spoke. "Be more thankful still that Edward does not think you a traitor."

Gryff looked at the cup of wine held out to him. He held his breath as he took it. The court, the king, power, games – he was back in a world where trust was a luxury few could afford, so he waited until Lord Robert drank before he put his own cup to his lips. The wine itself left him speechless for a moment. He had forgotten how delicious it could be, how well the wealthy drank and ate.

He swallowed it, and asked, "What does he think me, then, if not a traitor? Has he sought me these many years?"

"Aye, at first." Lord Robert sat across from him. "But you did not reappear to fight against him, nor has there been any whisper of you in Wales. And so he is inclined to agree with Will, that you are a loyal subject who fled in fear of your life from a greedy brother. Or that you are dead."

None of it meant that Gryff was safe, that the king would not lock him away or worse. This was what it meant to have the blood of princes running in his veins.

"I would let him think me dead."

He heard only the hard beat of his own heart in the silence that followed. It was presumptuous of him to even imply that this man, a stranger, might abandon honor for his sake. But it was a necessary part of this world, the continual assessment of potential allies and enemies.

"Hear me well, Gruffydd ab Iorwerth. I am a loyal servant of the king." There was a hint of apology in Lord Robert's face. "He will have truth from me, and know you live. Even if it means your death, I must tell him – though I think it will not be so dire."

Gryff nodded, glad to know exactly what he could expect. "I mean you no insult. I have lived in the wilds these many years, and know little of king and court. In faith, I have had little news since Wales fell."

"As I will give the king naught but truth, so too do I give it to you, and whatever news you seek. What would you know?"

Gryff took another careful sip of the wine, beating back the tide of questions that swelled in him. Better to learn what he could now, from this man who had no reason to twist the truth.

"Aderinyth." He closed his eyes briefly, bracing himself. He had always known, in his heart, that he might never go back – that there might be nothing to go back to. "What has Edward done to my people?"

"It goes hard in Wales, but Aderinyth is spared the very worst of it. The greatest wealth cannot be reached, for the falconers keep their secrets well. Only a dozen nesting places have the English discovered, and none of them the white gyrfalcons. Your people hold the knowledge hostage to good effect, despite all efforts to prise it from them."

A wave of relief came over Gryff, to know there was not the same devastation in Aderinyth as had been rumored in the rest of Wales. His breath loosed, and he brought the cup to his lips again.

"They killed Philip Walch," said Eluned softly from her place by the window, and he felt it like a stab to his heart. "He would not tell them. He did say that he swore a vow, as his father had done, and his father's father before him, that none but the prince and his falconers would ever know the nesting places. They hanged him, and three others before they saw the vow would not be broken no matter how many falconers died."

His knuckles had turned white where they gripped the cup. *The female is the fiercer creature,* he heard Philip say to him. It was true. But it was men who had murdered him, and men who had sworn him to a secrecy that killed him. And for what? Nests and birds. Wealth, pride, and a king's vanity.

He began to understand a little, what it might mean to have enough hate in his heart to burn down the world entire.

But he could also hear what his father had said so often, what Philip had taught him, too: *To rule well, you must learn what it is to be a servant to one who serves you.* He had fled, and Philip died because Gryff had not been there to serve his people. Hate would not change that, nor would it absolve him of his own transgression.

"Who rules there?" Gryff asked. The love he had for the place, that he had denied and hidden and tried to contain for so long, came vividly back to life, a ferocious protectiveness. Some cruel new lord was likely seated in his father's hall even now, hanging stubborn falconers and looking over his spoils of war. "What new barony has been made of it?"

"None." Lord Robert poured more wine. "Rhodri makes a claim for it, of course. Will has argued against him these many years. He has said to Edward that yours is the rightful claim, and you a true and loyal servant to the crown. Will argues that it is Welsh law, not Norman, that would allow a bastard to inherit – and that Edward should not rule with Welsh law."

Gryff snorted. "Ever has Edward chosen the law that serves him best." It was the cause of most Welsh grievances against the king. "Will has developed a silver tongue indeed, if he has held him off so many years."

"Is not commonly known, but when Edward divided the conquered lands among his barons, he did agree to Will's suggestion: to keep Aderinyth free of rule for five years, in case you should return to claim it. And here you are."

They stared at each other while the words sank in. Lord Robert was thoughtful and assessing. Gryff was stunned. Five years from the division of Wales – that would be only months from now, in the spring of next year.

"He would…" Gryff struggled for words, astonishment making his tongue slow. "I have only to claim it?"

A sound of derision came from Lady Eluned, who still stood at the window.

"You cannot know Edward well, do you think it so simple," she said. "There is no knowing what game he will play or what dance he will lead you. And at the end of it, you may have your lands or you may not. He holds all the power. It will be as it pleases him, not you."

Gryff looked to Lord Robert for confirmation of this grim declaration, feeling the hope of his home slipping away again.

"Never would I gainsay my lady wife in such a matter as this one. But I think me she will agree that Will is best positioned to know Edward's true mind." He paused, and Lady Eluned inclined her head, conceding this as truth. "Even now, Will is at court."

"So too is Rhodri there." Lady Eluned looked at him from her place by the window. Whatever she sought in Gryff's face, she seemed not to find it. Her cool gaze moved to her husband. "Does he know the true prince lives, Rhodri would not waste an instant to find him and see him dead."

Lord Robert nodded and looked into his cup, considering. Gryff had lately learned to hear words that went unspoken, to judge a mood and a moment by more than what was said. Lord Robert was straightforward, trustworthy, as cheerful and warm as Gryff had first perceived. Lady Eluned was none of those things, and though her knowledge was greater it seemed she was now giving a decision to her husband: the decision of what exactly to do with him. Gryff did not know whether to be glad of this or to despair.

"Is there no one else who knows you live?" asked Lord Robert finally.

"Only one man, and I will not name him." If he could do nothing else, he could keep Hal safe and free of all this. "He is no lord, and he will keep the secret well."

He told them then, of how he had been smuggled out of Lancaster's keep by a man now dead, and how at the abbey only Brother Clement had known his identity, and he was dead too. Gryff had thought it an advantage, that it would allow him to begin a new and nameless life of his own choosing. And it was an advantage – it had kept him alive. But as he told it, he could only see a long trail of broken ties and lost lives stretched out behind him. Somehow at the end of it, he still lived.

Robin appeared with a tray of food. He said not a word. He only set it down and left, but not before giving a look to Lady Eluned that seemed sorrowful, another to Gryff that seemed accusatory. As he walked out, he snapped his fingers at Fuss, who had been sitting unnoticed at Gryff's feet. The dog looked up at him as if asking approval before answering Robin's call and bounding out of the room.

When he had gone, they spoke at length of what transpired in Wales, of who had been given lands to rule there and why. Lord Robert told him who held power at court, which favorites held sway with the king and the matters that were most pressing. He had a clear distaste for the intrigues of court, and despite her aptitude Lady Eluned seemed to have no interest in it. She stood quiet at the window, listening while the food grew stale and her husband related only the most necessary information without embellishment.

But at the end of it, Lord Robert sat back and said, "I ask my lady wife what course she thinks best. We must tell Edward you live, and deliver you to him. But I would send word to Will in secret, and let him choose what is safest to tell the king and when."

"Safest for Prince Gruffydd, you mean," observed Lady Eluned, a pinch to her lips. "But I consider what is safest for you, my lord husband. There is risk in secrecy. Edward will not like to learn of this too late."

Lord Robert gave a reassuring smile, the kind that only cocksure fools or justifiably confident men gave. "I put it in Will's hands, and he is a trusted favorite at court. If he delays in telling the king, I do not doubt he will have ready explanation for it."

She looked like she might protest, but did not. She only gave a short nod and said, "William will know the risk, and handle it well. We will give the message to Robin to carry, and I will choose the words with care."

Lord Robert agreed and then looked at Gryff. "I will trust you not to flee again, and promise you my protection as long as you are in my household. Rhodri would be hard pressed to reach you here and do we stay alert, there is naught to fear of him."

He stood, saying he would show him to the chamber that would be made ready for him, and Gryff only briefly considered the possibility of fleeing in the night. To do so would be worse than foolish – it would make him seem guilty in some way, and they would hunt him down soon enough. If not the king's men, then Rhodri himself would find him.

Even those practical realities were nothing to the new realization that pressed in upon him: that if he ran now, he could only keep running, and forsake Aderinyth. What a child he had been, an impulsive boy who had thought only of his own life when he fled, and in the years since had thought only of his own longing to return. And while he feared for himself and dreamt of home, his people suffered and died.

They called him a prince, and so he must act as one. There would be no more running. It was time and past that he face his fate, no matter how cursed it may be, just as all other princes of his land had done.

It was only on his way out of the room, as they passed the window where Lady Eluned stood looking out, that he finally asked her. He knew she would know.

"My mother did intend to go to the sisters at Cairusk." It had comforted him to think of her there, knowing how greatly she preferred her prayers even to her family. He used to think she only waited for her husband to die, so that she might retreat behind a cloister's walls.

"She is there. She is happy to live much removed, from what little I have heard of her." Lady Eluned seemed strangely subdued. "Full well will it soothe her to know she has a child who lived."

There was no condemnation in it at all, but he felt damned by the words. Another sin to tally, that he had let his mother wonder and worry about his fate.

"My brothers," he said. "My father." He saw her close her eyes briefly, almost as in a silent prayer. "I would know how they died, and where they are interred."

It was Lord Robert who answered.

"Your father fell in battle, an arrow to the neck and a quick death. Aiden too was wounded and died quickly, a blow to the head." Here he put a hand on Gryff's shoulder, firm and bracing. "Owain was captured and imprisoned, but fell ill within a fortnight and died before he could be taken to the king for judgement."

Gryff almost asked what the illness was, but decided it didn't matter. It might have been poison sent by Rhodri, or only the flux, or a common sweating sickness. If the illness had not killed him, the king likely would have. Traitors to the crown did not meet happy fates, even if they were only boys.

"He was buried in Malmesbury, and your father and Aiden in a small churchyard near where they fell." It was Lady Eluned. She did not turn to him, but looked out over the fields and sky as she spoke. "I discovered the place, and two years ago was granted leave by the Church to move their bones to

Aderinyth. They rest there now, in the valley where your ancestors are laid."

Gryff looked at her profile, at the lift of her chin and the press of her mouth, at all the things she did not say. It was her doing, all of it, learning how they had died and going to such lengths to return them home. He had never thought of her as anything more than Will's mother – wife to a Marcher lord, clever and powerful, not to be trifled with. But now he saw she was more than that. She was Welsh. She loved, and lost. She understood it, at least this part of it.

He bowed deeply to her, in the way his father had taught him he must only bow to someone the equal of a prince, as he had only ever bowed to his king.

"My thanks to you, lady, for the honor you have shown them." He said it in Welsh, and the formal words came more easily than he would have guessed. "For this I will ask God's blessings on you with every breath unto my last, and hold you in my memory as dearly as my own family. Only say what you would have of me in return for the kindness you have done, and it is yours."

She turned to him then. He could feel her gaze on the top of his bowed head for a long and thoughtful moment.

"I do not do what is right for the approbation of princes – or of kings or lords or peasants in the field," she said. "I honor those who are deserving of my honor, be they high or low. And that is what I would ask of you, Prince Gruffydd. It will not be an easy request to grant. You will see."

He rose, and she turned back to her window,

leaving him to wonder what she saw when she looked out onto the world.

Chapter Twenty

Nan stood in the door of the manor kitchen, watching a boy sweep ashes from the hearth. It was a small kitchen, but as warm and welcoming as any other. The bustle of the evening meal was long finished, the cleaning done and the servants scattered, and now the sun had set.

She knew, long before he appeared beside her, that Robin had found her. He had probably searched for her all day, but she had discovered a secret stair that took her to the top of the tower where she looked out across the fields for hours and hours. For the first time in their friendship, she had avoided him, because to share this moment with him or even to look at him would make it real.

When he came to her, he stood close and gathered a fold of her dress in his fist. He had done that when he was a child, when he felt especially protective of her, or very lonely or scared for himself. It had been years. Now the fold he gathered was nearer to her hip than her knee, because he had grown so tall.

"Do you remember," she asked him, "the mice when we slept in the kitchen at Dinwen?"

He leaned against her a little, warm pressure at her shoulder. "And Hawys snoring, and the smell of dried fish when the wind blew southerly."

The boy at the hearth had banked the fire, leaving the embers faintly glowing. He nodded to them and stepped out of his wooden clogs as he left the kitchen, walking with bare feet toward the hall. Now he would go to his own bed, wherever it was, prepared to wake early to start the day's long labor. Stoke the fire, turn the spit, grind the spice. All of it was as familiar to her as breathing.

A prince. Not a falconer. Not even just a lord. A prince.

"Will you sleep with me by the fire?" she asked Robin.

"Nan –"

"Say you will." She was the one who used to say it wasn't right for him to sleep by her side in the kitchen, for all that he was a page at the time. "I want to be just Nan, with her Robin at her side. Just for a little while."

They made a place in the corner by the hearth, his cloak spread below them and hers over them. He grumbled a little about the hard floor and she teased him for growing soft. When they laid down, he did not curl his back against hers as he used to. Or maybe he did, and it felt different. Everything was changed. Everything.

Fuss settled at her feet and they all lay in the dark for hours, not sleeping. She thought of the steward at Morency, and how she had once considered becoming his wife because he was a good man and wanted her. She had let go of the idea easily, because she could not fathom marrying so high above her.

A prince. The last living prince of Aderinyth.

Deep in the night, she turned onto her back. Robin turned too, like he'd been waiting for it. He took her hand in his, and they stared up at the blackness above them a long time before he whispered to her.

"Do you love him, Nan?"

She tried to remember words. She seemed to have lost them. There were sounds that meant something, that would say what was trapped inside her. Breath and tongue and teeth and lips. Simple sounds. They would make it real.

"How can I love a prince?"

It was so plain, when she said it out loud. Princes were not there to be loved. It was as senseless as loving a barrel or a trout or the pope. She could still hear Lady Eluned reciting his string of names and title, word after word after word. Then her own name next to it, one little sound anchored to nowhere and nothing. How could she love a prince.

"You like him more than pork pie," said Robin quite reasonably. "That is no small thing."

Nan turned her face to him. She could barely make out the outline of his profile.

"Do you still love Ansel?" she asked, and felt his fingers twitch against hers.

Robin had loved him from their boyhood, though none but Nan knew it. He had gone to the tourney knowing Ansel would be there, and they would see each other for the first time in many years.

Last night he had whispered to Nan that Ansel was cordial and warm, with all the same passionate interests as when they were boys, and their meeting was joyful – until it was not. Ansel did not want him. Not that way. Robin did not say it outright, but he did not have to. She knew the sound of a broken heart.

"I know not," he answered at last. "I think me I know naught of love." He squeezed her hand, and twined his fingers with hers. "Nay, I know the hurt of it. But that is all."

She turned her face back to the ceiling. There were tears that spilled over and trickled their way to her hair. She could weep for Robin. It must be for Robin. If she were to weep for herself, she might never stop. Her brother, her mother, Oliver, Bea. The Welshman. There would be no end to her weeping, so she must not let there be a start.

"Only a fool could not want you," she whispered. "And he's worse than a fool, to hurt you."

She listened to the steady rise and fall of Robin's breath, and felt his hand tighten gently on hers.

"He cannot change what he is, Nan. Though it brings pain to one who loves him, he cannot change what God and his birth have made him."

The words were meant for both of them, a bitter truth. Her life had been spent in accepting injustice and sorrow, knowing from birth that to rail against it was wasted energy. But now there was something in her that seemed to beat against the bars of a cage, howling that it was not fair, it was not fair.

A prince. God save her, a prince.

✠ ✠ ✠

"Make haste, girl, she waits!"

The lady frowned at her amid the bustle of the kitchen, the morning light so bright that it blinded. Nan fumbled as she washed her face and hands. It seemed impossible to braid her hair neatly, and she wished her kerchief was cleaner. The knot in her stomach did not abate when she sipped the watered beer on offer.

Robin had left before the kitchen stirred, whispering to her that he was not a child anymore, and he would not have anyone think her lewd. He was ever chivalrous, even to a nobody like her.

"Honeyed water, not plain," Nan said to the servant assembling the tray. "And cheese. He won't ask for it, but he always likes a bit of cheese."

Both the lady and the servant scowled at her when she did it herself, but she did not care. This was something she knew, and she could not let it be done incorrectly. Her lady preferred honeyed water in the morning, and Lord Robert loved cheese. She chose the most pungent, then set a milder one next to it. And a pile of wastel bread for him, too, with bits of apple in. She looked for anything else to add, but the tray was already laden with a variety of food, more than two people could ever eat.

Her hands were empty as she followed the scornful lady, because they would not let Nan carry the tray or the jug. They treated her as guest and not servant – a guest who had slept on the kitchen floor but was summoned to a private audience. It was not the solar they took her to, but a smaller room next to it. There was a large window, beautiful tapestries, and two chairs at a table set by the hearth.

Her lady waited for her there, alone. Lord Robert would not come. It was not to be that kind of meeting.

Nan made her courtesy, troubled by her stained kerchief, the coarseness of her dress, and most of all that Lady Eluned stood at the window and did not look out at the sky, but at Nan. When the refreshment was set out and the others left them alone, she felt her lady's eyes on her. She could not seem to meet them.

"Sit, Nan, and eat."

Lady Eluned filled two cups with honeyed water and added a touch of the wine. It was the good kind, the best their French vineyards had to offer. Nan knew it by the color and the scent.

It should not be so difficult. She had done this before. But it always took every ounce of boldness she had, to sit down with a great lady and take a cup that had been poured by her hand. Now she clutched the cup and stared at the food until Lady Eluned tipped the jug of wine again, adding a bit more to Nan's cup.

"Drink, Nan." And because even her most gentle voice was bred to command, Nan obeyed.

When Lady Eluned had first given her a coin all those years ago, neither of them could have thought it would turn out like this. It started as a simple request, a moment's transaction that tangled the life of a serving girl with that of a great lady, whose rival was a monstrous and lustful lord. It ended with Oliver dead, and Nan scarred but saved – and with this undying gratitude, these deep bonds. There was no such thing as silence between them, not truly. Still, she braced herself for the words that must be spoken.

"Your sister," said Lady Eluned. Not a question or a command. Just an offering, an opening. Just a word, with a wealth of understanding behind it.

"She is a whore and a bawd, outside the walls of Lincoln." Nan watched shadows drift across the floor before the window, clouds moving across the sky. "You warned me, my lady. You said there are things worse than death that might befall her."

She had also warned of hurts from which Nan could not protect herself, because there was no defense against them. Sometimes she thought Lady Eluned saw everything, even before it happened.

"Is it worse than death, to be a whore and a bawd?" Lady Eluned asked, her voice mild. "If she lives that way unwilling, I know well you would bring her out of it, no matter the cost."

Nan fixed her eyes on the rich golden yellow of Lady Eluned's gown, a heavy silk velvet. Just one sleeve of it was worth more than the purse of coins given to Bargate Bettie, and that had been two years of Nan's own wages.

"She's not forced to be what she is, my lady. She likes it very well. And it's not that she's a bawd, but that she was intent on whoring a child."

She watched Lady Eluned's face harden, the familiar pinch that formed in her lips. It made tears press behind Nan's eyes. It was such welcome solace to see the instant disapproval, the outrage even to think of a girl treated so foully. The words poured forth then, and she told of how she had taken the girls from the brothel and found places for them, how she had crippled the tanner, how her sister had seen no wrong in what she did.

It was like it always was, when she put the worst into words and said them to Lady Eluned. It made her feel stronger, like telling it staunched the flow of blood from a mortal wound. When she said that Bargate Bettie had lied to the constable about the tanner's wound, Lady Eluned made a sound of disdain, but there was sadness written across her face.

"A checkmate wrapped in a sister's affection," she observed, an elegant way to state what Nan already knew. "You cannot speak out against her lest she recant her tale to the constable."

Nan nodded. "I can't know if she did it for that reason, or for love of me. It don't matter which, though. It all hurts the same."

Lady Eluned looked down at her hands folded before her on the table. The lines in her face were more defined now than when Nan had first met her years ago. The sprinkling of gray in her hair had become streaks of silver.

"It is often the way of family, that love and discord must live side by side, and so rend our hearts. But I did wish… I prayed for you, Nan, that you would find a sister worthy of you, and of all your earnest hopes."

"Nay, not sister. There is no more Bea, that's how I see it. There's only Bargate Bettie, and I'll never call her sister again. And what sorrow I feel for it is gone when I remember I have me such a one as Gwenllian." Nan had never said it, but if she could say nothing else of what was in her heart, she must say this. "It's you I have to thank for that, my lady. As if it weren't enough to give me my life and my strength, you gave me your daughter. I know I cannot call her family in truth, but in my heart she is my sister, and I want no other."

Lady Eluned nodded to acknowledge it, and her lips pressed together. No one else would know it from looking at her, but Nan knew she was biting back a rush of tears. As it receded there was something else, something that reminded her too much of how her own mother had looked at her at the end, and it made her turn her eyes away from Lady Eluned. It was worry, or fear – something that told her now they would speak of things she would not like.

"My daughter has taught you many things." Her voice was soft as a morning mist. "I must ask you, Nan, what she has taught you of herbs, those as might stop a child from growing in a woman."

Nan stared at the table before her. She wondered how it could be so quiet and still in this household full of people. She wondered where the Welshman was. The prince.

"I learned it," she said, and felt the warmth flood her face. "I put the knowledge to use as best I could."

Nothing was sure, they both knew that. Every woman knew that. She watched Lady Eluned's hands begin to move restlessly until they remembered the cup. Her fingers curled tight around it, a hard grip.

"Prince Gruffydd has put your life at risk, for if you bear his child there are some who will not abide it. They would see you dead first."

Nan almost said she knew no Prince Gruffydd. She only knew her Welshman, who would never put her in danger.

"And I would see them dead before their breath fell on me," she answered simply.

Lady Eluned inclined her head. "I do not doubt it."

She drank, then set a piece of bread before Nan and took one up for herself. Neither of them ate. The sun had dimmed, and the sound of a soft rain reached them as Nan looked at the bread and remembered his face when she had first set a loaf in his hands.

"I should have known he were a prince," she said.

He had been nothing but bones and beard. What meat the thieves had let him have, he had given to the hunting birds so that they would stay in perfect health. Nan knew starvation, how it drove pity from a man's heart and sense from his head. Most anyone starving would eat whatever they could, no matter the consequence. But he had seen past his own suffering and kept the birds alive. Not only because he knew if they died, he would die too, but because his duty to protect them was more important. That was what the truly great lords did, at least in all the tales she had heard: in times of crisis, they could see what sacrifices must be made, and took the cost on themselves.

"No matter who he is, if you have sworn vows to each other – even if they were spoken in secret with no witness – I will see that he holds to them, if you wish it." Lady Eluned's voice was gentle, her face stony. "And if you would deny those same vows, I will hold him to that as well. It is for you to say what the truth of it is, or what it will be."

Nan blinked at this offer to shape reality to her preference. But the truth was sufficient.

"We said no vows. He made me no promises."

A wellspring of misery and remembered joy sprang up in her. The way his face had filled with happiness when she said they would go to Aderinyth together – it would be in her mind forever. Now he would go alone. Or the king would kill him, or chain him up. She did not know what would happen to him, because these were the matters of great people who built castles and led armies, and what did she know but how to stir a soup and throw a knife?

"Why did you make me this, lady?" A sob wrenched from her, one she had not known was waiting at the back of her throat. She pressed her fist to her mouth to stop it. "Not a kitchen girl, but no more am I a lady."

Lady Eluned's face had gone pale. "It would be naught but vanity and pride, for me to take credit for any part of you," she said softly. "I but made it possible for you to choose better for yourself."

"Better? I go to my aunt and she thinks me above her." She could not stop the resentment that poured into the words. "I lay with a man who – I thought him a falconer to a great house and that were bad enough, because I dare not want someone so far above *me*." She leaned forward into her hands, her fingernails digging at her scalp. "I am trapped between, too good for one place and not good enough for the other. I know not where I belong, lady. Will you not tell me where I belong?"

"It is yours to choose," came the answer, calm and quiet.

A sudden fury lashed out from some hidden place within her. "Tell me!" Her hands came down, slapped hard on the table. "I cannot go back to the kitchens and I have no sister to save and I cannot have *him*."

It was impossible that she was shouting at her lady. Unthinkable. And she only sat there looking old and ashen-faced, bearing it. It was infuriating.

Nan stood suddenly, the heavy chair scraping backward. She leaned forward to strike the table again just under her lady's chin, making her flinch. Satisfaction and horror shot through Nan at the sight, because Lady Eluned did not flinch. Ever. "Tell me what I can have, lady!" she shouted. "Tell me what I should be."

She sat still, her eyes downcast and her voice steady. "I will not."

"You have cursed me, then." She spat the words, shaking her head in disgust when Lady Eluned finally looked up at her. "You should have left me to die all them years ago. Better you let me die than to make me this."

Such a look came into Lady Eluned's face as she rose that Nan forgot, for a moment, how to breathe. There was disdain and benevolence in her, both at the same time. She was an icy fire. She was the great lady who had saved her.

"Watch your tongue, child, and the things you think to demand of me. I do not apologize for the lives I save, nor those I risk – not to kitchen girls or gentle ladies or vile brutes who would have you worse than dead. You dare call yourself cursed!" She scoffed. "What you are, you have made yourself. Do you forget the only command I have ever given you, from the day I took you from that place, the *only* one?"

Nan stood still, caught between anger and fear, her tongue frozen in her mouth. She forced it free and said between gritted teeth, "I remember."

"Say it," she demanded. "Come, speak it if you remember so well."

"You commanded me never to swear fealty to you." Nan said it through stiff lips. "Not even in my secret heart."

"Aye, and you agreed to it. And I did say then as I say now, that I lay no claim to your life. Yet you beg me tell you what to be?" Her scorn at this was palpable, just short of sneering at such weakness, appalled at the very idea. "Very well, I tell you what I have ever told you: Be selfish. Swear fealty only to yourself."

Nan wanted to shake her head to deny it, but it was all truth. Her lady's stern face became a blur. She was only a smudge of yellow velvet amid the gloom of the day. It had been her guiding principle these many years in every moment of uncertainty. Be selfish. Serve no ends but her own, satisfy only her own heart's desires.

But she could not, this time. She could not change what her Welshman was, or how the world was made.

She blinked, and could not care about the tears that splashed down her cheeks or the sob she must push the words through. "God forgive me what I want, lady. I have no right to it."

Lady Eluned was there, crossing to her swiftly and standing before her. It was suddenly like it had been long ago, when Nan would weep as she tried to tell her story in those early days. But this time she sank to her knees, and her lady knelt with her and put her arms around her. *I am old and strong and weathered as an oak,* she had once said when Nan had worried she should not burden her with her own troubles. And the arms that held her as she sobbed felt just that strong and solid.

After an embarrassingly long while, she calmed herself and ended her weeping. She meant to pull away, and lament that Lady Eluned knelt on the floor and let her gown be dirtied and soaked with tears.

But instead, she kept her head on her lady's shoulder and whispered, "Will the king kill him? Like the…" Her voice trembled and cracked, but she must ask it. The vision had been with her all night. "Like them heads that are stuck up on the great tower in London?"

"Nay," she soothed, and she sounded so sure of it that Nan felt faint with relief. "Such ignominy is reserved for traitors, and Prince Gruffydd has only ever served the crown of England."

"He only wanted to go home." Nan wiped her tears and sat back on her heels. "What will happen?"

"In truth, I cannot say." Lady Eluned sighed. "I keep myself far from court. Robin has been sent there with a message for my son. William will know best, what the king is like to do. We can only await word."

Nan nodded, and tried to imagine Lord William fully grown. She had last seen him when she was a serving girl and he was an awkward youth making his oath to the king. She opened her mouth to ask where the king held court now, but she was interrupted by a lady at the door who made a deep courtesy despite the burden in her arms.

"Your pardon, my lady. I have brought the gown as you asked." She held a stack of folded clothes, snowy white linen and blue silk, with a crespinette set atop it all.

Lady Eluned did not rise, nor look at all as if she meant to be anywhere other than on the floor. "Leave it here." She waved her hand at the chair, and the woman readily complied. "Have water brought so she might bathe. I will help her to dress and call you to see to her hair."

Thus dismissed, the woman nodded and left. Nan stared in growing dread at the rich fabric, finer than anything she had ever worn – as fine as anything a real lady might wear.

"Nay, my lady," she said, looking up as Lady Eluned rose from the floor. "You cannot mean for me to wear it. I may be more than a serving girl, but not so worthy as to be wearing silks and pearls."

"I think me a better judge of your worth than you are." Lady Eluned took her hands and pulled her to her feet. She laid a hand on Nan's shoulder. "No more can you cover yourself in the roughest wool and hide in the kitchen, Nan."

Nan took a breath, trying to summon the words to protest. But Lady Eluned smiled softly and smoothed a hand over Nan's hair.

"You have been lover to a prince, and may yet bear his child. Silk and pearls are the least of what is owed to you."

Chapter Twenty-One

He knew it was Nan who had entered the hall by the change in the sounds around him, the sudden quiet followed swiftly by the excited murmurings, all attention drawn to where she moved toward the dais. She paid it no mind, though she must feel it – she must feel *him*, the fixed intensity of him taking in the sight of her like a drowning man takes in air.

She walked silently, never speaking to the ladies beside her, never looking up until she reached the table below the dais where he stood. Then her eyes went straight to his, a shock of blue that was almost unearthly. It was the gown she wore, the color of sapphires, that accentuated the blue of her eyes. Or it was the simple gold circlet set on her hair, a gleam across her brow. Her coiled braids glowed beneath a crespinette modestly studded with pearls. He could think of nothing but freeing her hair from its confines, watching it swirl around her face as those blue eyes moved across his bared body with fascination.

She looked at him for barely an instant, just a pause in her glance before she turned away and sat. It left him to stare helplessly in her wake, and he was hardly alone. It should not be possible for her to be yet more beautiful, and with only a fresh gown. But the rich color and stark simplicity of it made her beauty stand out, and those few women in the hall who dressed more opulently were hardly noticeable next to her.

"I would wager there is none more fair at Edward's court."

Lady Eluned had appeared beside him at the dais, watching him closely. This transformation was her doing, and her look told him it was calculated – not only to establish Nan's status as more than servant, but to emphasize her beauty to the utmost. He tried to imagine why, but he could not seem to think past the look of Nan, the luscious curve of her mouth and the gentle arc of her cheek, the way she had said not a thing to him with her look.

"You think you are worthy of her?" Lady Eluned asked it in an undertone, almost but not quite goading, making it clear that she doubted it.

Of course he was not, but there was no reason to admit it to her. He tore his eyes from Nan, knowing she would not look up at him again, and turned to meet Lady Eluned's shrewd gaze. "Are you?"

She was not flustered in the least by his challenging tone. Her chin lifted, a smile softened her lips as if his question pleased her, and she said, "I am least worthy of all, my lord. Shall we dine?"

So saying, she took her place at the high board next to Lord Robert. Gryff sat too, uncomfortably aware of the attention on him. His true name had not been given out, but it was a public declaration of his high status to seat him on the dais. He stopped himself from looking at Nan again, but noticed that Lady Eluned's eyes kept straying to where she sat.

"How come you to take such an interest in her?" he asked, careful to speak in Welsh.

Lady Eluned's eyes were on him instantly, a swift assessment. "Ah. She has told you her story." He was left to wonder what in his face could possibly have told her that, while she turned back to her plate and continued brusquely. "It was because of her service to me that she lost a husband and suffered great misfortune. I thought to pay that debt to her, though I know well it can never be paid in full. And then…" Her eyes found Nan again. "I discovered there is so much more to her than just serving girl."

It struck him as an unwelcome truth that this woman knew more of Nan than he did. He had thought he knew her because he had heard her story and met her aunt and saw her reunion with her sister. He had watched her kill men and marvel at cathedrals. But he had known nothing of these people who were so dear to her – Robin and Lady Eluned and Lord Robert – and wondered now what else she carried hidden in her silent heart.

"Will you tell me why it is that she speaks so rare?" he asked. Even now she sat wordlessly among the chatter of gathering diners.

"Because it suits her?" Lady Eluned shrugged a little, looking out at Nan, then grew thoughtful. "But there is a greater truth behind it: that the words of a serving girl are seldom noted. And so she did find a way through silence to her voice. It was only when she stopped speaking that she was ever heard."

This made a kind of sense that he could not deny. Nan spoke so little that all around her attended closely whenever words escaped her. She was so many things – strong and intelligent and competent at whatever she put her hand to. It was not surprising that she would be so clever as to have turned silence to her advantage in this way.

"She is no common woman," he observed.

"Is she not?" Lady Eluned picked up her wine and let her eyes drift thoughtfully over the other people in the hall. "In faith, that was my true discovery. Now I must wonder how many others there are under my very nose, whose worth is overlooked. Mark that lesson well, my lord," she said with a wry twist to her mouth as she lifted the cup. "I would that I had learned it sooner."

The servants came with ewers of fragrant water then platters of food, and Gryff made himself remember courtly conversation. One of the ladies who attended Lady Eluned was seated next to him, the one who had seemed familiar. It was because he had known her sister, he realized, though he bit his tongue against saying it. He had stolen a kiss from her once under a snow-laden tree, during a hunt – but only one kiss, because she had blushed prettily and then turned painfully shy.

It was a memory that made him smile fondly until he thought suddenly of how he had reached out that first time to touch Nan's hair. How sure he had been that she wanted it, and how wrong he had been. Even as this world of the highborn comforted him with its familiarity, he seemed to see it anew through her eyes. Innocent pleasures were not so innocent, frivolity and cruelty like two sides of the same coin. And he had never seen it before. He had never needed to, so occupied with his own concerns, so happy to indulge in what pleasures and privileges had been afforded him.

He could feel himself slipping back into it, if only a little, like it was the most natural thing in the world. The glib words, the excellent wine and rich foods, the attentiveness of servants, the coy attentions of the lady beside him who was daughter to a baron. It was an easier world, for all the dangers in it, and he could not help but welcome its embrace.

When the meal was done there was music and dancing, and he watched a few men pluck up the courage to approach Nan, inviting her to dance. To his relief, she did not, nor did she speak or smile or join in the merriment in any way. Instead she drifted closer to the exit and slipped out, accompanied by one of the other ladies who had attended Lady Eluned in her solar.

He followed within minutes, hoping he might at least learn which chamber was hers. In the morning, he could wait outside it and try to speak to her. He would be careful – they must be careful that none suspected what she meant to him lest it bring danger to her – but he must speak to her.

As he crossed the courtyard in the deepening twilight, he caught sight of Fuss running to a shadowed corner. There was a faint gleam of blue silk, and his heart lifted to see she was alone. He called her name softly as he approached.

She stepped out of the shadow and lowered herself into a courtesy, her eyes down, a perfect show of humility. Anyone would think she had been born and bred at court, the way it was executed. There was the old aura of untouchability to her, that sense that everything in her was perfectly contained and set apart from him. Worst of all was that she seemed to be waiting for him to tell her she might rise.

No, worse than that was how he could sense this deference was meant sincerely, because she thought it was expected of her.

"Stop this," he said, too terse. She immediately rose and began to hurry away, past him, always keeping her head lowered. She kept moving even as he said, "Nan."

He reached out to catch her elbow, and felt her go still beneath his touch. There was rejection in her, a stiffness that did not soften and melt as he expected. He waited, too happy to be touching her to break the contact, trying to judge her silence, desperately searching for the right thing to say. But she began to pull away.

He did not let go. He could not. He tugged at her arm to turn her to him and she spun, swift and sudden. She flung his hand off her in the same motion, a knife in her fist as she stepped within inches of him. It was the simple eating knife that hung from her belt, the only one she wore tonight – at least the only one that could be seen. She met his eyes, more threat in her look than he had ever seen directed at him.

The air froze in his lungs, but he did not flinch. "You would not." There was no doubt in his voice. "I know you would not."

Her look never wavered as she pressed the blade closer, the edge of it just under his ribs. Her words were cool, deliberate, spoken very clearly so that he would not mishear any one of them.

"I suffer the touch of no man without I ask it, be he prince or no."

She turned and made her way toward the manor, leaving him with only the burning blue of her gaze, her perfect Welsh ringing in his ears.

✠ ✠ ✠

Nan retreated to the tower roof again the next day. She should be attending her lady, or bent over an embroidery frame – something, anything. But she needed a kind of peace that could not be found anywhere except in this high corner of the manor, open to the wind and sky. A place where she could see the world but the world could not see her.

Word would come soon. The king held court barely a day's ride from here, hunting at some manor she had never heard of. Close enough for a pigeon to have carried a return message already, and she did not know what it meant that there was none. Perhaps it was not safe, or perhaps there was no news yet. But if nothing else, Robin should come back tonight. It might be any minute. She stared at the horizon, trying not to watch for riders.

At Morency she would have lost herself in sparring with Davydd and Robin, or listening to the unrelenting flow of Suzanna's chatter as they stitched an altar cloth. Or hours spent next to Gwenllian in the herb-house, her occasional murmur about this or that cure, the quiet companionship as they sorted and steeped and distilled.

Life had made sense there. *She* had made sense there, or felt she had.

Lord Robert found her at midday, and looked out with her at the sky for a long minute before saying only that there was no message yet. Just the sound of his voice was a comfort. It was him who had been the first to soothe her when she came out of that awful place, before her lady arrived to barter for their release. He had even wiped the blood and tears from her face, gentle as her own father – or as a father should be, if he cared more about his daughter than his drink.

So when, hours later, the Welshman appeared on the roof, she made herself stay still. She knew it was Lord Robert who had told him where to find her, and he would only do that if he thought she should hear what the Welshman had to say.

He held himself differently now. It had been there in the hall and it was here too. It wasn't just the fine new clothes they had given him. There was a sureness in his body, an absolute control of the space around him, the confidence like arrogance that was the birthright of highborn lords. It was so very far from the shrinking man she had found tied to a tree. When had it begun? Why had she not seen it for what it was?

She looked out at the horizon, and felt him looking at her. It was a long time before he spoke. He soaked in her silence first, fit himself into it in that way he had. For a moment it felt like it had only days ago, like she knew his every thought and feeling. *Hiraeth*, she thought – and knew it was not the distance from his lands that grieved him in this moment. It was the distance from her.

"It means naught to me that they call me a prince," he said quietly. "Is but a word. One that has damned me."

She tried to believe him. She tried not to remember how he had lain naked before her, all spread out like a banquet beneath her greedy hands, no shame in her as she compelled him to serve her hunger.

If it were but a word, she would not feel this way. If it were but a word, he would have told her.

"The Welsh have no kings, only princes with little wealth," he continued, so determined to explain it. "My only worth has been as pawn, to my father and to Edward."

Nan had no worth to any kings, and her worth to her father had fit easily into the palm of his hand. A few coins, spent and forgotten. Her worth.

"It is the Normans who rule, and it means little to them that I was called a prince. When I lived among them, they looked on me with contempt." It was there in his voice, how it still stung him. "They sneered at me. Every day, for years."

He made it sound like she should be amazed. If she felt like talking, she might tell him how she and Oliver were treated like dogs when a Norman lord had held them. Worse than dogs. But she had told him that already, all of it. He had seen the scars. So she stayed silent and tried to care about some sneering in his youth.

"I could not tell you for fear of my life. If Rhodri knew I lived, or the king… I could tell no one." She could hear the urgency beneath his calm coaxing, hear how much her silence unsettled him. "I verily believed I could live a simple Welshman, with none to remember my birth. I tell you, it is what I wanted." The yearning was in his voice, the same way he sounded when he spoke of his home. "I wanted that, and you."

She had imagined it. She had. No use in pretending otherwise. She had imagined a place in the green hills he had described, him flying falcons and Fuss hiding from the hawks. And now her imagination added a child – his child – in her arms, and she wanted it with a breathtaking ferocity. All of it: the place and the child and him.

It made her dizzy with longing, and then sick with hate. Hate for him because he made her want it. Hate for his murderous brother, hate for the king. Hate for all of them because they stole her Welshman and replaced him with a prince.

"It means naught to me, Nan," he insisted. "It is but a name."

A name, just a name. Gruffydd son of Iorwerth and grandson of Cynan the Red, that was what he was called. The leader of Aderinyth, who probably had a bard to sing the history of his family for ten generations.

She was Nan. Just Nan from nowhere, with a whore for a sister.

Though he stood close enough that she heard his every breath, all she could feel was the distance that had come with this word he said had no meaning. Even if a lesser prince, he was still a lord, like those she had served, those who felt free to grab and take as their right. Those who commanded serving girls to their beds, who had looked at her and seen a sweet morsel to get their hands on, who were the reason she had made herself strong and deadly: so that they could never hurt her again.

But one had found a way to hurt her in spite of it. Her heart seemed to bleed, a steady seeping as though from a skillful cut, no matter that he had not intended it. Any of it.

"Say something," he entreated.

She could not. She could feel how much he wanted to touch her. Her eyes stayed fixed on the horizon. The riders would come soon.

"Know you what has become of the other Welsh princes?" he asked suddenly.

She did not. She remembered hearing that the prince of all Wales who had died, Llewellyn, had a tiny baby girl. Nan had been vaguely aware that there were other Welsh princes but they were just more lords, to her. It had never been a thing that mattered before.

"Prince Llewellyn had no sons when he died. His daughter was taken from Wales and given to a convent as a babe in arms. She will never be allowed to leave it, for fear the Welsh will rally to her. They say she does not even know Welsh, and it will never be taught to her."

There was no anger in his tone but she heard it anyway, and understood why. They stole even her language from her, this orphaned Welsh princess, as though taking her land and her people were not enough.

"Prince Dafydd was executed for treason." He paused, and she nodded quickly to let him know he need not detail the execution to her. Everyone had heard of it, how the traitor Dafydd had been tortured. His skull still rotted on a spike in London. "He had two sons, both imprisoned at Bristol. The oldest was near my age. Last year he died in his prison. The younger prince…" His voice faded, and she glanced to see his face. His lips had gone white at the edges, and she looked away quickly. "He is there still. He is locked in a cage every night."

The sun seemed too bright, the air too cold. She did not know what to do with the images he put in her head. She pressed her tongue hard against her teeth and thought of her lady, wise and cunning, who said he would not be put to death. Nothing had been said about cages.

"It is a curse. All the misfortunes of my life have befallen me because they call me a prince. Believe me that I would live happily as your Welshman. I *have* lived happily as that." He stepped closer. Close enough to touch. "In all my wretched life, Nan, it is the only happiness I have known."

What was there to say – the truth, that it was the same for her? She stared out at the empty sky and remembered him saying simply, *And then I wake, and you are there.* He had said it like it was an answer to everything. And it had felt that way.

But it was no answer to this. There was no answer to this at all.

He turned from her to face the same sky, and they looked out in silence together. She could feel him giving up on her. Yet her tongue would not move.

"Tell me anything of what is inside you." He said it like a prayer, a supplication to her silence.

What was inside her. She thought of Oliver dead on a dirty floor. She thought of her mother telling her to care for her brother and sister. She thought of her aunt marveling over simple embroidery, of Bea with a blade pinning her sleeve, of Robin whispering in the dark. She thought of princes and cages and far green hills.

"Say something," he whispered.

But she did not, and he left her alone under the open sky.

Chapter Twenty-Two

The flame guttered, the wax dripped, the empty hours passed. His was a life spent in waiting. Waiting to learn when he would stop being a hostage, waiting until it was safe to come out of hiding, waiting for Baudry or one of his men to kill him. Waiting to go home.

Another day had passed. Three full days, when the journey to Edward and back should not be more than two. No message had come, no word of reassurance. Nothing.

It could only bode ill. Lord Robert was insistently optimistic, citing any number of harmless reasons for the delay – poor roads, an injured horse, the court moving to somewhere a little farther away for better hunting. He was sure it was nothing more than that. But Lady Eluned's face was carefully neutral, and her noncommittal responses filled him with foreboding. She knew Will as he did, and they both knew Will would send word if the news was good.

He would also send warning if it was bad – if he could. If it was safe to do so.

Gryff stared at the candle by his bedside. Those first years in Lancaster's household, when he was too young yet to fill the hours with welcoming women, he had spent his nights in this same way. He would watch the candle flame for hours, trying to burn the memory of home out of his eyes. Then at the abbey, he had spent every night for five years in the dark, wishing he could remember more.

Somewhere in the night he became aware of her. Outside the glow of candlelight, just inside the door of this fine bedchamber with its thick tapestries and carved oak furniture, she had slipped silently in. She brought her own peaceful variety of silence with her, somehow smoothing the jagged edges of the quiet that surrounded him.

He did not look toward her. All day he had paced the grounds of the manor, sure that at any moment a message would arrive. By late afternoon he had given into the sinking sense of doom. He could not eat, but could not resist going to the hall to look at her from afar, sure now that it was the last he would ever see of her. Blue silk, blue eyes, golden hair, and a mouth made for sin. No flame would ever burn the memory of it out of him, but he had let his eyes drink their fill.

"Do you come here to torment me with your silence?"

He asked it to the candle, his eyes following the dripping wax. He almost asked why she did not leave him alone, but stopped himself in time. She would take it as a command from a prince, damn her, and he would be left without even her wordlessness to keep him company.

Her step came closer, a soft footfall on the rushes behind him, but he did not turn from his place on the bed. There was a gathering glow, and he understood she must be holding a lamp. The light of it joined the light of his candle as she came closer behind him.

"Nay, not that." she said. "Far from that."

He held his breath through the rush of relief that flooded him. Her voice. It left him lightheaded, staring at his shadow on the wall while he prayed he would not say the wrong thing.

"Then why?"

Her slow steps carried her around the corner of the bed, just at the edge of his vision. He felt it again – that thin ribbon of her deepest self escaping its careful containment, flowing out toward him. He knew she was waiting for him to look at her. He thought he should fear whatever she had come to say. But he did not care, as long as he could look at her. As long as she spoke to him.

He turned his head to where she stood in the glow of her lamp. She was back in her coarse brown dress, her weapons glinting in the dim light. All her beauty was still there, and all her lethal strength, no matter the outer trappings.

"Robin has not come."

"Nay," he answered. "Haps he will never come, and I will bide here forever, waiting." The sight of the little lamp in her hand pierced his heart. It had burned beside them in their nights together, those nights he had dared to believe would never end. "Would you bide with me, Nan, through days and nights without number?"

There were signs of sleeplessness around her eyes. "What will happen?" she whispered. "What will the king do to you?"

"I cannot know." It seemed not to matter at all right now. Nothing mattered but her. "Would you bide with me?" he asked again.

She blinked, casting her eyes down to the floor. "You are a prince," she said, as though that were an answer. "You say the word means naught. You think it's naught to do with who you truly are." She looked up at him again. "But I see it in you, all the things that make you a prince. It's in your blood that you curse, and in your bones, and in everything that makes you. You were born to be Gruffydd ab Iorwerth, not a common Welshman. Just as I was born to be plain Nan and cannot be worthy of a lord, except as servant."

There was such sureness in her words that he almost missed the hint of uncertainty in her face. It was not to do with him. *I know my place even do you not know your own,* she had said to Robin.

But she wore silk and embraced a great lady like she was her own mother.

"You are more than what you were born to. Far more."

The shake of her head was faint but distinct, a rueful gesture that said she thought he did not understand. "You know little of me."

"Then tell me," he urged. "If you will scorn words, I am forced to know little of you."

She looked at him with a gentle furrow to her brow, blinking. He watched her search for words, as though he had asked an impossible question that pained her. Almost did he repent of it, fearing the impulse that had spurred her to come to him and speak at last, would fade. But he bit his tongue and waited, because he did not want to spend this night in thinking of his own fate. He wanted whatever she would give him of herself.

She took another step to reach the low table next to the bed, where his candle burned. She set her little lamp next to it. Her hand went to the eating knife at her belt and removed it.

"I had a baby brother who died starving in my arms, because there was no food nor pity to be had."

The words were like hailstones falling on him. The tension at the corner of her lips, the stiffness of her posture said what she did not put into words – that no matter his misfortunes, such things did not happen to princes. And if ever they did, all agreed that it was a horror, something that should never happen. Not to a prince.

But she blinked the bitterness away easily, it seemed, and looked down at the simple eating knife she held. She tilted it so that the handle caught the light and revealed a pattern of lines scratched deeply into it, and spoke into the hush.

"My mother died having him, and we were all starving, so my father looked to sell me into service. I would have gone to a man who was like that tanner, wanting little girls in his bed, but for Aunt Mary." Her finger traced over the lines and he saw suddenly that it was meant to be the letter M. "She shouted that she would not let it happen, and found me a better place. That were the first time I was saved from an ugly fate."

She put the knife on the table, kissed her fingertips and touched them to the M on the handle, a strange and sweet little ritual. She turned to face him but did not look up. Instead she reached down and quickly pulled her skirt to her knee, revealing her garter. The little silver knife was kept hidden there, and she pulled it out. It fit perfectly in her hand.

"So I went to work for a weaver's wife, cleaning and cooking until the weaver died." She kept her eyes on the knife. "I was more grown then, and the widow married herself to a man who took a fancy to me. Most women would beat me and throw me in the street, and say I tried to seduce him away. But Ida, she looked out for me. She found me work in a kitchen in Chester, and told the cook I was a good girl and should be treated well."

The silver knife was set next to the other, and he saw the I scratched into it. He had seen it countless times, but never thought it was meant to be a letter. Ida.

She bent again and brought the dagger out of her boot. It was tall and elegant, rarely used, and now he saw the letter I engraved in the quillon as she ran her fingers over it.

"Isabella," she said, almost with an air of shy apology. "She stood between me and that lord who killed Oliver. She were a lady and a stranger to me. Her disgust is what moved her, not any love for me. One night she came into the room and saw me there, and what he done to me. She put herself in front of me and would not budge until he left me in peace." She lined the dagger up on the table next to the other blades. "And so I was saved again."

Finally she looked at him, a shot of clear blue meeting his eyes through the lamplight. She reached behind her to the dagger that hid in her belt, the one she had first put to him when he had touched her hair uninvited. He did not look down at it. He did not need to. He remembered the twisting symbol and now understood what it was.

"Gwenllian," she whispered, like it was a word full of magic. "My teacher. It's how I know to speak Welsh, because a Welshwoman taught me this defense." Her eyes dropped to the dagger, resting on the G that was on the grip. "I didn't have no kind of strength or skill that could protect me until she gave it to me. She made it so I could save myself."

Her hands rested on the dagger a long time when she set it down. Finally she took off her belt and sheathed the blade before replacing it on the table. She seemed more content once the gleam of it was hidden, as though she could not be easy if it sat out in the open for all to see.

Now all that was left were the blades on her forearms. Perfectly fitted to her, small and wicked, designed with lethal efficiency. She ran her fingers lightly over the row on her right arm, touching the blunt end where an E was stamped on each one.

She laid a finger on the first blade in the row. "Lady Eluned tried to keep that lustful lord from me, and she did for a few days." Again that look of reverence that now he recognized as the deepest gratitude he had ever seen. She continued talking, touching a blade with each deed, counting them off, and she spoke Lady Eluned's name each time like it was a sacred word.

"When he captured me and killed Oliver, Lady Eluned gained my freedom. When I was swallowed up in fear, Lady Eluned taught me to speak of it, so I did not spend my life in shrinking. One of the knights in her hall got hold of me, and Lady Eluned stopped him." She moved to the row of blades on her left arm. "Lady Eluned sent me to Morency, so I might learn defense. She gave me Gwenllian, and Robin, and…everything." Nan closed her eyes and whispered the words like a long-practiced prayer. "Again and again, I am saved by good women. I will not forget their names, and I ask God and his saints to remember them."

Her eyes opened. He watched as she released the buckles on the arm braces and set them down carefully beside the lamp. They looked together at the pile of weapons on the table.

"Do you see now?" she asked softly. "I've spent my life in fighting against being made a whore, and worse. My fate was to be beaten and used, weak and wretched and lowly, and that's what I would be if not for others who took pity on me. I'm not more than what I was born to, as you say. It's only that I had them."

He looked at her, and then at the table laden with her many defenses. Everything in him rejected her words. He could not deny it was true that only chance had raised her above her birth. But there was more to her than chance, just as there was more beauty within her than there was without.

"You speak of what you were born to," he said at last. "And I cannot care. Were you born to more, or to less – still I would esteem you more highly than any lady I have known. Still I would want you. You and no other." He saw the doubt in her eyes, and the question that had lurked in him for days escaped. "Do you want me less, now that you know what I am born to?"

He did not breathe at all while she stared wordlessly at him. The candle flickered, sending light and shadows dancing across her face. Then she blinked, and let out a trembling breath.

"I should." She whispered it. "God forgive me, I should. But I want you all the same." She bit her lips together and moved her eyes over him like a caress. "More, even, when I think we will be parted."

She stepped forward, her dress hanging loosely, and sat beside him on the bed. He wanted to embrace her and say that they would not be parted, that he would never let anything take her from him. But he was at the king's mercy, and could promise nothing. His hand found hers, so small and delicate for all her strength and skill, and she gripped it tightly. She lifted his hand and pressed her lips against his fingers.

"What will happen?" she asked, and when he did not answer readily, she looked at him. She spoke in Welsh. "Say me the truth of it, for I know naught of the king and his commands."

He nodded. He could give her that, if nothing else.

"I wait to discover if Edward thinks me a threat. I am loyal to him, but my family has fought for generations against the domination of the Normans." How strange, that it was his father's words that came from him, the old avoidance of saying such things as traitor and treason and rebellion. "The king wants no more Welsh nobles to trouble him, or to stand as challenge to his authority in Wales. Yet do I think he may show me more mercy than he has shown many other Welsh princes."

Her eyes never left his. "Why?"

All the many things that signaled his fidelity to the king swirled through his mind, all the ways Edward would find him useful. But he chose the one thing he thought most important, that she would understand most easily. "Because I will forswear the title of prince." He watched her eyes widen in shock. "No prince of Aderinyth since my grandfather has been consecrated by the Church. It is but a word, as I have said. One I will gladly sacrifice."

He could feel the rise and fall of her breath against his arm where she clutched it lightly to her chest. Her eyes searched his.

"Will it be enough?"

There was so much more to consider. So much more that he did not care to think about now.

"I will do whatever the king demands. I want only my life." He dared to touch the hair that curled at her temple, freed from net and kerchief alike, arranged in the shining braid that he had followed out of hell. "And you, if you would have a simple Welshman."

She shook her head faintly, and he watched reluctant hope and doubt chase across her face.

"You cannot be that."

"I can. I will."

Her fingers squeezed his painfully. He could feel the reservation in her, how some part of her did not dare to believe it. He hardly dared believe it himself, knowing that it would be as Lady Eluned had warned: he was still a pawn, and the king had all the power. But he only wanted his life, and it seemed little enough to hope for.

Nan looked at the table where the candle guttered, light flickering across the blades. These were the stories beneath the silence, the defenses that were more than weapons, all laid out for him to see. All but one.

He moved his hand in hers, turning it to touch the hard lump that lay between her breasts. It was impractical, not easily reached beneath her linen, but still a defense. A last defense, when nothing else served. He had seen it against her naked skin, or else in her hand, so many times that the letter on it seemed engraved in his mind. He put a finger to it now, feeling the shape of the R through her linen.

In the end he did not ask it. He only looked at her, and waited to see if she would give him this part of herself.

She returned his look, a steady and clear gaze, then stood and, to his surprise, pulled the dress off. It left her linen to billow slightly around her, the silhouette of her nakedness barely visible beneath it. Her hand closed over the dagger and pulled it out, still sheathed, holding it close to her chest.

"I thought to myself that I should hate men," she said, still in Welsh. "All men, for how they have used me, and tried to use me, and how they have brought nearly all the sorrows of my life. But I do not, and it was a wonder to me until I considered why." She looked down at the dagger, ran her thumb over the engraved letter, and smiled a little. "Lord Robert, and

Lord Ranulf, and Robin. One dried my tears and treated me gentle in my worst distress. One put aside his own fears to help make me stronger, and faster, and better. And one has given me a brother's love, and asks for naught in return but that I am his friend."

She did not put it on the table with the rest. She kept her fingers curled around it as she pulled the cord from which it hung over her head. When she came close to him, the scent of her surrounded him, intoxicating.

"It may seem a strange defense, Welshman. But their tender care has protected me as well as any blade. Did I not know them, there would be naught left of my heart to give to you."

Her heart. His hands found the dip of her waist beneath the linen. He forgot, every time, how slight she was until he touched her. Solid, practical Nan, who was only a wisp of smoke, a sliver of flame against him. Her lips came to his, tentative and sweet until his arms went around her and she opened her mouth over his, bold in her hunger.

It made him weak with relief, to know her excitement. He had missed her so much that it was the sweetest pain to feel her again, the sensation of her body and breath flooding him like rain on parched earth. He had thought he wanted her before, but it was as nothing to the keen and ravenous hunger in him now that he knew she offered her heart to his true self, nothing hidden between them. He did as he had not done before this, and took control of their embrace. He pulled her down to him, hands gripping her tightly, urging her on to the bed beneath him.

When his palm smoothed over her thigh, she stretched and pressed herself up against him, demanding more. In the dim light, she seemed like a manifestation of his dreams, warm and welcoming, no part of her closed to him.

Beneath the linen shift her scars were a ghostly white, her skin glowing. He took down her hair and spread it over her, ripples of gold silk over the slight curves, the tips of her small breasts barely peeking through. His mouth went to them, his tongue caressing until she gasped, but he did not relent. He wanted the sounds that came from her because each of them, everything that came from her lips, he cherished. They were his riches, his treasure, as precious as jewels.

The sheathed dagger was still in her hand, and he could not resent it. Not when he knew what it meant that she had stripped herself of all other defense, and called him Welshman, and spoke of giving her heart to him. He pushed her arms above her head and sat back to look at her, all golden desire beneath his teasing hands, finding every place that made her gasp more.

"Welshman," she breathed, a command that set him afire. He kissed her, ravaging her eager mouth while his hands fumbled with his braies, and suddenly remembered the danger.

The thought that she could have his child released a flood of lust in him. It shot through his spine, a rush of blood and an animal desire to thrust himself inside her. He pulled away from her mouth, pressing his face to her throat, gulping air, stunned at the pleasure it gave him to think of putting a child in her.

He could not. Not tonight. One day, and he took a brief moment to say a blasphemous prayer it might be soon.

She moved a hand restlessly in his hair, her body straining upward, her legs open beneath him. He opened his mouth over her throat, her heartbeat on his lips, and pushed himself inside her heat.

She was bliss. She was heaven gasping beneath him, pulsing around him. He moved in her, his thumb on her to rouse her excitement to the utmost, following the sounds of her pleasure until she was writhing. Her release came hard and fast and lasted an infinity while he held himself still, committing it all to memory – the sight, the feel, the sound of her ecstasy. When he could hold himself at the brink no longer, he pulled himself out of her warmth, groaning, and spilled his seed on her belly.

One day. A child with her, one day. Plain Nan and a common Welshman. Soon, God willing. But not yet.

Chapter Twenty-Three

Nan did not sleep. No matter what he or her lady said, she could only envision the king's men arriving in force to drag him away with evil intent. When she whispered as much, he said that if men did come for him, they would not do him violence but only escort him to the king.

It eased her fear enough for now. She turned on her side to let his body cradle hers as she watched the lamp burn through the little oil it held. His breath was steady, his limbs heavy, and she hoped he slept. The dagger was still in her hand, her fingers loosely curled around the sheath. She watched the light play off it, and knew it should not be so difficult to let go.

He would be a common man. Not a prince. It was what he wanted. It would save his life.

She tried to imagine it. Likely he would never see, as she did, all the little things that marked him as better. She thought of how Aunt Mary had been in awe of the falcon, so beautiful and valuable, and how she had looked at the Welshman when he spoke his fine words. Then he had fetched water from the well, and repaired a crumbling wall, and slept on the floor, humble as any servant.

Her fingers uncurled and left the dagger lying next to her, inches from her hand. He was not like other lords. When he had spoken of his home, not knowing she understood, it was his brothers he spoke of – and the hills, the sky, the people and the legends. No word of a prized castle or manor, nor riches and comforts he sorely missed.

In the falconer's house, he had said he regretted the dishonor he had done her. Because he would not dishonor her, a servant.

She looked at the dagger beside her as the light changed, dawn beginning to filter in at the edges of the tapestry over the window as the oil lamp stuttered and dimmed. To lie next to him made her feel fragile, exposed. Vulnerable. Which was not the same as weak.

Soon he would not be a prince. And now, next to her, naked in bed, he was her Welshman and nothing else.

She lifted the dagger, carefully and slowly, so as not to wake him if he slept. At the edge of the bed, just within her reach, was the table where all her defenses were laid. Dagger in hand, her fist touched the table, cool air on her outstretched arm and his solid warmth all around her. Then she let it go, setting it among the other blades, and pulled her hand back to rest beneath her cheek.

His arm lifted to gather her in, his lips pressed to her hair. He would be hers. Her Welshman. She turned to him, skin against skin, and clutched him to her with both hands open. There was nothing between them. Nothing but their mingled breath and the new morning light.

✠ ✠ ✠

"Gruffydd! By God, it is good to see you at last!"

It was all Gryff heard before Will embraced him tightly, pounding his back and laughing. To his slight surprise, Gryff was every bit as glad to see Will, who had grown tall and handsome and powerful, but seemed just as eager and joyful as he had been as a boy. When he pulled back, Gryff could see him trying to rein in his emotion and put on a more sober face. It was unnerving, how quickly and easily he accomplished it. But it was good to know the old Will was beneath the mature facade, and happy to see him.

"In faith, I thought you had stopped growing," Gryff smiled up at him. "But that was a vain hope, I see."

Will's eyes strayed to Gryff's scar for only a brief moment before he blinked away his interest in it and smiled warmly again. They were in the yard outside the hall, standing in the midmorning sun with what felt like a hundred eyes on them. From the corner of his eye, Gryff could see Robin craning his neck, looking about.

He was likely hunting for Nan, who had left Gryff's chamber barely an hour before Will's party was seen riding toward the manor. Finally, just as Gryff had begun to despair, Will had arrived – with nearly a dozen other men, many of them armed knights.

"There is refreshment in the hall, if my lord of Ruardean would have his men take their ease." Lady Eluned spoke formally, her eyes not missing a thing. "More will be brought to the solar, if my lords will prefer to take their own ease in private."

"Aye, we would, Mother."

A few of the men ranged out behind him were greeting Lord Robert, all of them handing their horses to servants. Will called to one of the men to join them, waving the rest toward the hall. He must have seen the wariness in Gryff's face, for he put an arm around his shoulder as they walked to the manor house and leaned in close to say, "There is naught to fear, I swear it. The news I bring is happy. These men are come to protect you should the bastard learn you are here."

As they made their way up the stairs he explained that he had taken time to assemble these trusted men in secret, to consult most closely with the king, and to find a distraction to put in Rhodri's path. It was not safe to send a message; the court was filled with prying eyes. It pleased Will, this kind of intrigue and maneuvering. It was plain to see that he thrived on it.

When they reached the solar, he introduced the other man as a royal clerk of the chancery, a word that sent an icy wind down Gryff's spine. He thought he managed to hide his alarm but Will, like his mother, missed nothing.

"I have told you there is no need to fear," he said again as they sat. "I will tell you all, but first I would learn where you have hidden yourself these many years, my lord prince."

"Nay, Will, never call me prince." Gryff said it firmly, leaving no doubt he meant it. "The people of Aderinyth are Edward's subjects, not mine. So too am I his subject, and I would never be called prince again."

At this, Will's brows went up in surprise. His lips curved in an admiring smile and he glanced toward the royal clerk, exchanging a pleased look. "It will gratify Edward to know it," he said. "I will not fail to tell him these were the first words from you, even before you heard his offer."

All the air seemed to have left the room. This was not a word he had expected at all.

"Offer?"

At that moment, Lady Eluned came in with servants who carried refreshment. She bade them put it down and then depart. She remained to open her own offering – a bottle of mead, the finest and famed, from her own Welsh family's estate. While she busied herself, Will answered.

"Edward would give you much in return for serving him well in Aderinyth. Do you agree to his conditions, you will rule there as your father intended, and none of your lands sacrificed."

Gryff only blinked at him as Lady Eluned placed a cup in his hand. He concentrated on holding it, forcing his numb fingers to function as he tried to take in everything Will had said with so few words. He finally shook his head in confusion, and spoke to the part of it he was most sure of, only to gain time to absorb the rest.

"As my father intended?" he asked skeptically, almost laughing at the idea. He could not recall if he had ever told Will of it, how often his father had praised Gryff's brothers for being so truly Welsh, so like the princes of old. Gryff himself had not been told outright that he was less admired, but he did not have to be. "There is naught he could have wanted less. He gave me as hostage so his eldest son and heir need never be corrupted by Norman ways."

Will gave him such a look that he began to doubt everything he had ever known of his life.

"Nay, Gryff. He was made to give over his heir, and he gave you." He shook his head, as though it were the most obvious of facts. "How else do you think Edward would have been content with you and not your brother, may God assoil him?"

He was so utterly sure that Gryff could only stare, frowning. His father had declared that he would follow Norman ways of inheritance, and that Aiden would be the sole heir. Everyone in Aderinyth knew it. Yet it was not Aiden who was given as hostage, as he should have been.

Gryff looked down into the amber liquid in his cup. The scent that rose from it was indelibly linked to his childhood, the rich fragrance of the same mead that had been served at his father's table. He was transported, a boy again as his father commanded him to learn the ways of the Normans. But also to never forget that he was Welsh. *They cannot take that from you without you permit it.*

Lady Eluned had handed a cup to Will and was now setting the bottle on the table between them. She had known his father, at least a little. She would understand. She would tell Will it could not be true.

"My father," he said to her, and then was caught in her piercing gray gaze. "Aiden was eldest. Always was Aiden meant to be heir."

She stayed still, looking at him as she took a slow and careful breath. She clasped her hands before her, her face a careful blank.

"Your father played a deep game," she said. "Is true he meant always to follow Norman ways in allowing only one son to inherit, and by custom it should be his eldest. But he knew well that the Welsh were not likely to win against Edward, and that in victory the king would give land and grant power as it pleased him." She glanced at her son, and then at the clerk who only seemed bored by this conversation. "Did the Welsh prevail, your father meant Aiden to inherit. But did they lose, he would have a son with a Welsh heart who might yet rule as a Norman."

It could not be true. He stared hard at her, trying to discern if this was a convenient lie, or conjecture, or a truth his father had given her directly. But she was an unyielding wall. She gave nothing away, and in the silence he began to see how it was possible.

All those years, he had so rarely heard from his father, or his brothers. The sudden distance had become unbridgeable, and now he saw that his father had planned it thus. To sever the close ties and allow Gryff to give all his undivided allegiance to the English king – and so that it might be easily believed that Gryff shared no politics with his treasonous family.

Almost he could feel his father's satisfaction from the grave. This moment, this outcome… All of it was exactly how he had planned it, should the Welsh fail.

Except he had not planned for Gryff to run and hide. He had never considered what it would mean for his son to be caught in the middle, ignorant of any grand scheme and fearing for his life.

Gryff could not raise his eyes to Lady Eluned now, nor to Will. He could only stare into his cup and think of Philip Walch, murdered for his loyalty to a prince he believed would return any moment. How many others were there, dead and persecuted, living in fear and hunger and worse, because Gryff had abandoned his people?

"Edward does not forget how well you advised him in the Welsh campaign," Will was saying as Lady Eluned exited. But Gryff was preoccupied with the sudden realization that this was why Rhodri had tried to kill him, and not his other brothers. He must have known or at least suspected their father's plan. "The king wants only what is due to him," explained Will. "You must pay homage to him publicly, swear your oath and some other arrangements as are customary – and Aderinyth is yours."

The words made his heart speed up. Aderinyth. He could go home.

Now the clerk stirred to life, pulling out parchments, citing the terms of old treaties that had been violated on both sides for generations. Amidst it all came another realization: if Gryff had known his father's mind, if he had not fled out of fear, he might have gone home already. Years ago.

The clerk was saying there were details to be settled, conditions to which Gryff must agree in order to be declared the lord of Aderinyth. He launched into a lengthy explanation of how the disputed southern border would be determined according to English law and not Welsh, but Gryff barely heard it.

He had never thought to rule; he had only ever wanted to go home. But what would there be left of his home if a Norman lord ruled there, or Rhodri? Already the people suffered with no leader to protect them from greed and spite. All because his father had thought he was so clever to play both sides.

A sudden memory came to him, of how once he had dared to argue with his father, saying Aderinyth should stop fighting and live peaceably as vassals to the English crown. He had not meant it to be an argument – he thought it was an obvious fact, because a prince should want only peace and prosperity for his people. But it had infuriated his father, who had shouted about pride and courage and ancient lineage. Gryff had looked at his flushed and angry face and struggled to find the words to say that there were ways besides war, other paths that might be taken to preserve power and gain advantage. He had been a child, though, and could only shout back that his father was selfish and just as cruel as the king he hated.

Now he saw how right he had been. How selfish it had been of his father, who had not wanted to sacrifice his title or lands or allegiance. How much more selfish it was for Gryff to have run away, thinking only of his own life, blithely forgetting that it was the people who paid the price. It was they who suffered and died, for one man's pride and another's cowardice.

No more could he think only of his own selfish desires. The home he had longed for could be preserved, his people protected. No more falconers would hang, no more useless wars would be fought.

He would not be a prince. But he could not be only a simple Welshman.

She would understand it. She must. They would find a way.

He interrupted the droning clerk. He did not care about details. "The charge to care for my people will be given to me and no other?" he asked Will. "I will be allowed to go home?" He could not keep the emotion from his voice on the last word.

Will nodded, solemn. "I swear it. The king swears it, do you do as he commands."

"I will," he answered. Home. "Whatever he commands."

✠ ✠ ✠

They were so long in discussion that he was almost surprised to find sunlight when they came down from the solar and into the yard. It seemed deserted, everyone still in the hall. He could hear music playing there, and the noise of people.

Gryff knew he must find Nan, and quickly. Will was saying that they would begin the journey now so that they might be at court tomorrow. It would leave little time to explain everything to Nan, and he did not want to speak to her in the crowded hall.

But when Will fell silent, looking over Gryff's shoulder, he knew she stood there. He turned to find her half-hidden at the corner of the tower, watching, only a few steps away. She wore her cloak over the blue dress, and all her defenses. The belt was too thick and plain for such a fine gown and the braces were strapped clumsily over the silk sleeves.

From her anxious look, her stance, he understood she waited there in preparation for action. To defend him, did they seek to carry him away by force. Through a rush of affection, he shook his head faintly and smiled to reassure her that all was well. Still she looked anxious, because she could not know that this party had come to protect him in case his bastard brother should learn he was here. It was why Robin had not brought the message sooner by himself, for fear Rhodri would intercept him and make mischief.

"Go you to your men, Will," he said, turning back to his friend. Already a servant had appeared, and Will was telling him to prepare the mounts. "They will be loath to leave off their merriment."

Will nodded. He glanced again in Nan's direction, then seemed to pointedly avoid looking at her.

"They will find merriment enough in Chesterfield, and I am glad you will join us for it. I will command them to prepare to leave at once." He smiled and clapped a hand on Gryff's shoulder. "Do not be overlong, Lord Gruffydd. Is possible your betrothed will be at court, and you would not wish to be late to meet her."

He walked to the hall, leaving Gryff alone in the deafening silence to wonder if the words had been calculated, or if it was merely that Will could not imagine that Nan would care.

It was a long moment until he could turn to face her. He seemed unable to move or breathe, incapable of any thought beyond the memory of her hand this morning, illuminated by the light of dawn, putting aside her last defense. For him.

Alone in the solar with Will and the royal clerk, it had seemed almost incidental, one of the many details the clerk had been tasked with. The king wanted an alliance, owed a favor to some lord, and a lady of high birth and meager dowry met all Edward's requirements for an advantageous match. This was how such things were done. It was how it must be done, if he was to obey his king.

But now as he felt Nan's eyes on him, it was real in a way it had not been only moments ago. Now it seemed faithless, indefensible. He turned and made himself look at her.

Her face was devoid of any expression. There was no surprise in her, and that was the most damning thing of all.

"I must marry," he said, because he must say something. He must explain it. He stepped toward her, stopping when he was near enough to touch her. "At the king's behest."

He could hear the cowardice in his words, the defensiveness. She could hear it too, he knew, and that was why she looked him in the eye. The startling blue unnerved him, reminding him of his first sight of her, a shock of compassion amid the violence.

"It is a condition of the agreement." He would not be so craven as to say he must do it to save his life. She would forgive that. But it was not for his life. It was for Aderinyth. "I have said I will not be a prince. But I will rule in Aderinyth, do I obey Edward."

She lowered her eyes then, just a little. Just enough to cut off the connection to him. Her expression never changed, flat and closed off, an absolute silence.

"My people suffer, Nan. Too long have I abandoned them to cruelty and death. Nor can I continue to flee my duty to them. I am the last of my family, the last to whom they will gladly give their hearts. I must care for them."

Only last night she had said it, and he had been sure she was wrong – that he was born to be a prince, that it was in his nature. His inescapable fate. So well did she know him. Better than he knew himself.

"Come with me," he said, and it sounded so different than it had an hour ago, when he had imagined saying it to her. Now it was a plea, a breath away from despair. He reached out to put a hand to her hair, and she did not pull away. His thumb moved lightly over her temple. "Come with me now, as we planned. There is naught that will stop us being together."

Almost could he feel her go cold beneath his hand. Such a stillness came over her that she might be made of marble, a carved angel in a cathedral. All the words that had sprung to his lips – about how it was a political alliance, how it meant nothing, how it need not be an impediment – they all dried up.

Her eyes met his, a look that cut through him and spoke plainly the words she had said so long ago. *I am no whore. Nor do I wish to become one.*

Now he understood the enormity of his misjudgment, the carelessness of his presumption. It did not matter that he would give her an honored place in his household, and the only place in his heart. Her children would be bastards. She would be seen as naught but a servant to his lust. And he would never be her simple Welshman.

Her gaze was steady, even as he let his hand drop from her. Men began spilling from the hall into the yard, loud voices and music, horses being brought forth in preparation for the journey.

"Nan," he said, despair closing like a fist over him. He wanted to go on his knees and beg her to come with him, even knowing it would not move her. "You must understand."

But she did understand. She knew what it meant to have a lord's duties, why he went and what her place would be if she followed. She understood it all, and she quietly rejected it. No words were necessary, and so she did not speak them.

He looked at the knife on her belt where her hand rested. Her Aunt Mary seemed to whisper in his ear, telling him Nan used to be the most chattering girl. He waited for her to draw the knife, to plunge it into him. Then he prayed for it, because anything was better than this silence.

Of course she would not give him words. Not curses, or platitudes, or even farewell. Of course not. He did not deserve them, arrogant fool that he was.

He would lose her, and it would be silent, because nothing could be more devastating.

But then she proved him wrong, and finally uttered words that cut him deeper than any blade.

"I believed you."

No anguish or recrimination. Just simple truth, and it felt like a fatal wound.

She remained a statue, never moving, a perfect and untouchable beauty. He waited for her to turn and leave him, dreading the sight of her walking away. It would feel like death. Already it felt like death.

When one of the servants brought him a horse with his small bag of possessions hung from the saddle, he could not bring himself to mount. Even when Will called to him and said they must start out before the light began to fail, he could not move.

Finally he realized that she would not move from where she stood. He would be the one to leave, not her. Oh, the things she said without words.

He never knew how he mounted, or whose horse it was. The only clear memories were Fuss, and Lady Eluned. Fuss looked up at him, barking anxiously, confused as to why Nan did not command him to follow Gryff.

Then as he looked away from the dog, afraid he would weep at the sight of its sweet and eager face, Lady Eluned appeared at his knee. She bade him a formal farewell and murmured in Welsh, "If there is a child, it will not be yours. Do you understand?"

He closed his eyes against the sharp stab of pain. He understood. Of course he did.

The feel of it as it leaves your hand, Nan had said to him. *You will know if you've done right by how it feels.*

But he felt only a cold sickness as he rode away from her. He felt nothing but her silence like a cloak of condemnation, her words lodged like a splinter in his heart.

Chapter Twenty-Four

He had thought it might be the falconers who would resist his authority most strongly, but it was the bards with whom he clashed immediately and most frequently. It was not their counsel he objected to, nor even their politics. It was their poetry.

"Better to lament my brothers were sacrificed so young than to praise the battles they fought," he had said – mildly, he thought, which was no easy thing when he was so disgusted.

When he had first arrived, the chief bard seemed intent on performing poem after poem about the noble defense of Aderinyth, how its fallen prince had fought most valiantly against foreign rule. Gryff said they must stop singing of senseless death as a glorious thing, and was told that he had no right to dictate how the bards composed their record of history. His rule was temporary, after all, while their work lived on for generations.

"There will be no praise for Edward the Norman king, save this one verse where he does recognize your authority," the chief bard had declared one day.

"That he returned you to us is his only worthy deed, my lord prince."

After the first month, Gryff had given up on trying to stop them from calling him prince. So long as the title was not given to his sons, the king did not care. Edward almost seemed to prefer it, so that he could boast of how princes knelt before him.

"Nor do I wish your poems to praise Edward," Gryff had said to the old bard, his patience worn thin after weeks of this same argument. "I ask only that you not stand in my hall and sing how righteous was my father's cause, and how good that so many died for it."

The bard gave his answer like it was another performance in the hall, when it was only a handful of advisors in the solar. He spread his arms wide. "Your father gave his sons and his life, all for the people of Aderinyth, and I will praise each drop of blood he shed. What does Prince Gruffydd know of sacrifice?"

Sacrifice. The word had echoed in Gryff's head while he swallowed down the anger, and pushed aside the memory of her face. Finally, he said that the bard's services were no longer required in his court, and dismissed him. He turned to Rhys, who was much younger but fully trained, and appointed him the new chief bard of the household. It broke with tradition, but he refused to bow to the old ways in all things.

He had chosen well. The young bard Rhys was eager to prove himself, but not so eager that he spoke only flattery. The poems he sang about the old princes praised their wisdom and generosity more than their valor in battle, and spoke more of the alliances made than the discord and strife that had torn Wales apart. He proved a pleasant companion all through the summer.

"Will my lord tell me of that time before he returned to his home and his people?" Rhys asked, not for the first time.

It was his duty to learn everything he could of Gryff's life and be witness to his reign, so that he could commit it to song. This was the old way a bond was formed between bard and lord, hours spent together advising and reminiscing, ensuring there was no corner of his mind that was a mystery to the poet.

But Gryff had avoided telling him anything beyond the moment when the thieves were slain. He was dimly amazed, almost amused at how easy it was to speak of the things that still disturbed his sleep sometimes. He told the bard of the fire at the abbey, the villainy of Baudry's men, and even Brother Clement's death. But then he merely said an armed party had saved him by chance. When prompted for more, he answered that he had soon learned the king would allow him to rule in Aderinyth, and so he had come.

The bard Rhys was no fool for all that he was young, but was careful in how he pressed for more. Now it was the night before Gryff's betrothed would arrive. They drank too deeply, and when Rhys asked again, the words slipped out.

"There was a girl with golden hair." The light of interest in Rhys' eyes was so keen it sobered him a little. Gryff rubbed a hand across his face, thinking of how she had told him not to hide from memory. He would fail her in that, too. "When I am old and gray, ask me again," he mumbled, and then took himself to his cold bed, where he tried to forget her mouth, her sighs, the beat of her heart.

He spent the morning observing the progress with the youngest goshawks. The falconers had not liked being told there would be no more strict secrecy about the nests. They had spent these past five years resisting in their own way, pretending to the Normans there were fewer birds come to nest and giving less than the promised number to the king. Most had bristled at Gryff's command to give an honest account of the nestlings to the king's men, but they obeyed him to a man.

They respected him because he had been trained by Philip Walch, and they obeyed him because he was their prince. It was Philip's son, himself a falconer, who had told him that after his father's death the falconers had agreed among themselves to obey no one but Prince Gruffydd. This was his comfort, to know that no more of them would die needlessly. Aderinyth's one resource would no longer be held hostage to spite a king, and could be used to make a better life for his people. All of it was only possible because he had returned to them.

Now he watched two young gyrfalcons spread their feathers under the midmorning sun and wished he could keep one for himself. But one must go to Edward, and the other sold to bring in sorely needed coin. If his wedding happened soon enough, perhaps Hal would come and be able to see these two before they were traded away. He could bring Tiffin.

Even that thought was painful. Hal. Tiffin. Nan in a dark yard throwing knives into a post. All the memories he should not hide from but could not look at, even the happy ones. Especially the happy ones.

Word came that Will's party was traversing the final hills, and Gryff went to the wall-walk atop the keep to watch their arrival. The castle that Edward had commanded built was barely started, but there was this one tower and it was enough to house the guests. Even better, it was set in a perfect place to overlook the hills and valleys of Aderinyth. It was a glorious view.

This was the only thing about returning home that held no disillusionment or aggravation. When he had come to the manor that he had called home as a boy, it had felt very different from what he remembered. The hall he had thought so enormous in his youth was, in reality, smaller than Lancaster's stables. His mother's solar was as dark and cramped as the hut in Wragby that he had thought so poor.

But the hills, the sharp peaks and the glimmer of mountain lakes, the river winding along the valley floor, the hawks wheeling against the sky – that was even bigger than he had remembered, and he took any excuse to come up here and look at it spread out before him.

When he saw the party making their slow way through the valley, he understood why they were more than a week later than anticipated. It was an absurd amount of baggage for one lady and her few attendants. In the end, he had not met her at court because she had spent the week in prayer at some shrine or another. They had yet to agree on a date to be wed, but now she was come to see this place that would be her home, and be married here.

"On my honor, Gryff, I would have warned you had I known."

It was the first thing Will said to him, under his breath, after they had greeted one another in the forecourt. He did not look weary as so many travelers did after the arduous journey through the hills, but his face betrayed an exasperation that Gryff had never seen before, so practiced was Will at hiding anything as petty as annoyance.

The cause of his irritation was Gryff's intended, Lady Margaret, who seemed so devoted to prayer that she had little thought for any earthly concerns. This included the inconvenience she caused by insisting on traveling with so much baggage, and stopping several times every day for rest and prayer. Even in her greeting to Gryff, her first question was to ask where the chapel was so that she might give thanks for their safe journey.

He was happy to point her to it, and ignored her obvious disapproval that he did not join her. Instead he had some beer brought for Will and showed him the gyrfalcons, and the progress on the castle.

The servants were a mix of Welsh and English, and all were eager to see to the comfort of the guests. The feast was impressive and the entertainment in the hall was even better, to Gryff's mind, than what a Norman keep could offer. Hospitality and poetry were both held sacred here, and sincerely shared with every visitor. He had almost forgotten that.

"I vow it is more beautiful here than ever you could describe," said Will that evening. They sat together in the chamber set aside for him, with its window that looked out onto the northern ridge, drinking and talking into the night. "Will we go hawking tomorrow? Nor can I stay long, so much has your betrothed delayed me, but there will be time to fly a falcon or two."

"Aye, we will."

Gryff almost thanked him again for escorting Lady Margaret but thought it better to speak of anything else, so much did the thought of her sour his mood. She was a rather timid and bland-looking lady, who dressed so plain and modest that he wondered what she could have filled her baggage with. There seemed little to her character at all, aside from an overabundance of piety. It was probably why Will disliked her overmuch. He had a particular aversion to religious fervor.

Gryff turned the talk instead to affairs in Will's lands, and the prospect of Edward's intended crusade. It was pleasant, a welcome thing to see Will so relaxed and unguarded. "Time away from court suits you well, Will," he said.

"It does," he replied. "It can be a poisonous place."

A silence fell between them that went on long enough that Gryff knew it was not by chance. He braced himself to hear some bit of unwelcome news, some new thing the king wanted of him. But Will's words, when they came, were a different kind of blow. He did not look at Gryff as he said them, but at the fire.

"She is not with child," he said quietly, and took a long drink of his wine.

They had never spoken a word of it, but there was no doubt what he meant. Gryff stared at the embers. He wondered what exactly Will knew, and how he knew it. He wondered if he could be trusted, if his mother had confided anything about it, if anyone else at court knew.

He didn't ask any of it. He just looked at the embers for a very long time in silence, and mourned a child that had never been more than a forbidden dream.

"Where is she?" he asked. He had tried to imagine her at Morency, with Fuss at her heels as she tracked down thieves or chased off poachers. Now he wondered if she was with Lady Eluned in the north of Wales, and felt a violent stab of jealousy at the thought that Will might have seen her recently.

"She journeys to Burgundy, and then on to Basel." Will reached for the bottle and poured more wine into Gryff's cup. He very kindly did not look Gryff in the face. "Some task she has undertaken for Lord Robert, to see some cargo safely through England and then to distant shores."

Burgundy. Basel. They would not even share an island. No more could he imagine, when he looked at the eastern hills, that she was just beyond them. He fought down a sudden anger at her, the bitterness he carried every day in a secret corner of his heart, because she had not come with him. She should be here. She would never be here, because she rejected what little he could give her.

Never will she truly need you, Philip Walch had taught him about fierce and beautiful creatures. *She will stay with you so long as it suits her, but she will never be tame.*

He knew he must try to stop wanting her. He must. Even if he could do the impossible – find a way to give her more, or bring himself to abandon his people – it was too late. The knowledge sat like a heavy stone in his breast, a lifeless weight that threatened to suffocate him. She did not want him now. Her face when he left her was all he saw when he closed his eyes.

He was just another lord, like all the others who had used her.

"I would like to drink until I am blind with it," he announced.

"A fine idea," agreed Will. He drank down what was in his cup and reached for the bottle to pour more. "By God, I would like that too, after that journey. I hope you like your wife better than I do, or you will spend all your days blind drunk."

"Another fine idea," Gryff said, and held out his cup to be filled again.

✠ ✠ ✠

Will stayed less than a week, which was long enough to help negotiate a date for Gryff to be wed and to issue a warning about Rhodri.

"There has been no word of him. He is not in Rome and I would wager my own inheritance he does not journey there." Will looked around the crowded hall suspiciously, as though Rhodri might appear from the shadows. "You are certain sure these men can be trusted?"

Gryff shrugged. "I know they have no love for Rhodri. They have given proof enough, and I may put my faith in that."

Rhodri had left the king's court the same afternoon that Gryff had arrived. He had gone immediately to Aderinyth, hoping to claim it as his own with the support of the people – but he had found a cold welcome. For years, the story of how he had tried to kill Gryff had been sung by the bards, who painted him as the villain he was. The people of Aderinyth would not tolerate him, and he had barely escaped with his life.

Will loved that story, and asked Rhys to set it to verse and sing it every night of his visit.

After being run out of Aderinyth, Rhodri had announced that he would go to Rome and appeal to the Pope. It was too ridiculous to be taken as anything but jest; he knew as well as anyone that the Church cared nothing about this dispute. But Rhodri had disappeared and for nearly three months now, there had been no sign of him in England or Wales. Either he was licking his wounds in private or plotting to somehow usurp Gryff's place.

"Were I to die, would Edward grant him these lands?" Gryff asked.

"I hope not," was Will's answer. "But I dare not say it is impossible. We have a pragmatic king in Edward, and he sees the value in having a Welshman of the old blood as ruler here, one who owes his place to him."

More than ever, Gryff did not like to think how Rhodri would rule these people if allowed. It was another vindication of his decision to return, despite the cost.

If not for Will's persistence, they might never have settled on a date for the wedding. Lady Margaret seemed as disinclined to wed as Gryff did. She rejected every proposed date, citing Church restrictions on certain days of the week and saints' days and the many periods of abstinence – all of which, when considered together, did not allow any day of the year when they might hold a wedding feast. Finally, they had agreed on a day just after Michaelmas, and the decision hung like a millstone around his neck. Guests would begin arriving in only a few weeks.

His future wife's only redeeming feature was that she was not outright scornful of his people. She very obviously found their customs strange – the Welsh habit of warm familiarity that was more egalitarian than the Norman way seemed especially difficult for her – but she seemed to be attempting to adapt to it. Gryff saw little of her, as she kept to the chapel and her chambers in the tower, and he preferred it that way. He could not imagine their wedding night, or ever being happy to go to the bed of a woman so meek and pious.

One day after Will had left, Gryff came to the solar in the old manor house to find her there without her ladies, standing alone at the window. He felt a flash of anger toward her, because she stood where he had imagined Nan so many times.

They were nothing alike, in looks or temperament. Lady Margaret's silence was not soothing. There was no mystery to it, or quiet communication, or even peace. He only felt quietly judged with every breath.

"My lord," she said, and cast her eyes down demurely as she stood with folded hands.

It was not fair to her, or to the people who would soon call her their lady, to treat her as a stranger and a burden. It was not only the Welsh who called him lord, and his treatment of her would be seen as a reflection of his feelings for the English under his rule.

So he tried. He said that he hoped to keep this manor house despite the new castle being built nearby, but she only nodded. He asked if she liked the view of the valley from this window, and she nodded again. It was only when he said that this had been his mother's solar and that she too was very devoted to her prayers that Lady Margaret showed anything like interest.

"Your mother lives with the sisters at Cairusk," she said. Her voice was so timid he thought it must be an affectation, put on because she thought it would please him. "Always have I wanted… I have thought myself more suited to that kind of life."

This was hardly a surprise, but he bit his tongue against saying it. Her father gave her not to the Church, but in marriage. No matter her preference, she could not be married without her consent, so she must have agreed to this.

"My mother passed many hours in prayer, yet served as lady to her husband and her children, and to our people." He looked at her bowed head, her submissive pose, and felt more lonely than he had ever felt in his life. "In faith, I hope you will find such a life pleasing to you."

She nodded again, never looking up at him, and asked if he would join her in prayer this evening, after the meal. He declined as gallantly as he could manage, telling her it was not his habit, that he spent those hours in important tasks that could not wait for morning.

It was the first of what was sure to be many lies to this woman he must soon call wife. After the meal, he spent the evening in discussion with the master falconer, and an hour talking with the bard of inconsequential matters.

Then he went to his chamber and whispered his own prayers in the dark, as he did every night. As he knew he would do for as long as he lived. Mary, Ida, Isabella, Gwenllian, Eluned. He thanked God for them, because they had saved her.

He would not forget their names, because he could not forget her.

Chapter Twenty-Five

She knew the hills to the northwest were Aderinyth, and she felt a nervous fluttering under her skin every moment as she rode past them. She did not look in their direction, keeping her eyes fixed on the spot between the mule's ears and trying not to hear the other travelers talk about it – how the terrain made attack so difficult that it had protected the place for years, how it was famed for the falcons and hawks that nested there, how its prince was newly returned.

It took a full day of travel until the hills began to fade from sight. Suddenly panicked at the thought that she would otherwise never see it, she turned at the last moment. There were too many shades of green to count, and the evening light fell on shifting mists that clung to the high peaks. She looked for a glimmer of water high in the hills, remembering the lake where he had gone with his brothers to find the fairy queen, but saw only a falcon that soared out of the mists. Her heart gave a painful throb at the sight.

Even in that one glance, it was easy to see why he had longed for this place so deeply, and for so long. It was easy to see why he would do anything to return.

When there was no more to be seen, she turned her attention back to the road. She was not truly needed to guard this party. The men who did this work regularly for Lord Robert were more experienced and knew the road and its dangers far better than she ever could. They were efficient and courteous and – after a man twice her size had put a hand low on her back and she cut off half his mustache with a flick of her wrist – they left her alone. Fortunately that was the most trouble there had been on this journey.

At Whitting she had gone to Lord Robert, not even questioning why, only knowing that it would be a comfort just to be near him. He was looking out at the site where they were building a storage place for the wine, and she watched the progress with him. She thought of the time when he had wiped her tears and soothed her by telling her how a good wine was made. His was the only idle talk that she ever welcomed, because his voice was so warm and kind.

But he did not speak idly that day. He had asked if she would return to Morency.

He and Lady Eluned would go to their own home at Dinwen, and though she knew she was welcome there, it caused a searing pain to imagine herself in Wales. Yet the thought of going back to Morency made her want to weep, for no reason she could name.

"I know not where to go," she had answered. "If it would please my lord, I could stay here at Whitting." She could bide here through days and nights without number, just as he had asked her. She could haunt the place, useless and silent and solitary.

But Lord Robert knew her well enough to say, "It would please me to give you a task that I would trust to no other."

He told her that the wine was arrived from his lands in France and would be delivered to the buyers, who were in many places throughout England. In Lincoln, the carts would be emptied of casks and filled with wool to be taken to Burgundy. They would also carry Elias ben Joseph and his family, did they choose to come. Lord Robert trusted his men with wine and wool, but to guard and care for a family was different. "I know you will see them safe out of Lincoln," he said.

Could he know how she dreaded that place? Had he sent her there deliberately, to force her out of her listlessness? She would never know. Her only certainty was that she could not refuse him any request, no matter how difficult, so she agreed to it. He said she could even accompany the party all the way to Basel, if she wished. It was not necessary, but perhaps she would like to see more of the world.

As she turned to go and prepare herself for the journey, he said, "With time it will fade, Nan. The heartache. It will become more bearable."

She stared at his profile, her breath short. "My heart does not ache," she lied, because he had no right to speak of it. Because he could not know what it was like.

"Your pardon," he murmured. She had not thought it was possible to feel worse, but his kindness made her wretched. "When I was young I loved a lady who was far above me. My heart did ache to lose her. I have thought it is much the same for you."

She looked at the lines around his eyes, evidence of a thousand smiles, and tried to imagine him heartbroken for any woman who was not Lady Eluned. It seemed impossible. Yet he had married her only six years ago, which meant he must have spent many years in heartbreak.

"Was there no comfort for you?" she asked him.

"Only the knowledge that if she had abandoned all to be with me, many more were like to have suffered." He had looked at her then, kind eyes and a sad smile. "In truth, I cared naught for any suffering but my own, for that is the nature of heartbreak. Yet did it comfort me to know it was not lack of love that kept us apart."

She wanted to ask him how long it would be until the pain was bearable. Or how he knew the lady had truly loved him, if she had given him up. Or if he had felt a terrible anger, as she did, to be left behind. But she only looked at him and kept the words locked up inside of her, where they would burn for the rest of her days.

"It was my idea to send you to Morency, you know." She blinked at him, startled. "I told you once, that I did think my lady wife wished you to be a true friend, and not her servant. I knew if you did not leave her side and make your own way, you might never let yourself be her equal. And because she thought it best for you, she put aside her sorrow and bade you go."

Nan knew she could never bring herself to call Lady Eluned her friend, though she was that and more. Friend and mother and savior, her protector and her confidante. "Never could I be equal to so great a lady," she said.

He smiled fondly at her. "Already are you her equal. You have only to believe it, and you will be as great as she."

Perhaps it was true. But it could not make her a lady.

Soon after, she had left to meet the baggage train, ignoring Robin's request to accompany him first to Morency and then go on to Lincoln from there. She was too eager to be among people who had not known the Welshman, to have a purpose to her days again, to spend her time on the alert with a knife in hand, ready for something. Anything. So she had passed the summer guarding carts of wine barrels from one town to another. It felt strange to use the main roads, after so many months of disregarding them, but she grew accustomed.

They must pass some days in Lincoln, so she went to Wragby to see how Aunt Mary fared. She spent a day in cleaning again, and cooking, and refusing to take the mule back with her. "I have no use for him, Aunt Mary," she insisted. She endured the questions about her fine Welshman – where was he, and was it true he beat a man at the market? Nan said only that he had gone home, and then ignored the questions about her sister.

She made sure to avoid the southern road, and Bargate. Even to think of the woman who had once been her sister hurt, but she found she was accustomed to hurt. In Lincoln she tried to avoid the falconer's home entirely. But she must be sure little

Cecilia was well. She braced herself when she went to the door, but the falconer and his wife were not at home. The girl was thriving, so happy and smiling that she seemed a different person entirely.

When she offered a plate of stew to Nan, proud that she had made it herself, her face shining, Nan shocked herself by bursting into tears. Poor Cecilia – no, her name was Erma now, it had always been Erma. The girl could not know that it was little Bea that had appeared in Nan's mind. Bea as she might have been. Bea as she never would be, because wishes were nothing against the cruel realities of the world.

There was no trouble for Elias and his family when they left. They brought little with them, having sold nearly everything. Nan had to turn away from the sight of him as they left the house that his grandfather's grandfather had built. The look on him was one of such grief that it felt wrong to witness it.

It had been his home, his children's home, his father's home – and he must leave it, knowing he would likely never see it again. This was hiraeth being born.

Every night since, she had lain awake and thought of it. It made her understand the choice the Welshman had made, and took the sharpest edge off her anger. She had never had a home, not truly. As a child, her family had moved from place to place with the seasons, rarely the same village twice. There was no place she could call her own, and there never had been. Her heart dwelled in the people she loved. And if she had been forced to choose between keeping them safe and being with him, would she have chosen any differently than he had?

As the mountains surrounding Aderinyth diminished into the distance, she made herself imagine him not as her Welshman, but as their prince. Like the mountains that protected his land, he was the only thing that stood between the people, powerless and vulnerable, and the might of Norman lords who would take all that they could. He had been starving with a well-fed falcon on his wrist, because the great were not ruled – could not be ruled – by their own selfish desires.

He had always been a great lord. She had wanted him to be less than he was, only so she could have him.

"Have you never been on the sea?"

It was Marcus who asked it, one of the younger men of Lord Robert's hired guard. She shook her head and tried to look unfriendly, though he had always been respectful of her. He began to describe the upcoming journey, reminiscing with the other men over past bouts of seasickness.

They were at an inn awaiting the ship that would take them to France, and she was surprised and pleased to see how well the men behaved in this port town. Elias and his family were safely in their chamber above with Fuss guarding their door, and Nan had come to the common room below. It was filled with half-drunken travelers and there was no reason for her to be here at all – and many reasons for her to avoid such a place – but she did not want to be alone with her thoughts.

Soon she would cross the sea. She would not return for months. She might not return at all.

It felt like running away because it was. She wanted to be far away when he took a wife. If France agreed with her, she might find some kind of work. She would build a life that made sense, far from all of this. She would stop thinking of green hills one day.

The sound of men speaking Welsh nearby reached her, tugged at her though she tried not to hear. In France, she told herself, there would be no Welsh to haunt her. It would not drift to her when she least wanted to hear it.

But soon she would not hear it at all, and so she listened in spite of herself. Among all their drunken chatter, she heard a name that put a dread in her. *Rhodri.*

It might be any Rhodri. It was a common enough name. It was none of her affair. But then: Aderinyth. The prince. Wedding. Slay him.

She calmed her breath and slowed her heart. She did not think. She only eased away from her small party to move closer to the corner where three men sat talking. One seemed almost sober, at least enough that he warned the other two to keep their voices down. He was answered with laughter, and the insistence that there were no Welsh here besides them, so there was naught to fear. He looked up at that moment and saw her.

Nan knew the look. It was always either this wolfish look or the worshipful one. Always a whore or an angel.

He called out to ask if she was for sale, his eyes moving over every inch of her, and she pretended not to hear. It terrified her, that look. It turned her knees to water every time. She concentrated on not putting a hand to the knife on her belt, the only one she wore that they could see.

"Look at her, it needs a soft touch," said the man who was more drunk. He was older, the obvious leader of their group. "Put your eyes back in your head, for decency, if you will woo her."

This was where she would slip away, in the normal way of things. But they had said *the prince, Rhodri, slay him.* So when the more sober man switched to English and beckoned her, she came. She saw his face when she stepped into the light, her features no longer in shadow, and thought of what her lady had once said to her about beauty. That it was an asset, a power, a thing that might be wielded like a weapon.

Nan had never learned to use it that way, because the power to stir a man's lust only frightened her. She preferred a weapon that was under her control, not subject to the whims of others.

But she looked in this man's eyes and saw he was caught. He would let her near and tell her what she wanted to know and never even ask who she was. All because she had a face he liked.

"You are Welsh?" she asked him.

After he nodded, she feigned a shyness of his friends and he came to join her a little away from them. It was easy, except for the terrified pounding of her heart. She filled his cup with the strongest ale and made herself smile once or twice. She asked him if he knew of Rhodri, the bastard brother of the newly returned prince. She said little, and his eagerness to impress her made him talk too much.

It required less than an hour and two more servings of ale to learn everything. He and his companions were to travel to Aderinyth where Rhodri waited, their movements easily lost amid the many guests who had begun to arrive in the weeks before the wedding. They were part of a small party of mercenaries who would be paid well to aid him in his plan to slay the prince.

"I am promised enough land that I may keep a hundred sheep," he said, leaning close.

She did not recoil, even when he put an arm over her shoulder. She only smiled and looked right in his eyes, and when he sighed and said she was so very comely, she swallowed her fear and asked him what was the village where Rhodri waited. He said the name of the place three times, because her tongue tripped in trying to pronounce it, wasn't Welsh such a strange language? How kind of him to help her learn it.

She almost felt sorry for him when she slipped from under his arm, and she heard him lose his balance and hit the floor behind her. He would probably look for her when he was sober tomorrow, if he remembered. But she would be gone.

✠ ✠ ✠

"What is he like, your prince?"

It was impossible to refrain from talking with the Welsh whom she met when she crossed into Aderinyth. They opened their homes to her, and shared what little they had, and refused to take any kind of payment. It was their duty, they said over and over again, to welcome guests warmly and never leave them wanting if they could help it. All they ever seemed to expect in return was her company.

So she talked when they expected it, answering their questions and asking her own. The old man who served as her guide had brought her in four days to the heart of Aderinyth, taking her along hidden ways through the mountains, away from towns and villages. He was so hale that she was ashamed at how much more easily he climbed the hills while she struggled to keep up.

"I have heard as he does not like to be called a prince," said the old man. "He tells us the king in England is our true leader now, and we must remember Prince Gruffydd bows to him always. But no other man the king has sent has been so good, and the prince is one of us for all his Norman ways."

A young girl had joined them in this last leg of the journey, having business near the village they sought. She was daughter to a falconer, and said she had met the prince many times.

"There are some bards who like him not, and some of the falconers, too," she said now as they climbed the last hill. "In truth, their hate is only for King Edward. And their bitterness counts as naught against the many who do love our prince well. He has made a way for us to trade with the towns more easily. It will save many from hunger when the snows come. He'll not let it be like last winter, he said."

There was a reverence in the girl's voice, the kind of bone-deep gratitude that Nan recognized easily. The king had ordered castles built throughout Wales, and new towns founded for the English to settle. It was forbidden for the Welsh to live in the towns, one of many laws that seemed to Nan to impose an impossible hardship. But their lord had spent the summer in hearing their complaints and doing everything in his power to ease the pain caused by the new laws.

"Here it is," said the old man as they crested the hill.

A little village lay below, no more than a dozen small homes. In the distance she could see a keep – a single tower on a hill, the beginnings of a new castle. There was movement everywhere, builders moving stone and earth, visible even from this distance. Nan fixed her eyes on a figure standing at a wide window, just a tiny speck from here. It might be him.

This was his home. It fit him perfectly.

She paid the old man for his help in bringing her here, and watched him walk back over the hill after a lengthy farewell. The falconer's daughter looked suspicious when Nan had no ready answer for who she was visiting. But the girl pointed to a spacious barn at the edge of the village and said it must be where Nan was going, as some other guests had been brought there recently.

"Strange how they keep to themselves," she said. "Though always has it been a strange village. My father says the bastard's mother lived here, and is mostly her kin that live here now."

She bid Nan a farewell, and left her not far from the barn.

Even after days of travel, it seemed too sudden. She felt too alone – she had never done anything like this entirely alone, with no armed fellows or a careful plan. All she had was Fuss, who was like to be more trouble than not. If there were many men and much fighting, she would worry for him when she could least afford to lose attention.

"Stay," she whispered to him, and gave him the hand signal for the same.

He dutifully sat, hidden in this little cluster of trees at the edge of the village. She remembered him as a pup, how he had curled into the crook of her neck, pinning her hair, his comical little snores in her ear. He had soothed her to sleep when nothing else could, and then had learned to be useful to her in other ways – things she had taught him only as an excuse to keep him beside her.

She thought of her Welshman – no longer starving, nor captive to villains, nor flinching in fear of his own shadow. He was well and whole, soaring as high and strong as one of his falcons. But though she had wished otherwise, he was more than just her Welshman.

A prince had many defenses. He had knights and men-at-arms, a land full of people who would die to protect him. She could alert any one of them to the danger. But a prince – a good prince – would show mercy to his enemy. He would imprison him, or banish him. He would let the viper live.

"I must keep him safe, Fuss." She rubbed a hand over the dog's ears. "You understand."

The sun was beginning to set, so she took off her cloak and put down her small bag of belongings. She opened it, setting the last of the dried strips of meat before Fuss. He gave her his hopeful but suspicious look, unsure of this sudden bounty. She wished there was some way to tell him to go to the tower if she did not come back.

A man appeared at the side of the barn. The light was low, but she knew at a glance that he was the Welshman's brother. The resemblance made her angry, even as she felt a lurch in her stomach to see an echo of the face she held in her heart.

He slipped into the building, and she had a brief glimpse of the other men within. There was no way to say how many were there.

She breathed deep and reached behind her to pull out the dagger Gwenllian had given her so long ago. As night began to fall she whispered her prayers of thanksgiving, added another to ask for aid in her task, and yet another to ask forgiveness for the mortal sin she would commit. God would surely forgive her. He loved the Welshman no less than she did.

She gave Fuss one last scratch under the chin. Then she stepped forward into the darkness.

Chapter Twenty-Six

They brought him Rhodri's body a little more than a week before the wedding was to take place.

"There was one other dead, my lord prince, and three wounded who yet live. All have confessed that they followed his command, with murder in mind."

The captain of the guard continued, explaining that those who survived could not agree on who the attacker had been – only that it had been done quickly and suddenly, just as twilight fell – but Gryff knew it was her even before he saw the single blade that had been left in Rhodri's throat.

He removed it himself, slipping a nail into the hole where the hilt should be and pulling it free. His hand would not let it go. He looked down at the body and remembered the rat dead of a poison that had been meant for him all those years ago.

He gave orders for the surviving conspirators to be questioned further, and announced they would be judged according to Norman law. When his captain suggested that Rhodri's head be set on a spike above the tower, as Edward had done to his enemies, Gryff forbade it immediately. The men of his guard seemed to think this was because he thought it too gruesome a sight for the wedding feast, but he had not even considered that.

"We will not follow such a savage example," he announced. Not all Norman ways were superior. "Let him be buried in the valley where all princes of this land rest, for he was my father's son. But the ground will not be consecrated, nor will his grave be marked."

Later he would speak to Rhys and ask the bard to compose verses about how Rhodri need not have met such an end had he accepted Norman rule. Gryff felt no sympathy for his bastard brother, but he could not deny it was tragic that Rhodri had spent his life in resentment because he clung to a dead tradition. It was Gryff's duty to make sure his people understood that they must adapt if they were to survive.

Lady Margaret expressed horror when she was told of it that evening, and wondered if they should not be wed until the new year.

"What if others who wish you harm are among the guests?" she asked, and Gryff struggled to hide his amusement at this obviously manufactured concern. There was too much hope in her at the idea of postponement, just as there had been far too much difficulty in choosing a date.

He looked at her, so demure and colorless, overwhelmed by the stone walls of this place that she was meant to call home. Never would she slay an enemy. She was a lady, with all the docile virtues praised in courtly songs.

It suddenly seemed a great sin to give his people a puppet for a prince, and this subdued woman for their lady. She was perfectly acceptable, but not more than that. She would have pity for the Welsh, but she would never understand them or the deprivation they suffered. What children she gave him would be like her: dutiful and timid, removed and restrained. She could not teach them how to be fierce in defense of what they loved, nor how to survive unspeakable hardship. Never would she dare to tell him he was wrong, or move closer to his side when danger threatened.

There had been another wound just under Rhodri's ribcage, made by a long blade that would have reached his heart, as though she would not leave anything to chance. Now he looked at the blade he held, the one she had left behind. Short, sharp, wicked. Only a day ago – hours – it had been on her arm and felt the beat of her pulse.

She should be in France. But instead she was here. For him.

"I will not marry you," he said, the words spoken before he had even realized his intention. He did not let himself think of the consequences. He did not care. "Forgive me. I will not."

Lady Margaret blinked first in incomprehension, then stared at him in astonishment – and he realized it was the first time he had seen a frank reaction from her. She lowered her head slightly as though to hide it, and bid her ladies leave them. They hurried out of the room, leaving him alone with her.

"Have I so displeased you, my lord, that you will renounce the promise you have made to my father and our king?"

He did not know how to answer truthfully, so he did not answer it at all. Instead he read the silence that came from her and found that beneath her carefully composed, meek demeanor, her mind was working feverishly. It was entirely unexpected, as surprising as if she had sprouted wings.

"By Mary, I believe you are full relieved I will renounce it." He could not stop the incredulous smile that came over his face. "You do not wish to marry me?"

She gripped her hands together and blurted, "I do not wish to marry anyone, my lord!" She looked up at him with something like impatience. "Nor can I see that it matters what my wishes are. I must marry. My father commands it."

"You cannot be married without you consent to it. Would you not rather pledge yourself to a life of devotion? Would your father dare gainsay a calling from God?"

Her breath sped up. She glanced toward the door, where her ladies no doubt waited outside, trying to hear whatever they could. He could see the idea take hold of her, a spark in her eye as she considered it.

Will would hate him for this. It was he who had chosen her – there was some advantage to him in getting her married off to just the right man, some intricate web of alliances and favors that Gryff had not bothered to learn. It only made him feel a sudden sympathy for this woman, who was as much a pawn as he was. Now her eyes were alight with intelligence, the meek passivity tossed aside. What a terrible thing, that she had been so forced to hide her true nature beneath this submissive mask.

"Go now to the abbey of your choosing, and give yourself to God," he said. "I will send men of my guard as escort. You may say in truth to your father that I did refuse this marriage, and it is none of your doing."

She was frowning in concentration, her mind calculating. She nodded once, twice, then looked up at him again with a curious mixture of decision and doubt and, surprisingly, concern for him.

"But will there not be consequences to you, my lord? Why would you defy your king?"

He curled his fingers around the knife in his hand, evidence that she had been here. That she did not revile him. That she still cared for him.

For love, he might answer. For his people, for himself. For the blood he had cursed, for the title he had thought meant nothing. For her.

"Because I am a prince," he said, his eyes on the blade in his hand. "Because I was born to be Gruffydd ab Iorwerth, not a common Welshman, and I will defy the whole world if I must."

✠ ✠ ✠

A falconer's daughter said the fair lady who spoke their language so well was on foot, and could not have traveled far. He sent riders to the nearest villages to seek any news of her while he arranged an escort for Lady Margaret, who was quick enough to travel now that the destination was more desirable.

The abbey she named was not far from Will's home, so he sent word ahead to ask that Will would see her small party was accommodated as they passed through his lands. He told the cleric who wrote the message to be clear that it was not Lady Margaret at fault, that Gryff had chosen another bride, and that his most fervent wish was that Lady Margaret arrive at the abbey quickly and without incident. He could only hope that Will would forgive him for thwarting his plans, and smooth the way with King Edward.

Then he began preparations for his own journey. If he did not find her, he would go to Lady Eluned. He would prostrate himself before her, if he must, and ask where Nan had gone.

In the end he did not have to go further than a few miles. It was only the next day, just an hour after his former betrothed had departed, that he found himself outside the tiny village church. He remembered it well from his youth.

Father Ifor had heard her confession just that morning, and said she had gone up the mountain path to see the lake. The priest did not believe in any such pagan ideas as fairy queens, but he did recall that the princes had often wandered there when they were very young. It seemed to please her, he explained to his prince, and though she said she was headed north, she and her little dog had taken the path up to see the place. They had not yet come down.

It was the same path Gryff had imagined her on, a hundred times. The same lake where he had dreamt she stood, with flowers at her feet and dagger in hand.

He commanded his guard to stay at the foot of the path, and climbed.

He found Fuss first, waiting near the top of the path among the trees, keeping guard. The dog was overjoyed to see him, whining and dancing, falling to the ground on his back with tail thumping as Gryff rubbed his belly. When he moved forward Fuss did not run ahead to warn her, but stayed at Gryff's ankles, looking up at him with tongue lolling happily as they walked.

She stood at the edge of the water, looking out over it. She wore her cloak, the hood down and her hair pulled loosely back, falling free of its simple tie, the mountains rising up all around her. He felt the sight engrave itself onto his heart.

She must know it was him, because she only stood and waited. He knew every inch of her so well that though he saw naught but her cloak, he knew her hand had gone to the weapon at her belt and now eased away from it. Her breath was held as he came toward her.

When he stood beside her, an arm's length away, he held out her blade. She looked down at it, but did not take it.

"I dreamed of you here," he said to the tender curve of her lashes, the gentle flush in her cheek. "All my brothers and me, facing you. You were to choose one of us to be king, and I was filled with such a dread that I woke."

She looked up at him, blue eyes roaming over his face like she was learning it anew. The beauty of her struck him again, but it affected him far less than the simple fact of her nearness. Close enough to touch, when he had thought never to see her again.

"It is not mine to choose who rules here," she said, answering him in his language, and dropped her eyes.

"Nay, that choice is not yours." He reached out and took her forearm, slipping the knife into the brace. "Yet the blade is yours."

His hand held her wrist, thumb over her speeding pulse. There was a calm resolve in her, a certainty at the center of her unease. She waited to see what he would do, knowing she had slain men in the shadow of his keep, not regretting it at all though it may mean her own death.

How poor a prince she must think him, if she believed for one instant that this was why he sought her.

"You would have given him mercy," she said.

He did not deny it. He only set his thumb over the warmth of her pulse and remembered his first sight of her. "Will you always save me, Nan?"

Her fingers uncurled, knuckles brushing loosely against the inside of his wrist – and then moved against his skin with a purpose, a tiny caress.

"If I could."

It was barely a whisper. He watched her eyes press closed, just for a moment, savoring the touch. Then she lifted her hand away and turned, reaching to pull her hood up, stepping away as though she would leave now, already, with so few words.

"Stay." His voice too was barely above a whisper, because to watch her walk away closed his throat. But she heard him and halted, her hands still gripping the hood. "I have renounced my betrothal. I will marry no one but you."

She did not move for a long moment. There was no expression on her face, only a numb stillness. "You cannot renounce it."

"I can. I have."

It seemed to him his heart had stopped beating, lying dead in his chest, waiting for her to speak. After a moment she shook her head just barely, her brows drawing together in confusion as though she worked to decipher his words.

"You cannot." Her hands had dropped the hood to her shoulders and she looked up at him. "You must do as the king commands. You must, if you are to live, and rule."

He wanted to kiss the frown from her lips, but he only drank in the sight and sound of her. "I will rule with you by my side, or not at all."

She was shaking her head, denying it, staring at him until he saw her finally understand that he meant it. It did not gladden her, or make her throw herself into his arms. She only pulled her cloak tightly around herself and turned to look again at the sparkling lake.

"You belong here. It's why you felt the loss so keenly, because you are meant to be here." Her eyes scanned the peaks around them. "You are not meant to give it up."

"Nor am I meant to live without you."

She only shook her head again, so stubbornly sure, refusing to believe him. Of course she would not believe him. He had given her every reason to disbelieve.

"Nan, listen to me." Urgency strained his voice. "Think you that I do not know the risk? Think you that I would not give this and more – as much as you would give to keep me safe?"

Silence. Always silence, because she thought it was only words. He stepped closer to make her hear him.

"Let him take my land. Let him take my power and my title and my name. Let him take all of it, every possession to the very clothes off my back – and at the end I will come to you on my knees, pitiful and powerless, just as you found me. And I will call him a fool for making so poor a trade, for before God I swear that you are a prize greater than any kingdom."

She blinked rapidly. He could almost feel her barriers crumbling, all her feeling flooding free of its careful containment. She looked out on the green hills. It was the same way he looked at them, with love and wonder. "You belong to this place," she said. "It belongs to you."

"Aye," he agreed. "It is my heart. And my heart is naught but a desert without you." He looked at her in the midst of the mountains, the shimmering water, the wide sky. "Well do I know it is what I deserve for leaving you, that no place on this earth can be home to me, without you are in it."

She looked up at the sky and took a ragged breath, fighting off tears. Fuss was whining faintly, pressing himself against her feet but looking at Gryff, confused. "I think me it would be a great sin, to take you from your people."

"I care naught for sin or virtue." He looked at Fuss sitting at her scuffed boots, and at the purse of nails on her belt, and how a strand of hair clung to her neck. "Gladly would I give my soul into the fires of hell if you would have me, even if only for a day."

She made a choked sound, more tears than laughter. "And I would call you a fool to make such a poor trade."

He was a fool. Only a fool would ever have let her go. Only a fool would stand here, wanting to touch her, seeing her tears, loving her even more because she thought of his people and of him, but never of herself – yet still he was as uncertain as a boy, because she did not say yes.

"Will you have me, Nan?"

She was very still. Her gaze passed over him, from the scar at his ear to his fine woolen tunic, his belt studded with gems and the ancient golden brooch that pinned his cloak.

"I would have my Welshman," she answered, switching out of Welsh.

He heard the hope, the yearning for what they had been once – alone together and nameless as they wandered hidden paths – and shook his head. It could not be that again.

"You must take a prince," he said. "Though the king may strip me of all titles and possession, it is a prince you would take as husband now. And if God grants that I am permitted to rule though I have defied my king, then I will rule, Nan. With you at my side as lady."

The look she gave him was helpless, despairing. "I am no lady." Her eyes dropped to her hands where they gripped the edges of her cloak, as though they had never done anything but scrub floors and peel turnips. "You've seen it yourself, what I come from. I could never be no great lady."

He looked at the stubborn set of her mouth, the little frown that put a crease between her brows.

"Already are you greater than any lady I have ever known." She made a scoffing sound, opening her mouth to dispute it, but he would not hear it. It angered him beyond reason, that she believed she was so small. "You think yourself insignificant, born to naught, and yet you are here. You are *here*, Nan, and why? You have said it is not yours to choose who will rule this place, but it is you who has ended the last threat to its prince. With your own hands. Already you have chosen."

He stepped closer to her and took her wrist again, ignoring the tension in her as she resisted the movement. He pointed at the empty place on her forearm where a blade was still missing. "When you did see a girl in danger – just a girl, ordinary and humble, a stranger to you – did you leave her to her fate? Nay, because you are no meek and shrinking servant." She was looking down at where he held her, her hand tight in a fist, but she did not pull away. "Who could be more worthy to protect and love my people, to rule them as their lady? None but you."

She shook her head, a faint and bewildered rejection. "I am not... I am no one."

"No one!" He dropped her arm and put a hand to her chin, tilting it upward, making her look at him. "When I would have you come here as naught but my lover, you did scorn me. For dignity, for your honor, which you would not put aside for anyone. Not for *anyone*. You refuse a prince and call yourself no one?"

He shook his head, amazed. "Even great ladies do not scorn princes, Nan, nor yet queens. But you did. And you were right to do so."

She did not see it, this fairy queen who had stretched out her hand and transformed him from a shadow of a man into a prince. He took her face between his palms, soft skin beneath his fingers.

"Full well do I know I am unworthy of you. But all that I have, all that I am is at your feet, Nan. You have only to take it."

Her breath was harsh against his fingertips, shallow breaths as she gazed at him. "I want to." She blinked, and the tears spilled over, a delicate splash against her cheek. "God forgive me, I want to. But it is not how the world is made, Welshman. There is no way in it for one born so low to marry one so high."

There was a plea in her, as though she wanted only to understand how it could be, how it could possibly work. As though she had forgotten what she had taught him.

"The roads made by kings are not the only paths a man may travel," he reminded her. He brushed the tears away with his thumbs. "Is you who told me that we need not follow in the ways the world has fashioned for us."

Her eyes searched his face, like she looked for some way to dispute and deny, afraid to hope. He leaned his forehead against hers, willing her to believe. He waited – he would wait here forever, her breath against his lips, her warmth between his hands. Just this moment, forever. Just this place they made between them. There was nothing else he wanted.

Her hand came up to lay against his heart.

"Like a bird across the sky," she said. "It pays no heed to the paths laid out by men."

He pressed her hand tight to his heart, and nodded. "We will make a way that suits us. Every day, if you will have me."

Her hand came to cover his at her cheek, gripping hard. He pulled back to see her face and thought he might die of this feeling, of the happiness and the hope that leapt in him at the look in her eyes.

"Welshman," she whispered, her heart pounding so that he felt it against his fingertips. "We will make a way."

She kissed him then, fierce and eager, her mouth hard against his for a brief and dazzling moment. It was sudden, unforeseen, because she was as swift and fearless in her love as in everything.

"If you will defy the king then I will dare to be a lady, Welshman. I will have you. Be you beggar or prince, I will have you, and never let you go."

Chapter Twenty-Seven

Outside the tiny village church, the priest who had heard her confession married them. If he thought it strange his prince should marry this uncouth foreigner who only this morning had confessed murder, he hid it well.

Nan's breath caught when she saw the party that waited to bear witness to their vows. They were not as grand as the greatest lords of the king's court, but she knew the look of men of consequence. The one with the harp goggled at her when she looked at him direct, so she lowered her chin and averted her eyes, knowing it was not as graceful as it might be but at least it was better than her habitual glare.

She married her Welshman with her hair in a mess beneath the hood of a plain traveling cloak, Fuss at her feet, blades on her arms, and not a scrap of silk or pearls on her. Her tongue did not falter to say his many names, this prince who would defy a king to make her his lady wife.

She would not be daunted. She loved him. They would make a way together.

It was not the tower, but the hall of the ancient manor house where they had their impromptu wedding feast. It was filled with his people – her people now – who bowed to them and embraced them with equal fervor, as familiar as old friends. The man with the harp was Rhys, the chief bard, who was joined by many fellows. They sang poem after poem into the night. She pleased one by asking if he would sing of Arawn of the otherworld, and then spent a pleasant hour listening to one performance after another, all the bards having their own versions of the legend and competing to see whose was judged the best.

It made her Welshman laugh. "It is not a likely tale for a wedding feast," he said, and ordered them to sing instead of more cheerful things. They looked to her to confirm this command and just as when they bowed to her, she felt a mild panic. But her husband smiled so wide that her heart leapt in her breast to see it. "Already are they devoted to you, my lady wife."

They were so easy, and so forgiving, and so eager to have her as their lady. They almost seemed to love her more for having been wed in her simple dress, for having appeared as though from nowhere to claim a place at their lord's side. They did not expect her to put on fine airs, or to know a great many things. They only wanted her to love them, and him. Without a doubt, she was certain she could do that.

When her Welshman said to her that as lord and lady, they were servants to their people before all else, she was even more sure of herself. This was a different kind of service than she was accustomed to, but she would gladly learn it. For him and for them.

In the chamber behind the hall, she put aside her blades one by one, and looked at him. Her Welshman, her prince, her husband. "Even the king cannot sunder this union, do you take me to your bed now," she said.

"He cannot sunder it even do I not," he replied. "I have said my vows, Nan, and I will not have them broken by any man."

She meant to ask him if he was certain of this course, because the risk to him was so great – but he did not give her the chance to ask it. He only took her in his arms and kissed her. He bared her flesh to his touch and pleasured her, and then whispered into the night that he prayed their child would grow in her soon.

The light flickered dimly across his hair, his face. It made her heart beat fast only to look at him, every time. She had never thought it could feel so right to be soft and defenseless, but she felt more herself in this moment than ever in her life, anywhere. His eyes were drifting closed, but his arms were locked around her like she was a treasure he would hold close forever.

"Know you how happy you make me?" she whispered. The tenderness swelled in her, and she pressed him closer, her heart against his, as she silently prayed that he would never be taken from her. That God would keep him safe from the wrath of the king.

It was but a week until they had word. A week of learning her husband's people and their ways, and learning the kind of lady she could be to them. A week of seeing him among them, and how they looked at him, and how they needed him. A week of praying that God would not take him from this place, or from her. And soon enough they would know.

King Edward was in Wales, on his way to visit his lands in Snowdonia, and summoned Prince Gruffydd to him. It set a terror in her even to think of standing before the king and his court, but she would not let her Welshman see how her heart quailed. And she would not let him go alone.

His guard came with them, but she kept her weapons close. At most, the king would only shout and rage, her Welshman warned her. His famous temper was likely to be stirred by such blatant disobedience – but he could not undo the marriage.

To her relief it was not the full court that was assembled, but only a handful of retainers. Her eyes skimmed over the lords present, looking for any she had seen before, sure they would recognize her as the skittish serving girl who had dodged their grasping hands. A few she knew, but they did not seem to recognize her – either because they had not kept her face in their memory or because she was so changed in the gown of wine-colored velvet. They looked at her, some openly and some stealthily, but they gave their greatest attention to the prince who had come to beg his king's pardon.

It was a private audience, only the king and his closest advisors, and she was summoned too.

"I am grown tired of troublesome Welsh princes," King Edward said, with such a threat in the words that it sent a shiver up Nan's spine.

"My liege," said her husband from where he knelt before him. He spoke simply, begging pardon for renouncing the betrothal arranged by the king, swearing it was done not for any hopes of greater power, but for love.

At this, the king's regard fell on Nan where she waited with bowed head at the back of the chamber. He beckoned her forward, and for a terrible moment she could not move. For just an instant, she thought she should have a jug in hand to fill his cup – but no, even when she served in his hall she had never served the king himself.

Only the thought of her Welshman could make her move her feet. And only the thought of her lady could make her lift her chin and straighten her spine.

She made herself imitate Lady Eluned, the assurance she had seen so many times, the grace and the power. It was a poor imitation, for never could she have such magnificence – just as she could never swing a sword like Gwenllian, or laugh with carefree ease like Robin. But it was enough to bring her to stand before the king and raise her face to him.

Lord William was there; she had not noticed him until this moment. While the king looked her over and the eyes of all his advisors were fixed on her, it was William who spoke.

"She is no one of importance, my lord," he said to the king.

She was reminded of his mother, that careful cunning in how he spoke with just enough exasperation, just a little contempt. It was good that she was no one of consequence, and it was important the king knew that. She did not bring wealth or titles or a great alliance. Nothing that would give more power to a Welsh prince.

"I know her well enough," continued Lord William, "For she has attended both my lady mother and my sister. She has no wealth to speak of, nor family nor name. There is naught but her youth and her beauty to commend her."

"And those she has in abundance," said the king. There was appreciation in his eyes, a hint of the wolf behind it, and she prayed God to keep her fingers from the tiny jeweled knife on her belt. But he only turned to her husband and said, "You value your king's favor so little that you trade it for naught but a fair face?"

"Nay, my lord king. It is not your favor I hold so cheaply, but her honor I hold so dear." He stood now, and did not flinch when he looked Edward in the eye.

"How dear?" asked one of the advisors from behind her.

It seemed to amuse some of them, but her Welshman took it as a cue. He nodded at one of the servants, who uncovered the cages he had brought. Then there was only gasping to see the white gyrfalcons, so beautiful they made Nan forget to breathe when she looked at them. Now she only looked at the admiration in the king's face, his deep pleasure at the gift. It tempered the anger to almost nothing.

"Ever have my people given a portion of the falcons we trap and train to our king," said Prince Gruffydd. "And only months ago did we agree to increase that number, in exchange for restoring me to rule. Yet still we can give more, in thanks to a merciful king."

Nan did not understand all the words, but she understood bribery well enough. Lords and kings did not call it that, though. They called it a fine, and they spent much time in discussing numbers and nests and goshawks and peregrines. The sums made her head spin, and some concessions caused her Welshman to blanch so that she wanted to insist she was not worth so much. But she bit her tongue against it, because this was not about her or her worth. He must be allowed to rule, whatever the cost, for his people's sake.

In the end, they came to an agreement. The king would have a greater share of the wealth of Aderinyth, a claim to a number of nests and a portion of trained birds, and her Welshman would rule.

When she understood it, she was overcome by a rush of confused feeling: relief for her husband, faint dread for herself, and anger that the king had demanded so much. It so overwhelmed her that she was glad to lower herself into a deep courtesy and hide her face.

"Do you regret it?" her Welshman asked her that night as they lay in bed. "That I remain a prince and you must be a lady. Say me the truth."

"For myself? Nay, I cannot," she answered honestly, rubbing a lock of his hair between her fingers, still amazed he was hers. "So worthy are your people and so well do you love them, that I would feel only sorrow if you must be parted from them." She moved even closer, pressing her naked skin against his, and smiled. "Certes I will do my best to be worth the price you have paid."

They rode back to Aderinyth the next day. Already the sight of the hills filled her with a contentment she had never known. It fit into a place inside her that she had not known was empty.

Tell me where I belong, she had demanded of her lady. And here was the answer.

At the top of the mountain pass, they paused to rest before the descent, and looked out over the valleys, the high peaks and rolling green hills. She knew the falconers were even now planning which of them would teach her their sport, and the ladies waited to attend her as she learned the ways of her new home. There was much to do, and she found herself not fearful of her new place and purpose, but eager. She would serve them with all the strength and compassion in her.

She looked at him as he surveyed it, the wind lifting his hair, his face soft with love as he looked out at the land he had longed for.

"You are home, Welshman."

"Now it is home in truth," he said. He turned to her and took her hand. "You are here, and it is home."

THE END

✠

Author's Note

The conquest of Wales and subsequent oppression of its people represents one of the earliest instances of English colonialism. As such, it is a difficult topic to write about in an optimistic way – but not impossible. Though Aderinyth and its prince are entirely fictional, they are not entirely implausible.

As for the real Welsh princes, the fate of Llewellyn's daughter and Dafydd's sons as told in this novel is factual. Because Llewellyn – and upon his death, Dafydd – was recognized as Prince of all Wales, the consequences to them and their offspring were especially harsh. Llewellyn's daughter Gwenllian was a prisoner for life (she died at age 54) at a priory in Sempringham. Prince Dafydd himself was hanged, drawn, and quartered as a traitor. His eldest son Prince Llywelyn died 4 years into his imprisonment at Bristol Castle. The younger Prince Owain lived at least 42 years as a prisoner there, and Edward commanded "a wooden cage bound with iron in that house in which Owain might be enclosed at night."

Other Welsh princes were less powerful than Llewellyn, and how Edward dealt with each varied according to their relationship with him – and their value to him. Many sided with the king and bartered political autonomy for lands and other royal favors, even long before the final conquest. (In fact, the conquest was made easier by the lack of unity among the Welsh, and the nature of Welsh inheritance laws.) I often find that readers unfamiliar with medieval history assume that a king invariably said "off with their heads" if anyone displeased him, but it just didn't work like that. If it did, the two Barons' Wars of the 13th century would have wiped out the entire political structure of England. Politics made strange bedfellows even back then, and though Edward saw the value in being harsh with some Welsh nobility, he equally saw the value in making concessions and compromises so long as he could retain control. It is worth noting as well that many nobles – including Prince Llewellyn himself – famously married without the king's consent, and managed to retain power.

One other area of historical interest in the novel is prostitution, and though I have done my best to represent it with fidelity – women engaged in sex work then (as now) largely because of harsh economic realities, and they were as moral or amoral as anyone else – I can only recommend that those interested seek out the writings of Professor Ruth Mazo Karras and Dr. Eleanor Janega. Their writing is as entertaining as it is illuminating, and made me wish this story called for more on the subject.

Acknowledgements

I am indebted to Danièle Cybulskie, friendly neighborhood 5 Minute Medievalist, for keeping me from making a complete boob of myself on the historical front. (Or at least if I did make a boob of myself, it's because I didn't ask you about a historical fact first – or I conveniently didn't listen to you.) Thank you for always being there with a swyving whoreson when I need one!

Special thanks as well to Mer McGuire, who is exceedingly generous with both her emotional support and her skin care tips. (Which are sort of the same thing, when you get right down to it.) You are a true jewel among women. I hope this has enough angst for you.

Covering everything from emotional support to random horse-related fact-checks to actual betareading is the fabulous Laura Freaking Kinsale. I'll never write a book worthy of your generous time, effort, and talents, but I thank you for them nonetheless, from the bottom of my heart.

And as ever, the bulk of my thanks goes to Susanna Malcolm, forever setting everything aside to read (and re-read) every word at the drop of a hat, forever putting up with my ongoing meltdown as this book attempted to murder me, and forever greeting my text messages with "new number who dis?" Seriously, I wouldn't be a writer (much less an author) without you, and this book – as all my others – wouldn't be worth reading without your input. Thank you times a billion.

ABOUT THE AUTHOR

Elizabeth Kingston lives in Chicago, where she can be found gleefully subverting tropes and inventing new ways to make fictional people kiss. When there's time for it (hint: there's always time for it) she shouts loudly about the intersection of historical romance and white supremacist narratives. Lipstick, skincare, and baked goods all rank high on her list of Other Interests. She sincerely hopes you enjoy her writing, and that you'll share it with others.

More information can be found at
elizabethkingstonbooks.com

CPSIA information can be obtained
at www.ICGtesting.com
Printed in the USA
FSHW011411221219
65367FS